"Who . . . who are you?" Jessica whispered. "Why are you here?"

Jack glanced at Laurie before speaking. "We're . . . I suppose there isn't any other way to say this—we're sort of ghosts, Jessica."

Laurie smiled reassuringly. "I know you're scared. But you have to listen to me, Jessica. I was sent here to help you—"

"No, I was sent here," Jack interrupted.

Laurie glared at him before continuing. "Okay, *we* were sent here, except he's here by mistake."

"I don't need your help," Jessica countered. "Look, I don't believe in ghosts, so whatever you're planning isn't going to work."

"She needs proof," Laurie said. Turning to Jack, she muttered, "There's nothing personal in this," and extended her arm until her entire hand disappeared into his chest.

Jessica bolted out of her chair, sending it crashing to the floor behind her. "Go away! Both of you! I don't know what you are or why you're here but I want you out of my life!"

"We're not here to harm you, Jessica," Laurie said quietly. "In fact, it's just the opposite. Think of us as fairy godmothers." Glancing at Jack, she grinned. "Godparents, then. We're here to straighten out your life!"

KATHERINE STONE —
Zebra's Leading Lady for Love

CONSTANCE O'DAY-FLANNERY

SECOND CHANCES

ZEBRA BOOKS
KENSINGTON PUBLISHING CORP.

ZEBRA BOOKS

are published by

Kensington Publishing Corp.
475 Park Avenue South
New York, NY 10016

First Printing: November 1992

Printed in the United States of America

This book is dedicated to the memory of Roberta Grossman, and the conversation we had in New Orleans. That sincere dialogue was the inspiration for this story.

And

My sister, Virginia, my guardian angel . . . the love she gave will be carried in the minds and hearts of everyone who knew her.

Chapter 1

Closing her eyes, she shut out the image of the woman and breathed deeply, letting the cold air fill her lungs. Even though it was winter, the air was sweet and wonderfully fragrant. She could actually smell the sap of the pine trees, the dormant grass beneath her feet, the tangy scent of the river that was miles away. It was strange how much she had taken for granted, like the simple act of breathing. Now she felt almost feral, like part of the animals that inhabited the nearby woods. All her senses were more acute, more tuned in to her surroundings. She had slipped through life, always in a hurry, never really paying attention. How much had she missed along the way? Now she felt more alive than . . . She shook her head, not wanting to think about it. Not yet anyway. It was as if one sense had been awakened and all her others were quickly activated, producing a keen longing inside of her. To slide her fingers over a silk blouse. To touch the perfect skin of a baby. To sit on the beach and feel the heat penetrate her pores while a soft breeze played over her body. To appreciate the spicy taste of spaghetti and meatballs. Oh, and yes . . . to experience the tart flavor of lemon sherbet as it slowly melted on her tongue.

Leaning against the pine tree, she smiled with the memories. Just simple things, things she had always taken for granted—that's what she missed the most. Like snowflakes melting on her tongue, biting into a ripe peach and letting the juice run down her chin; the feel of a man's arms around her . . .

Suddenly she felt herself becoming a part of it, fading into the trunk of the tree, experiencing the moist and pulpy core. She sensed its age and its strength as it drew on her more deeply. *Focus*, she told herself, willing her mind to break the bonding. Finally free, she took a deep breath and felt foolish as she brushed the sleeves of her wool blazer and looked to the crowd of people before her. No one seemed to notice that for a split second she and the tree were one. But of course they wouldn't. How could she expect them to recognize something so spiritual? She didn't even know if they could see her yet. But she could see them, feel their grief, the way the old ones shivered against the cold wind as they waited in respectful silence. It was

8

all very strange. She wondered exactly what the rules were when one was a ghost.

Concentrating, she again focused in on the woman . . .

Jessica.

Soon they would meet.

It was over. It was finally over.

Jessica Meyers stared at the copper casket draped in sprays of white and pink carnations. Filled with a mixture of grief and an intense guilt over her sense of relief, she didn't hear the words of the priest as he prayed over her mother, nor did she meet the gaze of any of her mother's friends. What was there to say? That she had been a good daughter? That she had given up her job in Chicago six years ago and done the right thing when her mom had the first stroke? What difference did it make anymore? Her mother was gone. All those years of keeping house, of running her mother's dress shop, of nursing an invalid—it was all over.

What was she supposed to do now?

Making the sign of the cross with the others, Jessica smiled at the priest, silently thanking him, and then watched as her mother's friends shuffled away from the grave. Old friends. Old people. All dressed in somber colors. Their bent shoulders and gray hair signaling to the world that their own time of final resting was not that far into the future. When had she become one of them?

At thirty-four, Jessica admitted that she had no so-cial life. All her time had been spent either at home with her mother or running Sara's Closet, her mom's shop that catered to her old friends. For the last six years she had been surrounded by senior citizens. She sold them dresses that started at size twelve and went up to a hefty size twenty-six. She ordered brassieres and girdles and kept them happy. She served tea and scones when they came to the house to visit. She smiled at all their compliments, commiserated with all their complaints, and thought about when she could sneak back into the kitchen. On the top shelf, over the refrigerator, was a bottle of Old Grand-Dad bourbon and Scope mouthwash.

It was the one way she had gotten through the last six years.

Once she had had interests in concerts, plays, skiing and traveling. Once she had been the personnel direc-tor of a large insurance firm. She had one bad marriage behind her, had gotten through it without any major emotional trauma, and had been enjoying the freedom of dating when it all suddenly came to an end. Her mother needed her. It had happened so quietly and so easily that no one seemed to notice her fading away, becoming a shell of the woman she once was.

But now it was over, and she hadn't the slightest idea what to do with her life. She was too old, too plain, too damned tired, to start over. Tradition de-manded that she play the role for a little longer since all the funeral guests would be coming back to the house for something to eat. All she wanted to do was get through the next few hours, to feed everyone, to smile at all the right times. She would thank them and shake hands that trembled with age, kiss cheeks that felt as thin and brittle as fragile paper. And then she would usher them out. Out of her house, and out of her life.

She merely wanted to be alone, to drink herself into oblivion, to forget it all.

''C'mon, Jess. Let's go.''

She felt a tug on her coat sleeve and blinked a few times before recognizing her younger sister. Funny, Terry had stood next to her during the wake and the funeral and yet they hadn't really talked about their mother, nor the years Terry had stayed away. But what did any of it mean now? What was done, was done. And nothing could change the past.

Picturing the half empty bottle of bourbon in her mind, Jessica placed a white rose on her mother's casket, silently said her goodbyes, and turned toward the waiting car.

The tears would come later.

He couldn't believe it. No matter how many times he played it back in his head, he simply could not believe it.

His life had always been orderly and structured, and, yeah, sure, he'd been pissed off many times in his life when things didn't go his way. You can't spend twenty years on the Philadelphia Police Force working your way up to Vice Detective without a healthy share of frustration and futility. He'd accepted that.

But now . . . now Jack Lannigan was exceptionally pissed off.

Because he was dead.

It wasn't just that he was dead, hell, everybody's got to go sometime. It's the *way* he died. While playing touch football with the neighborhood kids he'd sprinted down the sidewalk, his head turned and focused on the spiraling football—an impressive pass from Joey Marchetti. His arms were outstretched. It should have been a sure touchdown for the Lardner Street Maulers. And it was so stupid that, even now, dead, he was embarrassed. He should have known that tree was there. He'd walked Lardner Street a thousand times; he'd even climbed it as a kid. The tree. That damned tree. He hit it in full stride, with total impact. His head slammed into the massive trunk, and there was a moment of surprise, then pain . . . then total darkness.

Final score: Tree:1 Jack:0.

It was a ridiculous ending for someone who had taken bruising hits as a wide receiver for Father Judge High School when they captured the city championship, who had survived thirteen months in the jungles of Southeast Asia, who while chasing a felon could negotiate fire escapes with the agility of a cat. It made no sense. How could he be dead? When the inevitable happened, he thought he would probably buy it from some coked-up dealer, or a drug-crazed gang member.

He'd always been so careful to minimize the risks. He'd been a professional, and he should not be dead. There was so much he hadn't done. He was only forty-four. His whole life, the best part, was supposed to be in front of him. He'd been two weeks away from getting a citation from the mayor, and he was finally dating a woman that didn't mind him being a cop. His number couldn't have been up, and if it was, it shouldn't have happened in such a humiliating way.

Closing his eyes, he shook his head with frustration. It was so damned unfair, he thought as he glanced at the small group of mourners, to find himself in a cemetery watching a burial . . . and it wasn't even his. This gathering is for some old woman that died in her sleep. Now that's the way it's supposed to be. That was the natural order of things.

But what did he know anymore?

His mission, *should he decide to take it*, is the daughter, the mousy-looking woman who appeared numb with shock as she stood before the grave and listened to the priest. How the hell is he supposed to help *her*?

It's funny how people imagine death, or what happens afterward. The nuns had taught him about Judgment Day, standing before God, or St. Peter, with all his bad deeds listed and checked off. That wasn't it at all. After hitting the tree he'd found himself in a room, seated on a metal folding chair, across a desk from a somber-looking man. The room, at least he thought it was a room, was so spartan that he figured he'd been called into a lieutenant's office in another district for

13

some imaginary infraction. He should have sensed his luck was on a downward spiral. There he had been told matter-of-factly that he had died from a broken neck, and that he wasn't ready to pass on to the next phase, whatever that was. It seems he still had some life lessons to learn.

He was to be given a mission, to help someone in need, and the outcome was stressed. He didn't argue. He didn't even question at the time. He was used to taking orders. But now he had to follow through, like it or not. And he didn't like it one damned bit. Why a woman? Especially this woman. If she wanted to drink herself to death, who was he to stop her?

Thinking there had to be a mistake somewhere, Jack watched Jessica place a white rose on her mother's casket and turn away from the grave.

Leaning up against the dining room wall, Laurie Reese felt the now-familiar tingling in her arm and quickly straightened before anyone could notice that she was disappearing right into the wall. Damn, she was going to have to get a better handle on this ghost thing. First the tree, and now a wall! Concentrate on the energy. Everything was energy. That's what she was told. And it was supposed to get easier to maintain her form as time passed. Yeah, right! Nothing about being dead was easy.

"Are you all right, my dear?"

Startled, Laurie spun around and stared at the old woman in front of her. "Huh? I'm sorry?"

The silver-haired lady smiled. "I didn't mean to frighten you."

Laurie almost laughed out loud. Frighten *her*? This poor grandmom would faint dead away if she knew who, or what, she was talking to. Oh, hell, might as well be nice. "That's all right. You didn't frighten me." Smiling, she asked, "Are you a friend of Sara's?"

The woman nodded and sighed deeply with sadness as she looked out to the table, ladened with food. "Poor dear. She had her troubles over the years. But she was blessed with Jessica. You must be a friend of hers."

Even though she had yet to meet Jessica, Laurie nodded. "Yes, I am. How long have you known her?"

"Jessica? Why, since she was a child. That one never gave her mother a moment of worry. She's a saint, taking over the shop and caring for Sara the way she did. You know she refused to put her mother into a nursing home? How many children would do that today?"

Laurie nodded and then shook her head, as if to say that she hadn't any idea.

"Not many, let me tell you. But our Jessica wouldn't even hear of it."

"Our Jessica? Are you related?"

The woman shook her head and chuckled. "Oh, no, but that's how we think of her—all of us that have been going to the store for years. She's such a dear. Never loses her patience, no matter what the situation."

Laurie wasn't listening anymore. *Our* Jessica? Boy, this was worse than she'd thought. When she first saw Jessica Meyers at the cemetery, Laurie's initial reaction was pity. She looked like a big brown sparrow, almost nondescript as she stood in front of the crowd of senior citizens. She had no family to speak of, except for the sister, the one who was so afraid of sickness and death that she could barely handle coming back home to visit the mother. So Jessica had assumed all the responsibility. Maybe she had lost her zest and vitality, but she still had something—something so precious that Laurie was going to make sure Jessica didn't flush it down the tubes.

She had life.

And Lauren Ann Reese had loved life and lived it to its fullest. She had gone from being a hippie in her college days, thinking she could save the world, into a more realistic adult. She didn't like to think of herself as a Yuppie, but maybe that's what she had turned into after all. Certain things in her life had become very important to her. Like her job. She'd specialized in marketing and communications for a prestigious advertising firm. She was good, and she knew it. It was more than selling soap to America. It was quietly getting an idea across to the masses. While the male account executives seemed rooted to the belief that one couldn't sell beer without boobs, Laurie had campaigned for years against it. Perhaps the changes were slow, but they were getting the point that a product could be sold without sex. And now . . . now that she was gone, who was going to take up the banner in her stead?

Moving out of the dining room and into the living room of the old Victorian home, Laurie watched an elderly man help his wife into her heavy woolen coat. She wondered what it was like to be married to the same person for fifty years. She'd never even had a relationship that lasted longer than three, and her marriage . . . it was hard to even think of it as a marriage.

At nineteen she had fallen in love at a protest march against the war and quickly eloped. She thought love would last forever. It lasted all of three months and her parents had it annulled. Since then marriage was not on her agenda.

The older couple smiled at her as they headed for the front door. They looked alike. They moved in the same slow way, knowing each other's movements and limitations. Laurie smiled back, wondering if maybe she had missed something. But she'd had it all, right? A great job. Financial security. A beautiful apartment on Rittenhouse Square that was often filled with wonderful friends. A terrific lover, even if he snored when she allowed him to sleep over. Life had been great, and she'd worked her butt off to be able to afford it. She had a housekeeper once a week and rarely cooked, eating instead at trendy Center City restaurants. She never even gained weight!

So what the hell happened?

How could it all be gone, taken away by what was

supposed to have been a simple tonsillectomy? Okay, okay, so she had lied to the admitting nurse. She was ordered not to eat or drink anything before coming to the hospital. How was she supposed to know that three sips of coffee and two tiny bites of toast could kill her? A complication with the anesthesia—that's what she was later told by the beautiful woman dressed in the flowing white gown.

The last thing she remembered was lying on the operating table, counting backward from one hundred. She had double vision for a moment, seeing two surgeons and mirror images of the nurses that surrounded him and then the comforting darkness had wrapped around her. When she was first enveloped by fog she had thought it was part of a dream, that she would wake up in the recovery room and go home later in the evening. That's what she had been told when she'd finally agreed to have her tonsils out. Ever since she was a child, every doctor that had looked down her throat had told her they should be removed. It was her impatience. She hated to be ill, to be stuck home. But lately she'd been nursing too many sore throats and bouts with swollen glands. And she always felt like she was missing out on something important—some event with her friends, some fantastic deal at work, some wonderful man that might have crossed her path. So she'd done it, made all the arrangements like an adult. And now she was dead.

Death . . . it was certainly a weird state of being. As she had walked through the fog, it had suddenly lifted and Laurie saw the most beautiful valley, presented before her like a gift. It was green and fertile. The air was filled with the wondrous scents of pine trees and spring flowers. Even a deer crossed her path, stopping and staring at her for a few moments, before slowly moving on. She'd heard soft, soothing music and somehow knew she was supposed to follow the sweet refrain. It had brought her to the woman with the peaceful voice, the one who had told her that she'd died from complications. She didn't even protest at the time. She silently listened as she was told there were certain areas in her life that were not sufficiently explored, that she was one of the chosen few that would return to earth in a limited form to work through these areas with someone in need. She was to be sent on a mission, to help a woman who is emotionally lost.

Laurie glanced over to Jessica as she smiled and kissed an older woman goodbye. It shouldn't be that hard to turn Jessica around. She just needed a little direction in her life, and Laurie was a great motivator. This should be a piece of cake. There weren't that many people left. A few couples getting ready to leave and the guy watching television in the corner. He must be the sister's husband. Once she cleared everyone out, she would approach Jessica, and figure the best way to let her know she wasn't alone anymore, that she had help now. Anxious to begin, Laurie turned and walked into the kitchen. Three women were washing dishes, and talking about Sara.

"Excuse me," Laurie interrupted, and picked up a dishtowel.

They turned around to her. "I'll finish up in here,"

she said. "You must be tired; I know Jessica is. It's been a long day for everyone."

"Are you sure?" an older woman asked, untying her apron.

Laurie smiled back at her and nodded. "I'll be staying with Jessica for a while, so I can clean up later tonight. Right now, I think Jessica needs to rest."

That worked. The women seemed to notice how tired they were and gladly left the task of washing dishes to someone younger. Once alone, Laurie looked about the old-fashioned kitchen, at the mountains of dishes, and wished with all her heart that she could be Samantha on *Bewitched*. Just tweak her nose and the kitchen would instantly be set to order. Or, Laurie smiled, as she put a container of cream back into the refrigerator, better yet, Mickey Mouse in the *Sorcerer's Apprentice*. If she could just wave her hand and command the dishes into the sink and cupboards.

Feeling foolish, she closed her eyes and concentrated on making the dishes on the table move to the sink.

She peeked. Nothing had changed.

"C'mon," she muttered. "Everything is energy. Move!"

Squeezing her eyelids shut, she tried harder.

Suddenly a crash made her jump in fright and she opened her eyes to see a cup and saucer on the floor. Reaching down, she ran her fingertip over a chip in the cup and marveled at herself. "I can do this," she whispered, her voice filled with awe. "All I need is practice."

"Is there a problem in here?"

Spinning around on her heels, she saw the sister's husband standing by the doorway. Laurie stood up and smiled.

"No. Not really. I just dropped a cup. I'll have to replace it."

He nodded, as if bored by the discussion and looked around the kitchen. "All of this has to be done yet?"

Typical male, Laurie thought. They eat and drink and never give a second thought about the work involved. Trying to be patient, she smiled politely. "I'll finish it. Why don't you and Terri take off now. Everybody's put in a long day. You're staying at a motel or something . . . right?"

He stared at her and Laurie felt like he was looking past her eyes and into her mind. "Who are you?" he demanded. "And who's Terri?"

"You're not Jessica's brother-in-law?"

"I didn't know she had one."

"Terri is her sister. I assumed you were her husband. I'm sorry." The guy wasn't bad looking, and there wasn't anyone under sixty in the house, except for Terri and Jessica. Hmm . . . maybe he was involved with Jessica. Now that would be an interesting twist. She was sizing him up—dark hair that looked black until the light hit it with a hint of brown. Piercing blue eyes that at the moment held little warmth or friendliness. Ruddy complexion, as if he spent a lot of time in the sun. Probably Black Irish. Not a bad picture. Definitely not her type, but not bad. Good for Jessica, but somebody should have filled her in about him. He completely changed the scenario. Perhaps she could use him to—

"And you are?" he interrupted her thoughts.

"Me? I'm a friend of Jessica's. I was trying to clear everyone out. It's been a long day for her and I thought she could use the rest." Seemed like the best reason to get rid of everyone, even the boyfriend.

"Good idea," he agreed. "I'll help you."

He waited for her, as if ushering her out of the kitchen, and followed as she walked back into the living room. Terri was pulling her coat on as she spoke with her sister.

"Are you sure you understand, Jess? I mean, if you really want me to stay, I will."

Jessica shook her head. "It's all right. I'll talk to you tomorrow. Go back to the hotel and get some rest. I'll see you in the morning and we can go over everything."

Terri, short and petite, reached up and hugged her sister. "Whatever you want, Jess. You're so good with all this stuff and I'm . . ." Terri couldn't finish her sentence and she pulled back to button her coat. "I can't believe she's gone," Terri muttered, sounding close to tears.

Jessica stared at her sister for a few moments, as if deciding whether or not to say something. Instead, her lips moved into a smile, one that was tired and strained. "We'll talk tomorrow."

Nodding, Terri quickly kissed her sister and walked out the front door.

Jess leaned up against the heavy wooden door and,

sighing, placed her forehead against the cool surface. They were gone, she thought. Everyone was gone. It was quiet. And private. She'd played her role right to the end. Now all she wanted was to make a drink, perhaps several, and then climb into bed. Molly Kellerman had given her two socially acceptable glasses of wine for her nerves, but that only made her crave the bourbon more. For the last hour, it had been all she could think of . . .

Pushing herself away from the door, she turned around and was startled to see a man and a woman staring at her.

She gathered her willpower around her, once more controlling the intense craving in her body, and straightened with a smile. "I'm sorry," she said, as she walked away from the door. "I thought everyone had left." She didn't recognize either one of them.

The attractive woman with the sandy-blond hair came forward and held out her hand. "Hello, Jessica. I'm Laurie Reese. I need to talk to you about something very important." She smiled and glanced toward the man on her right. "I can start cleaning up in the kitchen until you say goodbye."

Confused, Jess looked at the man who appeared annoyed by the woman's statement. "Do I know you?" she asked, wanting them out of her house.

"Not really," the man replied. "My name's Jack. Jack Lannigan. But I have to speak with you tonight. I can wait until you've finished," he said, nodding toward the other woman.

The one named Laurie shook her head and smiled

with strained patience. "I'm afraid you don't understand, Mr. Lannigan. I need to talk to Jessica alone."

"Did you two know my mother?" Jessica asked, trying desperately to figure out how they both got into her home.

"No." He glared at the woman.

"No." She glared right back at him.

"Then why are you here? On this day? We've never met before. You didn't know my mother. I'm afraid I'll have to ask you to leave."

The woman took a deep breath. "I have something extremely important to discuss with you—"

"So do I," the man interrupted.

"Look," Jess said, wringing her hands together at her waist, "you'll have to go now." Her hands were shaking and her brain was screaming for the bourbon. She had read about people who feed off obituaries, who track down grieving relatives and take advantage of them. "The house isn't for sale, nor the business. There isn't a large insurance policy, so there won't be a big inheritance. I don't know what you want, but I'm telling you both to leave before I call the police."

The man indicated his chest with his thumb. "I *am* a cop. At least I was," he added in a lower voice. "I have to talk to you, Jessica. In private." His last word was directed to the woman.

"Well, so do I," the woman insisted.

"I can't talk to either one of you right now." Her body was trembling with anger and a desperate need. One drink. That's all she wanted and she could handle this situation. "You've . . . you've both invaded my privacy. I insist that you leave right now."

"I'm sorry, Jessica," the woman said, "but I can't. Not until we've talked."

The man ran his fingers through his hair, as if the action might control his growing anger toward the woman. "Neither can I. Look, if I can just talk to you, I'll explain everything."

Jess held her hands up. "Okay, I've tried being polite. I'm calling the police." She walked into the kitchen, more determined to fix herself a drink than anything else. What more could happen to her? Why couldn't she just be alone? Hadn't she done everything right so far?

When Jessica left the room, Laurie turned to the man and said, "Hey, I don't know why you're here, but you'd better come back another time because I'm not going anywhere. I'm going to be staying with Jessica."

"Staying with her? You just admitted you didn't even know her. I think you're the one that better get out before the cops haul you in for invasion of privacy, harassment and maybe even fraud."

Laurie reached down to a table and touched a crystal ashtray. She ran her fingertips over the cuts and grooves, admiring the way the lamplight brought out the different colors in each prism. "Look, Lannigan, you might have been a cop, which I doubt, but you're the one in trouble here. You have no idea what you're walking into if you remain. I'm starting to lose my patience and, believe me, you don't want to see me angry."

His laugh was short and sarcastic. "Lady, move your butt out of this house right now or I'll do it for you. The woman just buried her mother. Damn! What kind of balls does it take to show up on the day of the funeral and fuck over the grieving daughter?"

It was in her hand. One second she was clutching the ashtray in her hand while she listened to the asshole yelling at her. She could feel the intense anger building inside of her turn to rage. She felt it in every nerve ending, every pore, his words filling her brain with a violent fury. And that's when it happened. As if of its own volition, the crystal ashtray flew out of her hands.

And passed right through his body.

Speechless, Laurie's jaw dropped open in amazement as she stared at him.

Jack held his stomach as the ashtray landed on the rug behind him. His eyes were wide with shock.

Jessica stood at the end of the dining room, a glass in one hand and a half empty bottle of bourbon in the other. She didn't see that! It couldn't have happened! She did not see her mother's ashtray fly out of the woman's hands and go right through someone's body!

"Oh God, help me . . ." Dropping the glass to the floor, she brought the bottle to her lips and swallowed half its contents.

Chapter 2

"Who *are* you?" Laurie whispered, suddenly afraid.

Jack's voice was low and shaky. "Who are *you*?"

"I asked you first."

He rubbed his stomach, waiting for the strange tingling to disappear. "I . . . I told you. I'm Jack Lannigan."

She shook her head. "That's not what I'm talking about, and you know it. *What* are you? How could that ashtray go right through you?" She appeared as frightened as he felt.

He opened his mouth to speak and then clamped his lips shut. Looking at her, Jack's years of police instinct took over. He saw a woman of average height with dark blond hair that was probably natural. She had blue eyes, faded freckles across the bridge of her nose and when she'd smiled earlier there had been dimples on either side of her mouth. She wore a silk dress under a navy blue blazer that he would bet was Ralph Lauren. And she looked just like all those rich snobs from the Main Line that wouldn't give a cop the time of day. It was for the last reason he disliked her on sight.

"How did you make the ashtray move?" he demanded, looking around her for wires. Just what he needed—some dame passing herself off as a psychic to exploit Jessica. She probably came in while everyone was at the cemetery to rig the whole thing.

"I asked the question, Lannigan. Why did the ashtray pass through your body?" Her voice was tense, anxious, as if she had already guessed the answer.

Might as well scare the hell out of her and make her leave, he thought. "Because I'm not a figment of your imagination, Miss Reese. I'm not some hologram that you conjured up to scare your victims into shelling over big bucks. I'm the real thing—a ghost."

It gave him a funny feeling to say that word, to finally admit the truth out loud. "Now get out. Run as fast as those skinny legs will carry you before I—"

She brought her hand up to her mouth and started shaking her head. "It can't be," she interrupted, her eyes wide with wonder. "Why are you here too?"

Her reaction was unexpected. Where was the fear? He could see she wasn't afraid of him, and he was

28

trying to figure out how exactly he could scare her when her last word finally registered. "Too? What the hell does that mean?"

She slowly walked around him, staring at his body, sizing him up, and he was taken back by her careful examination. She made him feel as if he belonged in some freak show at the circus. Why wasn't she running out the door? If he had seen an object pass through someone's body, he would have bolted for the nearest exit without the slightest hesitation. This woman either had cast iron nerves, or she didn't believe him.

Suddenly, without any warning, she stuck out her hand and it entered his shoulder. Reacting instinctively to the weird tingling sensation, Jack jumped back and yelled at her. "Hey! What do you think you're doing? Get away from me!"

"My God," she murmured, as she held her hand out in front of her. *"You really are dead!"*

"I told you," he said in an irritated voice, feeling that somehow the tables had been turned on him and he hadn't any idea how it had happened. Why didn't he have chains to rattle, or something? Where were the props for this gig anyway?

She picked up the ashtray from the rug and placed it on a nearby table. Turning back to him, she smiled in a superior manner and said, "Well, I'm sorry to tell you, Lannigan, but you've been sent by mistake. This is my mission."

He cocked his head to one side, as if he hadn't heard her correctly. "What?"

"I've been sent to help Jessica. This is my mission, so you might as well just pack it up and leave." She crossed her arms over her chest in that age-old feminine gesture of stubbornness.

Pointing at her, he asked, "*You've* been sent? By whom? And what for? *Just who the hell are you, lady?*" he demanded.

She brushed an imaginary speck off her impeccable blazer and said, "I'm Laurie Reese, newly departed—unfortunately—and I've been sent back to earth to help Jessica get her life in order. Obviously, there's been some mix-up and you've come to the wrong place."

"You're dead?"

"Newly departed. It sounds nicer."

Jack couldn't think straight. It wasn't bad enough that he was dead and given the assignment of helping a woman, now he had to fight some witch for the job? "You're the Antichrist, or something, right? You're like the devil—or, or one of his legion that goes out and tries to screw up people like me that have to perform good deeds."

She giggled and the sound of it grated on his nerves like fingernails scraping a chalkboard. "Oh, Jack . . . please. Give me a break. I'm just like you, only you're in the wrong place."

"I was sent here for Jessica." He wasn't scared anymore. He was back to being angry.

"So was I," she answered. "And obviously I'm the right one. You didn't even know Jessica had a sister."

"So what does that prove?"

They both heard the bottle hit the floor at the same

moment and they turned in unison toward the dining room. Jessica was passed out on the rug.

"Look what you've done," Laurie scolded as she hurried to Jessica's side. "She'd better not be hurt."

Unwilling to give up authority, Jack followed close behind her. He bent down and, after checking Jessica's pulse, lifted her eyelids. "She's drunk."

Laurie gave him a disgusted look. "No kidding, Sherlock? Great detective work."

"What do you want from me?" he said with exasperation.

"I want you to leave—after you help me get her to bed."

"Why don't you just get on your broomstick and fly back to wherever you came from? I'll take care of her." Jack tried to pick up Jessica, but his arm seemed to fade inside her body.

Laurie shook her head and sighed with impatience. "You have to concentrate. Didn't anybody tell you that? Everything is energy. That's why I could move the ashtray," she added in that superior tone.

"Why, aren't you the know-it-all little stiff?" He pulled his arm back, not really wanting to try again and fail.

"I'm just attempting to be helpful," she said, her feelings obviously hurt. "From now on I won't bother. And don't call me a stiff. You can drop the fake police jargon."

"No one asked for your help, you know?"

She shrugged. "I won't offer again. But we have to get her to bed. I won't be able to do it alone."

31

His eyes widened with feigned surprise. "Your little magic tricks don't extend that far? You really need *my* help? Why, I'm honored—to think someone of your immense talents would ask—"

"Knock it off, Lannigan," she ordered, placing the empty bottle next to the glass. "I don't need your sarcasm right now. Can't you guess why she's done this?"

"'Cause she drinks too much?"

She wouldn't give him the satisfaction of acknowledging his asinine question. "She must have seen that bit with the ashtray, and she probably overheard everything we said. What would you do if you saw two ghosts in your living room fighting over you?"

He looked at her, and then back at Jessica. "Yeah, I guess you're right," he reluctantly admitted. "So how do we get her upstairs?"

The doorbell rang before Laurie could answer. Startled, they stared at each other until Laurie whispered, "Do you think she really called the police?"

Jack glanced at Jessica and then back at Laurie. "You stay with her, I'll handle it." Sighing, he got up and walked toward the front door.

Laurie held her breath as she heard Jack talking to someone. What if it were the police? How could they ever explain themselves? What if they were asked for identification? The only proof she had was her ability to levitate a cup and saucer and an ashtray, and she was sure she wasn't supposed to do that in front of just anybody. This was not working out well. If only Lannigan hadn't shown up . . .

"They left."

Laurie looked up at him. "It was the police?"

He nodded and hooked a thumb into his pant's pocket. "I told them we were friends of Jessica's from Chicago, and that we were staying with her for a while. That there were two people who had remained after the funeral and tried to approach Jessica about investments, but I threw them out."

"And they believed you?" Laurie asked in a skeptical voice.

Jack grinned down at her. "It's amazing what a little fake police jargon will accomplish."

Ignoring his reference to her earlier remark, Laurie glanced back at Jessica. "We have to get her to bed."

Jack looked up at the long flight of stairs. "Okay. So tell me how."

"You have to concentrate on the energy. It was hard for me at the beginning, too."

"How long have you been . . . you know, been at this?"

Laurie shrugged. "I don't think it's been very long. We're here, or at least I'm here, in a limited form. I was experimenting in the kitchen with the cup and saucer when you walked in."

He knelt down next to her. "Show me," he said. "Show me what I have to do."

Needing his help, she dismissed her dislike for the man and said, "I'll take her shoulders and you take her legs. That way if you let go, she won't get hurt. Think of her as being weightless. That she's just one form of energy and you're another. It's easy. C'mon."

33

Standing up, Laurie bent over and placed her hands under Jessica's arms. She waited until Jack held onto Jess's ankles. "Okay, you try first," she said and watched as Jack's big hands seemed to disappear. "You're not trying hard enough," she scolded.

He glared at her. "I *am* trying!"

"No, you're not," she countered patiently. "Close your eyes and concentrate. Picture yourself picking up her legs and standing. If you believe you can do it, you will."

He shook his head. "You sound like a Dale Carnegie groupie."

"Well, I always have subscribed to the power of positive thinking theory. Why be negative?"

He touched Jessica's skin, feeling the texture of her stockings and the bones at her ankle. "'Cause it doesn't work in the real world, lady. Because for most people, to quote a bumper sticker: 'Life's a bitch, then you die.' "

"But this isn't the real world, is it?" she asked softly. "At least the two of us aren't in it any longer. So why don't you try it my way and give it a chance?"

He let her know by his facial expressions that he thought the whole idea was ridiculous, but he did shut his eyes. "Okay, I'm thinking. I can pick her up. She's just energy, and so am I—"

"And you're doing it," Laurie interrupted with a whisper and a giggle.

Jack opened his eyes and looked down to his hands. "Holy Shit!" He was holding Jessica's ankles about four inches above the floor, but as soon as he uttered the words, Jessica's feet slammed back to the rug.

Jessica groaned. "I'm coming . . ." she mumbled. "I'll be right there, Mom."

"You have to be more careful," Laurie scolded in a hushed voice. "You'll wake her."

"If she was awake, she could help," Jack whispered back and waited until Jessica settled down once more. "Okay. Let's try it again."

Laurie nodded and the two of them slowly picked up Jessica and headed for the stairs.

"She's not exactly weightless," Jack remarked, halfway up.

"Shh . . . just concentrate!"

"I am concentrating. I haven't dropped her, have I?" Yet he was struggling not to lose her. He stopped talking and tried to block out his resentment that the Reese woman was right. If he pictured himself carrying Jessica, he could do it.

At the top of the stairs, Laurie looked around her. "Which room is hers?"

"How would I know?" Jack answered. "Just pick one."

"We don't want to put her in the mother's room," Laurie said, trying to figure it out.

Jack nodded to the one on his right. "There. That one."

"How do you know?"

He sighed with exasperation. "Will you just listen to me? If you keep talking, I'm going to drop her."

35

Laurie backed up into the room he had indicated. They placed Jessica on the poster bed, stood next to each other and stared down at her.

"She wasn't weightless," Jack said again and pushed back the hair from his forehead.

"I know, but you did it anyway."

Jack glanced at the woman standing next to him. How come she knew so much? Why didn't he get any instructions, like she had obviously received? "Now what?" he asked, galled that he was the rookie on this mission.

"Now I'll take off her shoes and you pull the bedspread down. I'm going to leave her dressed."

"You should have pulled the spread down first," he remarked, wondering how he was supposed to do it while Jessica was lying on top of it.

Laurie gave him an impatient look. "Gee, I'm sorry I didn't think of everything. I'm only . . ." Her words trailed off.

"Human?" he supplied with a sarcastic grin.

"Just pull down one side and then roll her over," Laurie said as she removed Jessica's brown heels. When she opened the closet, she was surprised to see an orderly row of women's clothing and neat plastic containers of shoes. "How did you know this was her room?" she asked over her shoulder.

"Simple deduction. I could see the brushes, the hair dryer and perfume on a dresser. The mother was sick for years, so they had to belong to Jessica. Want to help me roll her over now?"

Once more viewing the plastic boxes of shoes, Laurie muttered, "Nobody's closet should be this neat," and dropped the heels to the floor. She closed the door and walked back to the bed.

Once they had Jessica settled in for the night, Laurie looked at the man standing next to her with his hands jammed into his pockets. "Now we have to clean the kitchen."

He turned his head to stare at her. "What do you mean *we*?" I thought you were going to do it."

"Hey, Lannigan, I said that when I thought you were one of the mourners. You and I have to talk. We have to figure this thing out, and we can do the dishes while we decide how you can return."

She walked out and left him staring after her.

"I said I'll wash them." Laurie stood at his side with a dishtowel in her hands.

"I hate drying dishes and putting them away," he whined like a teenager, and then cursed as another cup slid through his fingers.

"Look, you're having trouble concentrating with the water and the soap and—"

"Will you stop harping about concentrating? I swear if I hear that one more time I'll strangle you."

"Wouldn't do any good," she said with a laugh. "I'm already dead." She immediately stopped laughing and stared at him. "I can't believe I just said that. I'm really dead!"

She looked like she was about to cry and Jack lifted his hands from the water. Taking the towel away from her, he said, "I know how you feel. It's a real kicker, isn't it?"

She merely nodded.

Not wanting to deal with a depressed ghost, Jack said, "You go ahead and wash. I'll dry." She was bad enough to take when she was bossing him around. Depressed would be, well, depressing.

He waited until she had handed him a wine glass before asking the question that was uppermost in his mind. "How did it happen? I mean, you're young. You look healthy. Was it an accident?"

She smiled sadly. "I guess you could say that. I ate before going in for a tonsillectomy. The woman in the white gown told me there was a complication with the anesthesia. How about you?" She gave him a clean saucer with painted blue flowers on the rim. "Killed in the line of duty? You don't look like you were shot, or anything."

He wasn't going to tell her about the football game. "It was an accident," he said, which in his mind was close enough to the truth. "But back up there—what woman in a white gown?"

Her smile seemed genuine, as if recalling a pleasant memory. "You know—after you're taken. After you're pulled into that warm, brilliant light? Wasn't it beautiful? That valley . . . the birds and flowers. And the scents. It was so clear, like springtime—"

"Birds and flowers?" he interrupted. "It was an office. Plain and simple. A man, with absolutely no expression on his face, sat behind the desk and told me I was dead and that I had some life lessons to learn. He's the one that sent me on this mission.''

Laurie looked into his eyes and said sincerely, ''But you're wrong, Jack. It was beautiful. If I hadn't known that I had died, it would have been a wonderful experience. It was almost as if I had become one with the universe, with nature . . .''

''That's bullshit,'' Jack again interrupted, angry that she had this wonderfully spiritual encounter and his was as cut and dry as a job interview. ''Maybe you were on drugs or something when you checked out and that's why you think you saw all that.''

She didn't look at him, just continued to wash the dishes. Finally, she said in a soft voice, ''You know what I think? When we die, our experiences reflect our life, and our state of mind. You were a cop; you have linear thinking. Everything is right or wrong to you. Your mind is orderly and structured, with little room for creativity or imagination. So when you died, that's what you saw.''

Everything she said about him was true, yet he somehow felt insulted. ''Oh, and who were you? Some flower child? Little Miss Goodness and Light?''

She giggled, and for some unexplainable reason the sound continued to annoy him. ''Actually, I was a flower child in the seventies. I thought I could stop the war and save the planet.'' Shrugging off her past, she added, ''Then I grew up and got a job in advertising.''

''Oh, so you've got a real good grip on reality,'' he said with a measure of sarcasm. ''Advertising is just a glorified form of pimping, ramming stuff that no one really needs down the consumers' throats."

She stopped washing the dishes and turned to him. "Why are you so angry with me? What have I done to you?"

The dishtowel hid the clenching of his fist. "You want to know why? Because you've been pampered and sheltered from reality. You probably went to bed each night feeling safe and secure in your house on the Main Line or the high rise in Center City. You have absolutely no idea how the rest of the world survives. You've never held a dying thirteen-year-old in your arms that was shot because somebody who saw a Nike ad wanted his sneakers. You've never had to jam your jacket between the legs of a fifteen-year-old hooker to stop the bleeding because she'd given herself an abortion."

He was breathing heavily when he added, "And I know, Miss Flower Child, you damn well never spent thirteen months in the jungles of Viet Nam. I would have remembered you."

Chapter 3

"*You're* tired? I was up all night watching you."

Laurie spun around from the counter to face him. He did look tired, and rumpled from spending the night in a chair. She had taken possession of the couch. "Why? What did you think I was going to do?"

He ran his fingers through his hair. "I don't know . . . zap me into another dimension. That is, after you finally stopped arguing. What was it? Four or five in the morning before you shut up?"

She had to bite her bottom lip to stop the laughter. "You give me too much credit, Lannigan. The most I can do is zap cups and saucers."

"And ashtrays."

Bringing out a container of eggs from the refrigerator, she smiled. "And ashtrays. Are you hungry?" she asked, hoping to avoid another argument. Last night had drained her, and nothing had been settled. They had kept contradicting each other. It was her mission. His mission. She had insisted the afterlife was beautiful. According to him, it was cut and dried. Very business-like. They couldn't agree on anything. "Well? Are you or aren't you hungry?" she repeated.

He stared at her for a few seconds before rubbing his stomach. "I am," he admitted. "But why? I mean, if we don't really exist, how can I be hungry?"

She shrugged. "I don't know, but I am, too. Maybe the longer we stay, the more . . . well, human . . . attributes we take on."

"Damn, I hate it when you talk like that. We are human. At least I am. You make it sound like we're vampires, or something!"

She didn't answer him. Looking over his shoulder, Laurie saw Jessica staring at them. Jessica's mouth was opened in shock while her fingers clutched the molding of the door, as if it were the only thing keeping her upright.

"Good morning, Jessica," Laurie said, softly and calmly. "Would you like some coffee?"

Jack slowly turned around. "I'm glad you're up. We all need to talk."

"Who . . . who are you?" Jessica whispered. "Why are you here? It was a *dream*! It had to be a dream, or I'm . . . hallucinating!"

Laurie took charge. Placing the eggs on the counter, she took a mug from the shelf and filled it with steaming coffee. "Here," she said matter-of-factly, as if two ghosts showing up in someone's kitchen were an everyday occurrence. "What do you take in your coffee? Cream? Sugar? Equal? We have a lot to find out about each other. Personally, I always used Equal, but I could mainline sugar now and it wouldn't matter."

"You're rambling," Jack interrupted, before looking back at Jessica and mustering a smile. "I'm Jack Lannigan and this is Laurie . . . Reese, I think. Why don't you come in and sit down so we can all talk about this?"

Laurie watched as Jessica glanced from Jack back to her. She seemed to be trying to find her voice as she muttered, "Who *are* you? What are you still doing in my house?"

Tiny beads of perspiration broke out over Jessica's body and her hands were beginning to shake. Laurie sensed the intense fear rushing through Jessica, the surge of adrenalin as the fight or flight instinct took over.

Jack was watching her, staring at her hands, and Laurie saw that Jessica was trying to control them.

"Where do you keep it?" he asked.

Jessica didn't answer, and Laurie knew she wanted them to get out, to leave her alone. She thought it was all a dream, but now the reality of them was slamming back at her with a vengeance.

"The liquor," Jack answered for her. "Where is it? I guess you could use something in your coffee about right now."

"Lannigan!" Laurie scolded him, placing her hands on her hips with annoyance.

The need to ease the trembling in Jessica's body must have overcome everything else, even her fear. "In the cabinet over the refrigerator," she whispered. Jack brought out her bottle of Old Grand-Dad.

So that's where she keeps it, Laurie thought.

Watching as Jack poured a good measure into the mug of coffee, Laurie said, "I can't believe you're doing that! Aren't we supposed to be *helping* her?"

Jack didn't look up as he mumbled, "Right now, this is the help she needs."

He offered the cup to Jessica and Laurie watched her slowly walk toward the table. Grabbing hold of a chair, she sat down and clutched the steaming mug in her hands. "Who are you?" she repeated, staring at Jack.

He sat down opposite her and glanced toward Laurie before speaking. "I guess we didn't do a very good job of explaining last night. We're . . . I suppose there isn't any other way to say this. We're sort of ghosts, Jessica. Not the Patrick Swayzee kind. The real thing."

She gulped the coffee as she stared at them. Laurie knew it must be burning her throat, yet she probably didn't even feel it. Her fear was masking every other sensation.

"Please," she murmured in a frightened voice.

"Please don't do this. Just go. Okay? I won't say anything to anyone if you two leave right now."

Laurie pulled out the chair next to Jack and sat down. She smiled with reassurance. "I know you're scared. Anyone would be. But you have to listen to me. I was sent here to help you—"

"No—I was sent here," Jack interrupted.

Laurie glared at him before continuing. "Okay, *we* were sent here, except he's here by mistake. There really isn't anything you can do about it, and neither can we. I think we all should just accept the situation and get started."

"I don't need your help," Jessica countered, obviously feeling stronger. "What am I thinking, letting you two manipulate me like this?" She took a deep breath. "Look, I don't believe in ghosts, so whatever you're planning isn't going to work. Get out of my kitchen. Get out of my life. *Leave!*" She sat back, as if satisfied that she had finally asserted herself.

"What about last night?" Jack asked, after calmly sipping his coffee. "You saw us last night. You saw what happened when Laurie threw that ashtray. What did you think, Jessica, when you saw her hand pass through my body? You're an intelligent woman. Tell me, what did you think?"

"Stop interrogating her," Laurie said in an annoyed voice. "You're not a cop now. She needs proof."

He turned his head and stared at her. "What kind of proof? Last night wasn't enough?"

"C'mon, Jack. If it were you, would you take someone's word for this?"

He sat back in his chair. "Well, go ahead. You're the pro in this area. Show her some of your tricks."

Inhaling deeply, Laurie slowly exhaled and then muttered, "They're not tricks. In this case they're sort of like credentials."

He snorted with sarcasm. "Only if you're auditioning for the remake of *The Ghost and Mrs. Muir*."

Laurie smiled sweetly. "Why, Jack, I didn't know you were a romantic."

"I'm not," he grumbled.

She barely looked at him as she murmured, "No kidding. You're about as romantic as day-old bread."

"Why, thank you for that observation, but weren't you about to show Jessica our credentials?"

She wanted to punch him. He had the most annoying way of getting under her skin. "I was about to show her *my* credentials. You're on your own, buster."

Turning away from him she smiled at Jessica briefly, not acknowledging her confused expression, before staring at her mug of coffee. All she had to do was concentrate. Energy . . . everything was energy. She and the cup . . .

"Oh, my God!" Jessica whispered.

Laurie opened her eyes and was pleased to see the white ceramic mug suspended in the air before her. Letting her breath out slowly, she eased it back to the surface of the table.

"How did you do that?" Jessica demanded, frantically shoving the fringe of bangs off her forehead. "I mean, I saw it, but I don't believe it!"

Delighted with herself, Laurie pushed Jack's mug

in front of him and said, "Perhaps when you see his performance, you'll change your mind." Her voice conveyed her challenge.

"She doesn't need to see me do anything," Jack muttered.

"Of course she does. Don't you, Jessica?"

Jessica stared back at them, incapable of speech.

"C'mon, Jack. Here's your chance to prove this is your mission."

Laurie watched as Jack set his jaw and glared at the filled mug of coffee. She looked down to the table and had to bite her bottom lip to stop from laughing. The mug was rattling and dancing on the wooden surface like a broken washing machine, spilling its contents over the sides.

"Shit! Dammit!" With Jack's curses, the mug ceased its movement.

Laurie got up and grabbed a couple of paper towels to mop up the mess. She patted Jack's shoulder in a display of sympathy and said innocently, "He's just not very good at this yet."

Jessica swallowed several times, as if trying to bring moisture back into her mouth before she whispered, "I don't believe you're *ghosts*. I mean, look at you. You're not . . . ethereal, or anything. You look just like anyone else."

Laurie nodded. She knew this part wasn't going to be easy. "Okay, I'll show you something else." Turning to Jack, she said, "There's nothing personal in this," and extended her hand toward his stomach.

Realizing what she was about to do, he rolled his

47

eyes and muttered, "Oh, no . . ." just as her fingers entered his body.

When Laurie's entire hand disappeared inside Jack's torso, Jessica bolted out of her chair, sending it crashing to the floor behind her. "Go away! Both of you!" she screamed. Her hands were out in front of her, as if for protection. "I don't know what you are or why you're here, but I want you out of my life!"

Laurie pulled her hand back and calmly said to Jack, "I know why you're hungry. Your stomach's completely empty."

Jack groaned at the invasion of his body and he shot her a look of extreme displeasure. She ignored it as she got up and walked around the table to Jessica. Righting the chair, she nodded to it and said in a quiet voice, "Sit down, Jessica. We're not here to harm you. In fact, it's just the opposite. Think of us as fairy godmothers." Glancing at Jack, she grinned. "God*parents*, then. We're here to straighten out your life—"

"Who sent you?" Jessica demanded, collapsing back into the chair. "Was it my mother? She did this, didn't she? I'm never going to be free!"

"It wasn't your mother," Jack said. "These orders are from a little higher up."

"How high?" Jessica murmured.

Laurie could see that she was obviously still in shock, but she was starting to talk to them, and that was a good sign.

Jack looked to Laurie and shrugged. "I don't know. Maybe they were angels, or something."

"Well, mine was definitely an angel," Laurie said. "Oh, you should have seen her, Jessica. She was beautiful. All dressed in white. I've never seen skin that perfect or—"

"Give me a break," Jack interrupted. He looked at Jessica and added, "She was on drugs when she died, so you can't go by what she says."

"I was not on drugs!" Laurie insisted, highly offended. She glanced to Jessica. "A little operation that went wrong, that's all."

"And you were on drugs, admit it. That's why you got everything so screwed up."

"I got things screwed up?" Laurie demanded. "What about you? You're in the wrong place, at the wrong time, and you don't know anything about this mission. You have neither the skill for the job, nor the knowledge. And your incapacity for understanding women is appalling."

"Oh, really?" he sneered.

"Really," she sneered back.

"Well, I'll have you know that I haven't had many complaints from women."

"You must have dated mimes, then. And you never heard any complaints because, God knows, it would be so embarrassing to act out 'asshole.' "

"Oh—and the jerks you dated were real winners, I suppose. Pinstriped suits that were afraid to tell you to shut your sarcastic little mouth—"

"Excuse me. Excuse me," Jessica interrupted.

They both stopped and turned to the woman across the table from them.

"Are you two supposed to be partners, or something?"

They glared at each other briefly before Laurie said, "Or something is more like it."

Jessica drank some coffee and started laughing. She was laughing! Laurie grinned back at her. Okay, this was more like it. "What's so funny?" she asked.

Jessica wiped the tears away from her eyes and chuckled. "Isn't this perfect? If I'm to believe everything you've said, you've come here to help *me*? My life is a mess and I don't get the Charlton Heston version. I'm sent Maddie and David from the heavenly edition of 'Moonlighting?' My luck . . ."

The kitchen was silent, except for the sounds of Jessica's self-deprecating laughter. "I'm sorry," Laurie whispered. "We shouldn't have done that." She poked Jack in the ribs as Jessica really started to cry.

"I'm sorry, too. You're what's important, not us. We'll work out our differences, or we won't. But it shouldn't interfere with our mission."

"That's right," Laurie agreed, almost glad to hear him refer to it as *our* mission. "I don't blame you for crying. This isn't the best time of your life."

"Sure," Jack added. "Your mother just died. The dress shop's in trouble. You really don't have any friends your own age. And, quite frankly, you drink too much."

Laurie stared at him with disbelief. "Hey, don't sugar-coat it, Officer. Why not deliver it like a right jab to the jaw? In the 'good cop—bad cop' scenario, you must have been the sympathetic one."

"Your sarcasm is showing," he replied calmly.

"How do you know about the shop?" Jessica sniffled. She reached for a clean paper towel and blew her nose.

"Laurie told me."

It was hard not to flaunt it over him, the proof that she was better prepared for the job, but he was trying and maybe she should. "I was told by that . . . that woman. The one in the white dress. She said that you had given up a promising career to come home and nurse your mother. That you took over the shop and gave up on your own life. That you have a serious drinking problem and now that your mother is gone, you have no direction."

Jessica shook her head. "And now what are you two supposed to do? Make the store turn over a great profit? Fix my life so I meet some wonderful man and have 2.3 kids when at my age the chances of being mugged are better? Then take away from me the only thing in my miserable life that gives me pleasure?"

"Why, yes," Laurie said simply. "That's it, exactly." She looked at Jack and beamed. "Here we were trying to figure out how to help her and she just told us."

"It was my turn to be sarcastic," Jessica muttered. "I didn't mean it."

"She didn't mean it, Laurie," Jack said with caution. "We're here to stop her drinking—"

"Well, I think it's perfect," Laurie said. "We'll get her on a regimen of diet and exercise. We'll take a look at this shop and see what we can do." She looked at Jessica. "Although I have to tell you that survey you were quoting about your chances of being mugged are better than being married? It's a load of crap. That survey was done by a bunch of college kids. The media picked up on it and every woman past the age of thirty-five went into immediate depression. Talk shows and comedians had a field day, yet when the truth came out the media ignored it. It wasn't sensational, nor was it funny. So don't believe everything you read, Jessica. Your chances—"

The ringing of the doorbell interrupted anything more Laurie could say.

"Are you expecting someone?" Jack asked in an anxious voice.

Jessica looked as nervous as them. "I don't know. Maybe. Oh God, not Terri . . ."

The sister, Laurie thought. Just what they needed now that they were making progress.

"What will I say?" Jessica whispered. "How can I explain you two? Will she see you? Or is it just me?"

"I think she can see us," Jack answered. "Listen, just tell her we're good friends from Chicago and we'll be spending some time with you. It's what I told the police last night."

"The police were here?" Jessica squeaked. "They came?"

Laurie nodded. "Jack took care of them. Now take a deep breath and answer the door. We'll all get through this."

The difference between the sisters was striking. Terri Conway walked through life carrying a pair of aces in the pocket of her full-length mink coat. Everything she wanted eventually came her way. Jessica played the hand fate dealt out to her, and there were no aces for Jessica.

"Jess. My God, look at you," Terri nearly sang as she swept into the living room. "What did you do? Sleep in those clothes?" She dropped her fur coat onto a chair and turned back to her older sister. "You should have at least taken off your mascara. You look like a raccoon this morning. All those little particles are starting to embed themselves into your pores right as we speak. And moisturize. Moisturize, Jess! At your age your skin will show the neglect."

"Good morning, Terri," Jessica said with more than a hint of weariness in her voice, as she tucked her blouse into the waistband of her skirt. "I take it you slept well."

Terri brushed back her perfectly cut hair with a dramatic wave of her hand. Smoothing down the front of her white cashmere sweater, she said, "You would think a town this size would have a decent hotel. I had to go all the way out to Route 73 to check into a TraveLodge. It was either that or stay in one of those tacky motels on Route 130. And the TraveLodge is under renovation!" She looked up and smiled, showing the six thousand dollars of dental work for caps. "So, how are you?"

Jessica looked confused. "I . . . I have company."

"Really?" Terri asked, glancing around the empty living room. "One of mother's friends, I suppose." She leaned forward, as if to impart something of great importance. "You really need to get a life of your own."

Jessica's jaw seemed to harden with anger. "Actually, they're friends of mine. From Chicago. They . . . ah, they came when I told them about Mom."

"From Chicago?" Terri asked, suddenly interested. "Were they here yesterday? The great-looking guy and the blond? Where are they?"

"In the kitchen," Jessica answered, and watched as Terri checked the length of her designer jeans against her equally expensive boots before making her entrance.

"She's coming!" Laurie whispered to Jack as they hurried back to the kitchen table. "Sit down! God, doesn't she sound like a witch?"

"Sounds like she's got great taste," he answered with a smug expression plastered over his face.

More than anything else at that moment, Laurie wanted to wipe away that smirk, to put him in his place, but she never got the chance as Terri burst into the room.

"Well, hello, you two. I'm sorry we never got to meet yesterday, but the funeral and everything . . . I'm sure you understand." She gracefully held out her acrylic nails to Jack. "I'm Terri Conway, Jessica's younger sister."

He rose out of his chair. "Jack Lannigan. Nice to meet you."

Laurie's back teeth ground together in annoyance. It didn't matter if a man were dead or alive. Let a pretty woman fall all over him and he becomes stupid.

She forced a smile to appear at her lips and held out her own hand, so Jack would have to release Terri's. "And I'm Laurie Reese. We've heard *so* much about you, Terri."

The woman seemed startled for a moment, as if Jessica had given away family secrets. But her recovery was quick. Panther-quick. "You two aren't married? I mean the last names . . ."

"Of course we're married," Laurie immediately answered before Jack could open his mouth. She did, however, feel his body stiffen with shock. "Surely after two marriages you know that a woman doesn't have to take the husband's name." She derived a certain satisfaction in seeing Terri's uneasy expression. Obviously Terri didn't expect them to know her marital track record. "In fact, were you aware that a woman never legally gives up her maiden name? It's our choice which name to use, and I chose to use mine."

"Oh . . ." Terri glanced back to her sister. "And you knew Jess when she lived in Chicago?"

"That's right. When we heard about your mother, we flew in to help." Laurie put emphasis on her last word and was pleased to see the point was taken. "We'll be here for as long as she needs us." Smiling innocently, she added, "How long will you be here?"

"Oh, just until Mother's estate is settled." She glanced at Jessica. "That's why I came so early this morning. I thought we should get started."

Jessica came further into the room. "What are you talking about? What estate?"

Terri poured herself a cup of coffee and sat down

opposite Jack. She smiled at him once before answering her sister. "Mother's will. You knew about it, didn't you?"

Jessica seemed startled. "A will? Mom left a will?"

"Of course. She didn't tell you? She named me as executrix."

"*What?* She named *you*?" Jessica gulped her coffee, as if needing the jolt to soften the shock. "I can't believe it!"

Seeing her sister's reaction, Terri said, "I don't know why you're so surprised. Maybe we should discuss this at another time." She indicated the "company," as though embarrassed to have this particular meeting in front of strangers.

"No," Jessica insisted, her growing anger giving her strength. "Let's talk about it now. Jack and Laurie are friends," and she looked to them for support.

It was in that moment that she accepted them and the situation, as totally bizarre as it was, grateful for once to have someone on her side.

Remaining silent, Jack and Laurie looked to Terri. The ball was in her court. It was her move.

"Well, honestly, Jessica . . . if you insist on dragging out personal business in front of others, there's simply nothing I can do to save you embarrassment."

"Why would I be embarrassed? What does the will say? If you're executrix, then you must have already read it."

Terri took a deep breath and said, "Everything is to be divided equally in half between us."

"In half?" Jessica murmured. "The shop? Everything?"

"Everything." Terri delicately sipped her coffee, avoiding her sister's shocked expression. "I really would like to take care of this and get home. I'm co-chairperson with Vanessa Wainright on the AIDS ball next month and she's insisting on a purple and gold color scheme. Can you imagine?"

"Does that also mean this house?" Laurie asked, ignoring her last statements. "Jessica lives here." Why was Terri doing this? She was wealthy from the settlements she'd made with two ex-husbands. Vain and spoiled, she immersed herself in socially acceptable charity work. Was it only to meet husband Number Three? How could she be so charitable to others and be blind to her own sister's needs?

"The will states that the house be listed with a real estate agent one month after mother's passing. Of course, you can live here, if you want. In fact it would probably be best. We can take anything we want from it and the rest is to be sold at auction. Personally, I can't think of anything I'll take. Oh, except for my high school yearbook and things. If you come across any of them, would you save it for me?" Terri looked to her sister for a response.

Jessica slowly rose from the table and walked to the refrigerator. Reaching up, she opened the cabinet above it and brought out the bourbon. This time she didn't even bother with the coffee. She took a glass from another cabinet and filled half of it. With her back to everyone, she tilted her head and took a deep gulp of the alcohol.

"Jessica! What are you doing?" Terri demanded. "It's only ten-thirty, and you're drinking?"

"I think this has been a shock," Jack said in a flat voice.

Terri looked at him and then back at her sister. "I'm only carrying out mother's wishes. Think of it, Jess. We sell the shop and the house, and you can make a fresh start with your half. You can't want to live here forever. This is your chance to get out."

"I got out once, Terri," Jessica whispered, while still staring at the sink. "I had a life in Chicago, and it wasn't bad. But when Mom got sick I came home to help. I thought it was only going to be for a few months. It turned out to be six years."

She turned around and faced her sister. "Where were you in those six years? When did you visit? Maybe once a year? Always at Christmas, showering Mom with presents you must have known she couldn't use. What would a woman who's confined to bed do with a designer jogging outfit?"

Terri was surprised. "All the older women in Dallas were wearing them. I thought Mother could dress in something fun when her friends visited."

"Fun! *I* had to dress Mom. Do you have any idea how hard it is to pull spandex over someone's hips when they're dead weight and can't help you?" On a roll now, the anger returned to Jessica's voice. "What about the espresso machine and the Godiva chocolates? Oh God, those damn chocolates."

"Mother loved chocolate!"

"Right! And she finished the box in two days. She was confined to bed, Terri. In the last two years she couldn't use the walker to get into the bathroom, so I changed her—five and six times a day—and bathed her, rolling her over until my arms felt like they would fall off. I cleaned up those damned chocolates for a week!"

"I'm sorry. I didn't think . . ."

"Of course you didn't. Just like you never thought to call me and ask what you could do. Even if you couldn't stand to be around someone sick, even your own mother, then maybe you could have sent money to help pay for the rental of the hospital bed, or the mountains of adult diapers she went through in a month."

Jessica's eyes were filling with tears, but she couldn't stop now. Too many years of built-up anger were inside of her. "I'll never forget last Christmas when you came here and entertained us for over an hour with a detailed description of your holiday in the Caribbean, and how you were planning a skiing trip to Austria with your friends. Do you realize I haven't been away from all of this in six years? Six years! Not a single week, without worrying about the shop or whether this was the week I would wake up and find my mother dead in her room!"

Terri's face was red and she continued to stare at the surface of the table in silence.

Jessica finished her drink and quietly placed the glass on the counter. "And now you come here to tell me that the shop and this house are to be sold out from under me, and I have no say in the matter?''

"It's Mother's wish," Terri whispered, delicately touching the corners of her eyes with a fine cotton handkerchief.

"I think perhaps Jessica should read the will herself," Jack said. "Do you have it with you?"

Terri shook her head. "Harry Cohn, the lawyer mother used, has it. I read it right before the funeral, but I didn't want to say anything until it was over."

They all watched as Jessica poured herself another drink.

"Maybe I should go until Jess calms down." Terri stood up and clutched her handkerchief between her fingers. She glanced back to her sister and said, "I'll call you tonight, okay?"

Jessica didn't respond. She was staring at the amber liquid, as if it held all the answers.

When they heard the front door close, Laurie and Jack looked to Jessica. She turned around and tried to smile, but the strain showed around her mouth. "It's been quite a morning," she managed to say. "I think I'm going to take a bath."

Picking up her drink, she left them in the kitchen.

"Maybe you should go up and talk to her," Jack said to fill the silence.

Laurie was thinking. "We need a plan," she answered, deep in thought.

"What kind of plan? The woman's life is falling apart. She needs someone to talk to her."

"She's taking a bath and probably having a good

cry. Believe me, a woman doesn't want company for that. Besides, we can talk to her later. Right now we have to find a way to get rid of *her*."

Jack's eyes widened with dread. "Who?"

"The sister. Terri. Even if she did fall all over you when she walked in, you have to admit that she's arrogant, thoughtless and self-centered."

"So? She's executrix of the will."

"So, it's not fair. I've seen this happen before. One child stays home and devotes himself to the parent, and it's the one who stays away that becomes the favorite child. I'm glad I never had kids."

"And what do you think we can do? We can't change the will."

"C'mon, Jack," she urged. "This is our first challenge. I thought cops had backbone and determination. Where's your spirit?" She chuckled. "Okay, bad choice of words. How about imagination? We're ghosts. Let's haunt her."

He stared at her as if she had lost her mind. *"What?"*

"You heard me. Let's scare the little witch all the way back to Dallas. She doesn't need the money, and we can drive her nuts." It was hard not to rub her hands together with anticipation. "I like this idea."

"Well, I don't," Jack said with emphasis. "I don't think we're supposed to be doing stuff like that."

Laurie looked at him from the corner of her eye. "Did you get a booklet with instructions for this job?"

"No."

"Well, neither did I. So we'll try it my way."

Chapter 4

"I can't believe we're doing this," Jack muttered, as he walked into the TraveLodge.

Pushing open the front door, Laurie sighed with impatience. "You're just ticked off because I had to drive the car."

"I could have done it, if you'd given me time."

"We don't have time. Look, you'll get better the longer we're here."

"You drive like a maniac. Someone should have pulled you over and written you up." He hated being dependent on her.

"Were you a traffic cop?" she asked as they approached the front desk.

"No. Vice."

Laurie's eyes widened with surprise. "Vice? No kidding? Drugs and hookers and all that?"

She was so incredibly naive. "Yeah. Drugs and hookers and all that." Why bother to explain?

"Then this should be a piece of cake," she said and turned to smile at the desk clerk. "Terri Conway's room, please."

They watched as the young woman looked up Terri's name in the computer. Picking up the phone she punched in some numbers and waited for an answer. "I'm sorry," she said. "Ms. Conway doesn't seem to be in. Would you like to leave a message for her?"

Laurie shook her head. "No, but thank you." Pulling Jack's coat sleeve, she muttered, "Great, she's not here. How are we going to find out what room she's in?"

"Seven sixty-two."

"How do you know that?" she asked skeptically.

"Trust me," he said. "I've had years of experience reading phone numbers upside down. She's in seven sixty-two."

Suddenly Laurie smiled. "You know, Lannigan, I think you're going to come in handy."

He groaned. "Gee, thanks. It's great to be appreciated."

"C'mon," she said, again tugging on his coat sleeve, "let's find the elevator."

He looked at her, so full of direction and purpose. Once he had been like that, thinking he could make a difference. As the elevator started to rise, he thought about Viet Nam and later the police force. All he ever did was hold back the inevitable onslaught. For his whole life, he'd been losing ground. And now here he was, with it all behind him, and he's teamed up with Little Miss Optimism. He knew the reality of life. People were basically weak, and they only need the right circumstances before they crossed over the line.

"Do you think that stuff will work on the lock?" she whispered as the elevator left them out on the seventh floor.

He shrugged. "Jessica didn't exactly have a second-story man's kit in her basement, but I've worked with less."

"How come a policeman knows how to break into places? I mean isn't that illegal, or something?"

"Or something," he muttered.

"Oh, I get it," she said. "If you want to fight the bad guys, then it helps to know how they operate. Right?"

He gave her a look of impatience. "Right. Only this time it isn't going to help us."

"It isn't?"

Shaking his head, he pointed to the doors they passed. "These aren't ordinary locks. You need a pass card to open them."

They stood in front of Terri's room. Laurie stared at the lock with disappointment. "Then how are we going to get inside?"

"We're not," he answered with relief. The whole idea was dumb, and the last thing he wanted was to become her partner in a haunting. He may not have received instructions, but he was sure scaring people was not part of the job.

"We have to," she said. And he heard that feminine stubbornness enter her voice.

"Look, let's just go back to Jessica's. Okay? She's the one we're supposed to be helping. That's where our mission is. Not here at the TraveLodge."

But he could see that she wasn't listening. She was still staring at the door.

"We can go through it."

"What?" Surely he didn't hear her correctly.

She turned to him with an excited look on her face. "We can go through it, Jack. When I was at the cemetery, I was leaning against a tree and, well, for a moment I faded into it. I felt its age, how it needed moisture. Like with your stomach this morning. Did you see *Ghost*?"

"No," he said emphatically. "Every woman I know saw it, but I didn't."

"How come? Weren't you curious?"

"About what? Life after death? No thank you."

"You should have seen it. It might have helped you now. I mean they got some things wrong; how could they really know, huh? But I think they got the doors right."

"*What* are you talking about?" He was quickly losing the little patience he had left. "Let's just get out of here."

"No, wait." She reached out her hand and slowly stuck it into the door.

He took a step backward. "I'm not doing this."

With her hand still in the door, she turned her head to see him. "Don't be afraid."

"I'm not afraid! I'm—" He couldn't come up with an alternative. "We're not supposed to be doing things like this. This whole idea is crazy and—"

"Knock it off, Lannigan. It's not going to kill you." She grabbed hold of his wrist and walked through the door.

He found himself being pulled into it. As much as he tried to resist, she seemed to possess the strength of two men as she drew him through it. The tingling was now familiar, but it was more intense this time, entering his body like an electrical shock. "Oh, God . . ." he mumbled. It wasn't even wood. It was steel. Cold. Hard. And hollow.

Standing inside the room, he started breathing again as he tried to calm down. She stood before him, smiling, and he pulled his hand away from hers. "You could have at least told me you were going to do that!"

"Hey, if I did, you would have only argued with me. Now you can see for yourself. Wasn't it easy?"

Hearing the bright cheerfulness in her voice, he realized she annoyed him more than any other woman he had ever met. "It was cold."

"I know," she answered, while turning around to survey the room. "I guess I should have told you it wasn't wood."

"You also could have gone through it and opened the door for me."

"You needed the experience." She opened the closet and whistled. "Hey, will you look at this."

She inspected a few labels and shook her head. "Valentino. Donna Karan. Do you realize that this blouse would probably pay the rent on the dress shop for a month?"

"So? The woman's got expensive tastes." What did he know about clothes? They were never important to him. Jeans. That was his preference. In fact, he wondered how he could get a pair. Might as well be comfortable while he was here, instead of wearing the suit he'd come back in. He'd always hated suits and distrusted men who continually wore them.

"So," Laurie began as she pulled out the full length mink and slipped her arms into it. "How could Terri want half of her mother's estate when her sister's got almost nothing? I mean it's her sister. How can she be so greedy?"

"I don't think it's greed," Jack said, while walking around the room. "Terri thinks she's just following her mother's instructions. I don't think it even occurred to her that Jessica needed the money until this morning."

"Yes, but she didn't say she would do anything about it. She couldn't handle the confrontation, so she just walked out." Laurie ran her fingers up and down the soft fur. "You know, I always wanted a coat like this. I just couldn't stand the thought of those cute little minks dying for me."

"Minks are vicious, and you'd better take that off. We don't know where she is, and she could be coming back any minute."

Laurie sighed as she hung up the coat. "She's probably having dinner with some salesman she picked up in the hotel bar. After she saw that he drove a BMW, of course.''

''Why do you dislike her so much?''

''You only like her because she said you were good-looking. Typical male.''

''I believe she said great-looking. There is a difference.''

Rolling her eyes in disgust, Laurie groaned. ''Save me from the ego of a man! Okay, let's forget it. Something you said gave me an idea.''

Jack grinned. ''Don't tell me I was actually a help again.''

She held up her hand, as if to hold back any further sarcasm. ''You said Terri thinks she's just following her mother's wishes, right?''

''Right.''

''So what if her mother's wishes change?''

''I don't get it. The will's already been read. How can they change?''

Laurie smiled. ''Maybe not legally. But what if we leave certain messages that Terri should give up any rights to the house and the dress shop?''

''Messages?'' He looked confused.

Laurie nodded. ''You know, voices in the night . . . that sort of thing.''

Picking up a bottle of perfume, he smelled the expensive fragrance. ''I don't think we should mess around with a dead person's last requests.''

''Oh, really? Did you leave a will?''

''No.''

"Well, me either. But if I did, I would have tried to be fair. And as far as a dead person's last requests—I'm dead. You're dead. And I certainly didn't request this mission. Did you?"

"Hardly."

"Okay, so maybe last requests aren't the important issue here. Maybe fairness is."

"What kind of logic is that? You're dealing strictly from emotion—" He never got to finish his statement as he heard the door open.

Jack grabbed her hand and pulled her into the bathroom.

"Where can we hide in *here*?" she whispered. "At least in the bedroom we could have—"

"Don't you ever stop talking?" he interrupted in a near growl. "Just be quiet—for a change."

They listened as Terri came into the room. She threw something down on the dresser, probably her purse, and picked up the phone. After a few moments, they heard her voice.

"Jess, are you there? Pick up, okay? All right, look, maybe you're out with your friends. I'm going to have dinner with the auctioneer. We're going to discuss the best way to go about everything. I thought maybe you'd want to be there, but if you're not home . . . I'll call you tomorrow and tell you how it went. Bye."

"She's meeting with an auctioneer. We have to stop her!"

Jack glared down at the woman who had gotten him into this mess. "Shh . . . I think she's coming in here. C'mon."

He pulled back the shower curtain and shoved her inside. Getting into the tub, he stood behind Laurie and held his breath. Who would believe that he'd be hiding out in a bathtub? During twenty years on the force he'd never resorted to this!

She came into the bathroom and looked at herself in the mirror. Leaning closer, she brought her hand up to the area around her eyes as if examining it for signs of wrinkles. Just as quickly, she turned and pulled back the shower curtain about six inches.

Jack clamped his hand over Laurie's mouth to stop the gasp of surprise. With her back pressed against his chest, he could feel her lungs expand. He held his own breath as Terri turned on the shower and returned to the mirror. She began undressing, throwing her clothes on the toilet seat.

Laurie pulled his hand away from her mouth and wiped the water away from her face. Her hair was plastered against her skull. She lifted her chin and glared up at him. No words were necessary. Jack just wasn't sure if she was mad at him for getting her soaked, or the fact that his gaze kept returning to the edge of the curtain where he could see Terri performing a slow strip.

"This is ridiculous!" Laurie whispered. Unfortunately, the hot running water didn't completely muffle her voice.

Terri spun around and said, "Who's there? Is someone out there?" She grabbed her robe off the hook on the door and peeked into the bedroom. "Hello?"

Not receiving a reply, she tightened the belt around her waist and went to check.

As soon as she left, Jack pulled back the curtain and stepped out of the tub. "I knew this wouldn't work. C'mon, let's get out of here."

Laurie, dripping with water, emerged into the steam-filled room like a drowned rat. "Wait, there's something I have to do." She paused in front of the mirror.

Soon, she turned back to Jack and said, "All right. Let's go." Without asking, she took his hand and pulled him through the closest wall.

They emerged in the room next door.

"Is that you, darling?" they heard from the bathroom. "I didn't think you could get away from her this soon."

Jack and Laurie looked at each other. It was Jack who said, "Let's get out of this place."

This time Laurie didn't argue.

Terri stood in the bathroom, staring at the words written on the steamy mirror. Her heart was pounding. Her hands were shaking. Her mind refused to believe what was in front of her eyes.

I want Jess to have everything. *Go home.*

Chapter 5

"First you get me drenched by hiding in a *bath-tub* . . ."

"It was your dumb idea to go there in the first place."

"Then you make me walk down seven flights of stairs . . ."

"If we used the elevator, we would have come out in the lobby. I wouldn't want to try explaining the way we looked to hotel security."

"Then, soaking wet, you make *me* go for the car. I could have caught a death of a cold! It can't be forty degrees out there!"

"You're the one that can drive. And, Laurie? As far

as the cold goes . . . I don't think you have anything to worry about. You already bought it in the hospital. Remember?'' He wiped his hair with the towel hanging around his neck.

She glared at him as she waited for the teapot to whistle. Why did she have to be teamed up with him? Surely someone else must have died that was sane and had advanced further than a Neanderthal! ''How did you ever make Vice Detective? Blackmail?''

''I think it was my great looks.''

She ground her back teeth together. ''And how long do you intend to ride on a compliment by a self-centered, empty-headed woman?''

He grinned. ''As long as it continues to bother you. Question is, Laurie, *why* does it bother you?''

She silenced the shrieking of the teapot and poured the boiling water into the cups. ''Don't get any ideas, Lannigan. You aren't my type.''

He hooted with derision. ''Well, that makes two of us, Lady. I've never seen the attraction in tight-assed, uppity, broads.''

''Do not call me a broad,'' she said, slamming the mug of tea down in front of him. ''And I'm not tight-assed. I had lots of friends. Lots of them! And they all thought I was fun to be around.''

He used the edge of the towel to mop up the tea she had spilled. ''Oh, I'll bet you were.''

''Still arguing?''

Jack and Laurie turned to the doorway. Jessica stood in her chenille robe, an empty glass in her hands. There was a slightly glazed look in her eyes, as though nothing really mattered any more. She walked slowly into the room.

"Would you like some tea?" Laurie asked, watching her movements.

Jessica smiled. "No, thanks." She opened the cabinet over the refrigerator and poured the last of the bourbon into her glass. Getting some ice cubes, she muttered, "Guess I'll have to buy more tomorrow." She threw the empty bottle into the trash and again smiled. "Everyone comfortable, getting settled in?"

Jack pulled out a chair for her. "How do you feel?"

Sitting down heavily, Jessica sipped her drink and then stared at them. "I feel numb. I'm actually talking to two ghosts. I mean, I'm really starting to believe you guys are real." She waved her hand. "Well, not real. Like *real* . . . you know? Exist. That's it. Why are you wet? Is it raining out?"

Jack quickly said, "We each took a shower."

Jessica's giggle was slightly drunken. "I didn't think ghosts got dirty."

"Well, we do," Laurie answered. "Listen Jess . . . can I call you Jess?"

Jessica again waved her hand. "Go ahead."

"Jess, things aren't as bad as they seem."

Her chuckle of disbelief was short, but loud. "Oh, really?"

"Really," Laurie persisted. "You just have to get your life in order. Maybe you could move back to Chicago. You had friends there. You could start again."

"I'm too tired to start again. Chicago was six years

ago. Everyone's gone on with their lives. Everyone, but me." She shook her head. "There's nothing for me in Chicago anymore. My home is here. Now it's going to be sold off . . . along with everything else." She took another sip of her drink. "What's the point? Maybe I'll get a cheap apartment somewhere . . ."

"The first thing you have to do is stop drinking," Jack said in a quiet voice.

She looked up at him. "Give me one good reason why I should."

"Your health."

"I don't care about it. Look at you two. You're both young. You seem reasonably healthy. Or you were. Look what happened to you. I could get hit by a car tomorrow. At least my way I wouldn't feel it as much."

"What about the shop?" Laurie asked. "Maybe you could turn it around and make it work for you."

"It's going to be sold by my sister, remember?" Jessica grinned at them. "Look, I know you mean well, but there's nothing you can do. You seem like nice people . . . ghosts, whatever, but I wish you would go away. I really just want to be left alone."

No one said anything for a few minutes. Laurie looked at Jack and shook her head. "Okay, nothing is going to be settled tonight. I think we should all just go to sleep and start over in the morning. Are you going to the shop tomorrow?"

Jessica ran her fingers through her hair and shut her eyes for a few moments. "It's closed for three days because of the funeral," she said wearily. "I don't even know if I should reopen. What's the point? Terri's going to sell it one way or the other.''

''What's the name of it again?'' Laurie asked.

''Sara's Closet.'' Jess smiled. ''I guess it was my mom's idea of homey.''

''Well, we can talk about it tomorrow,'' Jack said. ''I think we're all about ready to put this day behind us.''

They got up and walked into the living room. ''Where are you two going to sleep?'' Jess asked. ''You can use my mom's room. They came and picked up the hospital bed this afternoon while you were out. I got them to put the double bed back in it, but it's not made. And there's a smaller bedroom behind that one, but it hasn't been cleaned in months.''

''I'll take the couch,'' Jack answered. ''Laurie can have the bedroom if she wants it.''

Jessica nodded and, still carrying her glass, murmured good night before walking upstairs.

''Forget the couch, Jack,'' Laurie said as soon as Jessica's bedroom door closed.

''Oh, come on. Give me a break. You had it last night.''

Shaking her head, Laurie said, ''You can have the couch, but we aren't going to sleep yet.''

''We're not?''

''Nope. I have an idea.''

''Forget it. Whatever it is, just forget it.'' He picked up the cranberry colored pillows from the couch and threw them on a chair. ''I'm going to sleep.''

Laurie took the pillows and threw them back on the couch. "I want to check out this dress shop, and I might need your help. C'mon, Jack. Jessica needs something to be excited about, to give her a reason to get up in the morning. I think it might be the shop."

He looked at her as if she had lost her mind. "Did you forget the shop is about to be sold?"

Laurie grinned. "Oh, you of little faith . . . I just bet Terri is shaking in her designer boots about now."

"Oh, right. Like she could even decipher that message you scrawled on the mirror."

"I think she did. And we're almost dry. Just come with me, okay?" Laurie would have batted her eyelashes at him, but she knew it wouldn't work. "Or are you afraid?"

He put his hand on his hip. "Afraid of what?"

"Afraid that I may be right." Oh, yes. The way to motivate Jack Lannigan was with a challenge. "That I might succeed in this mission, while you were resting your laurels on the couch. I'm sure they're keeping track of us somehow."

"You don't know that."

"But you don't know they aren't. Come on, Jack. Just for a little while. It won't take long."

He sighed with exasperation. "Do you even know where it is?"

Laurie smiled. "It's got to be listed in the Yellow Pages." She picked up the heavy book from under a nearby table and flipped through it. "Here. Right here. On Main Street. Shouldn't be too hard to find."

"It's not finding it that worries me. It's what you're going to do next."

Poor Jack, Laurie thought as they headed for the door. If he only knew.

Five minutes later they were standing in front of Sara's Closet. It was sandwiched in between a florist and a gift store.

"First thing I'm going to do is change the name," Laurie whispered into the night. "Something with a little more pizzazz, to shake up this neighborhood." She gestured to the rest of the street.

Main Street in Moorestown looked like Beaver Cleaver might appear at any moment. It was pure Yankee North East, with mansions converted into community and art centers. Tasteful stores were nestled next to doctor's and lawyer's offices. Among the ancient oak trees were beautiful Victorian homes that had been renovated, transformed into art galleries or antique shops. Lanterns lit the street, reminders of an era long past. At Christmas they would be decorated with evergreens and tiny white lights. In summer, baskets of colorful flowers would be hung. The community spirit was strong. Neighbors were important. The school system was the best in the state. Its library was private, yet larger than a town four times its size. Old families hung on to estates, reluctant to sell out to the nouveau riche who didn't seem effected by the recession. They built their homes in the fast diminishing fruit orchards on the edge of town, right next to the new golf course designed by Arnold Palmer.

Moorestown was the American Dream. But there

was money, old and new, and Laurie decided to try and get Jess some of it.

Jack shivered in the cold night air. "Change the name? You actually think that's going to help? The place is going to be sold in a month."

"Then we don't have time to waste. Let's see inside." Laurie walked toward the front door.

Jack pulled her back. "Hold on a minute. You didn't say anything about going in. You said you only wanted to check it out."

Laurie glanced up at him with impatience. "Look, if you're worried about going through the door, I'll do it and then open it for you."

"Maybe you'd better check the door out first. It's wired. There's an alarm system. Open that door and you'll set it off. I don't know how many times I can sweet talk the Moorestown police force into believing we're two innocent friends from Chicago."

Laurie took a deep breath and stared at the door. "Okay," she finally said, "then you have to go in my way."

"Huh ah. No way. Not me." Shaking his head, he jammed his fists into the pockets of his suit jacket. "First steel, now glass . . . No thanks. Get the key from Jessica and come back in the morning. Like normal people, Laurie. Try it, you might even remember what it's like."

"That won't work," she persisted. "I don't want Jess to know what we're doing."

He stared down at her for a moment, recognizing that fanatical gleam in her eyes. It was the same look she had when she'd announced her haunting scheme. "And what *are* we doing?" he asked, afraid of her answer.

She winked at him. "I'll tell you when we get inside."

Grabbing his wrist she leaped forward, propelling him through the glass.

He stood with his arms out in front of him trying to catch his breath. "I *hate* it when you do that!" he gasped.

Even though anger clearly showed in his expression, Laurie smiled at him as she brushed imaginary glass off the sleeves of her wool blazer. "Oh, come on, Jack. You would have stood out there in the street and argued for an hour, rather than take one little step forward. Admit it, it wasn't as bad this time."

Jack looked around the shop. "I'm not admitting anything, except that you're crazy. And I'm not following any more of your harebrained schemes."

Inspecting the shop, she spun around to face him. "But this is a good one. I promise!"

"Yeah?" he asked in a disbelieving voice. "Okay, we're inside. Let's hear it."

She came forward, an eager expression on her face. "Do you remember the fairy tale of 'The Shoemaker and The Elves?' "

He rolled his gaze toward the ceiling. "Oh, God . . . I'm getting out of here. I don't care if the cops come or—"

"No wait," Laurie said and pulled on his arm to

stop him from leaving. "Don't you remember how the elves worked during the night, making beautiful shoes for the old shoemaker?"

He looked down at her with an incredulous expression. "Are you suggesting we make shoes?"

"Where's your imagination, Jack? Look at this place. It's worse than I thought. No wonder Jess isn't making any money with this kind of inventory. It's all for grandmoms, so dark and depressing."

"That's what grandmoms wear. Dark, depressing clothes." He pulled his arm away from her fingers. "I'm leaving."

"You'll have to go through the door yourself. I'm not going to help you." She was desperate. She just knew this plan would work. "Jack, listen to me. I know what I'm talking about here. I was in advertising, remember? I've studied trends, and one of the fastest growing businesses right now is one that offers pretty clothes to women who aren't built like Barbie Dolls. Good clothes that are current with the styles. Not everyone is a size four to ten, yet until a couple of years ago women weren't offered anything but this stuff Jess has. Can you imagine being twenty years old and forced to wear a dress like this?" She grabbed a black and white flowered nightmare and made him look at it.

"We've got three days to fix this place up with some paint and lighting. Maybe a couple of plants and flowers. Bright, cheerful flowers. And great pictures. We can FedEx overnight the new stock, and I can organize an ad campaign that would draw in women from all over. We can do it, Jack. It would work. I know it.''

He didn't say anything for a few moments, just continued to stare at her. Finally, he drew in a deep breath. ''How can you be so optimistic? Didn't life teach you anything? There isn't always a happy ending.''

''But we can't just give up. We can't let Jess lose everything without even trying. If our mission is to help her, then let's really help her. Sure, she has to stop drinking. But there has to be a life after bourbon, or what's the point? This could be it, Jack. Something to build her self-esteem.''

He looked around the shop and said, ''Everything you're talking about is expensive. Where would we get the money?''

Afraid to shout out her joy at his acceptance of her plan, she said calmly, ''I thought that's where you'd help out.''

''Me? I don't have any money.''

''Well, we could just go into the hardware stores tonight and walk out with paint and—''

''Forget it. I'm not going to become a thief.''

She nodded. ''I didn't think you'd go for that one. There has to be some place where we can get some money, without hurting honest people. I know of this place in Philly that can renovate a store like this overnight. We would use them to design a set if we were rushed for a commercial. It costs a fortune to pay triple time to unions, but they get the job done.''

He wasn't looking at her. He was deep in thought. "Maybe I can come up with something," he said in an absent voice. "But I'm going to have to think about it for a while. Let's go home."

Smiling, Laurie answered, "Sure, Jack. But first we have to make a side trip."

"Now where?"

Laurie walked to the door and held out her hand to him. "I think Terri needs another nudge in the right direction."

He stared at her, as if not believing he had heard correctly. "You've got to be kidding!"

She took a firm hold of his wrist and, just before she entered the glass, looked back at him and grinned. "I'm not kidding, Jack."

She was asleep when she heard the voices. She thought at first that it was a dream, that her mind was playing tricks on her because of the bizarre writing on the bathroom mirror. Opening her eyes, she held her breath and listened, terrified that she would see the specter of her mother at the foot of the bed.

The voices, low and muffled, seemed to float out from the wall . . .

"Go home. Don't take anything away from Jessica."

"You have more than you need. Go away . . ."

She had earlier complained to the hotel's management of bad pipes making noises. Of the people in the room next door being too loud, of the maid writing things on her mirror, but this . . . Nothing could explain this! It was an outside wall, seven stories up!

She felt dizzy. Her heart was slamming against her rib cage and her breath was caught at the back of her throat, but she forced it out to whisper, "Stop it! Please . . . Please!"

A picture fell off the wall, crashing to the rug.

Two hands, women's hands, seemed to reach out of the wall, as if wanting to grab her and—

Screaming, Terri flipped on the light and threw her clothes into the black leather Georgio case.

"Ahhh, c'mon . . . you have to admit that was fun, Jack," Laurie said after they returned to Jessica's house. "I'll bet she's on her way to the airport still dressed in her nightgown and mink."

"That's the last time I'm doing it," Jack answered, taking the pillows off the couch. "She was really scared."

Laurie moved the pillows from the chair and sat down. Still grinning, she said, "Of course she was. That was the whole point. How are we supposed to fix up the shop with her poking her nose around along with auctioneers? Did you see how fast she was packing?" She knew he was angry, so she didn't expect an answer. "Okay, maybe my methods are a little unorthodox, but I told you it would work."

He spun around to face her. "A *little* unorthodox? You never said anything about throwing pictures around. And what was that bit with showing her your hands?''

''I thought it added a . . . a dramatic flair.'' Why couldn't he get into the spirit of the thing? They had done it! Terri was gone.

''Dramatic flair? She could have had a heart attack!''

Laurie made a face. ''Nonsense. She's young and healthy. We just got her adrenalin pumping, that's all.''

He opened his mouth to come back at her, but was stopped by the frantic pounding on the front door. He looked to the door, then back at Laurie. ''Who could it be? The police?''

Laurie shook her head. ''I don't know, but we'd better answer it before Jessica wakes up.''

She stood behind him, afraid of what was on the other side.

Nothing could have prepared her when Jack opened it.

''I . . . I've been driving around, not knowing where to go,'' Terri said, in between tears and hiccups. She looked like she had just been dragged through a field. Her hair was a mess; her face was puffy and red. Her mink hung off her shoulder.

Wiping at her eyes with the back of her hands, she sniffled and said, ''But then I remembered that the voices said I should go home. So here I am.''

Chapter 6

Handing her bag to Jack, Terri walked into the living room. She turned back to them, still standing in the doorway, and smiled with embarrassment. "You must think I've lost my mind."

Jack shut the door, glaring at Laurie before walking up to Terri. "Jessica's asleep. She's had a rough day."

Terri pulled her mink tighter around her shoulders. "She's not the only one. All these strange . . . things are happening. I know you won't believe me, but I think my mother is haunting me."

Laurie cleared her throat and joined them in the living room. "Why would your mother do that?"

Terri sniffled. "I don't know. She's the one that

wrote the will. I was just trying to carry out her wishes.''

"Her wishes?''

Nodding, Terri said, "About the house and the shop. But now . . . what does she want me to do? I'm so confused.'' She started crying again. "Nobody would believe what's happening to me!''

Jack looked uncomfortable. "Maybe you should follow your conscience. The truth is, Terri, your sister needs something in her life right now to hang onto. The house and the store are very important to her.''

Terri looked over her hands at him. "The will states they have to be sold.''

"Sell them to Jess,'' Laurie quickly said. "She could buy them for a token amount and then your mother's requests would be satisfied.''

Terri appeared groggy, as if she were having a hard time understanding. "I . . . I think I need to lie down. I took two Valium in the car.''

Jack nodded with relief. "We can discuss this in the morning. It's time we all went to sleep. Jess said your mother's room has a double bed in it now, so you can take that one.''

Horrified, Terri vehemently shook her head. "I couldn't sleep in there. You two take it. I mean, you're married and all. I'll just use my old room. The voice said to go home, so that's what I'll do. Get in my old room and think about everything. If I stay in there I know nothing will happen to me.''

She picked up her leather suitcase and started for

the stairs. On the third one, she stopped and turned back to them. "Aren't you coming up?"

"We'll be up later," Laurie said, not daring to look at Jack.

"Oh, please, come up with me. I would feel safer if I knew you two were in the room next to mine." Her pleading expression left little room for argument.

Filled with guilt, Laurie and Jack shut off the lights and followed Terri upstairs. Once they got her settled into the room she had used as a child, they stood at the doorway to the largest bedroom.

"Now what bright ideas do you have?" Jack whispered in disgust.

"How did I know she was going to come *here*?" Laurie whispered back.

Terri's door quickly opened. "Oh, it's just you two," she sighed with relief. "I thought I was hearing voices again."

"Just us," Laurie said with a strained smile. "We were . . . wondering where to find sheets."

"Mother always kept them in the closet to your right. I guess Jess does too."

"Thanks," Jack said and went to the closet. The women watched as he pulled out several sheets and pillowcases.

"Good night," Laurie said, waiting for Terri to close her door.

Terri seemed determined to see them inside the room, as if afraid they might sneak back downstairs and leave her without protection.

Waiting until Jack walked into the bedroom, Laurie whispered good night to Terri and closed the door. She turned back to Jack and saw him staring at the sheets he had thrown on the bed. "Look, I'm sorry. Okay? When I said for her to go home, I was thinking about Texas. I thought she would too."

"Well, she didn't. Now what? She's right in the next room, and has us trapped in here together." His voice was filled with anger and accusation.

Laurie picked up the sheets, looking for the fitted one. Finding it, she flipped it out over the mattress. "So we'll sleep in here tonight and figure out something for tomorrow."

"Sleep in that bed together?" He sounded as if he'd rather bed down outside.

Offended, Laurie straightened from fitting the last corner of the sheet. "There isn't even a chair in here and I'm not sleeping on the floor, are you?"

He looked around the room with disgust. "I can't believe this."

"Look, Lannigan, I'm not going to attack you. I barely like you. So your virtue is intact. Besides, in our state, we probably couldn't be tempted by Kevin Costner and Michelle Pfeiffer." She almost laughed as she threw him a pillow. "I'll do the sheets; you handle the pillowcases."

He caught the pillow and grabbed a white cotton case. As he began stuffing it, he muttered, "I must be being punished. This has to be Purgatory, or something real close to it."

Laurie looked in the closet and brought out a yellow woolen blanket. Smoothing it over the sheets, she glanced up at him and smiled. "I'm not going to argue with you anymore." She removed her blazer and started to unbutton her skirt. "I'm going to bed."

He continued to stare at her as she stepped out of her skirt. "You're getting undressed?" he asked in disbelief as she took off her pantyhose and folded it into her shoes.

She glanced up at him. "I'm sleeping in my blouse and slip. I haven't been out of these clothes in two days." She pulled back the blanket and got into bed. When her head hit the pillow, she closed her eyes and sighed with pleasure.

Jack kept watching her, unable to believe this was the same stuffy woman who had driven him crazy. Now here she was, half undressed, expecting him to get into bed with her.

Laurie opened her eyes and looked at him. "What are you doing? Aren't you tired?"

"I was tired three hours ago when you dragged me out of this house to go haunting. I was just wondering how you expected me to sleep."

She looked puzzled. "What do you mean? I don't snore."

"I mean I've been in these clothes for the same amount of time. It was one of the reasons why I wanted to sleep on the couch."

Her gaze left his face and traveled down his body

to his pants. "Oh. Oh, yeah. Well, I guess you can take them off. Just stay on your side of the bed."

He unbuckled his belt. "Why, thank you for your permission, but you've already taken possession of my side of the bed."

"I always sleep on the right."

"So do I," he countered.

"You can have it tomorrow then," she said and turned on her side so she wouldn't have to watch him undress.

"I don't intend to be in this room tomorrow night," he answered, hanging his trousers on the door handle of the closet.

"Fine. Do what you want."

He flipped off the light. "I will." He got into bed and punched his pillow down before turning his back to her and staring at the moonlight that was coming in through the sheer curtains. He simply couldn't relax with her behind him. She was the most irritating woman he had ever been around.

"Jack?"

"What?" Why couldn't she just go to sleep?

"Do you think we should tell Terri to go home again? I mean if she heard it in this house then she would know we meant Texas."

He quickly turned around and grabbed her arm. "Don't you dare move out of this bed tonight," he ordered. "Don't call out. Don't stick your hands through walls, or levitate anything! You are to stay right here with me. Do you understand?"

She looked down to his hand on her arm and then back to his face. Her smile was sweet, almost serene. He should have been warned. "Gee, Jack, I didn't know you cared."

He dropped her arm and closed his eyes, trying to control his temper. "Just go to sleep," he muttered.

"I can't. I wish I could, but I keep trying to figure out a way to make it all happen for Jessica. I just know if we fixed up the shop she would take an interest in life again and stop drinking."

"Everything isn't that simple. The reasons why she drinks go a lot deeper than a depressing dress store."

"That's just it. Her whole life is depressing," Laurie said. "We have to start somewhere, and the shop is the perfect place. All we need is money to begin. Why can't we be invisible, so we can walk into a bank and—"

"I already know where to get the money," Jack interrupted.

Laurie leaned up on her elbow. "You do?" she asked in an excited voice. "Where?"

He hesitated telling her. Knowing he would need her assistance, though, he decided to answer. "Drug money."

"Huh? You're not going to sell drugs, are you? I mean you didn't even want to steal paint out of a hardware store!"

He couldn't help it. He laughed. "I'm going to take money that was already used for drugs."

"Like evidence money they keep locked up?"

He shook his head. "No. That would jeopardize

pending cases. I'm talking about taking money from the dealers themselves.''

He could tell she was thinking. Finally, she said, ''Won't that be dangerous?''

''What are they going to do? Kill me?'' He laughed and she joined in.

''You've got a point there. How are we going to do it?''

He stopped laughing. ''I never said anything about you getting the money. I'll do it. I just need you to drive the car.''

She smiled. ''Ah. The getaway car.''

''That's right. Now all I have to figure out is how to launder the money.''

''I don't get it. Launder it?''

''It's dirty money, and probably marked by the dealer. We're talking about a big business here, and in that particular one there isn't a whole lot of trust.'' He linked his fingers behind his head and sighed before closing his eyes. ''I'll figure it out by the time we get the money tomorrow morning.''

''We're going in the morning?''

''To Philly.'' He actually smiled, thinking about going back across the bridge. Philadelphia. That was familiar turf. Suddenly, he couldn't wait until daybreak. It was finally his turn to be in control.

He stood on the steps in front of his district, looking up at the old brick building. A familiar knot formed in his belly. It was automatic, the edge he had needed to

93

stay sharp. In that moment he realized how vital his job had been to his perception of well-being. It was the only thing in his life that gave him a sense of purpose.

A blue uniform nearly walked into him and he looked down with a wide grin. "Shultz! How the hell are you?"

The stocky man breezed right past him to the parking lot where his cruiser waited.

Jack stared after the man, confused. He had to have seen him. Probably preoccupied, that's all. Pushing open the glass door he walked inside, eager to see his old life.

He was assaulted by the routine chaos of the place. What was once commonplace now seemed like mass confusion. Junkies, hookers and DWI's were being processed either in or out—social misfits that society had forgotten and were now a part of the revolving system. Cops were moving about with a purpose. Phones were ringing. Reports were being typed. The smell of burnt coffee, cigarettes and disinfectant permeated the building. In the corner cage a man screamed out for someone to get the snakes off his head. A voice shouted back telling him to shut up.

He saw several men that he knew, officers he had worked with during the years. They all looked right through him, as if he wasn't there.

"Hey, handsome, you a lawyer?"

Jack turned at the sound of the woman's voice. Her skin was the color of warm caramel. The long black wig she wore was tilted to one side, and caked with too much hair spray. Her makeup was heavy and smeared, as if she'd been crying, and the skin-tight dress she wore left nothing to the imagination.

"You can see me?" he asked the hooker.

She smiled with a practiced seductiveness. "Well, I sure do like what I see. You a lawyer? Maybe you can help me, huh? I'll make it worth your time."

"Hey, Lucy, who're you talking to over there?"

She turned her head back to the arresting officer. "My lawyer. He's going to get me out of this dump!"

Looking back at him, she fluttered her long eyelashes. "You will, won't you? I can't stay here."

"I'm not a lawyer," Jack said absently, wondering why Phil Polis didn't recognize him when he'd looked at the hooker.

"Then what are you?" the woman demanded.

"I'm . . . I was a cop," he answered, as a strange thought came to him.

"Shit! A cop! Get the hell away from me!"

Phil Polis walked up to them and took hold of his collar's upper arm. "What's wrong with you? Are you back on smack, or something?"

Lucy tried to pull her arm away. "I was just talkin' to this cop, is all."

Phil looked right past Jack. "What cop?"

"*This* one," Lucy said, and gave Jack a disgusted look.

Phil shook his head and pulled Lucy toward his desk. "Now you're seeing things, huh? Well, come on, sweetheart. Let's get started. You know the routine."

They couldn't see him! Jack started to wave his arms around, drawing attention to himself. The only ones that looked at him were people he didn't know. That explained Shultz on the steps and Phil. It made a strange kind of sense. His life was over; he didn't exist for anyone who knew him.

He realized he had to find Mike. Mike Rafferty had been his partner for six years. They had worked together, gotten drunk together. Laughed and cried together. They had each saved the other's life more than once. Mike was more than a partner—he was his best friend. If anyone in the whole damn precinct could see him, it would be Mike.

He almost ran to the Vice Department. Vinny Scampeca sat at his old desk, and there were pictures of Vinny's kids where Jack's '80 World Series baseball had been. Then his gaze shifted to the desk in front of Vinny and a smile appeared at his lips.

Mike.

Short and skinny, Mike Rafferty looked ten years younger than his forty-four years. He always wore a White Sox baseball cap, a sentimental reminder of spending his youth in Chicago.

"Hey, Vin, what do we got on this son of a bitch Nast?" Mike threw the manila folder on Vinny's desk and sat back to play with one of the cigarettes that he hadn't lit in two years.

Vinny pored over the contents of the folder. "Let's see . . . Frankie Nast. Two priors. One for armed robbery in '81. Served five years at Graterford. Last one was for dealing in coke. Somehow the evidence disappeared and the case was dismissed.''

Scanning the thick file, Vinny lit a Marlboro and absently blew the smoke across his desk. As if by reflex, Mike leaned forward and inhaled.

"Likes to call himself 'The Untouchable,' " Vinny said. "His uncle's a capo in the Gamballi family. Nast runs his operation in North Philly out of his house. A pig sty on the outside, but I've heard inside it's a nightmare of black velvet. Paintings. Furniture. Rugs. He's a mean bastard. Brought in four times in the last year for assault and battery. Mostly women he's lived with. Each time the charges are dropped. Word is out that anyone who crosses him is beat shitless and never seen again.''

Mike closed his eyes for a moment, as if in meditation, and then slowly asked, "So how come this human excrement is still walking?''

Vinny shrugged. "Every time we manage to get a search warrant, by the time we get there the place just looks like a bad Vegas lounge. Clean as a whistle.''

"So he's being tipped off by someone here or in City Hall,'' Mike said, shaking his head.

Vinny nodded. "Seems like it. Makes sense, with Nast's family connections.''

Jack leaned over and looked at the picture in the folder. Frankie Nast had stared at the camera lens with a cold-hearted, cruel expression. His face was long and angular; the skin under his cheekbones was marked by a childhood disease or adolescent acne. There was more than a hint of arrogance around his mouth, as if he knew he'd be back out on the street within hours.

"I want this son of a bitch," Mike said with a calmness that Jack recognized. It was a familiar serenity that always preceded an explosion of temper. By tomorrow morning, Mike would have come up with a plan to bust Nast. It would be rash and high risk. And this time Jack couldn't stop him.

Memorizing the address, Jack grinned at Mike and said, "A farewell gift, partner. Somebody's got to look after you."

With one last glance around the squad room, Jack fought off the depression and turned to walk away.

Mike lifted his head as a weird chill ran up his back to settle in his scalp. "Hey, did you say something, Vinny?"

Scampeca shook his head.

Looking around the department, Mike whispered one word.

"Spooky . . ."

Diamond Street. It was like a war zone.

Shells of burned-out row houses, littered with glass, were the playground for children. Others were just abandoned and boarded up to keep out the junkies. Frames of cars that had been stripped sat deserted next to Mercedes, BMW's and Jaguars that were watched over by ten-year-olds. White, black and Hispanic teenagers stood huddled in doorways, pockets of color and race, looking for a handout or their next vial of crack.

"I want you to stay in the car," Jack ordered, as he stared at one of the few houses on the street that was inhabited.

"But I don't want to stay out here alone," she answered, already afraid of her surroundings.

He turned to her. "Don't argue with me on this, Laurie. Now we're in my territory, and I know what I'm doing. Do not get out of this car." Unlocking his door, he got out and walked up to the house.

She immediately locked his door and sat back, shivering in the freezing morning air. A huge mural had been painted on the side of a brick building, depicting men and women dancing. The faces looked happy, almost carefree. The clothing was bright, cheerful and sexy; in the background was a blue sky, palm trees and a turquoise ocean. She wondered who had painted it, who had decided to bring such a startling contrast to this decaying neighborhood of poverty and apathy. Perhaps the artist longed for the country he had left behind. And then she thought of her own neighborhood. Uptown. Upscale. Not so very far away from this horror. How could she have lived in the same city and have never seen this in person? She knew it existed, had seen pictures of it on the nightly news, but she had felt removed from it. Helpless to bring about any kind of change, she had isolated herself from the reality of it. Now it surrounded her, a menacing presence that forced her to acknowledge it.

She heard the yelling and a woman's scream. Even the kids on the street looked up to the house Jack had entered. Fear suddenly ran through her. What if Jack were in trouble? He had difficulty in washing dishes. How could he handle whatever was going on in that house? Without thought, she pushed open the car door and ran to help him.

"Please, Frankie, I'm sorry! I . . . I won't ask anymore." The woman wiped at the blood dripping from her bottom lip and backed away in fear. "I pro—promise."

Frankie Nast slowly walked in her direction, enjoying the smell of her panic. "What'd I tell you, huh? What *I* do is my business. This is my house. It's my money you use. I put the clothes on your back. You don't question me. You *never* question me!"

"I won't! I swear, I won't. It's—it's just that Carmen said you were in Merinos with another woman and—"

His fist shot out and connected with the side of her head, sending her sprawling onto the black velvet rug. Breathing heavily, he leaned over her as he felt the power surge through his body. "You never learn, do you, Nina? Now I'm going to have to teach you again. I want you to remember that you're makin' me do this to you."

Just as he grabbed a fist full of her hair, he felt himself being jerked back and thrown to the floor. Recovering, he looked up at the man standing before him. "Who the hell are you? Get out! Get out of my house."

Jack watched as he crawled to his knees. "Stand up, you son of a bitch. Or is it just that you get off on beating women?"

Nast rose to his feet and straightened his silk shirt. "You got any idea who I am?"

Jack laughed. "Oh, I know exactly who you are. You're every low-life bastard I've tried to get off the street all rolled into one. Now where do you keep it, Frankie?"

"Keep what?"

"Don't get cute with me. The money. Where is it?"

The corner of Frankie's upper lip rose, as if in a snarl. "You got balls, motha'fucker. You come in here without so much as a baseball bat and expect me to hand over my money." He shook his head. "Why don't you just get the hell out?"

Watching as Frankie walked over to a table, Jack said, "I'm not leaving without the money. I would say you can make it easier on yourself, but . . . I don't think so. I'm gonna enjoy beating the crap out of you."

Nast spun around with a thin, five-inch blade in his hand. He waved it back and forth in a small arc. "I think you just made a mistake, big mouth. Nobody threatens Frankie Nast."

"Nobody until now," Jack whispered with a smile of anticipation.

He knew exactly when Frankie was going to make his move. Instead of getting out of the way when Nast lunged at him, Jack stood still and felt the cold knife pass through him. Seeing Frankie's stunned expression, he laughed before seizing the man's collar. "Ever hear of the Angel of Mercy, Frankie?"

Nast could only blink.

"Well, I'm not him," Jack pronounced, just before

he brought back his fist and slammed it into Nast's stomach.

When Frankie doubled over, Jack grabbed his hair and lifted his face. It gave him great pleasure to connect his fist with those cruel eyes. Frankie went down on one knee, but Jack wasn't finished.

"The money, Frankie. Don't make me ask again. Dead men can get real nasty."

Frankie brought a shaky hand up to his eye, saw his own blood, and then pointed to a huge black velvet painting of Elvis over the bar. Jack made him stand up and then shoved him toward it. "What a way to desecrate the King. Open it."

Frankie stood before the painting and hesitated.

"Don't even think about it," Jack warned. "If there's an iron in there and you touch it, I'll use it on you. Just one less piece of shit walking the streets. The knife didn't work and neither will the gun. I'm already dead, but if you want to join me, it makes no difference."

Pulling back the painting, Frankie fumbled with the combination to the safe. When he finally got it right, he opened it and stepped back.

Jack looked inside and whistled. "Looks like business has been good."

Frankie took that opportunity to run for the door, as if the hounds of hell were at his heels. Three feet from it, he stopped dead in his tracks as a woman seemed to leap right through it.

Jack caught him from behind and slammed him against the wall. Another velvet painting, this one of a mean-looking Mexican smoking a cigarette, crashed to the ground.

Jack turned to Laurie. "Didn't I tell you to stay outside?"

"I couldn't," she answered, looking from him to the man against the wall. "I thought you might need help."

"Help?" Frankie's voice was incredulous. "What are you people?" he demanded in a state of shock.

Jack looked at Laurie and grinned. "You still haven't gotten it yet, have you, Frankie? To use a cliché, we're your worst nightmare."

Grabbing Frankie's arm, he pulled him toward a huge velvet chair. "Laurie, I want you to call the police and ask for Mike Rafferty in Vice. When you get him give him this address and tell him to get over here fast. Frankie Nast is out of business."

Jack waited until she made the call and then he ripped the phone cord out of the wall. He used it to tie Frankie to the chair and stood back to admire his handiwork. Walking over to the safe, he said to Laurie, "Get a towel out of the bathroom and come over here."

In less than a minute, Laurie stood next to him with the black towel. "There's a woman moaning in the corner. Shouldn't we help her?"

Jack began dropping stacked bills into the towel. "I'll check her before we leave. If her injuries aren't serious, Mike will take care of her. Well, well, well— what do we have here?" Pushing aside Zip-loc bags filled with eight-balls and twentybags of coke, Jack brought out a small brown leather book. He thumbed through it, saw it was Nast's score sheet of pushers, and smiled with satisfaction. "I think we just hit the mother lode."

Nervous, Laurie looked up at him. "What?"

"Never mind. I'll explain later; we've got to get out of here. Put the rest of the money into the towel." There was a kilo in the rear of the safe the size of a tissue box. It had to be worth twenty-five thousand, but he decided to leave it as evidence. Instead, he grabbed the plastic bags of coke and turned back to the room. "I have to take care of our benefactor."

Walking up to Nast, Jack said, "Open your mouth, Frankie."

"What're you gonna do?" Defenseless, Frankie's eyes were wide with fear.

"I'm going to make sure this time you don't walk." Jack forced open the man's mouth and began shoving egg-sized balls of cocaine inside. "It's up to you how you want this to go down. You can sit here, very still, until they come and find you, or you can screw it up, in which case you'll probably bite through the plastic bags. I would imagine this amount of coke would kill anybody—even you. Maybe you should just sit and pray the cops aren't held up in traffic."

When he couldn't jam anything more into Frankie's mouth, Jack pulled back the dealer's waistband and dropped the twentybags into his pants. He put more into Nast's pockets. "I don't think there's going to be any question about evidence this time, Frankie."

Nast made some noises and Jack pretended to understand the garbled sound. "Yeah, yeah, whatever. Remember you have the right to remain silent. I suggest you try it."

He checked the woman on the floor, found her to be coming around, and quickly rose. "Are you finished?" he asked Laurie. "We've got to get out."

Standing in front of the safe, she looked back at him from over her shoulder. "There's still some money," she said in a high, nervous voice.

"Leave it," Jack stated, coming up to her and taking her arm. "Whatever you've got will have to be enough. The rest is evidence."

Completely out of her element, Laurie merely nodded. She hugged the bulging sack to her stomach and allowed him to lead her out of the house. Once in the car, her teeth started chattering as Jack slammed the car into drive and left Diamond Street behind them.

"I can't believe we just did that!" Shock was quickly turning into excitement. "I mean, we walked right in there and cleaned out that guy's place. Think of it! We could go into banks and . . . and help all the homeless. And—"

"Calm down," Jack said as he turned the car toward downtown. "And you can forget about any more heists. That's not our mission. Jessica is. The only reason we—"

"Jack!" Laurie interrupted in an astonished voice. "What?"

"You're driving. Look at you!"

Jack glanced at her, saw a wide grin that seemed to light up her face, and he started smiling. "I am, aren't

I?'' He sat back, more relaxed. ''I guess you were right about concentrating. All I could think about was getting away from that place.''

''Well, we did it. God, I felt like I was watching 'Miami Vice,' or something. Did you really shove those drugs in his mouth? What if he chokes?''

''Then I just did the city a favor. Forget about him. If everything goes right, Frankie Nast will be spending the next twenty years behind bars.'' He looked at the large lump in the towel she still held to her chest. ''What's important is that we got the money.''

Laurie peeked into the towel. ''How much do you think is in here?''

Jack shrugged. ''I don't know, but we can't pull over and count it yet. Wait until we get into Jersey.''

His words seemed to break through her shock and she quickly lifted her head. ''Wait. Don't go back yet. I have to go to the office and get the contractor's name and number.''

He looked at her. ''You don't remember it?''

Shaking her head, she said, ''Turn right here and follow this until you get to Walnut Street. It's on a big rolodex; won't take me a minute.''

When they pulled up in front of her office, Jack took the money from her and said, ''Wait a second, Laurie. There's something you should know.''

Impatient to see her old digs, she turned back to him. ''What?''

''Nobody who knew us when we were alive can see us now. We don't exist to them, so . . . I guess we're not here for them either. Don't try and talk to them. No one will hear you.''

She stared at him. "How do you know this?"

"It happened in my district. My best friend, my old partner, he didn't even know I was standing right next to him. I just don't want you to be upset when you go in there. Believe me, it's depressing as hell. Just get in, get the name, and get out. Okay?"

She looked at the huge building and murmured, "Okay. I'll be right back."

The elevator opened on the fifteenth floor directly into the lobby of Baynard, Henderson and Royce. The contrast to Diamond Street was startling. Trendy pop art lined the walls next to copies of ads. Everything was bright and cheerful. As she passed Jeanine, the receptionist, she realized Jack was right. No one could see her. She walked down the hallway to her office, seeing colleagues laughing together. The women were stylish and confident. The men were Center City preppy. Why hadn't she noticed before that every single one of them wore suspenders? Like trademarks of their station, bottles of Evian water sat atop each desk. As she approached her office, she heard a female voice inside. Looking in she saw a young woman, no more than twenty-four, sitting at her old desk. Her long blond hair was straight and shiny, and she absently flicked it back over her shoulder as she talked to Ray Newman about an account. She was eager, enthusiastic and . . . and bubbly.

Laurie felt like someone had reached in and twisted

her stomach muscles. She had been replaced by this child. It all seemed too easy. All her plants and paintings were gone. There was no sign that she had ever been here. It was as if she had never existed in this office. Feeling sick, she backed out into the hall and took a deep breath. She had to leave, but first she needed the name of the contractor. Rushing to Sam Henderson's office, she ignored the two men in deep discussion and flipped through the rolodex until she found what she wanted. As she memorized the name and number and turned to leave, Sam whispered in a stunned voice, "Did you see that, Barney? The rolodex! It was turning by itself!"

Laurie couldn't even smile at her boss's words. She was too depressed.

Fighting back tears when she sat in the car, she looked at Jack and said, "I guess you really can't go home again."

Chapter 7

Jess was stunned when she walked into the kitchen and found her sister. "Terri? What time did you come? You should have woke me."

Terri turned from the stove and said, "I came last night after you fell asleep. Jack and Laurie let me in." She smiled shyly, as though trying to find out if Jess was still upset with her. "There's coffee. I was going to make breakfast, but it's nearly noon, so I went for grilled cheese sandwiches and tomato soup."

Astonished by the sight of her sister actually cooking, Jess poured herself a cup of coffee and sat down at the table to watch. "Mom would always make grilled cheese and tomato soup on snow days when we had off from school," she murmured.

Terri glanced over at her. "She did, didn't she? I remember that." She looked back to the frying pan. "Maybe that's why I made it. It must remind me of a time when I felt taken care of. Of course, there's probably enough cholesterol here to give us both heart attacks."

In spite of everything, Jess grinned. "I don't think one time is going to hurt us."

Terri shrugged. "Still, it's going to be terrible for our complexion. Not to mention our hips—"

"Then let's not mention them." Being a size fourteen with a sister who probably wore a six was not easy.

"What the hell. It's already made."

For the first time in Jess' recollection, Terri served her. It was an odd sensation. Eating the soup brought back memories—memories of waiting for her younger sister to finish breakfast so she could walk her to school. Helping Terri with her homework. Celebrating with her when she finally got her period and consoling her a few months later when the novelty had worn off. She remembered defending her to their mother when Terri would come home late from a date, or wear too much makeup, or was caught smoking. She had even tried not to mind that her younger sister was asked to her senior prom. But she did. There was a tiny spark of resentment that she had kept under control since she was a teenager. Resentment that Terri was prettier, more popular, that everything seemed to come so eas-

110

ily to her, whether it was geometry or a date to her older sister's prom.

In contrast, Jess felt like her own life was a series of delays, of waiting. Waiting for her breasts to grow, to shave her legs, to wear a bra, to stop being clumsy and awkward. Waiting for a boyfriend, to be asked to dance, for her pimples to go away, for a first date— Always waiting. Even as an adult in Chicago the scenario had been the same. Only the circumstances had changed. Then she had waited to lose her virginity, for a man to show interest, to make the first move. She had waited for Mr. Perfect to come into her life and change it, to take away her loneliness and uncertainty. She had married in haste and divorced just as quickly. She had waited all these many years for the right person, the one who would make her happy. But no more. Now she was realistic. The time for fantasies was over. Wrinkles were beginning to form around her eyes. Her breasts were starting to sag. Her hips were nearly Rubenesque. Clearly, her time had passed. If Mr. Perfect was even in the same hemisphere, by this time he was married to Mrs. Perfect with children, dogs and the white picket fence . . . everything that would never be hers. Now all she waited for was the end of the day, for night to come, for sleep, for the bourbon to take the edge off the pain of reality . . . for release.

"Listen, Jess. I've been thinking."

Jessica looked up from the creamy red soup that seemed to hold the memories of a lifetime. "I'm sorry. I wasn't listening."

Terri put her sandwich back on the plate. "I said I've been thinking about Mother's will. You're right. It isn't fair. I don't need the money and you seem to want to stay here, so if I sell the shop and the house to you then I could still carry out her wishes."

Jess shook her head. "Terri, what are you talking about? Yesterday you were so adamant. You had the lawyer and an auctioneer all lined up."

Holding up her hand, Terri quickly said, "I know. I guess I was confused, and I wanted to have everything handled so I could get back to Dallas."

"What happened between yesterday and today?"

Terri sighed and gazed around the kitchen. "Let's just say I'm seeing things more clearly now. The shop and the house are yours if you really want them. Although I still think you should make a fresh start somewhere else."

Jess looked at her in amazement. "I . . . I don't know what to say. Thanks . . . for the offer, but I couldn't get the money together to buy you out."

"I think you can. I'll take a dollar each. For the house and the shop."

Slowly placing her spoon in the bowl, Jess said, "A dollar!"

"It was your friend, Laurie's, suggestion. Mother said sell them. She didn't specify an amount. We can go to the lawyer's this afternoon and take care of it."

"Are you serious?"

Terri's eyes seemed to fill with moisture as she nodded. "You were right yesterday, Jess. I stayed away. I pretended I was so busy with my life, but the truth is I was scared to death. I was so afraid because I knew she was never going to get better and I didn't want to see it. If I didn't see it, I wouldn't think about it. And maybe it wouldn't happen. I was never very practical and . . . and you were." The tears were falling down her cheeks and she quickly wiped them back with the side of her hand. "But I should have helped. You were right. I should have been here—for both of you."

Jess felt a burning at the back of her throat. "She missed you. She talked about you all the time, bragging to her old friends about your glamorous life—all your friends, your adventures. Even if you weren't here, you added something to her life. And she was proud of you."

"Hah!" Terri sniffled. "If she only knew."

"Knew what?"

"The lie I've been living."

"What lie?"

It took a few moments before Terri could speak. When she did, her voice was low and she had to stop several times to swallow back the tears. "I'm so lonely, Jess. I have this . . . this big house and I wake up in the morning and wander down to the kitchen alone. It's so empty. There's no one to share it with. I spend my time trying to figure out ways to fill the void. Charities. Parties. Traveling. Golf. God, can you believe I've even taken up golf? Just about all my friends are married. At least the ones who still remained friendly after Tom and I got divorced. It's weird what happens. It's almost as if you have a contagious disease. Get too close and you're a reminder of a failed marriage. They might have to examine their own situations and see the cracks they've been patching up over the years. And if it could happen to you, then it could happen to them.''

Sympathy welled up inside of Jess. ''But I always thought you had this wonderfully fulfilling life.''

No longer interested in lunch, Terri pushed the bowl of soup away from her. ''Look . . . I've had two marriages, both of them failures. When I'm not married I seem to attract the wrong men. And what's really available out there, anyway? Especially at my age. Someone else who's failed at a relationship? I keep thinking I need a man to feel complete and I go from one to another, searching for happiness. But I can't find it.''

Jess stared at her in amazement. ''I thought you were so happy. I guess I was even jealous. It's hard to think of you as being lonely. You always seemed like you had everything anyone could want.''

''I'm a good actress. You learn how after two divorces. Nobody wants to hear how miserable you really are, so you give everybody what they want, what they expect.''

''I know what you mean,'' Jess said, not quite believing that she and her sister were really communicating. ''I feel like I've been doing that my entire life.''

Terri shook her head. ''Why is that? Why do we do it? You thought I had everything. And all I want is to find a partner to share my life. Who would think it would be this hard?'' She looked over at her sister and said quietly, "You know, Jess, what I really miss? The attention. Not just the sex. It's the touching, holding hands, sharing at the end of the day. Waking up in the morning with someone that cares about you. Yeah . . . I miss it." As if catching herself getting melancholy, she laughed. "And the sex. Who am I kidding? It's been over three months."

Jess picked up her sandwich and examined the browned crust. "Three months, huh? Try almost seven years."

Terri was speechless.

Jess saw her expression and laughed. "Now, don't you feel better? Three months is nothing."

"Are you serious? Seven years?"

Taking a deep breath, Jess nodded. "I'm serious."

"My God, I've heard about celibacy, but I never thought—"

"Celibacy, Terri, is usually a choice someone makes. I sort of just fell into it." She pushed Terri's sandwich in front of her. "Stop staring at me and eat your lunch. It isn't so bad any more. There were a couple of tough years after I moved back here, but then . . . I don't know. I don't think about it any more. It just isn't a part of my life."

"But seven years," Terri protested. "I can't believe it! I'd go crazy."

Jess smiled. "No, you wouldn't. You'd find ways to fill the void."

"Like what? What can fill that kind of void?"

Shrugging, Jess glanced at the cabinet over the refrigerator. Was she out of bourbon? She couldn't remember. Suddenly, it was very important to know. She got up and walked over to the refrigerator. "Do you want ketchup on your sandwich? Remember how Mom thought it was disgusting?" she asked, while pretending to search the inside of the fridge. "I can't find it. There has to be some in one of these cabinets." She opened the one where she always kept the bourbon and saw it was gone. She did finish it. Why didn't she remember to replace it? Her shoulders sagged in disappointment.

"How do you fill the void, Jess?" Terri repeated.

"Huh?" She glanced at her sister. "What do you mean?"

"Do you fill it with drinking? Is that how you do it?"

She turned around and leaned back against the countertop. "What are you talking about?"

Terri shook her head. "I do it with shopping. I'm addicted to it. If I don't have anything fulfilling in my life then I go out and buy a handbag for six hundred dollars. It makes me feel better. Some people substitute food for sex. Maybe that's what you do with a bottle."

Jess could feel her defenses rise. "Listen, Terri, if I have a drink it's because I want to unwind at the end of the day. It's not because I've been without sex."

"It wasn't even noon yesterday, Jess."

"Mom was just buried and then I heard about her will. If I needed an excuse, that was it." Jess returned to the table and toyed with her food. "Let's not get into an argument, okay?" She looked over at her sister.

"This is the first time in years you and I have sat down and really talked."

Terri nodded. "Okay. But if you need me, Jess? If you have a problem . . . this time I won't stay away. I promise."

The tears that were always so close to the surface emerged and ran down her cheeks. She reached across the table and held out her hand. Terri immediately took it and smiled. Seeing the tears in her sister's eyes, Jess grinned and said, "No kidding? Six hundred for a purse? The best male prostitute in Dallas wouldn't have cost that much!"

Terri laughed and the awkwardness between them was gone. "You're probably right, but who knows where to find them. It's weird that you should say that because I've actually thought about it."

"What?" Jess chuckled. "A male prostitute?"

Nodding, Terri tried to stop laughing long enough to say, "I know they're out there somewhere. Classy. Clean. With good references. I just don't have the courage to ask around. But if they have bordellos for men, then they should have them for women."

"Yeah," Jess agreed. "But the real question is, could the men put in an eight hour day?"

Jack and Laurie walked into the kitchen to find the sisters laughing hysterically.

"Did we miss something?" Laurie asked with a smile. The laughter was contagious. She grinned at Jack and saw his confusion.

Jess wiped at her eyes and said, "Just girl talk. It's been a long time."

Laurie glimpsed the affection between the sisters and asked, "Are you two okay now?"

Terri and Jess looked at each other and nodded. "We're okay," Jess whispered and felt the first spark of happiness. It was true. She had made peace with her sister.

"Jessica, do you have an attache case, or a duffel bag?" Jack said, obviously uneasy with female bonding.

She looked at him and noticed for the first time the bundle he carried in front of him. "What is that?"

Jack looked down at the towel and answered, "Ahh . . . clothes. That's why we need the duffel bag. Laurie and I are going to Atlantic City."

"Atlantic City?" Why were two ghosts going to Atlantic City? "When?"

"In a few minutes. Do you think we could have the bags?"

Jess looked at them. They were like two children that had a secret. Too tired to figure it out, she said, "Sure. I'll go up and get them."

"And Laurie could use a purse," he added. "A big one, if you have it."

"A purse?"

"In case I win," Laurie remarked with a quick laugh.

As they followed her up the stairs, Jess knew the two of them were up to something. She just couldn't figure it out. What were they going to do in Atlantic City?

* * *

It stood before them, like Sodom and Gomorrah, a city of light and temptation. It beckoned to them with its multicolored lights and laser beams that shot out into the early night. Bally's. Trump. Caesar's. Taj Mahal.

"Are you sure we can do this?" Laurie whispered with excitement while taking in the spectacle. "It can't be legal."

Jack rolled up the window after paying the last toll on the Atlantic City Expressway. "Of course it isn't legal." He passed a Ford Escort and settled into the right hand lane. "Neither was relieving Frankie of eighty-six thousand dollars. Besides, even if we're caught, what can they do to us?"

She nodded. "You're right. I keep forgetting." Taking a deep breath, she asked, "Well, where do we start? Bally's?"

"We might as well hit Caesar's first. We're going to drive right up to it."

"I'm nervous," she said as they left the expressway and entered the city.

"I've already explained it to you."

"Do it again, okay?" They were stopped at a red light and Caesar's was a block away. His plan had sounded plausible three hours ago after they had given the contractor a sizable deposit to begin work on the shop. But now? Now when it was time to carry through with the scheme, Laurie was having doubts.

"All we have to do is get ten thousand dollars worth of chips at each casino. We play with the high rollers for about an hour. Lose a couple of thousand, and win what we can. Then we cash everything in, get clean money back, and move on to the next casino." He pulled into the valet parking and stopped the car.

"Do we have to lose two thousand at each place? I mean, Jessica could use it."

Jack laughed. "Yes, we have to lose some money to appear credible. Believe me, it's a small price to pay to launder this amount of cash. It's like acting. You just assume the role of some rich snob who's so bored she can afford to drop two grand without blinking a false eyelash. Oh . . . sorry. That wasn't meant as an insult." He looked at her. "Are you okay?"

"I was neither rich, nor a snob."

"I said I was sorry. Now, are you ready?"

She watched the valet walk around the car and open Jack's door. "I guess so," she whispered.

Jack left the young man waiting. He grabbed her hand and squeezed hard. "Laurie, you can't guess with this. It isn't a dress rehearsal for some college play. I have to know that I can count on you."

She took a deep breath. "I'm ready, Jack."

At Caesar's she found out the quickest way to lose money was playing roulette. She lost eight hundred. Appalled, she switched to blackjack. Surprisingly, she won three hundred—which wasn't all that hard since she was playing with hundred dollar chips. She figured the three hundred was hers, and she planned to use it for clothes. She knew there were fabulous shops right above the casino and she was sick of the suit she'd been wearing. Slacks. Jeans. Sweaters. Before she left Atlantic City, she was going to ditch the suit.

If Caesar's was garish, Bally's was tasteful by comparison and this time it was Jack who couldn't seem to lose. After an hour and a half he exchanged twelve thousand of the drug money and walked away with three thousand more. When Laurie told him of her shopping plans, he heartily approved. Since the shops were so outrageously overpriced, they agreed on one outfit each. Anything else they could purchase back in Moorestown.

"C'mon, pick something," Jack muttered as he stood watching her sift through a rack of clothes.

"Don't be so impatient," she answered, trying to decide on the green silk pantsuit or the black rayon one. "I didn't harass you when you were shopping." She turned back to him and held up her selections. "Which one do you like?"

He leaned closer to her and whispered, "What does it matter what I like? I've got drug money in this duffel bag and clean in here." He held up the attache case. "And we've got more casinos to visit. Let's go."

"I know. But maybe I should try them on. If I get the green I can wear my navy blazer. It is still winter and—"

"Fine. Fine. Get the green. Pay for it and put it on so we can get out of here."

She gave him a look filled with annoyance and put the black outfit back on the rack. Taking the silk up to the sales clerk, she wondered how he found the gray pleated pants, steel blue shirt that perfectly matched his eyes, and the deep gray jacket in less than ten minutes. And that included paying for them and changing clothes. Men were just different, she decided while taking out the cash. And it wouldn't be quite so irritating if he didn't look so damn good in such a short time. His appearance was more like an elegant version of "Miami Vice" than northeast Philly cop. Although she thought he should undo the top button of his shirt. Still, he looked handsome . . . and just a little dangerous. But he was so impatient. Why couldn't he understand that shopping wasn't a chore for her. It was something she missed from her past. If they were at a baseball game, she wouldn't demand that he leave in the second inning. She would have understood, and let him enjoy it.

While changing in the dressing room, she thought of all the time she had spent shopping. Not just for clothes. She loved exploring stores, looking at furniture, kitchen items, gifts . . . it was hardly ever a task. Most women loved it, for it was the female equivalent of the hunt. Seeking that perfect dress or sofa or birthday gift. Men simply didn't have the patience. Like Jack, they wanted to streak through and get out. With women, it was a lifetime passion.

Suddenly, she stared at her reflection in the mirror as the thought came to her. A wide grin spread over her face and she hurried to get dressed. She couldn't wait to tell Jack.

Everyone turned as she left the dressing room and walked in his direction. The men who were waiting for their wives or girlfriends stared at her with admiration. Even the women had to look at her. And Jack had to admit what all of them saw. Laurie really was pretty. But it wasn't just that. There was an aura about her, of energy and enthusiasm, of happiness. And what he had thought was so phony and irritating when he first saw her, now seemed genuine as she stood in front of him with a dazzling smile.

"Guess what?" she asked in an excited voice.

This time he was drawn in to her joyful mood. He couldn't help returning her smile. "What?"

"I have the name for the store. It just came to me in the dressing room."

He knew what was expected, so he played along. "What is it?"

"Are you ready?"

He nodded.

" 'A Woman's Passion.' What do you think? Isn't it great?" She never gave him a chance to answer as she hurried on. "I can already see the game plan. Picture this: a full page ad, because we certainly have the money, both in a Philly paper and a local one. I'm going to base it on the Nike ad. The one that was running in *People* and *Time* magazines. Did you ever see it? About a woman's statistics, 36-24-36, how it's all lies, how most women aren't like that and never will be. What could be more perfect for a store like Jessica's? I can't wait to write it. Oh, Jack, it's all going to work. I can feel it!"

There was a click inside of his head, as if someone were fine tuning the picture he had of her. It all came into focus. She wasn't silly, spoiled and self-centered. A job needed to be done and she had taken charge. Her methods might have been unorthodox, but he had to admit she'd been right about Terri. In one afternoon she had organized the impossible task of renovating the store. Work was to begin at seven the next morning. She had already contacted clothing manufacturers and catalogues were going to be overnight expressed to the shop. She was actually achieving what he had first thought to be a harebrained, impossible mission.

"You're right, Laurie," he admitted. "It's perfect."

Her smile was nearly blinding and he saw such happiness in her eyes that something tugged deep within him. He knew, in that moment, that he had never experienced such complete delight in anything, or in anyone. Not in his job. Not in a relationship. Something was always missing . . .

"How many more casinos are left?" she asked, reaching for the attache case.

He handed it over and she held it with the bag containing her old clothes. "Four, maybe five."

"Well, let's go. We've got a lot of work to do in the next two days." She started to walk away from him and when she saw he wasn't following, she stopped and turned around. "Are you coming?" she asked with an amused smile.

Seeing her, the total picture of her, he wished with all his heart that he had met her before—before everything was taken away.

She walked back to him and slipped her arm through

his. Leading him out of the casino, she glanced up and said, "You know, Lannigan, I think we do make a good team after all."

He smiled, even though he was suddenly filled with regret. It really didn't matter. A vice cop never would have stood a chance with her anyway. And he figured there was no such thing as second chances. Not now. Not in his situation. Now all he could do was keep the attraction under control, because he might not know much about this crazy assignment, he might be the novice, but one thing was certain.

Falling in love was not part of the mission.

It could only mean trouble.

Chapter 8

The soft mix of color and texture was soothing to the eye. She tried to pattern the store after Victoria's Secret—old world respectability saturated with seduction. The ceiling was covered with yards and yards of a flowered cotton fabric, pleated and gathered at the center. Hanging from that was an elegant brass chandelier. The wallpaper was muted, yet rich, and the rugs were thick and plush. Dark, warm, cherry wood drawers would be filled with sexy lingerie. Designer ensembles would hang from ornate brass stands, as well as along the walls. Lush botanical prints were matted in a moire fabric and framed in gilt. Exquisite silk arrangements of calla lilies that stood three feet high were covered in sheets and waiting to sit atop the pink faux marble counter.

It was almost finished, Laurie thought, as she clasped a copy of the camera-ready ad in one hand and a large box of doughnuts in the other. She had just returned from Philadelphia where she had hand-delivered the ad to the city's largest newspaper. Considering her budget, she had to settle for a half page advertisement, but the local *Courier Post's* full page ad would cover most of south Jersey. It had been wonderful to feel like an account exec again. She was proud of herself to have accomplished so much in such a short time, but there was still plenty to do.

Over twenty men were busy with the final stages of the transformation and Laurie grinned as she inhaled the scents of new wood and fresh paint. "Doughnuts, gentlemen—to keep you going," she announced, as if being paid triple time wasn't enough.

Laying the box on the marble counter, she took two out and sidestepped a saw horse as she made her way to the back storage room. "Jack? Are you in here?" she called out, squeezing through a maze of boxes. It looked like mass confusion.

"Back here," he yelled from behind a wall of boxes.

She walked to the rear entrance and saw him helping a UPS driver with even more. "Hi. I wanted to show you the ad." She would have offered him the doughnut, but his hands were full.

"Are there any clothes left, at any manufacturer, on either coast? Or did you wipe them out when you

127

ordered all this?'' He threw the box on top of another and turned back to the driver.

"I know where to sign, Dave,'' he said as the man held out the form. He scribbled his name and glanced over his shoulder.

"Laurie, this is Dave Sawyer, the man whose back you've severely strained.''

She looked at the driver and smiled apologetically. It's funny how some people perfectly fit their jobs, she thought. Dave's light brown hair, brown eyes, and tortoise-shell glasses all matched his brown uniform and truck. "Hi, Dave. It's nice to meet you. Sorry about your back.''

The man smiled and shook his head. "Hey, it was easy. Even if this delivery took up half the truck, at least it was all at one stop. You're the ones that have to deal with all those boxes.''

Laurie looked at the large cardboard containers that surrounded her and groaned. "You're right. We'll probably be here all night.''

Jack stared at her. "All night? You've got to be kidding. You can't expect us to unpack all this!''

She walked up to him and stuck the doughnut in his mouth. "Sustenance, Jack. I think that one's jelly. And we'll do it. We really don't have any other choice. Grand opening in the morning, remember?''

"I haven't seen Jessica around,'' Dave said as he backed up to his truck. "She must really be excited about all this. When you see her, tell her I'm sorry about her mother. I just heard.''

Laurie nodded. "I'll tell her. Thanks, Dave.''

Jack waved to the driver and shut the door. He looked at her and said, "Laurie, there isn't any way in hell that you and I can do this. Look around you. There have to be seventy-five boxes here."

She did look, and he was right. It did seem like an impossible task. Taking a deep breath, she squared her shoulders. "Then we'd better get started. But first I want to show you the ad." She held it out to him. "Didn't it come out great?"

She watched him read it and waited for his reaction.

When he finished, he raised his head and looked at her. "This is terrific, Laurie. You managed to make a statement about women and at the same time attract them to the store. You must have been really good at your job."

She stared at him as something dormant inside of her sprung to life. It was the first sincere compliment he had given her. "Thanks," she said quietly. "It really wasn't that hard, since I had free rein. There wasn't anyone telling me what I couldn't do."

"What's this flower thing in the corner?" he asked, pointing to a calla lily.

"That's the logo. I saw it when I was picking out the new shopping bags for the store. Embossed white on white. I put it on everything, the tissue paper, the stationery. Oh, and while I was at the newspaper, I put an ad in the classified for two sales clerks to help out."

He finished off the jelly doughnut while he was listening to her. "You don't think we're placing Jessica in a little over her head? This inventory, bags, stationery, and now hiring two people—what if it isn't the big success you're planning on?''

''Don't worry, Jack. It will be. I know it,'' she stated, while staring at the powdered sugar on his bottom lip. She had the most ridiculous urge to run her finger over it, wiping it away and feeling the texture of his mouth. ''Let's get going,'' she said suddenly, confused by her reaction to him. ''Let's start unpacking this stuff.''

She looked around her to the sea of boxes. ''First we have to find the hangers and the steamer.''

''A steamer?''

She nodded. ''Sure. Everything we've ordered has to first be pressed.''

His mouth hung open. ''You're joking, right?''

Grinning, she shook her head. ''Look, the contractor is right on schedule, which means by the time they clean up tonight we can start putting things in the store. I'm telling you, it'll all work out. C'mon, we can do this.''

Defeated in the face of her enthusiasm, he started looking through the boxes for the hangers.

Laurie took a bite of her doughnut and watched as he bent down to read a label. She had to revise her initial opinion of him. He didn't seem uptight and sarcastic any longer, and he looked good in those jeans, too damned good. A familiar drawing sensation started at her inner knees and slowly crept up her legs. Totally confused, she tried to dismiss the sudden awareness, but her will power wasn't strong enough.

Why was this happening to her? Especially now? She shouldn't be feeling like this. She was on a mission from . . . well, from God, she guessed. She should be pure of mind and heart. Maybe it was a test. That's it. That could be the only reason for feeling aroused. It was merely an earthly sensation, and she should be beyond it. She was a heavenly emissary now, and must be strong and turn away from temptation.

Putting her ad down on the old desk, Laurie took a deep breath and focused her attention on a stack of boxes. As she ripped one open, she couldn't help glancing in Jack's direction. Her breath caught at the back of her throat as she watched him lift a heavy box. Every muscle was outlined by the cotton shirt he wore. She could see the way his back tapered in to his waist, the way those jeans clung to his hips and his . . .

Closing her eyes, she willed the traitorous thoughts away. One thing was certain. She wasn't pure of mind. Not yet.

Jess walked into the house and dropped her purse on the kitchen table. Terri was gone. Each time her sister left, the house seemed quieter, but this time it was more sharp. She had just taken her to the airport for a ten o'clock flight back to Dallas, and she missed her sister. For the first time in years she missed her. The last two days had been an emotional reunion for them. They had handled all the legal matters. The shop and house were hers. They had stayed up half the night talking, laughing, crying. And this afternoon they had visited the cemetery, holding and supporting each other, as they said goodbye to their mother.

She opened the cabinet over the refrigerator and stopped as she stared at the bottle of bourbon. Was Terri right? Did she use it to fill the void in her life? Maybe she was drinking too much, too often . . .

The phone started ringing and the decision she had to make was put off as she closed the cabinet and picked up the receiver.

"Hello?"

"Jessica? This is Grace Armstrong. How are you, dear?"

"I'm fine. How are you?" Grace was one of her mother's oldest friends and best customers.

"Oh, a little tired. Margaret and I were at choir practice. Not that I can sing any more, but it gives me peace to listen. I don't suppose it will be long before I join your mother—"

Jess closed her eyes and interrupted. "Oh, Grace, please don't talk like that." The woman had an inoperable brain aneurysm, and it was true—she was on borrowed time. "How was choir practice?" she asked, to change the subject.

"Lovely, just lovely. Maybe you could come some Sunday and hear them."

Grace was still trying to get her back to the church. "Maybe." She gave the same answer she had given for the last five years.

"Anyway, dear, that isn't the reason for my call at such a late hour. I just wanted to congratulate you on the store. We passed it on the way home and it looks beautiful. *A Woman's Passion*. What a clever name, and the facade is so elegant. It looks just like a little shop in London. Like that lingerie place in the malls.''

"Grace, what are you talking about?"

"You know the place, Jessica. The one that has all those revealing lacy things."

"That's not what I'm talking about. What about my store?" A knot formed in her belly and she immediately reached up to open the cabinet.

"Why, it appears completely renovated. Margaret and I can't wait to see the inside. There was someone working, but Margaret said it was your friend from Chicago, so I thought I would call to congratulate you. I'm so glad you decided not to sell it."

It all made sense, she thought as she poured the bourbon into a glass. She'd been so busy with Terri that she hadn't realized Jack and Laurie hadn't been around.

She gulped the bourbon and then said, "Listen, Grace, thanks for calling, but I have to get down there and . . . and help them. I'll see you at the store, all right?"

Grace sounded surprised at her quick dismissal. "Well, certainly, dear. Goodbye."

Jess hung up and grabbed her purse and coat. All the trips with the car. Atlantic City. The secrecy. Now it all added up. They were like two juvenile delinquents that couldn't be left alone. What had they *done*?

Ten minutes later she stood in front of her store. Her hands were jammed into the pockets of her coat.

Her mouth hung open in shock. It was just as Margaret had described.

A Woman's Passion stood out in neat gilt letters against a warm brown background. Behind the new paned windows was a display featuring three gorgeous outfits. She didn't even have to see the price tag to know they were expensive. A surge of anger rushed through her. It was *her* store and they had taken over. She wasn't even consulted. Inhaling a deep breath, she moved forward and opened the door. A bell, like soft wind chimes, tinkled overhead.

The interior was breathtaking, and her anger immediately dissipated. Her first impressions were of old world charm, sophistication, discreet money, class.

"I'm sorry, but we're not open. Tomorrow—" Laurie's words were cut off as she saw Jessica standing in the center of the store. "Ahh . . . Jack? I think you'd better come up here," she called out as she cautiously approached Jess.

Laurie's smile was uncertain. "How do you like it?" she asked.

"I'm speechless . . ." Jess whispered. "How . . . how did you do it?"

Jack walked up to them and grinned. "Laurie's responsible. She's a genius at organization."

Laurie actually blushed. "That isn't true. I didn't do it alone. Jack got the money, or none of this would have been possible." She looked at Jess and asked, "Does this mean you like it?"

"Like it?" Jess' voice was incredulous. "I *love* it!"

Her eyes filled with tears. "How can I ever repay you? All the money and the work . . ."

Glancing at Jack, Laurie said, "You don't have to repay anything. The money was . . . donated, and the rest was our job."

"What about Atlantic City?"

Jack cleared his throat. "Okay, so we won some of it."

She looked at the two of them. "You didn't do anything . . . spooky, did you?"

"Spooky?" Laurie laughed. "Oh, you mean did we use our powers? I'm afraid what powers we do have are limited. The only way it might have worked was if we could have levitated the blackjack dealer's hand to see his cards. And we didn't. We were lucky, right, Jack?"

He nodded. "Right. But this was supposed to have been a surprise for you, Jess."

"It *is*! I can't believe it," she said as she looked around her again. "It's absolutely beautiful. Thank you. Thank you both."

Laurie gave Jack a pleased look and said to Jess, "It made sense. I remember some of the research I had read once. It said that two-thirds of the female population was a size fourteen or above and clothing these women was a billion dollar industry. Why shouldn't you get some of it? All you needed was a little window dressing and a new inventory."

Jess ran her fingers over the marble counter. "A *little* window dressing? This is magnificent."

"Actually," Jack said, "there's more than a little inventory. I think Laurie went overboard in ordering stock. There must be thirty or forty boxes in the back that we still have to unpack."

"And steam," Laurie added with a grin.

Jack gave her an impatient look. "She's a slave driver."

Taking off her coat, Jess said, "Then I'm glad I found out tonight. You two take a break. It's time for me to go back to work."

As she walked to the rear of the store, she suddenly turned around and smiled at them. "If I told anybody about this, they'd lock me in a padded room. Who in their right mind would believe it? But I have to say this: when you first came I thought I was cursed, that I was losing my mind, all you did was fight with each other, but now . . . well, now I guess I'm blessed. You took care of Terri and the will, and this . . ." She looked around her and sighed with appreciation. "You guys really must be my guardian angels."

Jack and Laurie stared after her as she disappeared into the back, then they slowly looked at each other.

"Geez, Jack," Laurie whispered. "Do you think we did it?"

"What?"

"Our mission. Do you think it's over?" She looked up to the ceiling, as if they would be sucked back into wherever they were before.

He couldn't help glancing upwards with the same thought. "I don't know," he whispered back. "Maybe . . ."

She wanted to hold his hand for support, for courage. She didn't want to go back yet and was instantly frightened that it might happen.

"We'd better get to work," Jack said. "It's nearly ten o'clock, and there's a lot to do."

"You're right," Laurie answered, the moment of closeness now gone. "Tomorrow's going to be a big day."

The three of them were working on four hours sleep, but none of the nearly two hundred women that came into the shop could tell. Jess, Laurie and Jack were riding high on adrenalin. *A Woman's Passion* was a huge success. Women from Pennsylvania crossed the Delaware River to check out a store that sounded as though it respected them. Five even carpooled up from Wilmington, Delaware. The phone rang constantly for directions. It got so bad that Jess finally left it off the hook. Jack took charge of ringing up the sales and Laurie and Jess ran around like track stars, trying to keep up with the fashion demands. The only ones who weren't pleased were the older customers. Margaret and Grace returned right before closing to speak with Jess.

"You're back," Laurie said as she recognized the women.

Margaret looked uncomfortable, but Grace nudged her forward. "Yes. It was so busy before and . . . and we thought we'd stop back to discuss something with Jessica."

Laurie called to Jess, who was trying to explain her system of accounting to Jack. When Jess approached the group of women Laurie could see that she was tired. There was tension around her eyes and she was holding her hands together at her waist, an action Laurie knew was to stop them from shaking.

It was late, almost nine o'clock, and she hadn't had a drink all day.

The ache in her temples was more annoying than painful. Her feet hurt. In the last hour she had broke into a sweat, just thinking about the bottle over her refrigerator. All she wanted was to get out, to leave, to get home.

"Margaret. Grace. What can I do for you?" She knew her smile was strained and she tried to relax her mouth.

Margaret returned her smile. "Jessica, dear, Grace and I have . . . well, we've been asked to speak with you on behalf of your old customers."

"My old customers?"

"Those of us who have been coming here for years, since your mother opened the store," Grace said. "All of this is quite lovely, Jessica, but it's geared toward a much younger woman. Where are we supposed to go now? It's nearly impossible for us to special order something at a department store. That's why Sara's Closet was so wonderful. It was . . ."

Jess was having trouble concentrating. She didn't even hear the rest of Grace's statement. For the last six years she had tried to please everyone—her

138

mother, her customers. She was tired of it. More than tired, she was mentally and physically exhausted. The store should have excited her, and it did, until around six o'clock when Jack left to get sandwiches. It was then she realized that she wanted a drink more than food. For three hours she had been thinking about it, knowing the bourbon would take away the stress and anxiety.

Suddenly she was aware of the three women staring at her, and she had no idea what they had been saying. Something about the store?

Laurie filled in the silence. "Grace, we still have the old stock. How would you feel if Jessica allotted a section for her most loyal customers? That way you could still shop here and she would be able to order anything else you needed."

Grace nodded and Margaret said, "I think that sounds wonderful. Everyone should be happy." She looked at Jess and added, "You look tired, dear. This must have been quite a strain after everything you've been through. You should get some rest."

Jess ran her fingers through her hair. "Thank you, Margaret. You're right. I am tired." She managed to resist the urge to dig her fingernails into her scalp, a distraction she used to stop the ache that seemed to settle right under her skin. "I think Laurie had a great idea. We'll get started on it tomorrow."

The women said good night and Jess knew she couldn't handle any more. She had to get out. Immediately. She went into the back room and picked up her coat and purse. When she returned to the front of the store, Jess looked at Jack and Laurie and said, "Do you two think you could close up? I'm really beat."

Heading for the door, she didn't even wait for them to answer.

They stared after her as the door chimes slowly settled into silence. It was Laurie who said what they both were thinking. "She's going home to drink."

"I know," Jack answered, slipping the cash into a metal strongbox. "We'd better hurry."

Laurie turned her head to look at him. "The store didn't work," she said in a hurt voice. "She's still not happy. I thought once she had something to make her feel better she would stop."

"It isn't that simple, Laurie. Nothing in life is ever that simple."

Chapter 9

He'd taken over the smaller bedroom that Terri had used. Lying in bed, with one arm behind his head, Jack stared up at the shadows that the moonlight created on the ceiling. Both he and Laurie agreed that they had been too optimistic. Their mission definitely wasn't over. It was four days since the store had opened and every night, at dinner time, Jess volunteered to go out for food. When she had returned, they both knew she had made a stop at the house. They couldn't smell the alcohol on her breath, but they could see it in her eyes, the way the tension was eased from her expression.

Laurie had hired two women to help out at the store. They were both in their thirties and experienced in retail sales. The addition of two employees was a relief, especially since Laurie was constantly coming up with new ideas. Like compiling a mailing list and sending out handwritten thank you notes to every customer. The women were paid fifty cents for each card and seemed happy to take them home and earn the extra cash. He thought it was a waste of time and money, and told her that he'd never received a thank you note from a store and it wouldn't make any difference if he had. Laurie said he didn't understand the female psyche. Well, she was right about that. He never did.

Closing his eyes, he felt the weariness of the day fold down around him. It was funny, but at the beginning he and Laurie didn't really need sleep. It seemed the more they remained earthbound, the more they acquired all the human attributes. The only difference was that they were out of their own surroundings, that they weren't permitted any connection with their old lives. It made him mentally examine his past. If this was all really happening, then how many times had he walked past others who were on missions? It made him question people who had briefly come into his life, like strangers who perform good deeds and then disappear.

A soft knock on the door interrupted his thoughts. "Yes?" He watched as Laurie walked into his room.

"Jack, are you asleep?"

He smiled, wondering why she would ask when he had already answered her. But that was just like Laurie. For all her shrewdness in business, there was still a childlike quality about her. "No, I'm awake," he answered, looking at her as she came closer to the bed. She wore that heavy white terrycloth robe she'd taken from the store, and he immediately wondered what she was wearing underneath. Did she go for silk and sexy, or cotton and comfort? Forcing the thought out of his mind, he brought his arm down and sat up against the pillow. "What's up?"

"Do you mind if I sit?" she asked.

He moved his feet. "Go ahead," he answered, though he did mind. He wasn't sure it was a great idea, considering the thoughts that had been plaguing him about her lately.

She sat at the bottom of the bed, bringing her knees up to her chest and wrapping her arms around them. "I've been thinking a lot about Jess, and what we can do to help her."

"I know. Me, too. Maybe we should just convince her to check into therapy, or AA. I don't know what else we can do."

"Well, I don't think she's at the point where she would do that. If she is an alcoholic, then she's a functioning one. I still believe that if she had something in her life to bring her happiness, then the bourbon wouldn't be that important to her."

He sighed. "The store didn't work. It eased her money problems, but it wasn't the answer. What else is there?"

"A man."

"What?" He heard her. He just couldn't believe she said it.

Running her fingers through her hair, she almost laughed. "I know. It goes against every feminist thought I've ever had. That's why it's taken me two days to bring up this new plan."

"You have a plan?" He should have known it.

She nodded. "Tell me something, Jack. What do you think of Jess?"

"Jess? What do you mean?"

"As a man. When you look at her, what do you think?"

He took his time, picturing Jessica in his mind. Finally, he said the truth. "She's nondescript. There isn't anything unattractive about her, yet there isn't anything to attract attention."

"Exactly. Did you ever notice that she has gorgeous eyes, or a wonderful smile?"

He thought for a moment. "No, not really, but then she doesn't smile very often. She always looks under stress, like she's minutes away from crying."

"I think Jess needs a make-over."

"A make-over?"

"Sure. We do something with her hair. Teach her how to use makeup. You must have noticed that she's starting to wear clothes from the store. She just needs a little help."

"Hair and makeup. That's your department. Do you really think that's going to make her feel better?"

"About herself? Yes. But I need a man's perspective here. When you were . . ." She hesitated and started again. "Before all of this, what attracted you to a woman? Be honest. Was it her appearance? Her

144

personality? What was it that made you want to meet a woman?''

He blew his breath out in a nervous rush. What was he supposed to say to her? Tell her the truth? Betray his gender?

''C'mon, Jack. I need to know. I mean, what does it matter now? If we're both here to help Jess, then we've got to cooperate.''

''There has to be a physical attraction,'' he finally said.

''But attracted to what? Her smile? Her body? Some invisible pheromones?''

How was he supposed to admit this without sounding like a jerk? ''Look, Laurie, I don't know how typical I am, but with me it was the whole package. If there was a—a chemistry when I looked at a woman, then I would follow through.''

''But if a woman was nondescript, if there wasn't a sexual chemistry, then you wouldn't even bother to get to know her?''

''I didn't say anything about sex.''

''I know you didn't. But that's what you were talking about.''

''Well, what about you?'' he asked, uncomfortable with the conversation. ''How many nerds did you date?''

''I'm not condemning you, Jack. I'm trying to get a handle on this male/female thing to help Jess.'' She looked out the window to the winter night. ''When I was in it, I wasn't real successful with the whole process.''

"Me either," he whispered.

She turned her head and stared at him. "You know, it's really weird that we know so little about each other. I don't even know if you were married, if you had kids."

"No to both."

"Never? You were never married?" She sounded more than a little surprised.

He shook his head. "After I got out of the service I wasn't ready. When I thought I was, all I had to do was look around me. Cops don't have good marriages. Funny thing is, when all my friend's marriages were falling apart, I never blamed the women."

"Why?"

He shrugged. "Cops are a strange breed. They see so much crap during the day that they can't just go home and dump it on their family. So they meet after work and let off steam. Their social circle consists of other cops, and most cops drink to forget. Then they go home to the wife and kids and find they can't communicate. It's as if the rest of the world speaks a foreign language, one that's squeaky clean and naive. There's a lot of anger and frustration from the family, especially from the wife, who's trying to hold it all together by herself. It ain't exactly June and Ward Cleaver."

Laurie smiled sadly. "What marriage is? I think all us baby boomers forget that was fiction."

Even in the moonlight he could see her serious expression. "A statement like that surprises me. I would have thought that was your background."

146

"What? June and Ward Cleaver?"

He nodded. "That, or something better. Main Line aristocracy. House in the suburbs. Country club. Private schools—"

"Hold it," she interrupted. "I let people believe that. I *want* them to." Her voice trailed off. When she again spoke, it was a mere whisper. "It couldn't be farther from the truth."

He unconsciously leaned forward. "What do you mean?"

Shaking her head, she softly laughed and then again looked out the window. "What I mean is that my background could be termed lower middle class. My father held a job—barely. He was a salesman. Always looking for that pot of gold. New cars. Used cars. Encyclopedias. Water purifiers. A real Willy Loman. A charmer of women—at least my old man *thought* he was a charmer, except with my mother. She was mostly angry and frustrated."

She rested her chin on her arms and said, "One of my childhood memories of my father is of him taking me with him to work because my grandmother was sick and my mother had to be with her. He was selling new cars then and was closing a deal with a woman. A widow. For him, it was a rare occasion and he was in a good mood. I remember him talking to another man about the widow and laughing. I couldn't have been more than ten or eleven years old and I had only a vague idea of what a widow was, but I couldn't wait to see her. She had to be special from the way the men were talking about her, and she was. She was so quietly beautiful. Everything was understated, from her voice to her clothes.''

She blinked several times and Jack thought he saw a tear slide down her cheek, but he kept silent and allowed her to continue.

''When her car was ready, my father was holding the keys and he kept talking to her. I didn't know what he was saying, but I could tell from the woman's face that she was uncomfortable, that she wanted to get away from him. I can remember thinking, *Give her the keys, Daddy. Let her go.* I was too young to recognize flirting, especially by my own father, but I instinctively knew that he, in his shiny shark-skin suit that barely closed over his beer belly and his flashy, fake gold rings, wasn't in the same league with her.''

Looking at him, she added, ''You know, Jack, thinking back on it now, that woman was everything you described. Wealthy, but with dignity and class. Even as a child, I knew I wanted to be like her. I knew there had to be a better way of life than the one I was living. There was so much fighting, so much ugliness. Arguing about money and bills and other women.''

''Is that why you weren't married?''

She smiled. ''I was. You're going to hate this, but I married a fellow protester. At eighteen I thought love would last forever. It took all of three months for both of us to realize we'd made a major mistake. My mother insisted that my father pay for an annulment. It's one of the few times I can remember my mother sticking up for me against him. His motto was 'you made your bed, now lie in it.' Of course, my mother didn't want to jeopardize my scholarship to Temple, so she would have done anything to keep me in college. Even take on my father.''

"And you never married again?'' he asked quietly, wondering why he wanted to know every detail of her life.

She shook her head. "Never. I concentrated on school, on re-inventing myself. I was determined to build a different life from my parents. I didn't want to turn into a bitter woman who depended on a man and was ultimately disappointed when expectations weren't met. I knew if I depended on myself, if I worked hard and pushed myself, I would succeed.''

"And you did,'' he added. But he silently questioned whether it had been a satisfying life. He couldn't imagine a woman like Laurie living out her time alone.

"What about you?'' she asked, crossing her legs and brushing back the hair from her forehead. "I've just spilled my guts, Lannigan, and completely shattered your image of me as the rich, spoiled bitch.''

"I never called you that. Rich and spoiled, yes. I guess I should apologize.''

She laughed and he was glad she wasn't sad any longer.

"You may never have said it out loud, Jack, but you know you thought it.''

He grinned. "Maybe.''

She lifted her chin and studied him. He was uncomfortable by her scrutiny, but kept his silence.

She was the one that broke it. "I think you're avoiding my question.''

"Which one?"

"How was your childhood? Were you a happy kid? Cub Scouts. Little League. All the male bonding stuff that begins so young."

Nodding, he quietly answered, "I suppose I was."

"You don't sound convincing. I just opened a vein for you," she said with a chuckle. "I'm not asking for a show of blood, but you could reciprocate with a little background."

He didn't want to do this. It had been too long since he had thought about it and it wouldn't serve any purpose now, except satisfying her curiosity.

Without warning, she brought her leg out and play-fully kicked his thigh with her toes. "C'mon, you're holding back, and it isn't fair. What could be worse than living out *Death of a Salesman*?"

"I was adopted."

She immediately sobered. "Oh, God, I'm sorry."

Neither of them spoke for a full minute. He knew she didn't know what to say, and it would hurt too much for him to recall memories that he had tried so hard to bury.

"I found out when I was twelve years old," he finally said, not knowing why he was volunteering the information. He hadn't talked about it since he was eighteen with anyone except Mike, and then he'd been drunk. But once he started, he couldn't seem to stop. "My parents are good people. I know they love me and they thought they were protecting me. It's just . . ."

He didn't know how to say it. He had spent too many years burying his emotions.

"What?" she asked softly, cautiously.

"I was playing catch in the driveway," he began in a hesitant voice. "This kid, Tommy Forchetti, told me. He said he heard my mother talking to his. I called him a liar. I even punched him in the face when he wouldn't stop. And then, later that night, I asked my mother. She finally told me the truth."

"Oh, Jack . . ."

He held up his hand. "Hey, I know all the platitudes—that I'm special because my parents chose me, that I'm twice loved. I know all of that logically, but there is still the fact that my birth mother gave me up for adoption, and my mother, my adopted mother, lied to me."

"Did you ever try to find her? Your birth mother?"

He looked up at the ceiling and attempted to push back the tightness in his throat. "When I was eighteen I called her."

Laurie leaned forward. "And?"

"And she didn't want to see me. I wasn't a part of her life. She had married and had children and none of them knew about me. She was afraid I was going to make trouble for her." He laughed with bitterness. "I never contacted her again."

As if they had known each other for years, Laurie crawled up the bed and wrapped her arms around him. "What a shitty thing to do," she whispered and sniffled.

He immediately stiffened at her touch. He didn't want her sympathy, her compassion or kindness. He had built a wall around his heart and he didn't want anyone to enter ever again, especially not now, especially not her. If he let her in, if he allowed a crack in the wall, then he might crumble along with it. He had learned survival. First as a kid, then in Nam, and later on the force. You couldn't depend on anyone but yourself. Especially for love, because if you do you'll always be disappointed.

She must have felt his rejection and she pulled away from him. He experienced an immediate sense of regret, of loss, for the moment of intimacy was gone. She sat back at the bottom of the bed and he felt he had to say something, to fill in the awkward silence. "I think we got off track somewhere. We were talking about Jessica, and what we could do for her."

Laurie slipped off the bed and took a deep breath. "You're right, of course. Like you said, the make-over will be my department. Thanks for the conversation, Jack."

Without saying good night, she quietly left the room.

He stared at the closed door, knowing full well she was hurt and angry. He'd seen it too many times in his past when a woman tried to get beyond the wall. Looking back, he knew it was the reason why every female relationship in his life had failed.

Loving, intimacy, trusting, just hurt too damn much.

Her brown hair was streaked with blond and given a body perm. A session with a professional cosmetologist had taught her to make the most of her features. Suddenly she had fantastic eyes, high cheekbones, a full mouth. The designer clothes accented her long legs and generous bust, yet camouflaged those body parts that were less than perfect. Heads actually were beginning to turn when she walked down a street. However, there were no offers of a date. Everyone Jessica met was either too old, too startled by the drastic change in her, or happily married. It was time, Laurie thought, to become proactive. She wasn't going to meet anyone staying in her own surroundings. She obviously needed to enlarge her social circle.

"I say we go out tonight after work," Laurie announced. The three of them were on break from the store, having dinner together at a small local cafe.

"Go out?" Jack asked, looking up from his plate of ravioli. "Where?"

"I don't know," she said, stabbing at the romaine in her Caesar salad. "Maybe a dance club."

Lifting a spoonful of soup to her mouth, Jess looked almost frightened. "Why? Why would you ever want to go to a place like that?"

"Geez, I don't know—maybe to have fun?" She sat back in her chair and stared at them. "What's wrong with you two? Haven't we been working hard? I think we need a little time to relax."

"We could go to a movie," Jack suggested.

"No thanks, Mr. Excitement." She couldn't keep the sarcasm out of her voice. It had been there for two weeks now, ever since the night in his bedroom. They had been polite to each other, but there was an undercurrent of tension whenever they were together. "Sitting in a dark movie theater wasn't exactly what I had in mind. I want to listen to some music, dance . . . have fun." How could he be so dense?

"Laurie, you aren't . . . you're forty years old," Jess said. "Those places are for young kids."

"There's got to be places for people our age. There was in Philly—and so what if I'm forty. I'm not—" Her words trailed off into silence. She was about to say "dead," when she realized she was. But it didn't feel like dead, or what she thought it would be like. She felt alive. Okay, so her life, her job, her friends, everything that she once had was gone. But she could smell and taste and feel things that she never had before. And she wanted to go out tonight. Not just for Jess. She wanted to be carefree again.

Finally Jack looked at her and then Jessica, and seemed to catch on. "Okay. I'll go if you want."

"Well, you two can go. I think I'll—"

"Oh, no," Laurie interrupted. "You're coming with us, Jess. It's time to get out of this town."

Jess shook her head. "I've gone along with everything—the store, which is terrific and I thank you both, and then the make-over. I know you're trying to help me. It's your job, your . . . your mission, and I'm sorry you got such a sorry assignment, but I can't do this. It just isn't me."

"What *is* you, Jess?" Laurie asked, thinking it was time to get tough. "Staying home night after night with a glass of bourbon for company? I've never seen anyone give up on life like you! God, if you could

154

only appreciate it while you've got it. Don't wait until you're like Jack and me wishing for second chances, for something that's gone forever. This is it, Jess. Right here. Right now. It's the only game in town and if you want to flush it down the tubes out of self-pity or fear then—''

"Okay, Laurie," Jack firmly cut in. "I think we all got your point."

He turned to Jessica and saw that she was close to tears. His smile was warm and inviting. "Jess, will you come out with us tonight?"

His voice was calm, almost soothing, and it grated on Laurie's nerves to see Jess nod. She was doing all the hard work on this one, while he just had to smile and ask.

Taking a deep breath, she tried to calm down. "Great. I'll ask Mari where we should go." One of the women she had hired was thirty-eight, divorced and full of life. She was sure Mari didn't sit home on a Saturday night.

"Loser. Loser. *Major* loser," Laurie remarked over Jess's shoulder as she checked out the men in the club. They were either at the bar, or standing around staring at the women. Nothing had changed. It was still the same old story . . .

"Laurie, please," Jess muttered. "I'm not here to find a man. We're here because you wanted to dance. So why don't you?"

Well, she might not be here to find a man, but Laurie

was certainly going to find one for her. There had to be one man in this place that was right. Even if he wasn't Mr. Right, he could be a start.

Leaning over in the other direction, she nudged Jack's arm. "Dance with her," she ordered.

"What?" He looked down at her as if she'd lost her mind. "First you drag us to this place, where everyone is drinking, I might add. Great choice. Then you tell me I have to go out there and *dance*?"

She felt the anger building again. Why did he have to wear that baby blue shirt under his sports coat? That shade of blue matched his eyes and made him seem so healthy, so handsome, so . . . so damn sexy. Disgusted with herself, she whispered, "Look, pal, I've done all the ground work on this plan. Now it's your turn. Showcase her."

"It was your plan," he answered, moving aside as a tall blonde passed him and gave him the once over. "What do you mean, showcase her?"

Laurie didn't miss the blonde with the big breasts and she mentally sized her up. The woman's dress was too tight. She wore too much makeup. She had too much hair and it looked like it would stand up to the force of a wind tunnel from the amount of gel and spray. She looked cheap and eager. Dismissing her, she turned her attention back at Jack. "Take her out on the dance floor so the men will see her. You're decent enough looking. I know how men think. If you look like you're interested, then they will be too."

"Oh, is that right?" He appeared amused by her observation.

"That's right. Now will you do it? Or can't you dance?" It was a challenge all the way, from her words to her expression.

He took a long swallow from his Coke and placed it back on the table. "C'mon, Jess," he said, taking her hand. "Let's dance."

Jess tried to pull back from him. "Oh, no. I couldn't!" she protested. "It's been too many years."

They were standing by a table and Jack took the glass from her hand and said, "It'll all come back. Come on."

Laurie watched as he took Jess out to the dance floor. Jess was a little stiff as she moved, but Jack was a natural. Damn, the man could dance!

A smile appeared at her lips as she continued to look at them. It stayed there until she noticed the blond on the edge of the dance floor watching Jack. She was moving to the music and trying to get Jack's attention. And it worked. Every so often Jack would look over at her, and the blond would give him a knowing smile. *The whole package, huh?* Well, this package was wrapped in blatant sex. He wasn't any different. He was just like every other male. It was sex that attracted them.

"Would you like to dance?"

Laurie turned her head and saw a man in his mid-forties. He was decent-looking and seemed harmless. She looked at Jack and then back at the man. Smiling she said, "Sure, why not?"

Chapter 10

She walked out to the dance floor, leading the man to a spot right next to Jack and Jess. She saw the surprise in Jack's expression and was pleased. She, too, was a good dancer. And she ought to be; she'd had enough practice. It seemed to her that she'd spent years in places just like this. She'd go with her friends, telling herself that she was going to listen to music, to laugh and have a good time. That she wasn't expecting anything to happen, that Mr. Wonderful wasn't going to be there. But she always looked, and was always disappointed. Even if she met someone and dated him, it inevitably turned out the same. Whatever she was looking for, maybe a great love like in the storybooks of her youth, wasn't in the cards for her. She had spent years looking for it, then fighting it, and finally took the path of least resistance. She gave up. Several times she'd had long lasting relationships, but she always saw something that eventually made her lose respect for the man. And that was it for her. Respect. It was the one thing she needed to stay in a relationship. Well, it was too late now.

She looked at Jack with a smug expression as she moved her hips in time with the beat. Maybe she could have respected him. He was the first man she had told about her childhood. But what did it matter any more? They were here for Jess. Not for anything else.

Laurie smiled at the man she was dancing with and glanced at Jess. She looked really pretty tonight, and it was odd to see the transformation and know she was a part of it. In her past she never would have taken someone under her wing like that. Was it because she thought it would be pushy, or because she was more concerned with her own life? She thought of her friends. Had she taken enough time with them? Had she given of herself? Had she listened to their tales of woe with sympathy, or with impatience? Was she doing all this work now because she finally had nothing to gain for herself, except the completion of the mission? Or was it because she wanted to help Jess?

Seeing Jess before her, she knew in her heart that she was fond of the woman. She really wanted her to be happy. But, although her dancing had improved, her expression was still strained. Leaning over, Laurie whispered in her ear. "Hey, this isn't torture. It's supposed to be fun. Smile!"

Jess obliged, yet she continued to look like she couldn't wait for the music to end. When it did, Laurie thanked the man she was with and walked off the floor with Jess and Jack.

"Well, there. That was a beginning," Laurie remarked, handing Jess her Perrier and Jack his Coke. She took a sip of her Diet Coke. "You were really good, Jess. I bet you loved to dance when you lived in Chicago."

Jess shrugged. "I went out sometimes . . . but it was so long ago. I'm not really comfortable here, Laurie."

"I know, but it'll get better. You'll see."

Jess looked back to the dance floor and Laurie turned to Jack. "Okay, if you can drag your attention away from the blond, I think we should look for a nice man for Jess."

He let his breath out in a rush and glanced down at her. "What are you talking about?"

"Which remark needs an explanation? The blond? Or the man?"

"Both."

She grinned. "Let's just say the blond is definitely eye-catching, but your interest in the obvious is a bit surprising. And we're here for Jess, remember? Now, look around."

"How would I know what she wants?" He sounded annoyed.

"See if you can spot someone nice."

"There," he said, nodding toward the corner of the room. "How about him?"

"Where?"

"The one in the green sweater. He looks *nice*."

"Geez, Jack—he's a nerd. All he needs is a pocket protector."

He gave her a disgusted look. "This is so stupid. How can we pick someone? And what are we going to do? Drag her up to meet him?"

She nudged him with her elbow. "Knock it off and look around. There has to be someone. Hello, handsome . . ." Her words trailed off as she saw an extremely attractive man across the dance floor. He was tall, dark and dressed in an expensive suit.

Jack looked in the same direction and smirked. "You've got to be kidding. He looks like an aging John Travolta. I'll bet he's real good at disco."

"Very funny. Disco's making a comeback, in case you haven't heard. Though I couldn't stand it the first time around." She glanced back at the man. "He could be a doctor or a lawyer. Maybe a CEO of a small company. You never know."

He turned and stared at her. "Laurie, do you honestly think a doctor or a lawyer or a CEO is going to be hanging out in this place?"

She looked around her. He was probably right, but she didn't want to admit it. "Well, maybe. You never know."

"And maybe not. What about the guy in the gray jacket? He looks responsible."

"Too short."

He pointed out several more men and Laurie found something wrong with each of them.

"Too intense."

"Too tall."

"Bad dresser."

"Smiles too much."

"Too desperate looking."

Exasperated, Jack finally gave up. "I can't believe you're picking apart these men like that."

"Why not?" she answered. "Isn't that what men do? At least mentally? Look, we've all got our criteria for what attracts us, for what our perfect mate should be. It's a psychological fact that it's stored in our subconscious. We've developed it since childhood, when we first became aware of the opposite sex. We like 'em tall, short, dark, fair, skinny, more defined, hard, soft. We go for the eyes, the smiles, the long legs, the firm butts, moustaches or smooth skin. You name it. Whatever it is that turns us on, it must be met, at least most of it must be met, or we pass over that person and look elsewhere. It all happens in a matter of seconds."

She gave him a knowing smirk. "Like when you walked into this place, your eyes went right for the blond. You must like blonds with big breasts and big hips, ones that wear cheap dresses at least a size too small."

He laughed. "You are something else, you know that? And what about you? Every man you picked was dressed in a suit. What does that say about you?"

162

"I like successful men."

He shook his head. "I think it goes deeper than that. I think it has something to do with your father."

Her eyes narrowed. "You'd better be careful, Jack, where you're treading. I could have pointed out that big breasts and big hips are maternal, and what you are looking for is your—"

"All right," he interrupted. "That's enough. I'm sorry I brought up your father."

She took a deep breath and tried to calm down. Nodding, she said, "Sorry about that maternal remark."

"Okay. Let's just forget it and—hey," he whispered. "Look behind you. Look at Jess."

Turning, Laurie's jaw dropped in amazement.

Jess was actually talking to a man. A *nice* looking man. While she and Jack were searching and arguing, Jess had done it on her own!

"Can you believe it?" she whispered, pulling Jack the few steps back to Jess . . . and her new friend.

"Hi," Laurie said, looking at the man and liking what she saw.

Jess seemed embarrassed and made the introductions. "Laurie. Jack. This is Keith . . . ?"

"Keith Williams." The man supplied his last name and shook hands with them.

He was about five inches taller than Jess. Light brown hair, hazel eyes and a great smile that lit up an average face. And he wore a suit. Laurie was pleased.

"Nice to meet you, Keith," she said.

Jack smiled and nodded.

There was an awkward silence and Laurie rushed to fill it. "Are you from around here?"

"Actually, I'm from Scarsdale, New York. I'm here for a few months doing consulting work for Eastern Technologies on Route 73."

No one said anything, so again Laurie spoke. "What do you do?"

"I'm an engineer. We're designing a new computer system for the space program."

"How interesting. Isn't that interesting, Jess?" Boy, Laurie had heard about shy, but this was ridiculous. Jess was staring at the floor. And Jack was even less help.

"Do you, all of you, come here often?" Keith asked. "It's the first time for me. Somebody at Eastern told me about it."

Still tongue-tied, Jess shook her head.

"We're here celebrating the re-opening of Jess' store."

He turned to her. "You have a store?"

"Yes."

Finally, Laurie thought. She speaks!

"Really? What kind? What do you sell?"

"Clothes. Women's clothes."

"It's a specialty shop on Main Street in Moorestown," Laurie volunteered. "It's called *A Woman's Passion*." Okay, so he was only here for a few months, but he could be a beginning. Jess could learn to date again, and she had to start somewhere.

"I like that," he said and smiled at Jess. "It's a great name. How long have you had the store?"

164

Jess answered him and Laurie smiled with satisfaction, feeling like a Jewish grandmother, one that specialized in matchmaking.

"Would you happen to have a light?"

She and Jack both turned around at the sound of a deep, sexy voice.

It belonged to a woman. The blond.

"I don't smoke," Laurie said, clearly annoyed. But the blond wasn't looking at her.

Her gaze was centered on Jack. "I know I shouldn't," she said, making Laurie wonder whether she was talking about smoking or the way she was devouring Jack with her eyes. She put the long cigarette back into the pack and added, "Some things are just so hard to stop."

Oh, brother . . . Laurie looked up at Jack and had to give him credit. His expression never changed.

A waitress came and gave the woman her drink, one that she had obviously ordered before approaching them. She paid the woman and then sipped her fruity concoction. Holding the glass right at her chin, she said to Jack, "My name's Cindi, with an *i*."

"How cute," Laurie said, not bothering to hide the sarcasm. "This is Jess and that's Keith and I'm Laurie." She stopped for effect. "Oh, I'm sorry. I forgot someone, didn't I? Jack? This is Cindi—with an *i*."

"Hi, Jack," the woman said in an inviting voice, and then suddenly giggled. "That sounded so funny. Hijack, you know?"

Laurie gave Jack a look that spoke volumes. The woman wasn't exactly a Rhodes scholar.

Jack ignored her and smiled politely. "Hello, Cindi."

"You're a good dancer," she answered, bringing her drink up to her mouth. "I was watching you."

No kidding, Laurie thought, as she stared at the woman sipping her drink. How could she flirt so openly in front of everyone? It was blatant and shameless. How did she know that Jack wasn't with either Jess or herself? Someone ought to teach her a lesson in club etiquette.

Laurie was concentrating so hard that before she knew what was happening, Cindi's drink splashed up in her face. The woman was so shocked that she dropped her clutch bag.

"Oh . . . I don't know what happened," she sputtered and wiped at her face with the cocktail napkin. When she bent to pick up her bag the seam at her hip split open, exposing her pantyhose. The coup de grâce was her shriek of embarrassment as she tried to clutch the two ends together as her left heel suddenly broke.

Keith and Jack could only stare as the woman seemed to fall apart in front of them. It was Jess who started laughing first. It was a tiny giggle and then a cough, and then another giggle and more coughing, until she had to turn away. But her shoulders were still shaking.

Cindi seemed immobilized, frozen in shock, and it

was Jack who said, "Maybe you could get help in the ladies' room."

She still didn't move and Laurie's eyes narrowed more dangerously. As the music slowed, she heard Jack's voice. It sounded as though it were coming from far away. "C'mon, Laurie. Let's dance."

When she didn't respond, he took her arm and dragged her out to the dance floor.

It took two or three seconds before she realized where she was. When she did, she blinked several times with a questioning look in her eyes.

"You shouldn't have done that," he scolded, as he pulled her into a slow dance.

"Done what?" Her voice was low and breathy, as if she'd just run up four flights of stairs.

"Oh, give me a break. Even Jess knew it was you. It wasn't fair."

Laurie looked back to Jessica and saw the blond limping away. "*I did that?*"

"Don't tell me you didn't know. I had to get you out of there while the woman still had clothes on her." Angry with her, he looked over her shoulder and shook his head.

"Jack, I don't even remember doing it. I mean, I didn't plan on doing anything to her. It must have just happened."

"Sure."

"I'm telling you, I didn't . . . you know. Okay, so I shouldn't have done it, but she made me so angry." Laurie settled into the dance and looked up at Jack. "You have to admit she was pushy."

He almost grinned. Almost—not quite. "She was . . . friendly."

Laurie laughed at his choice of words. "And you loved it, too, having that club bimbo fawning all over you."

"Club bimbo?" This time he chuckled. "I never heard that expression before."

"In this case it's self-explanatory. Cindi with an i? Hijack? And that hungry look in her eyes? I was worried about you there for a minute."

"You shouldn't have been. I can take care of myself."

She nodded. "I guess you can." She didn't want to question why she was so jealous. The woman should have produced amusement instead of anger. If she thought about it too much then there would be a whole string of inconsistencies that she didn't want to answer. It was a paradox, a riddle without a solution.

"Look, Laurie. Jess is dancing with that guy."

Jack turned her around and she saw Jessica Meyers, scared and insecure, pushing herself back into life. "Well, will you look at that? She's even smiling. I am *so* proud of her! And isn't Keith nice?"

Jack shrugged. "I suppose so."

She looked up at him. "Why do you say it like that?"

"What do you expect me to say? We don't know him. He seems all right."

She turned her head toward where Jess and Keith were dancing. "But doesn't she look happy right now?"

He nodded. "I guess."

She smiled with satisfaction. "So everything turned out okay then. Even zapping the blond bombshell. It broke the ice with them. They're laughing and talking and I'll bet it's about how Cindi with an i came apart at the seams." She glanced at him from the corner of her eye. "The dress *was* too tight, Jack."

"No comment."

"Oh, well. Look at them—they make a cute couple. Once more the team of Reese and Lannigan comes through."

Grinning, he said, "I should have expected that you would put your name first."

Her eyes were wide with innocence. "But, of course. In case you've forgotten, I've had to drag you, kicking and screaming, into every one of my schemes."

"Shut up and dance, Laurie," he answered, pulling her closer until they were cheek to cheek. "I like this song."

And she did shut up. She could barely breathe, let alone talk. His breath tickled her earlobe with his last words, sending shivers of excitement running down her body. This wasn't supposed to happen. She wasn't supposed to feel anything sexual, and she closed her eyes, concentrating on removing any impure thoughts from her mind. It didn't work.

When he started humming along with Taylor Dane's "I'll Always Love You," she gave up and enjoyed whatever was happening between them. It felt good to be held by a man again. Better than that, it felt right to be held by this man. They fit together so well, like sections to a children's puzzle, one part smooth, one a little jagged at the edges, pieces that when next to each other formed part of something whole. It was dangerous to be thinking like this, she thought. It could only be trouble. But she didn't care. Not now. Not tonight. When she moved her hand at his shoulder, he moved his at her waist, spreading his fingers up her back to guide her around the floor.

"You're a good dancer," he whispered by her ear.

She resisted the shiver that instantly followed his words. "Thanks," she whispered back. "So are you. But then Cindi already told you that."

She winced and could have bitten her tongue.

Instead of being angry as she expected, he laughed. She felt the laughter ripple down his body and nearly moaned. She was definitely treading on dangerous ground here.

"You were doing pretty well with that guy earlier."

She was surprised by his remark. "He was nice."

"They're *all* nice to you," he said with more than a hint of amusement in his voice.

"That's not true," she answered and pulled back to see his face. "I know from past experience that they aren't all nice."

"Well, that's a cryptic remark. Care to explain?"

She shook her head. "I don't think so," she murmured while looking into his eyes.

The song changed and she forgot about Jess and her new friend, the blond, this place. She even forgot that she was no longer a part of this world. In that moment,

170

with Jack staring back at her, neither of them speaking out loud, she felt more alive than she ever had in her past. The lyrics of the song, "Always and Forever," swirled around in her head and took on a new meaning.

It was as if they were communicating in their minds. She was telling him that she was scared. He admitted the same. She told him there was something happening between them, an intense drawing sensation, more powerful and sexual than anything she had experienced before. His gaze said that he felt it, that he wanted her and was fighting it, too. Her smile was tender and romantic; his was gentle and intimate.

When the music ended, they found themselves almost trancelike, still holding each other, trying to communicate the thoughts that were impossible to put into words. The crowd walked off the floor, or started to fast dance to a Madonna song. Yet, they continued to stare at one another, willing the rest of the world to go away.

Jack was the first to break the spell. He blinked several times and looked around them. "We'd better get back to Jessica," he murmured.

Laurie nodded, knowing instinctively she had finally met her match. How ironic to have it happen now.

Chapter 11

"I can't believe you didn't give him your phone number." Shaking her head, Laurie hung up her coat and scowled at Jess.

"I couldn't. I wasn't comfortable doing it." Jess waited until Laurie left the hall closet and then brought out a hanger. "I said I would meet him there next week."

After hanging up her coat, Jess went into the kitchen where Jack was already picking at the leftover chicken from dinner. "Still hungry? I never saw Casper, the friendly you know what, chowing down." She leaned against the refrigerator and grinned. "I didn't think ghosts ate and slept. If I didn't see with my own eyes the stuff you two could do, I'd swear you were real."

Jack nodded while he swallowed. "Laurie and I were talking about it. She thinks the longer we stay here, with you, the more human attributes we take on. I guess she's right," he added, pulling more chicken off the breast bone. "And if you think all this is hard to believe, try having it happen to you."

"Who's right?" Laurie asked, joining them in the kitchen.

"You are. Jack was just giving me your theory about why you two seem so real." Jess looked up at the cupboard over the refrigerator. "About the longer you stay here . . ." She hadn't had a drink all night.

"I don't know what else could explain it," Laurie answered, watching as Jess opened the cabinet door. "We're going dancing again next week, Jack. Think you're up to it?"

"Next week?" Jack looked at Laurie and she nodded to Jess. He saw her staring at the bottle of bourbon.

"Jess is going back to meet Keith. What do you think of him? I think he's nice."

"You answered your own question. It doesn't matter what I think. How does Jess feel?"

They both stared at her and waited.

Jessica slowly closed the door and turned to smile at them. "I think he's very nice. Now if you two little matchmakers will excuse me, I'm going to sleep. Good night."

When they were left alone, the air in the kitchen suddenly seemed heavy and weighted with uncertainty. Neither of them knew what to say, or even how to begin. Embarrassed, Laurie murmured a quick good night, and left the room. Jack started to call out to her, but abruptly changed his mind. Instead, he cleaned up the mess he had made and then turned off the light.

As he passed her bedroom door, he stopped and stared at it. There was tension between them. It wasn't anger any longer. This was something more dangerous. He raised his hand to knock, hesitated for a few seconds, and then his knuckles connected with the wood.

When she opened the door his breath caught at the back of his throat. He finally had his answer. She went in for cotton and comfy. And the short, peach-colored nightshirt was sexier than any silk negligee he'd ever seen. Finding his voice, he managed to say, ''Could I talk to you for a few minutes?''

She appeared startled, but quickly recovered. ''Sure. Come in.''

She sat on the edge of the bed and looked up at him with expectation. It took every ounce of willpower he possessed not to join her. Instead, he cleared his throat and began to tell her what was on his mind.

''I don't know what happened tonight when we were dancing. Well, I know what happened. I just don't know *why* it happened. And why it's happening now.'' He began pacing in front of the bed. ''I mean, what the hell are we doing? We're on a mission here and this—this attraction can only get us in trouble. Did you see Jess down in the kitchen? She didn't drink. I know she thought about it, but she didn't. You were right, Laurie. Meeting someone has made a difference to her. This is working, and now we have to stay on course. We can't let . . . well, we can't let anything distract us. This could be some kind of test. You know they have to be aware of everything we're doing, and this isn't going to look good for either one of us.''

He stopped and turned to her. ''What do you think?''

''I think you're right,'' she said softly.

''You do?'' Why was he surprised, and maybe a little disappointed, that she agreed so readily?

She nodded and got up from the bed. ''Sure. You're absolutely right. Jessica is our mission, and we shouldn't forget that. I'm so glad you feel the same way I do.'' She walked to the door and opened it wider. ''Now I think we should both get some sleep. Tomorrow's Saturday, and we still have to work.''

''Okay,'' he said as he walked to the door. ''Well, good night.''

She smiled. ''Good night.'' And then shut the door at his back.

He stood in the hallway for a few seconds wondering why he felt like she had just rejected him. It didn't make any sense. She agreed with everything he said. She wasn't upset or hurt or argumentative. He had expected that she would have debated him, or something. Shrugging, he walked down the hall to his bedroom while trying to figure out why he didn't feel more virtuous about his decision, and less foolish.

*　*　*

Saturday was the busiest day of the week. The store was hectic and, even though there were two additional workers, it still seemed like they were short-handed.

"I just love those little thank you notes you send out. It's the reason I came back from Media, Pennsylvania. An hour in the car, but it's worth it." The woman handed over her VISA card to pay for the three hundred dollars worth of clothing she was purchasing.

Laurie glanced at the credit card before handing it to Jack. "Thank you, Carol. We just want you to know that we appreciate your business." The look she gave Jack spoke volumes. It had to, since she tried not to speak with him at all. Of course he was right last night. Jess was their mission, but he'd acted as if it had only been a mild flirtation between them. And she was hurt because she had felt something far stronger. He could have admitted that he'd felt it, too.

Placing the clothes into a shiny white shopping bag, she again thanked the woman from Pennsylvania and hurried to her next customer. As she was bringing a smaller size into the dressing room, Dave walked in with a special delivery.

"Must be pretty important for a Saturday delivery, Jessica," he said, walking up to her with a long, flat package.

Jess handed the appliquéd sweater to her customer and looked down at the label. "Oh, thanks, Dave. It's a special order. The woman's coming in this afternoon and I promised her it would be here." She smiled at the UPS man as he gave her his pen.

"I can't believe how busy this place is," Dave commented, as Jess signed for the package. "You should be really proud. It looks great." He took his clipboard back, and added, "Come to think of it, you're looking pretty good yourself lately. I'm glad everything's turning around for you."

Jessica was about to thank him when a young man came in with a huge floral bouquet. "Jessica Meyers?" He called out her name.

Jess was too startled to reply and Jack pointed her out. She felt everyone's attention on her as she accepted the beautiful flowers and couldn't help the blush from creeping up from her neck.

"Who're they from?" Mari demanded with that eternal feminine excitement flowers seemed to bring out in all women. Even the customers waited for an answer.

Jess handed the flowers to Mari and opened the small envelope.

I can't wait a whole week. If you won't give me your number, here's mine. 235-8859. Please call me?
Keith.

"Well?" Laurie asked, a wide grin on her face.

Jess looked up and smiled. "They're from Keith." She showed Laurie the card.

"Yes!" Laurie's response came out as a whoop of triumph. "I knew mentioning the shop was a good idea."

Taking her flowers and the card, Jess smiled at Laurie before walking into the back room. She placed the flowers on her desk and sat down to stare at them. It had been so long since a man had sent her flowers that she wasn't sure how to react. She glanced down to the card in her hand. How could she call him? What would she say? She *should* call him to thank him. That's it. Thank him. It was only politeness. All she had to do was pick up the phone. She reached for the receiver, but hesitated. What would she say after she thanked him? What if it were awkward—those dreaded silences in a phone conversation?

She shook her head, as if trying to dislodge the fear, and picked up the phone. Without any further thought, she punched in the numbers. When the phone rang, her stomach muscles clenched with apprehension.

"Hello?"

"Keith?"

"Yes?"

"This . . . this is Jessica."

There was surprise and maybe pleasure in his voice. "Well, hi. I'm glad you called."

She touched the soft petal of a yellow rose. "The flowers are beautiful. Thank you so much, but you really shouldn't have."

"I wanted to, and I couldn't think of any other way to speak with you before next Friday."

Smiling, she said, "Well, it worked."

"Are you busy? At the store, I mean."

"Saturdays are always the worst, though I shouldn't complain. Especially in a recession."

"What time do you close?"

She knew where his question was leading. "Nine. But it takes about forty-five minutes to an hour to get out of here."

"How about a late dinner?"

She closed her eyes. "I can't."

"Why?"

"Well, first of all, I'm going to be exhausted. And by the time I got ready it would just be too late." She should suggest another time, but was too shy.

There was a pause and Jess was starting to think about the dreadful silences when he said, "Okay. I can understand that. But you don't work tomorrow, do you?"

"No."

"How about showing me the area? A trip to the zoo?"

"In the middle of winter?" She laughed.

"That's the best time. No crowds. All those carnivores to ourselves. I always take my kids in the winter."

She stopped laughing. *Kids?* "You have children?"

"Two of them. Boys. They live with their mother. I usually see them on the weekends, but since this is my first week down here I'd already explained to them that I'd have to skip this one."

She didn't know what to say. He was obviously divorced, in a new place, and didn't know that many people. Maybe he was just as lonely as she was.

"Jessica?"

"Yes?"

"Would you take pity on a dislocated man and go with him to the zoo?"

She hesitated for a few seconds and then took a deep breath. "Sure, I'd love to go. It sounds like fun." Talk about one giant leap! She'd just plunged, head first, back into dating.

"Great! We can have lunch first, if you'd like."

"All right. What time?"

"How does eleven sound? Too early?"

"No, that's fine. I'll see you then."

"Jessica?"

"Yes?"

"Maybe you should give me directions to your house?"

She laughed. "I'm sorry. I guess I'm a little rusty at all this."

"Yeah, I know what you mean. Me, too. I thought perhaps the flowers might have been a bit old fashioned, but I couldn't think of any other way to contact you."

She told him how to get to her house and he repeated the directions. Finally, she gave him her number, in case he got lost. "I really should get back to work," she added, not really wanting to get off the phone, but knowing she should end the conversation before she said something stupid.

"All right then—I'll see you tomorrow."

"Okay . . . and, Keith?"

"Yes?"

"The flowers weren't old fashioned. They were perfect. Thank you, again."

"You're welcome. Dress warm tomorrow, Jessica."

"I will," she said softly, already impatient for the morning. "Goodbye."

After hanging up the phone, she sat back and stared at it. Well, that was relatively painless. He'd even made her laugh. But . . . a date! She hadn't dated in over six years! Suddenly the knot in her stomach tightened and she stood up. She put the card into her purse and brought her flowers with her as she returned to the front of the store.

Placing them on the counter in back of the register, she leaned down to smell a rose when Laurie appeared at her side.

"Did you call him?"

Jess nodded.

"*And* . . . ?"

Smiling, Jess said, "And I need an outfit for the zoo tomorrow morning."

She knocked, and then poked her head around the door. "Jess? Can I come in?"

"Sure? What's wrong?" Reading a mystery novel while in bed, Jessica placed it on her stomach.

"Nothing's wrong," Laurie said as she stood by the bottom of the bed. "I was just wondering if you wanted to talk."

"Not really. Well, the truth is I'm so nervous I can't sleep. I don't think talking about it will help."

Laurie wrapped an arm around a high wooden post

and smiled. "Yeah, I know what you mean. Dating. Especially first dates. They can be scary."

"Try not having one in over six years," Jess groaned.

Laughing, Laurie sat on the edge of the bed. "It doesn't matter how long it's been. I think all women are anxious on every first date. For that matter, so are most men. I used to think of them as auditioning. Do I look right? Do I sound fairly intelligent? Will I get the part? A second date?"

"You thought that way?" Jess sounded surprised.

Laurie nodded.

"I never would have thought it. You appear to be so . . . I don't know, together. Like you can handle any situation."

Smiling, Laurie said, "I'm a good actress. Most of the time I'm uncertain, but I brave it out with instinct and guts. Believe me, I've made mistakes. I've had my share of bad relationships."

"You never married?"

"Once."

"No kidding? I just thought you were a career woman with—"

"I was a career woman," Laurie interrupted. "I was married before I had a career. In college." She shook her head, as if remembering her distant past. "It was brief and disastrous. After that I had several relationships and I tended to crash and burn with every one of them. But there's something wonderful about the human spirit. I guess we lick our wounds, hopefully learn from our mistakes, and then we venture out again. I suppose it's the joy we experience when a relationship works that makes us so brave."

"And you've had relationships that work?" Jess asked in a disbelieving voice. "I guess I have bad memories."

"I've had several that lasted for a couple of years, and good memories from each of them."

"Really?"

"Yup. I think sometimes we outgrow people or situations, and something must be forfeited because the relationship has outgrown its usefulness. It's like cutting away the old to make room for the new. It's the cutting away that's painful. But that's growth, and maybe it's the only way we learn." She leaned forward to make her point. "But, I'll tell you something, Jess. No matter what, if you find happiness, even temporary, it's all worth it. I wouldn't give up one good memory."

Jessica closed her eyes for a brief moment and then whispered. "I'm scared. I really like this man, and it's been so long that I'm afraid I'll either screw it up or appear desperate."

Laurie smiled with sympathy. "You won't screw it up. Just be yourself. And you didn't look desperate the other night when you were with him. You looked happy. I guess I didn't appreciate happiness before. Not really. Now I believe that a person shouldn't look toward tomorrows. Take it for what it is and enjoy the time you spend with someone now. You can't count on forever, so just count on today. Or in your case, tomorrow morning. Have a good time. Maybe you

183

won't see him again, and maybe you will. So forget all the anxiety that goes with a first date and enjoy the day."

Nodding, Jess said, "You're right."

"Hey, you haven't even gone out with him and you're already trying to figure out how you'll screw it up. Does that make sense? You're over-analyzing this whole thing because you're nervous."

Neither of them said anything for a few moments and then Jess murmured, "Thank you. I suppose I did need to talk. I guess I felt a little guilty—going out dancing so soon after my mother's death. And now dating." She shook her head. "I don't know. It seems my whole life has turned around since she's gone, and . . ." Her words trailed off as the tears came into her eyes.

Laurie leaned over and took her hand. Squeezing it, she said, "Jess, don't feel bad about being happy. Do you really think your mother would want you to grieve? You've been grieving for six years. It's time to start living again. I'm going to tell you something, give you a gift. Dying isn't what's hard. Living is. It's the giving up, the giving in . . . surrendering to a force more powerful than your will. Your mother finally surrendered, and it must have been so hard. I didn't have a choice. But I do know one thing for certain. Wherever your mother is, she's found peace. Take it from one who knows."

Chapter 12

Over brunch she learned that he was a good father, that he missed his boys and intended to spend every weekend with them. He showed her pictures, boasted about their ability in soccer and their marks in school. He talked about his sorrow over the death of his marriage and how he tried to maintain a friendly relationship with the mother of his children. He drew her out, asking about her life. He wanted to know what she was like in high school and college. He had been transferred to Chicago for a few years and they reminisced about favorite haunts, restaurants and museums. They got along so well that by the time they arrived at the zoo, Jess felt like she had known him for years.

"They remind me of my boys," Keith said as Jess laughed at the antics of the otters.

"Oh, to have that much energy," she said in a wistful voice. "They have such joy and playfulness. They seem so happy just to be alive."

"Maybe we should take a lesson from them," he answered.

She looked at him from the corner of her eye. Really looked. Another woman probably would have said he was average-looking, but to her he was more than that. He was intelligent, warm, exciting . . . and stimulating.

Smiling at the otters, she realized that she felt more alive today than she had in years. Even though the air was brisk, the winter sun shined down on them, warming the senses.

Keith consulted the map of the zoo. "Let's go to Bear Island," he suggested, touching her elbow.

She turned and walked toward the polar bears, feeling content to be with him. How many times in the past had she observed couples together, and wondered what was wrong with her? Why she had to miss sharing the day with someone?

They sat for a while outside, below water level, and watched the bears swim. They talked about everything. Her store. His job. Made comments about the people who passed before them. If there was a silence it wasn't awkward. It was peaceful.

"Are you cold?" he asked.

She grinned. "I wasn't when we were walking, but I have to admit my hands are reminding me that it's really winter. I should have worn gloves."

"C'mon. We'll visit the birds. At least that's inside."

It was as if they had walked into a tropical rain forest. The air was hot and humid, and Jess felt a little dizzy as her body adjusted to the extreme change in climate. What was worse was that she immediately broke out in a sweat.

"Are you okay?"

Jess nodded. "I think I'm going to take off my coat. It's *hot* in here."

"I know what you mean," he answered, as he helped her.

They were surrounded by greenery and noise, the wild calls of the birds that flew around them. As he removed his jacket, Keith ducked his head when a dive-bombing red finch seemed to zero in on him. Laughing, Jess watched the flight of the bird.

"Did I tell you that you look very pretty today?"

Startled, she tried to recover with a smart reply. "Oh, yeah. Sure. I feel real pretty with sweat dripping off my forehead."

He didn't laugh. He continued to stare at her. "I like sweat," he finally said. "But I was just reminded of how pretty you are when you laughed. You should do it more."

She wanted to tell him that there hadn't been a whole lot to laugh about in the last six years. But she didn't; now was not the time. Instead, she smiled and said,

"My mother used to say, 'Ladies don't sweat; they glisten.' "

He looked her straight in the eye and answered, "Well, with all due respect to the memory of your mother, I prefer a woman to sweat. It's healthy . . . and sexy as hell."

She couldn't help it. She blushed. Just like a fifteen-year-old virgin.

"I'm sorry. I embarrassed you." He grinned at her and held out his hand. "C'mon. Let's check out those parrots in the back. The brochure says something about a Purple Victoria Crown Pigeon."

She hesitated and he added, "May I hold your hand, Jess?"

Her answer was to place her palm into his opened one.

She knew, as soon as skin touched skin, that she was in trouble.

"Well, I think you should look up your birth mother. You haven't seen her for twenty years. Maybe she's changed."

"Will you just drop it?" Jack asked in a strained voice. "I'm trying to watch a game here."

Laurie threw the Sunday paper to the rug in annoyance. "What are you so afraid of? She won't know you. And even if she did, don't you think she has a right to hear about your death?"

He turned away from the television to stare at her. "What rights? She gave them up forty years ago. I don't want to see her. I don't want to talk to her. There's no point in this.''

The truth suddenly hit her. "You're afraid," Laurie whispered.

"What? I don't think I heard you."

"You heard me."

He shook his head, trying to control his anger. "No. I don't think so."

"You're afraid she'll reject you again." This time her voice was strong enough so that he couldn't misunderstand her words.

"That's bullshit. I have no interest in seeing her. I don't even know if she's still alive. And I couldn't care. She's nothing to me."

"That's not true. She's your mother."

"She's my birth mother. Period. It was a biological circumstance. My mother is the woman who raised me, and she's very much alive in Philly."

"But you can't approach her, any more than I can see my parents. We can't be seen by anyone that knew us. But don't you understand, Jack, your birth mother never knew you. You *could* talk to her."

"What for? Exactly what would be the purpose in talking to her?" The basketball game was forgotten as his words became a challenge.

Laurie remembered the night they had talked in his room. She would never forget how he had turned stiff and cold when she tried to comfort him. Walls that high and that thick take years to build. Changing tactics, she asked, "Were you ever in love, Jack?"

189

His expression reflected his confusion. "What?"

"Have you ever been in love?" she repeated.

"What does that have to do with seeing my birth mother?"

"I think there's a connection. Why are men so reluctant to talk about love?" she asked and then laughed. "You'd think you were revealing some terrible secret. I'm talking about love, something wonderful."

"Why do women want to talk about it so much?" he countered, while giving up on his game. "There's books, songs, movies devoted to something that should come naturally."

"Maybe because it reaffirms our basic instinct. And maybe human beings don't get enough of it, so if we can't experience it ourselves, then we look for it elsewhere. Love, in some form, is the driving force behind everything."

"You're talking to the wrong person," he said skeptically. "I've seen too much to accept that statement."

"I think it's the opening of your heart, whether it's to another human being, community involvement, or even the environment. It's still opening up to love." Her smile was gentle. "And you still didn't answer my original question."

He stared at the television screen for a few moments and then said, "You're relentless when you want something, do you realize that? It doesn't matter whether it's renovating an entire store in three days or prying into my psyche."

She didn't answer him. The only sound was the announcer's voice on the TV. She wasn't going to let him slip out of this one. Instinct told her she was right about him.

"I don't think I've ever really been in love," he finally muttered. "At least not in the way you're describing it."

"You've never really opened up to anyone, to a woman?"

He thought for a few moments and then shook his head. "And it's been a contributing factor in why every relationship I've ever had has failed."

"If you've realized that, then why didn't you change?"

He looked at her. "I just realized it thirty seconds ago."

She laughed. "Fair enough. Did you ever think of settling down? Of marrying?"

His answer was immediate. "Never."

"Why?"

Shrugging, he said, "Because I don't think I'd be successful at it. And what's the point, anyway? It rarely works."

She sat up straighter, pleased with the way the conversation had progressed. "Would you like me to tell you why you believed it wouldn't work for you?"

"Do I really have a choice? If I say no, will that actually stop you?"

Her smile was almost serene. "If you don't want to hear it, then I won't say anything."

"Yeah, right." He took the remote and started to flip through the channels. "I can't imagine you having an opinion and keeping it to yourself."

She merely smiled.

"Then I don't want to hear it." His statement was thrown out like a challenge.

It was her turn to shrug. She picked up the paper from the rug and pretended to read while listening to him switch channels. He must have gone through the entire cable listing, and was starting over again with the basketball game when he suddenly threw the remote down on the couch.

"Okay, let's hear it," he said with exasperation.

"I don't think you trust women," she said slowly, as she looked up from the paper. "I think you've been deeply hurt by the two most important women in your life. Your adopted mother, by lying to you when you were a child. And your birth mother, by rejecting you at birth and then again as an adult. Buried in your subconscious is this belief that all women will eventually hurt you, so you don't let any in. That way you protect yourself. And if you find yourself weakening, you sabotage the relationship and drive the woman away."

He listened in silence, yet she could tell by the way he was clenching his jaw that he was angry. Finally, he said, "And what if I told you that's bullshit? That you're practicing Psych 101 on me? That you don't know me well enough to come to that conclusion?"

"I'd say you're protecting yourself again. Our survival instincts are very strong, and when someone gets too close and threatens that structure we've set up around us, we either back off or attack. What you're doing now is a combination of both, don't you think?"

"Oh, I'm being asked for my opinion now?" His tone was sarcastic and defensive. "You want to know what I'm thinking? I wish I never said anything to you about the circumstances of my birth. Just to have you throw it back in my face—"

"I'm not doing that," she interrupted. "I'm trying to understand you."

"Don't. Who asked you to understand me? We're here on a mission. Period. When this is over, who knows what's going to happen. We've got a job to do, and we have to work together. So let's just leave it at that, and drop this subject. All right?"

Before she could answer, the front door opened and Jessica walked in from her date. "You're home?" Laurie asked with surprise. The clock showed that it was barely five-thirty. "Did you have a good time?"

She nodded as she hung up her coat. "I had a great time. Lunch was delicious and the zoo was a lot of fun." She turned and walked into the kitchen.

It was as if she were giving a weather report, Laurie thought. Something was definitely wrong. Walking into the kitchen, Laurie saw Jessica in the act of pouring herself a drink. "What happened? What's wrong?"

Jess didn't even look up. "Nothing's wrong," she said. "And nothing happened."

"Then why are you drinking?" Laurie held on to the back of a chair and felt that knot coming to life again in her stomach.

"Because I want one." Jess swallowed a deep gulp.

"But something must have happened," Laurie

193

insisted. "You'd been doing so well lately, and now—"

"And now I'm having a drink." Jess spun around from the counter. "Look, nothing happened, all right? That's just it! He didn't kiss me goodbye. He didn't ask to see me again. Nothing. Just a quick thanks and he had a great time." Finishing off the drink, she turned back. "I must have done something wrong. I just can't think of what it is."

Desperately wanting to help her, Laurie blurted, "But he said he had a great time."

Jess glared at her. "Oh, yeah. Right. He had such a great time, he didn't want to see me again!"

Laurie needed to find a way to salvage her remark. "I don't think he would say that if he didn't mean it. Maybe he's just taking it slow."

"And maybe he just felt sorry for me. Take the lonely woman out for a nice day. Feed her. Walk her through the zoo. Make her feel special and then drop her off at her door. Why didn't he just pat me on the head and tell me to get straight A's on my next report card?" Pouring another drink, she added, "I'm going upstairs."

Laurie could only watch as Jessica pushed past her.

Jack, coming into the kitchen, stopped and stared, first at Jess and then Laurie. "Was that alcohol she's got in that glass?" he asked, pointing toward the stairs. "What's going on?"

Laurie could only shrug.

It was nearly ten o'clock and Jess still hadn't read more than four pages—and she'd re-read two of them, because she couldn't concentrate. Her thoughts kept returning to her date. What could she have done wrong? He'd asked to hold her hand. She didn't refuse. He'd drawn her out and they talked easily. On the way home they laughed about the animals. She simply couldn't think of what went wrong. Maybe she was too quiet, not vivacious enough. Maybe he thought she didn't really have a good time. Maybe—

The phone next to her bed rang and, as she reached for it, she tried to imagine who could be calling her so late.

"Hello?"

"Jessica? It's Keith. Is it too late to call?"

The weight on her chest immediately lifted and she smiled. "No. Not at all. I was just reading."

"Well, I wanted to call to tell you again how much I enjoyed today. I did have a great time."

"Me, too. It was a lot of fun."

"Being with you was fun. Actually, the real reason I'm calling is to see if you want to do it again."

Thank you, God. "Go to the zoo?" she asked and giggled.

He laughed. "I was thinking maybe dinner and a movie."

"Sure. I'd love to go. When?"

"I'll leave that up to you. You're the one with a busy schedule. I'm free any night."

"Okay, how about tomorrow or Tuesday? We close early both nights."

"You pick one. If it was up to me, I'd see you tomorrow. But listen, I might as well tell you this now.

We'll go at your pace. I don't want to rush you into anything. No pressure. I was happy walking around the zoo and holding your hand.''

There was a slight crack in the steel wall around her heart. ''Thank you for that, Keith,'' she said slowly, and then took a deep breath. ''Tomorrow night will be fine. I'll be home from work around six-thirty.''

''All right. If I pick you up at seven-thirty, will that give you enough time?''

''That's fine.'' Jess thought he sounded pleased by her answer.

''We'll have dinner and then take in a ten o'clock movie.''

''Sounds great. Thanks for asking me.''

''Well, thank you for accepting. I'll let you get back to your reading, and I'll see you tomorrow night.''

''Okay. Good night.''

''Sweet dreams, Jessica.''

After she hung up the phone, she dropped her book to the rug and turned off the light. Laying in the dark, her smile was serene. Her heart was light. And her imagination was in high gear. He liked her! She hadn't done anything wrong. And he was so sweet. They would go at her pace. If he only knew that her pace had suddenly accelerated. It had been so long since a man had paid attention to her that she craved it, like . . .

Like bourbon, she realized.

They say if you break one habit you replace it with another. Well, Keith held a heck of a lot more appeal than alcohol. She would stop drinking. She could do it. Maybe she'd only been using it as a substitute anyway, something to fill her empty life. But her life wasn't empty any more. She had the shop. A successful career as a businesswoman. She had friends. She had *ghosts* living in her home. And she had a date tomorrow.

Things were certainly looking up.

"She's drinking again. This dating was definitely a bad idea." Jack poured himself a cup of coffee and then sat opposite Laurie at the kitchen table as she ate her grapefruit.

"It was not a bad idea," Laurie countered. "Okay, so maybe this Keith guy didn't pan out. There are a lot of men out there. We just have to look further."

"I'm not looking—period. We have a mission, remember? We're not here to be a dating service."

"Oh, c'mon, Jack. Where's your romance? Women need it in their lives. It adds something. Makes them feel more alive."

"I could see that last night when she came in," he said sarcastically. "Why can't you just admit this isn't working? We can't find the magic solution to making her happy. She's got to do that."

Laurie finished her breakfast and picked up her mug of coffee. "You understand so little about women, Jack. It's amazing you ever had a second date."

"Let's forget my track record in dating. I did just fine—"

"Good morning, everyone . . ." Jess nearly sang

197

as she breezed into the kitchen. She looked rested, relaxed and happy.

Laurie and Jack stared at her with confusion.

Taking out a container of milk, Jess opened several cabinets while searching for something. "You know, we're going to have to go food shopping. I can't believe I don't have any cereal in the house. We'll have to make a list. Something really healthy, with all those grains and fiber." She put the milk back in the refrigerator and took out orange juice.

"We could go tonight after work," Laurie suggested, giving Jack a questioning look. He merely shrugged, silently conveying that he didn't understand Jess' changed mood either.

"I can't," Jess said. "Not tonight. Tonight I'm going out."

"You are?" Jack and Laurie both asked the question.

Turning from the counter, Jess smiled. "Keith called last night. We're going to dinner and a movie." She glanced at the wall clock and added, "C'mon, guys, we've got fifteen minutes to get to work. I'll warm up the car."

As she left the room, Laurie and Jack stared at each other. It was Laurie that smiled and spoke first. "See what a little romance can do?" She picked up her mug of coffee and walked to the sink and set it inside. "Hurry up, Jack. We don't want to be late."

He sat for a few seconds and watched as she walked out of the kitchen. At least she didn't say I told you so.

Women. It simply didn't pay to try and figure them out.

"She went to lunch. That was three hours ago. Where the hell is she?"

Laurie leaned up against the counter and sighed. "What do you care, Jack? She's been dating him for two weeks now. I think she's safe."

"I care because it's busy. This is her store. She should be here."

"It's busy and we're managing. She's happy. Isn't that what we wanted? What does a three hour lunch date mean to you?"

"It means she's being irresponsible, that's what." Jack straightened out the charge receipts, while acting like Jessica's father.

"Do you think they've had sex yet?"

"Jesus! What business is that of ours?"

Laurie giggled. "I don't know—all those late nights, those smiles, the faraway looks and day-dreaming." She nodded. "If they haven't, I'll bet it's soon."

"Grace," Jack said in a loud voice. "Good to see you again."

"Thank you, Jack. It's nice to see you, too. How are you, Laurie?"

"I'm great," Laurie answered and waved as her customer came out of a fitting room. "Excuse me, if you need anything Jack will take care of you."

Grace appeared embarrassed as Jack said, "What can I do for you today?"

"Well," the older woman began, "Jessica ordered . . . she ordered a few things for me and I was wondering if they came in yet. She usually calls, but it's been over a week now, and I thought I'd check myself."

"Jess has been a little busy lately. What was it? I'll see what I can do."

Grace seemed to stagger for a second and then righted herself as she clutched the edge of the marble counter.

"Are you okay?" Jack asked.

"Oh, this is so silly. You're such good friends of Jessica's, helping her so much. I can't imagine staying here as long as the two of you have. She's a very lucky girl to have you and your wife staying with her. And I shouldn't be embarrassed. Not at my age anyway." She took a deep breath and said, "Jessica ordered some . . . some undergarments for me."

Jack could only stare at her.

Grace rubbed her temple. "Now I've embarrassed you. Perhaps Laurie, or one of the—"

"No. No, not at all," Jack quickly recovered. "I'll go in the back room and see if there's anything with your name on it."

Smiling weakly, Grace said, "Thank you, Jack. I'll just wait here."

He hurried into the store room and started searching the shelves. Where would they put it, he wondered. Poor Grace. It must have been hard to ask a man to search for her—what did she call them? Undergarments? What was that? Panties, slips, garter belts? Nah. Not garterbelts. A girdle, maybe.

"Jack! Come quick," Mari yelled with a frightened voice. "Mrs. Armstrong just collapsed!"

He ran past her and saw Grace sprawled on the floor in front of the counter. Laurie was kneeling by Grace's head, and he called out over his shoulder, "Mari, call an ambulance!"

He squatted down as Laurie looked up at him with a helpless expression. Grace was in the midst of a seizure. Her eyes had rolled back and her arms and legs were shaking.

"Help me move her," he ordered. "*Now!* She may break her wrist against this counter."

"She's bleeding," Laurie whispered in a scared voice.

"She's already bit her tongue. Now! Help me lift her now—hold her head and shoulders."

Laurie did as she was told and then fell back on her legs as she watched Grace flail about on the rug. Something snapped inside of her when she thought how aptly this woman had been named. She was a lady. She always carried herself with dignity and grace. For this to happen so publicly was unfair.

Crawling to her feet, Laurie announced, "Everyone, please leave. We'll be open later this evening. I'm sorry."

Customers filed out in silence as the paramedics came in. Grace's seizure slowly ceased and she was put on a gurney.

"How do you feel?" one of them asked her.

She appeared dazed and frightened and tried to speak. Only garbled noises emerged.

"I'm going to the hospital with her," Jack stated, as he held the older woman's hand. "Laurie, you stay here and wait for Jess. She'll want to know."

Laurie could only nod as she watched them leave.

"She has a brain aneurysm," Jack told one of the paramedics as Grace was placed in the ambulance.

"Well, it looks like it just blew," the guy muttered under his breath as he jumped into the back of the vehicle and held out a hand to Jack.

He sat next to her and held her. He'd done this before. He'd watched too many people die, and under worse conditions than this. So why was he so tormented by the thought of this old woman dying in his arms? She'd lived a full life. Nobody snuffed it out because of drugs or war or poverty.

"Her blood pressure is going right off the monitor. I think we're in for something major here."

Grace had another seizure, a bigger one, and the paramedic told him he'd have to get out of the way. Sitting on a narrow bench, he knew she wouldn't survive this one. And if she did, she'd be a vegetable. She might hang on for a few hours, or maybe even a few days, but she'd never recover. Not from this. She was starting to bleed from her nose and her ears.

When it was over, and the paramedic sat down by the back doors, Jack knelt next to Grace's face.

He put his mouth right next to her ear and whispered, "Don't be afraid, Grace, of where you're going. It's like . . . like leaving a smoke-filled room where there are too many people talking and . . . and emerging into fresh air and peace and quiet.'' He thought of Laurie and her experience and prayed that Grace's would be like it.

''If you see the light,'' he whispered, while swallowing the thick lump in his throat, ''then go toward it. It's the only part you have to do alone. That's the only scary part; that this last journey is alone, and you can't hold anyone's hand. But beyond that light someone is waiting for you. Maybe it's your husband, or a friend. Let it go, Grace. Just let it all go. There's nothing left here for you. Your task is finished . . .''

The heart monitor beeped erratically for a few moments and then ceased. The paramedic listened to her heart and checked for vital signs as the ambulance pulled up to the emergency room òf the hospital. As the doors were flung open, the man looked at Jack and shook his head. ''Sorry. She's gone.''

Jack nodded and sat back on the bench as they took Grace out. When he was alone, he buried his face in his hands and cried like a ten-year-old kid who had just lost his mother.

Chapter 13

"I just feel so guilty that I was out with Keith when she died in my store." Jess wandered around the living room, as if lost.

"There was nothing you could have done," Laurie answered.

Jess barely heard her. While Grace, a good friend, was dying, she was in Keith's arms. And it had been wonderful. For weeks she had only kissed him. He had left it up to her, and she was scared to take it further. Today, as they sat in his car after lunch, it had gone further. In her day they'd called it petting or necking, but she had stopped it before it had gotten out of control. She used daylight as an excuse, even if they were in a deserted park, but what really held her back was fear.

She was falling in love.

It was that simple—and that complicated. He was only here for another month and then he would return to New York. His life was there. His sons were there. Her life was here. There was no future in this. But what was the future? What could she really count on?

Her mother had died. Grace had died. She was sick of death, for it was the only certainty.

She walked into the kitchen and opened the refrigerator, but she wasn't hungry. Slowly, she lifted her chin and stared at the cabinet above her. Maybe Jack or Laurie had thrown the bourbon out. She told herself it was curiosity that made her open the door.

It stood there, half full, and she felt a drawing sensation inside of her. She realized that it had been almost three weeks since she'd had a drink. It would calm her nerves, make her forget that she'd lost another person close to her. It would be a familiar comfort, a temporary remedy for the aching emptiness.

Suddenly, she slammed the door shut and rushed out of the kitchen, knowing it wasn't bourbon that she wanted. She picked up her purse and opened the hall closet.

"Where are you going?" Laurie asked. "Mari's closing up tonight."

"I've got to get out of here. I'm going to Keith's," Jess said as she jammed her arms into her coat. As she headed for the door, she added over her shoulder. "Don't wait up. I might be late."

She drove to Marlton like a woman on a mission. Keith had already shown her where his apartment was located, but she hadn't gone in. Then, she hadn't been ready. She hadn't even been ready this afternoon. Now she was. Grace's passing had reawakened something long dormant. Life was too uncertain, and she knew she would always regret it if she missed intimacy with this man.

She knew if she thought about it she might lose her nerve so, as soon as she parked the car in front of the townhouse, she turned off the ignition and got out. She forced her legs to move up the sidewalk and held her breath as she knocked three times.

She was thinking how ironic it would be if he weren't at home when the door opened.

"Jess. What are you doing here?" Keith seemed more than surprised to find her staring at him.

"I had to see you. Do you mind?" Oh, God. What if she had made a mistake?

He smiled. "No. Never. Come on in."

When she was inside, he added, "I'll just be a minute. I'm talking to the kids."

She nodded and took off her coat. As she sat down she looked around the townhouse. It was a typical corporate apartment. Sparsely furnished in male contemporary, but functional.

He got off the phone and walked up to her. "Are you all right? You look upset."

She forced the tension out of her smile. "I had some bad news when I got back to the store."

"What was it? Do you want something to drink?"

he asked before she could answer his first question. "Coffee? Hot tea?"

She shook her head. "One of my customers, one of my oldest customers and a good friend, had a seizure in the store and died on the way to the hospital."

He hunched down in front of her. "God, Jess . . . I'm sorry." The phone rang and he ignored it.

"Aren't you going to answer it?" she asked.

"No. The machine will pick it up. You're what's important now. What can I do?"

It stopped ringing and she realized he had put his answering machine on mute so they wouldn't be disturbed. She knew why she was here. Now if she could only find the courage to tell him. She thought about all those years alone, feeling cut off from the rest of the world. It was as if something was wrong with her, that she couldn't find a mate or a partner. Or even a date on a Saturday night. And now a man cared about her. Maybe he wasn't falling in love, like her. Maybe he was only looking for companionship while on an extended business trip. It didn't matter. He was right in front of her, asking what he could do to make her feel better.

She swallowed the lump of fear at the back of her throat and took a deep breath. "You can make love to me, Keith. I don't want to think about death anymore. It's been hovering in corners all around me for six years and I've had enough. I want to concentrate on life, on living." Her eyes filled with tears. "I want to feel alive again."

His smile was warm and sympathetic and he gathered her into his arms. "Do you know how long I've waited for this moment? For you to make that decision? I've wanted you from the night I met you at that dance club."

He pulled back and stared into her eyes. "But it had to be your decision, Jess. I didn't want to push you into anything."

"I know," she whispered, as the tears ran down her cheeks. "And I appreciate that." What he didn't know was that by giving her the control, she wanted him more than any other man in her life.

Leaning forward, she kissed him.

It was sweet and tender, yet quickly grew into something more. Slowly, she lifted her gaze to his. He'd been watching her. A sudden erotic awareness, an undeniable passion rose up between them.

"C'mon," he whispered in a hoarse voice. Rising, he held out his hand in an invitation.

She couldn't refuse. Knowing it was what she wanted, she placed her hand inside his and stood up.

He led her into the bedroom and Jess experienced a moment of fear that she tried to reason out of her brain. He was a good man, a kind man. He would be tender and considerate. The time for repression, for holding back, was finished. She was finally free to start over, yet it was like being with a man for the first time again.

She refused to think about it. Jess' searching lips grazed over his, tasting a hint of coffee and something sweet with the tip of her tongue. Twice he allowed her to tease him and then his mouth became hungry, demanding more.

"Jess . . ." Her name sounded almost like a plea just as his lips crushed her own in a breathtaking kiss.

Her breasts melted into his chest and her arms wrapped around him, pulling him even closer. She felt the muscles of his back tighten under her fingers and reveled that she could bring about such a reaction. She cherished each awakened yearning, for it was proof that she was alive. The lonely, empty years were behind her . . .

There was no sanity, no logical thinking, as they shed the barriers of clothing. She wanted the exquisite friction of skin against skin, of his body pressed tightly against hers.

His hands slid over her, feeling, exploring, the way her rib cage tapered into her waist and then flared out again at her hips. She sucked in her breath when his fingers began their ascent, hoping this time he would discover her breasts. She wasn't disappointed.

Moaning with satisfaction, she flung her head back and closed her eyes, wanting to memorize everything—the way his lips teased her, the way his hands pleasured her. It was better than she remembered. Hard and soft. Feminine and masculine. One seeking. One giving. Every nerve ending in her body seemed sensitive to his touch.

"My God, Jess, I want you," he murmured against her neck. His voice was hoarse and passionate, and it excited her to know that she was once again a desirable woman.

It was like coming awake after a long sleep, almost as if she were being returned to the woman she once was, the one that had lain dormant inside of her all of these years.

Fully awakened, she took his hand and led him to the bed.

"She just went out?"

Laurie nodded as she prepared the BLT's. She'd forgotten how good fried bacon smelled, and her mouth watered in anticipation. She hadn't eaten bacon in years since all the fuss about fat and cholesterol came out. Now, who cared? She could eat anything she wanted. There were *some* advantages to this ghost state. "She said she was going to Keith's." Glancing back at him, she added, "She also said not to wait up for her. What do you think that means?"

Jack shook his head and shrugged. "I guess it means she's going to be late. But why would she run to him when you told her about Grace?"

"Because you and I couldn't give her the kind of comfort she needed." Laurie brought the sandwiches to the table and sat down. "I think she's falling in love."

"Oh, God . . ." He gave her a disgusted look. "Just what we need now."

"Maybe it's what she needs now. She didn't drink. She went to the cabinet, but she didn't do it." Laurie picked up half of her sandwich. "Instead, she went to Keith. I think that's healthy."

She bit down and moaned with pleasure at the combined taste of bacon, tomatoes, lettuce and toast. The effect on her taste buds was so sensual that it felt sinful. "Oh, Jack . . . you have to taste this. Isn't it great to eat anything we want and never have to worry about what it's doing to our bodies? We could go on binges. Pizzas, with everything on them. Ice cream sundaes, dripping with hot fudge sauce. Oh, yes, and thick, juicy steaks. We should do it, Jack. What do you think?"

Staring down at his sandwich, he didn't answer.

"What's wrong with you?"

He slowly raised his head. "How can you eat and go on about food when a woman just died?"

She stared at him. "I don't know. Maybe I'm handling it the same way Jess is, only with me, at this moment, it's food. She's finding comfort in someone's arms. With me, all I've got right now is this BLT, and I'm trying to make the most of it. Because it's pretty damn sad to realize at the end of my lifetime that's it." She sat back in her chair and sighed loudly. "And now I'm depressed, thank you. Question is, why are you? You really didn't know Grace. And you, above all others, know what awaits her."

He shook his head, unable to speak.

"I don't get it, Jack. Why are you grieving?"

"I don't get it either. I don't even know why I was helping this woman to go . . . into our world." He ran his hand over his eyes, as if he had a headache. "It's . . . it's just that she was so sweet, so nice. So damn scared. There was this old woman with this horrible fear in her eyes. And I *knew*, you know? I had the answer for her. I wanted her to go peacefully.

211

I wanted to make it like you described, all calm and beautiful.'' His eyes filled with tears. "And she did go peacefully in the end. She didn't give up. She just let go.''

Laurie swiped at her tears with the back of her hand and stood up. She walked around the table until she was in front of him. Bending down, she wrapped her arms around his shoulders and brought him against her chest. "That was a beautiful thing you did, Lannigan,'' she whispered above his head and then gently slapped his back when she felt his muscles tighten in withdrawal. "And you can relax. You can even put your arms around me, if you want. This is nothing more than two friends trying to get through a rough time, okay?''

His answer was to slowly slide his hands around her waist.

She smiled and stroked his hair. "Sometimes you surprise me. You can be so rigid and methodical and if you only let yourself go, Jack, you might just find someone you're real comfortable with. Yourself.''

"I am comfortable with myself,'' he muttered into her chest.

Laurie tried not to think how right it felt being this close to him. Instead, she concentrated on the conversation. "No, you're not. Not really. Do you want to know why you helped Grace? Why her death is bothering you so much?''

He groaned, and his breath went right through the thin material of her blouse, sending shivers down her arms. "Please, Laurie. Don't start. Not now.''

212

"But I think it's all tied together, Jack. Don't you see, Grace represented your mother to you. Both your mothers. And you need to make peace with them—"

He pulled away and shook his head. "That's enough," he interrupted. "I feel fine now. Look, thanks for listening. Hey, you're right. This sandwich looks great." He picked it up and took a bite.

Knowing she was dismissed, and again feeling rejected, Laurie turned away from him and sat back in her chair. "I don't know why you have this mental block about this subject."

"Hey." He dug into his pant's pocket and flipped a nickel onto the table. "Remember Lucy from the Peanuts comic strip? Well, here you are. Five cents worth of amateur psychiatry. Paid in full. Now let's drop it, okay?"

"Okay . . ." Although she said the word, she knew she didn't mean it. If Jack couldn't do anything about it, then maybe she would. She never promised not to explore the possibility of finding his birth mother. All it would take was a little time and research. What were friends for, anyway?

"And what about this guy?" Jack threw out as a weak attempt to change the subject. "How come she never sees him on a Saturday night?"

"Are we talking about Keith and Jess again?" Laurie asked with a smile. Sometimes he was so transparent.

"Yeah. What's his story?"

"Jess says he's divorced and he goes back to New York to see his kids on the weekend. He's a devoted

213

father." She picked up her sandwich, determined to enjoy it this time.

"I don't know . . ."

"Well, if I didn't know better, Jack, I would say you were jealous."

"Of him? You've got to be kidding." He looked insulted by the thought. "It's just—"

Her laughter interrupted him. "Relax, Officer Lannigan. Jess is happy. That's all that counts right now."

The next morning everyone was rushing out of the house because of a power failure during the night. The digital alarms failed and Jess' old manual was the only one that worked. And she had decided to sleep in for fifteen extra minutes.

"You have no idea how difficult it is living with two women," Jack grumbled as he grabbed his coat from the hall closet. "The two of you hog the bathroom. What the hell do you do in there for twenty minutes apiece?"

"Oh, knock it off, Jack," Laurie said as she reached past him for her coat. "We were taking showers, just like every morning."

"For twenty minutes? Your bodies are only so big—"

"We have legs to shave. And armpits," she said, halting anything further he could say. Grinning at his expression, she added, "Any more questions?"

Even if he had a reply, he never got the chance as Jess rushed up to them. "Could you hand me my coat, Jack? The green one."

While she was buttoning it up, she looked at them

214

and smiled. "Listen, before we leave, I want to say something to both of you." She appeared embarrassed and actually blushed before continuing. "I'm sorry I ran out last night. We'll do something special in Grace's memory. She loved gardenias. I'll call this morning and make sure she has them. The funeral is tomorrow morning and I'm closing the shop. I'd appreciate it if you both came with me."

"Sure," Laurie said. "We were going to go anyway. Right, Jack?"

He nodded.

Jess took a deep breath. "And another thing. Thank you both for . . . well, for forcing me back into life. If that was your mission, then you've done a good job. I'm actually happy again."

Laurie smiled. "Keith?"

Nodding, Jess said, "He's wonderful. He's so kind and sweet and—"

"Maybe we can continue this in the car?" Jack asked with impatience. "We're going to be late."

Laurie gave him a look of irritation before grinning at Jess. "Maybe he's Mr. Right?"

Jess' face shined with pleasure. "Maybe," she whispered shyly and hurried from the house.

"Oh, great . . . *Mr. Right.*" Jack scowled at Laurie.

Laurie stared after Jess. "I think she's in love, Jack."

"Of course she is. What did you expect? She hasn't been with a man for over six years. She'd fall in love with Captain Kangaroo if he paid attention to her."

215

When she didn't answer him, he indicated the front door. "Come on, pal. Looks like this mission is almost over."

The truth of his statement suddenly hit her. If it were so, then she didn't have much time left.

How did one go about finding a woman that, forty-four years ago, had given her baby up for adoption?

Well, Grace, you finally got me in here to listen to the choir. Smiling sadly, Jess sat in the pew and tried to find comfort in the funeral service. It looked like the entire town had turned out to pay tribute to one of the finest ladies that had lived among them. The casket was draped with the blanket of gardenias Jess had ordered and the church was filled with floral arrangements. The choir sang softly, beautifully, for one of its own. Tears welled up in her eyes when she remembered sitting in the front pew for her mother's funeral. Strange that it seemed so long ago. She had wanted to fade away that day, to slip into bed and never get up again, for she was sure life held no promises for her. So much had changed in such a short time.

The store was a success. The feature editor of the local paper even wanted to do a story on it and the changing woman's retail market. It seemed good fortune was finally shining down on her. And then there was Keith. She breathed deeply and closed her eyes as a rush of warmth spread through her body. The first time they had made love he was slow and gentle. The second time was . . . unbelievable. Thank God he'd had condoms, even though he didn't like to use them. Last night she'd brought her old diaphragm. Still fit after six years. And she was seeing him tonight at the apartment. As she sat between Laurie and Jack, she started to fantasize about what they would do.

Suddenly, she realized where she was and sat up straight. Ashamed to have such thoughts at her friend's funeral, Jess tried to say a prayer for Grace. It had been a long time since she'd prayed. For years, she thought God had simply forgotten about her. Somewhere in her mind the prayer for Grace's soul turned into a prayer of thanksgiving, for Laurie and Jack . . . and especially for Keith.

Laurie wanted to stand up and tell everyone not to be so sad. That Grace was in a beautiful place, and even if she could she wouldn't want to come back. But this whole process of grieving was for those that are left behind. She listened to the prayers for Grace's soul and wondered about the concept of God, of a Supreme Being. Was it the brilliant light that had called to her after rushing through the dark tunnel? Was it the beautiful woman in the valley that had given her this assignment? Was she God, or an angel? Or was God beyond all of that? Jack had talked to a man behind a desk. It was weird and indescribable for someone who hadn't experienced it.

She leaned forward slightly and glanced at Jack. He was sitting absolutely still, staring at Grace's coffin. What was he thinking? The only reason Grace's death had affected him like this had to be because of his mothers. Okay, so it really wasn't any of her business. If he wanted to carry that chip on his shoulder throughout eternity, that should be his decision. But he had this chance, this second chance, to make it right. To clean out old wounds and let them heal.

Even if he hated her for it, she was going to find his birth mother and then leave it up to him.

He wanted to get up and run out, to leave this place that seemed to be closing in on him. It was too hot. There were too many people. The incense the priest was waving about the coffin felt like it was crawling down his throat and choking him. Why did he feel like this about an old woman that he hardly knew? There was an emptiness inside of him that actually hurt, and he didn't know how to make it go away. The last time he had felt like this was in Viet Nam, when he had seen his first dead body. Jamie Koenig. That was his name. He had played Crazy Eights with him the night before a mortar had blown him to hell and back in the DMZ.

After throwing up his guts in the tall elephant grass, he'd been assigned the job of helping to carry Koenig back to their base. The Marines didn't leave their dead. That was the one thing they could all count on. Even if you bought it, you knew your own would bring you back. But nobody told a green kid what that kind of heat could do to a body in seven hours. When they'd gotten back to the camp, he knew he'd never be able to wash the stench of death from him. So he'd accepted it, made it part of him, and turned his mind and his soul cold to it. That was why he was a good cop. He could stay detached.

So why was it slamming back into his consciousness now? Why was the armor cracking and falling away from him?

Scared, more terrified than when he was eighteen years old, Jack muttered something about needing air to Jess and left the church.

Chapter 14

Miriam Koslowski

Laurie stared at the name and felt a rush of triumph. It had taken her three weeks of phone calls and inquiries, only to be told that the records were sealed and Jack would have to petition a judge in Family Court to have them opened. Knowing that was out of the question, she had been stalled for the last week until the solution had suddenly come to her . . . She didn't need anyone's help. All she had to do was wait until dark and then walk right in. No one could stop her. And they didn't. Doors were no obstacle, nor were locked filing cabinets or computers. And she was grateful for all the hours she had spent in the college library researching a subject on microfilm, for that's where she had found her answer.

John Michael Lannigan had been born Paul Andrew Koslowski at Frankford Hospital in northeast Philadelphia. The adoption had been arranged through the Silver Cradle Agency, a place that still advertised on billboards and in the newspaper. She'd heard of it growing up as a home for unwed mothers. The father was noted as unknown. Jack had been eight pounds, three ounces, and twenty inches long.

Laurie took a pen and a small notebook out of her purse and began writing down all the information. On the third screen was a notation with two asterisks, followed by three pound signs. She sucked in her breath and held it in awe as she stared at the short paragraph.

Mother notified court (11/27/51) of married name. Miriam Stanton. Residing in Langhorne, Pennsylvania. Notification requested only in case of mortality.

Blinking at the screen several times, Laurie slowly exhaled. Surely his mother must have wanted to keep in touch or be informed, even if only on a subconscious level, or she wouldn't have given her married name three years after Jack's birth. It was over forty years ago. The woman had to be in her sixties, or close to it. So much could have changed since Jack talked to her. Her children were grown and perhaps had families of their own. Maybe her husband had died, or she had finally told him.

It was worth a shot.

Now if only Jack would see it like that.

* * *

"You did *what*!"

"I found your mother. Her name is Miriam Stanton and she still lives in Langhorne. I have her phone number and her address." They were driving home from work and, as usual, they were alone. Jess had been going straight to Keith's every night after work. The only time they saw her was on Friday night and Saturday when Keith went to New York to see his kids. Laurie had put this conversation off for three days, waiting for the right time to break the news to Jack. For some reason, tonight, the words spilled right out of her mouth.

"I just walked into Family Court when the place was closed and pulled up your records. Then, while I was in Philly, I went to the main telephone office and—"

"That's not what I mean," he interrupted in an angry voice. "And you know it. How *could* you? Why can't you leave things alone? This is none of your business." His hands were gripping the steering wheel as if to keep them from striking out at her. "I'm not your mission!" he nearly yelled. "You can't just charge in and do whatever you want with someone's life."

"But I thought—"

"No, Laurie. Your problem is you never think, you just react. You're so out of touch with reality. You think the whole world is a damn "Oz" movie. That you can just click your heels and make everything

222

right. Give this one hope. This one love. This one a mother. Did you ever bother to think that it doesn't mean squat unless that person does it himself? And that they do it in their own time?"

"Jack," she said his name steadily, trying to calm him down. "If you'll just listen to me."

"I don't want to listen to you," he answered as he squealed into the driveway. He turned his head and stared at her.

Even in the dark, his expression sent a chill down her back.

"I'm tired of listening to you, and all your crazy schemes. It was bad enough when you did it to Jessica, but now you're doing it to me. I told you something in confidence and you've been rubbing my face in it ever since. I won't have you meddling in my past. Do you understand?"

When she didn't answer, he pulled the key out of the ignition and threw the car door open. Right before he slammed it, he muttered, "Christ! This is what happens when you trust a woman."

She sat in the car, stunned by his reaction. Sure she had expected him to be angry, but she'd thought he would have at least listened to her. Maybe she shouldn't have just blurted it out like that. But he sounded as if he thought she had betrayed him. She'd only been trying to help. And he was wrong about her meddling. If she didn't care about him, she would have let him carry his emotional baggage around for eternity. And he was wrong about Jess, too. Just this morning, Jess had told her that she was happier than

223

she'd ever been in her life. That everything was finally falling together. She had bought two Nintendo games for Keith's sons and had spent over twenty minutes wrapping them. And she was humming a Bonnie Raitt song. Humming! Jack was wrong. She hadn't messed up Jess' life.

He just needed time, that's all. She only hoped they had enough left . . .

Tucking the games under her arm, she smiled as she saw that Keith's mail was still in his box. Picking it up, Jess walked up to his door and knocked. As she waited she looked down to the regular junk mail and saw a large white envelope, like a card. Maybe his sons sent it to him because they missed him. She looked at the return address and saw the same last name as his. It was definitely a woman's handwriting. A sinking feeling started in her stomach and she tried to will it away. Probably his ex-wife had addressed the card for her children. And her stomach had been bothering her for days, so this whole thing was silly. It was the way she'd been eating lately. On the run, or skipping meals altogether. What was that old saying? Someone wrote it in her eighth grade autograph book. "Don't trouble trouble till trouble troubles you?" Yeah, that was it.

Shoving the card back in with the rest of the mail, she pasted a smile on her face as Keith opened the door.

His answering smile was slow and easy. "Hey . . . come on in."

"You forgot your mail," she said and handed it to him. "And I brought these for the boys. They're those games you were talking about. At least two of them. The football one is still out of stock."

He threw the mail on a table without looking at it and took the games from her so she could remove her coat. "That's really nice of you, Jess, but you shouldn't have. I would have gotten them."

She shook her head as she hung up her coat. "It wasn't a big deal. I was passing by Sheurman's on my way to the post office and I thought I would see if they had them. You said they were hard to find, so I thought, why not? I guess I lucked out, huh? At least with two of them."

He nodded. "They'll be thrilled. Here," he reached into his pant's pocket. "Let me pay you for them. These video games are expensive."

She stared at him. "Absolutely not. They're gifts, Keith." He appeared uncomfortable and she was wondering if she'd made a mistake. It's just that she was so happy and she wanted everyone else to share in it— even his sons.

"Okay," he finally said and placed them on top of the mail. "Thank you. They'll love them."

Don't trouble trouble, remember? She did, and smiled back at him. "So how was work?"

He shrugged as he moved into the kitchen. "Some glitches are showing up on the prototype and we have to iron them out before the government rep comes next week. How about some tea? Earl Gray? Black Currant?''

She wrapped her arms around her waist. ''Black Currant sounds good.'' She watched as he prepared it and smiled with contentment. Everything was going so well between them. It wasn't just the lovemaking, though that was fantastic. It was the communication, the laughter, the sharing. All the things she had missed.

''Busy day?'' he asked, as he waited for the water to boil. ''You look tired.''

''No, I'm okay,'' she answered and pushed back her hair. The truth was she was tired. Sometimes she felt euphoric and then plunged into exhaustion. When it hit her she had no energy, and her arms left like dead weights hanging from her shoulders. It was all the running around, she thought, as she started to unconsciously rub her arms. She just wasn't used to the high volume of business at the store and then being here with a man. Though it was strange that taking care of an invalid hadn't wiped her out as much the next morning as after making love. There were times she felt like she was swimming upstream, trying to recapture her strength. And then it suddenly would return.

He came up to her and took her in his arms. She relaxed against him and sighed with contentment.

''What were you thinking about?'' he asked, his mouth against her hair. ''You looked so serious.''

She smiled. ''I was thinking how happy I am.''

''And for that you looked serious?''

She shook her head. "I was also thinking that I wished you would be able to stay here longer. There's only another week left and you'll be gone."

She felt his body tense and immediately knew she had said the wrong thing. "But let's not think about that," she whispered, as she fought the moisture building in her eyes. "Let's just enjoy the time we have together. Right?"

"Right," he agreed, and his muscles relaxed. He pulled back from her so he could see her face. "Hey, I just realized I haven't kissed you hello yet."

His mouth came down on hers. It started out soft and gentle, almost as if he were testing her. She responded in the same way. When his lips became demanding she summoned all she had and put it into that kiss. She wanted to communicate what she was feeling inside. Even if he didn't want to hear the words, she needed to tell him in some way how much he meant to her.

"Wow," he murmured against her mouth. "That was some kiss."

She could feel his immediate arousal against her stomach and smiled lazily. "I missed you today."

He grinned. "Yeah?"

Nodding, she whispered back, "Yeah."

His hands slid up from her waist to capture her breasts. "How much?" he asked and squeezed.

She cried out in sudden pain and instinctively pulled back from him.

"What's wrong with you?"

She heard the impatience in his voice and tried to

smile. "I don't know," she said honestly. "I'm just tender, I guess."

Leaving her to turn off the gas under the tea kettle, he nodded. "Maybe it's your time of the month."

She thought of the date and forced the embarrassment out of her voice. "Well, actually, you're right. Any time, that is. I'm sorry, Keith, for jumping away from you. I don't know. I guess you took me by surprise."

"You were never surprised before," he said as he poured the water.

There was a defensive note in his tone and Jess thought, well, this is the first time I've been around you when I'm expecting my period. But she didn't say it.

He handed her the tea and walked into the living room. "There's a basketball game on tonight," he threw out over his shoulder. "Do you mind if I watch it?"

"No. Go ahead," she said and looked at him as he walked over to the table with the mail. He flipped through the junk stuff and touched the card before covering it again, as if disinterested. "Is it the finals, or something?"

He glanced at her and shook his head. "No. It's just a game. The finals aren't until late spring."

Sitting down on the couch, Jess smiled. "Thank you. Now I know."

Something was wrong. She could feel it. Hell, she could see it in that look he just gave her. How was she supposed to know about basketball? She never had any

228

brothers, nor a husband, and her father had died when she was a young girl. Why didn't he open that card, if it was from his sons? And why was the answering machine always on mute when she came over?

Her mind was going through the possibilities and each of them nauseated her. In every other relationship in her past, she had kept her doubts quiet, silently torturing herself with nagging uncertainty. She didn't want to ruin this one because she was lacking in communication skills. It was okay to open her mouth and voice her concerns. How else would he know? How else would she? Hugging her stomach, she looked at him and asked, "Is something wrong, Keith?"

He turned his head away from the TV screen. "What are you talking about?"

She shrugged. "I don't know. You seem upset, or at least angry. I'm trying to figure it out."

He continued to stare at her for a few seconds, then he broke into a smile and held out his arm. "Come here. Nothing's wrong. Put your head down on my lap and rest. You really do look tired."

Smiling, Jess curled up next to him and he played with her hair while he watched the game. It felt so good, so right. Someone finally cared about her. She took a deep breath and closed her eyes.

She wasn't going to trouble trouble again.

He had turned into a real couch potato. Every night when they closed the shop, they would return to the house and barely speak to each other. No, that really wasn't accurate, Laurie thought. She would speak. He would answer in single sentences, as if he were preoccupied with his television shows. He was using the TV to block her out, but the truth was he was still angry. Three days were enough, she had decided, so she'd gone out and bought a peace offering.

Walking up to him, she placed two six packs of beer down on the coffee table by his propped-up feet.

He glanced up at her and raised his eyebrows in question.

"A peace offering," she said, and sat Indian-style on the floor. "We can't keep this up, Jack."

He didn't answer her and Laurie handed him an ice cold bottle of beer. "I'm sorry, okay? I mean it. I didn't think I was betraying you or your trust. We don't know what's going to happen to us after this and . . . well, I didn't want you carrying around that kind of burden. I guess I didn't understand how deep all of this goes for you. I apologize. I was everything you said. Rash. Unthinking. Unrealistic. Meddling."

The corner of his lip lifted in a hint of a smile, and Laurie felt the knot in her stomach muscles ease. She held her bottle of beer out in a salute. "To a truce then? I promise to stay out of your past, and you'll stop giving me the cold shoulder? Geez, Jack, with Jess always gone now, it's like we're living alone. And if you don't talk to me, I'll go nuts."

He smiled then, a genuine smile, and tapped his bottle against hers. "A truce, then. No more meddling?"

She shook her head. "I promise."

"Good," he said, then laughed. "I was getting pretty sick of TV. How can people sit every night and watch for three hours?"

"I don't know. Can I turn it off now?"

He grinned. "Go ahead."

"Great." She got up and shut it off. Pressing the power button on the stereo, Laurie listened as the room was filled with a Lionel Ritchie song and asked, "Do you play cards, Jack?"

"Cards? Like poker?"

"More like gin rummy, or casino. I used to play that in college."

Jack took his feet off the coffee table and made space for them. "Do you know where Jess keeps the cards?"

Laurie nodded. "I saw them in a kitchen drawer. I'll get 'em."

When she returned, she had a bowl of fruit and a box of pretzels. "Sustenance," she declared. "I'm about to beat the pants off you, Lannigan."

He laughed as he took the pretzels from her. "Oh, you think so, Reese?"

Sitting back down on the rug, she looked him straight in the eye and said, "Absolutely. Now, what's your game?"

He took the challenge, answering, "Gin rummy. Loser has to do all the laundry for the next two weeks."

"What?" Since Jess was never home, it had been a source of irritation for both of them. He hated doing it, and so did she. "Okay," she conceded, and grinned. "Just remember I like lavender fabric softener in with my underwear."

He swallowed hard and muttered, "Just remember I don't. Now deal."

She won three hands. He won two. She drank four beers. He drank five. It was his turn to deal and she watched as he shuffled the cards. "You know, Jack," she said, feeling very relaxed and happy, ". . . we're like an old married couple. It's like Jess doesn't even live here anymore. She just visits on the weekends. We work all day and now here we are comfortable with each other's company until it's time for bed."

"You make it sound like we're over the hill."

"I guess we are," she said and giggled. Four beers were a lot for her. "Over the hill, I mean. Not a married couple."

He smiled. "I know what you meant."

"We aren't even a couple, married or otherwise. Except a couple of ghosts." She waved her hand lazily, maybe a little drunkenly. "And that doesn't count in this conversation."

He dealt the cards. "It doesn't?"

"Nope." She ignored the cards laying face down in front of her. "Did you ever wonder, Jack, what it would be like to be married? I mean for a long time?"

"Sure. Are you going to play?" He nodded to her cards.

"In a minute. Sometimes I look at old couples and they barely talk to each other. It's as if they have nothing to say anymore. I think that's so sad, and I can't figure why they would go on like that."

232

"Probably security. Financial and emotional."

"How can living in near-silence be emotional security? I'd probably go insane and wind up in a mental institution."

He laughed. "Good thing you never married."

"You think so?" She stared at him. "Could be I missed something important. Maybe if I had married, I wouldn't have let it get like that. I'd force my husband to talk to me."

"I bet you would've, Laurie. You got me talking to you again."

"You're right." Her expression was filled with satisfaction.

"Are we going to play, or what?"

"I don't want to play anymore. Not just yet." She giggled. "That didn't make sense, did it?" She sighed and propped her chin up with her hands as she looked at him. "Ahh, Jack . . . so what do you think?"

He smiled. "I think you're a little drunk."

"You may be right," she answered with a smile. "Shh . . . listen to this song."

They sat in silence as Phil Collins' voice seemed to fill the room and their minds. "Hold On My Heart." How prophetic. The words mirrored what she was feeling about falling in love and being afraid. And then the reality of what she was thinking hit her. Dear God, could it be possible? She was falling in love with *Jack*?

They stared at each other for the entire song. Nothing else existed for those few minutes, except the music and holding the other's gaze. She tried to read what was in his eyes. Did he feel the same? Did he want her as much as she wanted him? And she did want him. She wanted him to take her in his arms, to kiss her, to make love to her. She wanted, for just once in her life, to feel as if she belonged somewhere, with someone.

He would never do it. She knew he would never make the first move. And if she thought about it, neither would she.

She leaned toward him, so that she was at his knees. "Would you hold me, Jack?" she whispered in a frightened voice. She felt so raw, so vulnerable, to rejection.

He slanted his body forward and gathered her into his arms as she knelt in front of him. She smelled the clean scent of his shirt, the faint masculinity of his cologne, and wrapped her arms around his waist. If eternity was like this—this peacefulness, this security, then she would want to stay forever.

Jack's hands roamed over her back, calming her, soothing her, and she sighed with pleasure as her sexuality was once more awakened by his touch.

"Laurie," he whispered her name, and she leaned back to see his face.

There was uncertainty in his expression, and she smiled with confidence. Suddenly she wasn't afraid. Reaching up, she gently pushed a stray lock of hair back off his forehead and ran the tip of her finger over his eyes, his nose, the slope of his cheekbone and, finally, his lips. She glanced up and saw a dark passion in his eyes, one that answered what she was experiencing.

"Jack?" Her voice was low and husky and questioning.

His lips were soft and warm as they brushed across hers, and she wanted to memorize each incredible sensation that was speeding through her body. When the kiss deepened, she pulled him closer to her chest, wanting to make him a part of her, and that's when it happened . . .

She started blending right into his body.

Frightened, he pushed her away and stood up. "Jesus! I can't do this," he stated in a disgusted voice. "*We* can't do this, Laurie. Do you understand?"

She was so shocked by his reaction that she could barely speak. "Listen, Jack. It's just a little harder for us, that's all. We're not like ordinary people and—"

"You're right," he interrupted in an emotional voice. "We're not ordinary people. And it's obvious we aren't supposed to be doing this." Running a hand through his hair in frustration, he said good night and left the room.

She cursed as she hit a red light a block from Keith's apartment. With any luck she would catch him before he left for New York. Waiting for the light to change, she looked at the bag on the front seat and smiled. This afternoon Walt Shuerman had called to tell her that the football game was in, and she wanted Keith to bring it with him tonight when he went back to see his sons. She was tired and had a headache, and promised herself that when she got home she was taking a hot bath and going straight to bed. All this rushing around was getting to her.

When Jess turned into his apartment complex, she sighed with relief as she saw that his lights were still on. Luck was on her side, she thought, as she shut the car off and hurried up to his door.

Knocking, she tried to block out the headache and plastered a big smile on her face. Moments later, the smile was frozen in shock when a woman answered.

"Yes?"

Jess merely blinked for several seconds while she attempted to find her voice. She looked at the number on the door for confirmation and then mumbled, "Is Keith here?"

The woman's eyes narrowed slightly. "May I help you?" she asked. "I'm his wife."

Chapter 15

She saw two little boys behind the woman, laughing and teasing each other. They looked like Keith. Light brown hair. Same easy smiles.

Pull it together, Jess, she silently commanded. He's divorced from this woman. Taking a deep breath, she held out the video game. ''Would you please give this to him?''

The woman was short and attractive, and thoroughly confused. She took the package and Jess murmured a quick thank you before turning to walk down the drive.

''Excuse me . . .''

Slowly turning around, Jess saw the woman walk away from the door.

"He's doing it again, isn't he?"

A terrible cramping started in her belly, as Jess answered, "I beg your pardon?"

"Keith. He's playing around again." The woman shook her head, as if angry with herself. Wrapping her arms around her waist to ward off the cold air, she said, "You're not the first, you know. Are you recently divorced or widowed, or coming out of a bad relationship?"

Jess could only shake her head. This could not be happening. It couldn't be true!

"Well, then he's breaking a pattern. He usually picks some lonely woman and romances her. He loves the chase and seduction. And with his job and the amount of traveling he does, it's fairly easy. I think he sees himself as some kind of rescuer, and that way he can live with his conscience."

Jess could feel her throat closing up, taking away her breath and her ability to speak. "I . . . I'm sorry."

"No," Keith's wife said, as her eyes filled with tears. "I'm sorry. For both of us."

Jess ran to her car. She had trouble putting the key into the ignition and started crying with hurt, anger and frustration. When the engine finally turned over, she threw the gear shift into drive and roared away from the apartment complex.

She had no idea where she was going. Her hands gripped the steering wheel and her gaze was riveted to the long ribbons of asphalt in front of her. Tears streamed down her cheeks and she kept blinking them away so she could see the road.

He was married! It kept repeating itself in her brain, along with his wife's words . . . *He usually picks some lonely woman.* God, it was pathetic! She was pathetic. She must have been, for him to have picked her. She felt so . . . dirty, used. How could she have been so gullible? Was she so starved for affection that she showed it? He had picked her. *Picked her!*

Her entire body started shaking and she pulled over into a Burger King parking lot. Her breath was coming in gasps, trying to stop the nausea that was building up. Suddenly, she flung the door open and ran toward the grass.

"Mommy, look! That lady is throwing up."

"Come away, Brian," the mother said in an angry voice. "Honestly! There's a bathroom right inside!"

Jess ignored the woman as she fumbled through her pocket for a tissue. Wiping her mouth, she gulped in the night air and held onto the side of the car as she made her way back inside. Once seated, she leaned back against the head rest and let the tears come. How could she have let this happen? How could she have been so blind?

He never said he was divorced, not really. She just assumed from his conversations. He talked about his wife as his children's mother, not his ex. That's why he didn't open that card in front of her. Why the answering machine was always on mute. That's why the decision to have sex had to be hers. He didn't want the guilt when she finally found out.

And they all must have found out he was married . . . sooner or later.

The chase: flowers at the shop, the zoo, lunches and dinners, long walks and longer conversations. The seduction: only holding hands, chaste kisses, making her want him because he was so considerate, so thoughtful of her feelings. God, it was sickening! And she thought she was falling in love with him . . .

Closing her eyes, Jess realized love wouldn't happen for her. She had known it, had accepted it, until Keith. How could she have been so naive to think anything would change?

Sitting in the parking lot of a fast food restaurant, she accepted the fact that she was alone and would remain alone for the rest of her life.

The dark tunnel of loneliness once again wrapped around her. She tried to find comfort in it, for it had been so familiar in the last six years. She should welcome it as an old friend, but her heart was breaking. For a few weeks she had lived in sunshine . . .

Laurie came downstairs to find a book and make a cup of tea. It was a Friday night and Jack was still holed up in his room, afraid, perhaps, that she would get him drunk and throw herself at him again. Dressed in lycra leggings and an oversized sweatshirt, she decided to venture out of her room in the hopes that Jess was home. She needed to talk to someone about Jack, and what was happening between them, and Jess was the only person on this planet that wouldn't think she was crazy.

When she walked into the kitchen, she wasn't prepared to see Jess sitting at the table with a bottle of bourbon and a glass in front of her.

"Ah . . . hi," Laurie said, as she walked up to her. Jess' eyes were red and her makeup was smeared from crying. Laurie slid into the chair opposite her. "Want to talk?"

Jess glanced up and shook her head. "There's no point in it anymore. And I really don't have much to say, Laurie, except two words: he's married."

Laurie's body jerked upright. "What? Keith? How do you know? Did he tell you?"

Jess issued a sarcastic laugh. "Tell me? He's too much of a coward for that. I met his wife tonight."

"Oh, my God." Laurie stared at her. "Are you okay?"

Jess didn't answer.

"Look, Jess, maybe you've got a reason to drink tonight but I don't—"

"I haven't had a drink—yet." Jess wiped fresh tears from the corners of her eyes. "I keep looking at it, knowing it will make me forget. You know his wife says he does this all the time? He looks for lonely women when he's away from home on business and seduces them. God, I feel so stupid . . ."

"Maybe you shouldn't forget," Laurie said. "Before tonight, you were happy, Jess. Keep remembering the good parts. He was just the wrong man, that's all. You'll find someone."

"Oh, please," Jess answered. "They're all the wrong men. At least for me. I just have to give up my dreams. Home. Family. All that stuff we're made to believe in from the time we're little girls. It just isn't going to happen for me. I'm going to be alone for the rest of my life, and I either have to learn to accept that or pour this drink and slowly kill myself.''

Jess looked so miserable, so distraught, that Laurie reached across the table and grabbed her hand. ''Jessica, listen to me. Don't let him do this to you. He's already hurt you and deceived you. How much more power are you going to give this son of a bitch? Are you going to let what he did destroy the rest of your life? You're a wonderful woman with a lot of love to give someone. You just wasted it on the wrong person, that's all.''

Laurie felt tears well up in her eyes. ''Part of this is my fault. I'm the one that pushed you into it. I'm sorry. I should have listened to Jack. He never trusted Keith from the beginning.''

Jess shook her head. ''It isn't anyone's fault, except mine. I'm an adult. I guess I didn't want to really look beneath the surface.'' She wiped the tears away from her cheek with the heel of her hand. ''I was so happy, Laurie. For the first time in so long, I was happy . . .''

Laurie nodded sadly. ''I know,'' she whispered. Standing up, she came around the table and stood beside Jess. ''C'mon. Let's go upstairs. All these years, Jess, you took care of everyone. Now it's your turn. I'm going to put you to bed.''

Jess looked up and tried to smile through the pain. ''You don't have to baby me.''

Laurie grinned back. ''I'm not going to baby you.

I'm going to pamper you. There's a difference. And we're going to start with a bubble bath.''

An hour and a half later, Laurie quietly closed Jess' bedroom door so she wouldn't wake up. After the bath, they had sat in bed and talked until Jess finally broke down and sobbed. The anger slowly left, leaving only raw hurt and disillusionment. She was a woman that couldn't trust herself or her feelings, or anyone else. And it was a hell of a place to be. Laurie had held her, rocking her back and forth, letting her cry it out, until she fell asleep. This was a wound that would take a long time to heal.

And Laurie felt responsible.

She was about to open her bedroom door when she turned her head and looked down the hall. She should tell him. He had a right to know.

She knocked and waited for him to answer. When the door opened he didn't even look surprised.

''Laurie, this isn't a good idea. What happened downstairs was a—''

''Forget downstairs,'' she interrupted, brushing past him to sit on the bed. ''I've done something terrible.''

''What are you talking about?'' he asked, leaving the door open.

She shook her head. ''You were right. Everything you said earlier. I am meddling in people's lives. And all of this is the result.''

''Do you want to explain?'' His voice was patient, as if talking to a child.

Laurie looked up at him and tried to keep the emotion out of her words. "Keith is married. Jess went over to his apartment and his wife answered the door. That son of a bitch was using her! He's been having these affairs for years."

Jack let his breath out and leaned against his dresser. "I knew it. I knew something bothered me about that guy. How's Jess taking it?"

"She's devastated. This was all my idea, and now I think I've set her back. She's worse than when we first came."

"She's drinking again?"

Laurie's eyes widened. "No. No, she's not. But you should see her, Jack. She looks like a lost child, as if the things she's trusted, everything she's believed in, has been taken away. Why do people do this to each other? How can Keith live with what he's doing to women, and to his wife?"

Jack stared at her for a few seconds. His expression was set and the color in his face turned a deep red. Suddenly, he walked over to the bed and picked up his shoes. "Where's Jess' purse?"

"Downstairs. What are you going to do?"

"I need the car keys, and I want to look in that little address book she carries. What's that bastard's last name again? Williams?"

Laurie stood up. "I don't know if you should do anything. Look what's happened already from my interference," she said in a worried voice. "I didn't come in here for you to go over there and confront him."

Jack finished tying his shoes. When he looked up at

her, he had a sinister grin. "This clown's been getting away with this for years. What's the worse he's faced? Some women crying? His wife's threats? I think it's time he gets what he deserves."

It took less than twenty minutes for him to find the apartment. When Keith opened the door, Jack pushed him back and walked in.

"What do you want?" Keith asked, a scared look on his face, as he back-peddled into the living room.

"I'm here to teach you a lesson, loverboy," Jack muttered, right before his fist connected with Keith's jaw. "That one was for Jess," he said calmly, as Keith reeled away from him.

Following like a lion about to strike, Jack brought back his arm and landed a blow to the man's midsection. "And that's for every other woman you charmed into your bed," he added, as Keith doubled over.

"And this," he said as he grabbed Keith's hair and lifted his face. "This is so you'll remember never to do it again." He let him go, and spinning, with a back-kick to the groin, sent him across the room.

Keith landed, a heap of broken humanity. His face was bloodied and he was gasping in a high, raspy voice.

Jack knelt down in front of him and muttered, "I want you to pay attention to this, Williams."

He spread his fingers out and stuck them into Keith's bruised abdomen. When they disappeared inside of him, Keith's cry was a strangled whimper of fear and disbelief.

"Just so you know you're not dealing with an ordinary person. This isn't a dream, and you're not punch drunk. I work for the Man upstairs, so you'd better listen." He paused for effect. "If I wanted, I could reach down right now and pull your balls out through your belly. And I will, if you ever go near another woman again. Do you understand?"

When Keith seemed incapable of speech, Jack jerked on his hair. "Do you understand?" he repeated.

"Yes!" Keith gasped.

"Good." Jack stood up just as a woman entered the room and screamed.

"My God, what's going on out here?"

Walking toward the door, Jack said over his shoulder, "If you still want him, I don't think he'll give you any more problems, ma'am. Have a nice life."

"Jess, c'mon. We're going to be late."

She looked up from the bathroom sink and stared through the mirror at the locked door. She couldn't go with them. For the last week she'd been forcing herself to follow her usual routine, but she didn't have the strength this morning. She simply couldn't face the store, or anything else.

Walking out of the bathroom, she stood at the top of the steps and looked down. Jack and Laurie were in their coats, waiting for her to join them. "You two go on ahead. I think I'll stay home today."

"You're still sick?" Laurie asked with concern, as she buttoned her coat.

Jess nodded. "It must be the flu."

"Everybody that comes into the store is concerned about it. Maybe you should call a doctor," Jack suggested. "Can't they give you a shot, or some pills?"

"I may call later, if I don't feel any better."

"Okay, don't worry about the store," Jack said, heading for the door. "We'll take care of everything."

Laurie started to follow him, then turned back. "Do you want me to stop in at lunch time and check up on you?"

Jess shook her head. "Don't bother. I'll probably be sleeping. But thanks."

When they left, Jess stood for a few moments, afraid to go back into the bathroom. The thought had come into her head yesterday and she couldn't shake it out. She had to know, to relieve her mind, yet she was terrified of the answer.

Forcing her legs to move, she went back in.

Pink—she was.

Blue—she wasn't.

She stared at the tiny dot on what looked like a thermometer. She couldn't blink. She couldn't breathe.

It was pink.

There was a mistake. That's all. Those things weren't a hundred percent accurate. When Doctor Greenspan came back into the examining room, he would tell her she had the flu and to go home and rest. She wouldn't even be angry at the manufacturer of the home pregnancy kit for the last four hours of anguish.

Hell, she'd be so grateful for the mistake that she'd gladly go home and relish each ache and wave of nausea. At the moment, the flu seemed like a wonderful alternative.

The doctor walked in and smiled reassuringly. Good sign, Jess thought as she clasped her hands tightly together on her lap. The paper gown she wore rustled softly under her wrists.

Sitting on a movable stool, Doctor Greenspan said, "Besides the state of your cervix, I wanted to make sure with the urine sample. The results were positive."

Her head moved forward slightly, as if to hear him better. "Positive what? Positive I'm not pregnant?"

"Positive you are."

She didn't speak for several seconds. A cold dread washed over her, making her numb. "I—I thought I had the flu," she said weakly.

He smiled. "No. You're pregnant."

She suddenly came to life as the words poured out of her mouth. "But, you don't understand. I can't be. I was very careful. I used protection—"

"You said you weren't on the pill," he interrupted.

"I'm not. He . . . he used a condom and I had my old diaphragm. I was careful. Responsible. This can't be possible, doctor!"

"All right. Calm down. First of all, a condom isn't one hundred percent safe. It's a product, subject to defects . . . tiny rips or holes that can't be picked up with the naked eye. And how old is this diaphragm?"

She stared at him, as doom settled in her stomach. "Six years. No, seven."

He sighed and shook his head. "Jessica, even if it wasn't cracked from age, it would never still fit you correctly. You should have seen a doctor first."

"I haven't seen a gynecologist in seven years. I . . . I didn't have a need." This was all a bad dream. None of it was happening!

"Well," he said patiently. "I want you to make an appointment for next week and I'll do a more thorough examination." He hesitated for a few seconds, and then added, "I take it this pregnancy isn't welcomed."

She could only stare back at him.

"Then you have some serious options to think over."

"Options?"

"You can terminate the pregnancy. It's early enough. You wouldn't reach term until Christmas. Then there's adoption. Your record shows you aren't married, but a growing number of single women are raising their children. Can you talk this over with the father?"

"He's out of the picture," Jess said in a stilted voice. *The father!* It sounded so real . . .

He stood up. "Okay, listen. I want you to get dressed, and then come into my office. I have some pamphlets that might help explain each of your choices. You're thirty-four and this is a first pregnancy. You can start taking prenatal vitamins now, or wait until you know how you're going to proceed."

Numb with shock, she nodded and he quietly left the room.

She sat on the table and looked at the stirrups, the

metal instruments, the jars and tubes and machines. It was a bizarre chamber of torture for most women, and one of the reasons she had avoided it for seven years. Now it surrounded her, closing in on her like the set in a horror movie. Any moment now someone would shout "cut," and she would return to normal. Her mother would still be alive. Two ghosts wouldn't have taken over her life and moved in with her. She never would have met Keith and been humiliated. And she wouldn't be pregnant. *She wouldn't be pregnant!*

There had to be some kind of mistake. None of it could be real. God wouldn't do this to her. He wouldn't! Hadn't she gone through enough pain and sorrow in her life?

What had she ever done to deserve this?

Chapter 16

"What did the doctor say? Did he give you anything?" Laurie sat on the edge of Jess' bed as she asked the questions. What was odd was that Jess looked worse than when they had left in the morning. And she seemed to have been crying.

"Did he *give* me anything?" Jess almost laughed and then sniffled as she pointed to her night table. "Oh, yeah, Laurie . . . he gave me something."

Laurie picked up the large container of pills and read the label. "Vitamins? Prenatal vitamins? *Prenatal*?" She stared at Jess in shock. "What does this mean?" she whispered, her mind refusing to accept what she was reading.

"It means I'm pregnant," Jess cried and, turning over in bed, buried her face into the pillow.

Laurie stared at the pills, then at Jess, and then back to the pills. "Pregnant?" It was as if her brain couldn't assimilate the statement.

Jack stuck his head in the doorway and asked in a low voice, "Is she any better?"

Laurie blinked a few times before muttering, "She's pregnant."

"What?" He came into the room and stood before the bed. "What did you say?"

"She's pregnant. *Pregnant!*" It finally kicked in, and the full impact of her words slammed into her brain as she picked up the pamphlet entitled, "Alternate Choices."

"Stop saying it!" Jess moaned and started crying again. "Please, just leave me alone. I . . . I want to sleep and forget everything. Leave me alone . . . *please!*"

"Okay," Laurie whispered and stood up. Without looking at Jack, she motioned for them to leave the room. She didn't say anything as she led him downstairs and into the kitchen.

Sitting down heavily at the table, she stared at the wooden surface while saying, "She's pregnant, Jack. I can't believe it. She doesn't have the flu."

"Do you understand what this means?" Jack demanded as he slid into the place opposite her.

She merely stared back at him, too shocked to think clearly.

"It means," he said, "that we've completely

252

screwed up this mission. We've ruined a woman's life. And we'll probably be damned to hell!''

"Oh, shit!'' Laurie's eyes widened in horror. "You're right! What are we going to do?''

"What do you mean, *we*? This was your idea, remember? Find her a man. She'll be happy! She looks real happy up there in bed, doesn't she?''

"How dare you blame this all on me? Where were your ideas? Lock her up in rehab?''

"Well, she wouldn't be pregnant.''

Laurie glared back at him. "No, she probably would have tried to commit suicide.''

"Okay, let's forget arguing. We've got a real problem here. I'm sure getting her pregnant was not part of our mission.''

"*We* didn't get her pregnant, Jack. Keith did. And now I'm glad you beat the hell out of him. I wish he was still around, so I could have a go at the creep. Pregnant! My God, what's going to happen now?''

They both looked around them and then up to the ceiling, as if expecting to be pulled into another dimension for a severe reprimand. Or worse.

"What do you think they'll do?'' Laurie whispered, really afraid. It was one thing to botch up matchmaking; screwing up someone's life was quite another.

"I don't know,'' Jack answered. "There's got to be repercussions from this. I can just picture that guy sitting behind the desk. I've obviously failed whatever task he was assigning me. And I don't know what life lessons I was supposed to learn from this, except to mind my own business.''

"Now wait," Laurie said patiently, trying to stay calm. "Maybe this isn't so bad. Maybe we can fix it."

"What!" Jack looked incredulous. "Don't you ever learn?"

"There has to be something we can do."

"Stay out of it, Laurie. I'm warning you. We've obviously done enough to Jess—"

"What have you done to me?" Jess asked, sniffling while walking into the kitchen. Her eyes were red and ringed with smeared makeup. Her robe was hanging open and her hair looked like she had stuck her finger into an electrical socket.

Jack was uncomfortable. "I . . . ah . . . I was just telling Laurie that we've sort of contributed to your . . . your problem."

Jess sighed and a tiny shudder raced down her body. "My problem has nothing to do with either one of you. I'm an adult. It's just too bad I couldn't have acted like one, instead of an infatuated teenager with her first boyfriend. Dear God, if this wasn't so pathetic, it'd be laughable."

Shaking her head, Jess shuffled over to the cabinets. She took out a bag of English Muffins and opened the refrigerator. "Don't we have apricot jam?"

"I finished it this morning," Jack said in a guilty voice. "I'm sorry."

Jess merely shrugged. "It doesn't matter. I don't even know why I wanted it." She looked in the refrigerator for a full minute, searching for something that might appeal to her. Finally, she closed the door and inspected the freezer. Taking out a plastic bowl of raspberry sherbet, she got a tablespoon and sat at the table.

"I'm sorry I snapped at you two earlier," she said, trying to get the tight lid off. "I'm sorry about a lot of stuff." Her words trailed off as she continued to struggle with the lid.

"You don't have to be sorry." Jack took the sherbet from her. "Here, give me that." Removing the lid, he slid the container back to her.

Jess dug into the hard confection until her spoon was filled. She seemed to concentrate on the sherbet as it melted in her mouth, and then quickly went back to chiseling more.

Laurie had seen her share of depressed women before. Heck, *she'd* been through the same routine herself, and Jess was a picture of depression. At least she was finding comfort in ice cream and not alcohol. Knowing she had to get her talking, she quietly asked, "What are you going to do?"

Jess didn't answer for a few seconds. She appeared stunned and didn't look up from the sherbet as she answered, "Do? I don't know. My life is over."

"Are you going to tell Keith?" Laurie asked in a gentle voice. "Maybe he could help."

That seemed to shake Jess out of her lethargy. "I won't have anything to do with that man again. And I don't ever want to hear his name mentioned. Do both of you understand?"

Jack and Laurie nodded.

"This is my problem, my life, and the decision has to be mine." The sherbet was melting on her spoon, but she didn't seem to notice. "How can I raise a child?" she asked as tears came back into her eyes. "I've made a mess out of my own life. How could I take care of it? I'm all alone in this. And can't you just hear the gossip? The town spinster winds up preggy? Since her mother died, she's just gone to hell in a hand basket."

"You're not a spinster," Laurie said with a smile. "Nobody even talks like that anymore. You're younger than I was, and I certainly didn't consider myself a spinster. What did the doctor say to you?"

"He said I have alternatives. I can still terminate the pregnancy, or opt for adoption. Or I can try single parenthood. Hell, Murphy Brown's made it almost respectable. Of course, she doesn't live in Moorestown. And she has money and a supportive circle of friends. I don't have anyone to turn to in this."

She looked up at them and tears were streaming down her cheeks. "But I've got you two."

Laurie smiled. "We'll help you any way we can. Right, Jack?"

Jack looked like someone had punched him in the stomach. He was biting the inside of his cheek and abruptly nodded. "Right."

Jess tried to smile, but wasn't entirely successful. "This is the worst thing that's ever happened to me. I . . . I thought I had gone through so much already that God was rewarding me with some happiness. I should have known. Nothing good in my life ever lasts. It never did. And now this is growing inside of me and it doesn't even ask my permission to take over my body—"

"Excuse me. I'm sorry," Jack said as he stood up. "I'm going to get you that apricot jam for the morning. I'll be back later."

They watched as he left the kitchen. Laurie waited until she heard the front door close and then said to Jess, "Jack's adopted. I think this is hitting pretty close to home for him."

"I'm sorry. I didn't know."

Laurie got up and found another spoon. Coming back to the table, she scooped up the now soft sherbet. She remembered when she had seen Jess for the first time at her mother's funeral. Then she had thought about sherbet melting on her tongue. It seemed so long ago . . . "Jack's had a tough time with this issue. He found out he was adopted from some kid on the street and beat him up. Then his mother told him the truth. When he was eighteen he found his birth mother and she didn't want him to be a part of her life. I think it's profoundly affected his life. He doesn't trust women. They'll all betray him in the end."

Jess stared into the container of sherbet. "I don't think I could carry a child for nine months and then give it away. I know it's the right option for some women, but not for me. I just couldn't do it."

"Okay," Laurie said in a serious voice. "We've eliminated adoption."

Jess sighed deeply. "So it's either terminate, or go full force on my own."

"How do you feel about abortion?"

"I'm pro choice, but that doesn't mean I'm pro abortion. I'm against eight men on the Supreme Court telling women what they can do with their bodies, when none of them will ever have to face that decision. The same thing about men standing in front of picket lines and at rallies. Men shouldn't even have a voice in this. If men got pregnant, this probably would have been written into the constitution two hundred years ago."

"Well, now it's your decision, Jess. There aren't any men here telling you what you can, or can not, do. How do you feel about aborting this pregnancy?"

The kitchen was filled with silence as both women thought about the toughest judgment a woman would ever have to make. Finally Jess said, "I'm thirty-four years old. I thought by this time I would be married. That I would have a child with someone I loved. That my life would be settled. I never thought this would happen to me." Jess ran her fingers through her hair, and closed her eyes briefly before adding, "Although I'm for it in certain circumstances, an abortion for me seems like a quick solution to a long-term problem. I don't know if I could do it, or get over the guilt. And, yet, when I think about bringing up a child alone, without any support . . . it scares me to death. I want to run out screaming into the night. My life—it feels like it's over already. That there's no hope for real happiness now."

Laurie took her in her arms and let her cry. Sometimes only another woman can understand and bring

258

comfort. Crying along with Jess, Laurie whispered against her hair, "Did you ever think, Jess, that at thirty-four, this just might be your hope for real happiness?"

Later that night, Jess forced herself to leave her bed and go to him. It had been on her mind and she knew she would never fall asleep until she spoke with him. Knocking softly, she waited for him to answer.

He looked sleepy as he opened the door. "Jess? What's wrong?"

"I'm sorry, Jack. Did I wake you?"

Shaking his head, he said, "What's up? Are you okay?"

She smiled. "I don't know if I'm okay. I have some heavy thinking to do, but I just wanted to apologize. I didn't know you were adopted."

At his look of surprise, she added, "Laurie told me. Don't be mad at her. I couldn't figure out why you ran out of here to get jam."

"I'm not mad. And you don't have to apologize. It's a pretty rough situation to be in." He appeared emotional. "I guess I never realized before . . ."

"Are you thinking about your birth mother? She was probably young, younger than me."

"She was nineteen."

Jess nodded. "I can't imagine being that young, with your whole life ahead of you, and being faced with this decision."

Although his expression was a non-verbal agreement, he seemed uncomfortable. "Do you know what you're going to do?"

She looked down to the rug. "I've eliminated adoption. That's all I know for sure. And picturing the other alternatives won't let me sleep."

He cleared his throat and Jess looked up.

"I wish I could help you, but I can't," he said in an hoarse voice. "I can't be unemotional and objective. It's all too close."

"I understand," Jess said as tears once more came into her eyes. "But, Jack? I think your birth mother must have loved you very much to carry you for nine months and then want a better life for you than she could provide. I'm not that brave. I'd rather stop everything now . . ."

Suddenly, Jess stopped and stared at him. He'd had a life, and in that life he'd given happiness and joy. He'd accomplished things, and affected others. Maybe his beginnings weren't perfect, but he had made a difference in this world.

She tried to control her voice as she stood on tip toe to kiss his cheek. "Thanks, Jack," she said in a trembling voice. "You just helped me make my decision."

Kneeling in front of the commode in the storeroom, Jess shuddered and pushed herself upright. She stared at her reflection in the mirror, as she brought out the toothbrush and paste that was now part of the small bathroom at the shop. She was pale and her eyes were red and watery. Dear God, when would this end? She was nauseated as soon as she sat up in bed. But the real thing seemed to come around eleven o'clock each morning. For the past two months she had tried everything every woman had readily advised, and nothing had worked. The doctor said it was a good sign, that her hormones were working properly. She wondered why nature couldn't have come up with a less distasteful sign.

Her body seemed to take on a life of its own. She had no control over it. If she wasn't clutching a toilet bowl, then she was crying over stories on the news. It could be a disaster on another continent, or the saving of a goat that had gotten stuck in a well. It made no sense. Like her diet. She had to have apricot jam in the morning on her toast. And raspberry sherbet before she went to bed. Maybe that's why she was nauseated when she woke up.

Running a brush through her hair, Jess wondered for the hundredth time about her decision. She really shouldn't think about it when she was like this, because she was trying to eliminate any negative thoughts. Sighing, she figured it was time to visit the infant's department at Strawbridge's. For it was there that everything seemed best. She could touch the tiny undershirts and daydream. The perfect little dresses made her feel right in her decision . . . a daughter might be fun. And once she had picked up a miniature sized baseball cap and actually laughed with joy to think of it on a son's head. Yeah, she needed a trip to the department store.

She left the bathroom and was surprised to find Dave Sawyer from UPS standing by the desk.

"Hi, Jess. I carried these boxes in for Jack. He was busy at the register, and he told me you were back here." He smiled for a moment and then frowned. "Are you all right?"

She touched her mouth to check if any toothpaste remained. Oh, no. He didn't *hear* her? "I . . . I'm fine," she said, gathering her pride around her. Since making her decision to keep the baby, she had almost become defensive about it. There wasn't even a faint flutter yet, but she had the protective instincts of a lioness.

Sticking her chin out, she said, "I'm pregnant, Dave." There. Let him tell everyone on his route.

Dave's brown eyes widened and he took off his hat to run his fingers through his hair. "Pregnant?"

She nodded, waiting for the scorn to follow his shock.

It never came.

He suddenly recovered and broke into a wide grin. "Hey, that's great! A baby! Always wanted kids, but they say a man over forty is pretty set in his ways. Congratulations!"

It was so unexpected that Jess found herself smiling back and allowing him to pump her hand up and down. "Thanks, Dave. I . . . well, I guess I appreciate— you know, that you're not too shocked by it. I'll be raising the child alone," she added, taking back her hand. He might have thought she'd eloped, or something.

He stared at her for a moment longer than she

thought was necessary, and then said, "I think you'll make a great mother. You can bring her to work with you." He looked around the store room. "Organize this place and you can stick a crib back here."

She gazed around her. "I don't know about a baby sleeping in here. I haven't figured it all out." She unconsciously rubbed her stomach. "I've got time yet."

"When are you due?"

"Around Christmas. December twenty-sixth, to be exact, but I've been doing a lot of reading and it seems first babies can come early or late." She stopped speaking and looked at him. "Dave, you and your wife don't have children? I wonder why I thought you did."

"I've been divorced for ten months now."

It was her turn to look shocked. "I'm so sorry. I didn't know." And suddenly tears sprang to her eyes.

Embarrassed, she reached for the tissues that were on the desk and apologized. "Don't mind me. I cry over everything lately. It's these hormones."

He grinned. "I think it's kind of cute. I mean, you're the first person I've told about my divorce that's burst into tears. Most of my friends were relieved to hear it was over."

"Well, I'm sorry," she mumbled into the tissue. "It must have been painful."

He shrugged. "Yeah, well, life goes on. Listen, I've got to get going. Let me know if you need help back here when you figure out what you want to do."

"Thanks," Jess said and then called out to him just as he was about to go up front. "Dave? Why did you say she? Like you thought it was going to be a girl?"

His grin widened. "I don't know. It's kind of weird, isn't it? I mean, everybody always says he." Shrugging, he said, "Take care of yourself, Jess. And congratulations."

She stared at the doorway for a full minute.

He was right about one thing. Life does go on.

Chapter 17

It was happening again, and Laurie was getting more frightened with each occurrence. The first time was when Jessica and Jack were talking about the time they had all gone to the Camden Aquarium. She didn't remember. She swore it didn't happen, until Jess showed her the brochures, even a tee shirt. *Why* couldn't she remember? And, now, when Jess came down for breakfast she was dressed in maternity clothes!

"Aren't you going to be hot in that?" Jess asked. "I just heard on the news that it's going to be eighty-four and humid."

Laurie sat very still and slowly looked down to the

deep green sweater she wore. If she were alive, she would swear she was losing her mind. Glancing at the wall calendar, Laurie held her breath as she read the month.

June.

No. It couldn't be possible!

Leaving the kitchen, she heard Jess say, "When you change, remember the shop has air conditioning. Wear something with sleeves."

She raced up the stairs and didn't even knock on Jack's door as she flung it open. He looked up in surprise as he was zippering his pants. "What's wrong? Is it Jess?"

"Jack . . ." She couldn't find the words. She could only stare at him as her body started shaking.

He immediately came over to her and grabbed her shoulders. "Is it the baby? Laurie, what's wrong?"

She shook her head. Swallowing down the fear, she whispered, "Something's happening to me."

"What do you mean?"

"I . . . I can't remember things. I go to sleep and Jess is just pregnant, and I wake up this morning and—and it's June! And she's in maternity clothes. Where was I? What happened to me?"

"You were right here. It's okay, Laurie. You're not going crazy," he said, holding her close to his chest. "Unless I am, too."

She pulled her head back so she could see his face. "What do you mean?"

"I'm having blanks, too. The first time was in May.

266

On Mother's Day. You were making a big dinner for Jess, and I couldn't understand it. I thought it was the middle of April. I lost a whole month and was afraid to say anything to you."

"Try four months. I don't remember Mother's Day, or making dinner. God, Jack, what's happening to us?"

He shook his head. "I don't know. How can we participate in things and have no memory of them?"

"Maybe—maybe we're starting to go back. When I was getting dressed a little while ago, I was looking in the mirror and I became fuzzy."

"Fuzzy?"

"Like I needed glasses. Just my reflection was sort of hazy, not the bed behind me or anything. It only lasted about ten seconds. Jack, maybe we're going to start fading away."

He thought about it and then shook his head. "I don't think so. If we go, *when* we go," he corrected. "I bet it's going to be the same as when we came. Quick. One moment we're talking to someone about a mission and the next moment we're here."

"I'm sorry," Jess said, looking embarrassed as she stood in the doorway. "I just wanted to hurry you two along. Mari has off this morning, and we're opening."

Laurie was suddenly aware of the fact that Jack was only wearing a sleeveless undershirt and his trousers. She stepped away from him and muttered, "I'd better change," before hurrying out of the room.

Jess looked at Jack and smiled with happiness as

she unconsciously caressed her rounded belly. "I just knew you two were meant for each other." Turning, she walked down the hallway before he could react.

"Dr. Greenspan says I need a Lamaze coach. The classes start on Monday and, well, I'd like to ask you guys—if you think you're up to it. He says he'll clear it with the instructor for me to have both of you."

It was lunch time and the store was slow. Jack and Laurie were behind the counter and Jess laughed at their expressions. Laurie was surprised, and Jack— Jack was speechless. "Hey, c'mon. If you'd rather not, it's okay. I'll probably be screaming for drugs in the first hour."

Laurie recovered first. "No. I think it's a great idea. It's just that . . ." and she leaned forward, ". . . I don't know if we'll be here that long. We don't know what's going to happen with us."

"Oh, you'll be here," Jess said with confidence. "You were sent to me because I was in need, right? Well, when would I need you more than the birth of my child? You'll be here," she repeated.

"If we're here, then I'd love to do it," Laurie said, and glanced at Jack.

He looked like a man stuck in quicksand up to his waist. It was a no-win situation with two women waiting for his answer. He knew if he struggled and tried to worm his way out of it, he'd sink like a bowling ball. And if he remained motionless, the inevitable would just be slower. Why did women think men wanted to share the experience? He'd seen a birth when he was a rookie cop, and it was something he'd never forget. There was a lot of screaming and a lot of blood. He'd rather face a coke-head with a razor blade than a woman in labor.

"Sure, why not?" he heard himself saying to end the inevitable. What choice did he really have? He couldn't hurt Jess by saying no. And Laurie would never let up on him until he gave in. Besides, he found this child meant something to him. It was crazy. He wasn't the father, so he shouldn't feel responsible, but he wanted to make sure this kid was taken care of. So if it meant being a labor coach, then he'd simply have to do it. Only it wasn't going to be simple.

Nothing concerning these two women was ever simple.

"So who's going to sign for these?"

All three of them said in a chorus, "Hi, Dave."

Laurie stepped forward. "I'll sign."

Jack took the boxes into the back room as Laurie handed the clipboard back to Dave. "So, how are you doing? Is it hot out there yet?"

He shrugged. "It's not bad. I don't mind the heat. It's the detour on Chester Avenue that's killing me. The traffic is murder."

Remembering the road construction they had slowly passed through on the way to work, Laurie agreed. "I know. Excuse me, Dave. I think I have a customer."

As Laurie left to assist an older woman, Dave turned to Jess. "How are you? You look great," he added.

Jess smiled. "Well, thank you. I feel pretty good.

In fact, I feel wonderful." She giggled. "I haven't felt this good since I was twenty. It's weird."

"It's not weird. I think it's normal. They say women . . . I don't know, sort of glow. Don't they?"

"I guess they do. I never thought of myself as glowing, though. I'm just happy."

"Good," he said, tucking his clipboard under his arm. "You deserve it. I guess your life has really changed, huh?"

She shrugged. "I don't know. Outside of this," and she touched her stomach. "Everything's just about the same. I am, though, about to begin work on a nursery. In fact, poor Jack's going to lose his room on Sunday. I feel bad about it, but he and Laurie are anxious to start."

"Anxious about what?" Jack asked, as he rejoined them.

"Jess was telling me you're doing some renovating on Sunday."

Jack nodded. "Right. We're going to take the smallest bedroom in the house and turn it into a nursery."

"I'm pretty good with a hammer and a paintbrush, if you need help," Dave said as he backed up toward the door.

"Yeah, right, Dave," Jack answered with a laugh. "Show up on Sunday and tell me that."

"I've got to get back to my route, but who knows? Maybe I will. See you."

After Dave left, Jack was still smiling. "Nice guy," he remarked.

Jess barely nodded. "Very friendly. Listen, I think I'll go in the back and unpack those boxes."

Jack watched her as she walked away. Why couldn't she see it? And Laurie didn't either. In the six months they'd been here, every week Dave Sawyer walked into the store at least three or four times. And each time he either found a way to talk to Jess or ask about her. Jack couldn't figure it out. How could he, a man, see what was so obvious, and the women miss it? Maybe it had something to do with what Laurie had said a long time ago. About that mental criteria each of us has stored in our subconscious. He knew it was true. He'd always liked 'em tall, willowy, with long dark hair.

Looking across the store to Laurie, he wondered why he was so attracted to her. She was short and blond. When he'd first seen her, he dismissed her as not his type. It wasn't until they had gotten to know each other that the attraction had started. So if Jess got to know Dave away from his delivery route, she might actually see him for who he is. Maybe he didn't meet all the requirements on Jess' list. Maybe he wasn't a hunk, or a doctor, or a high-powered business exec, and that's why the women passed him over as not suitable. The trouble with that was in doing so, they'd overlooked a diamond in the rough. Now all he had to do was figure out how to make Dave shine. Shaking his head, Jack almost laughed out loud. Who'd believe he'd turn into a matchmaker?

He was sure Laurie would never let him forget it.

* * *

She felt a kick, and stopped brushing her hair. Smiling, Jess went over to the window seat and glanced out at the midsummer morning. The sun was shining. The birds were singing. The grass was green. And the flowers were in bloom. It was perfect and peaceful. Sighing, she realized that, at this moment, all was right with her world.

"You feel wide awake, sweetie," she whispered, while gently running her fingertips over her abdomen. She couldn't seem to stop doing it. If she wasn't able to hold her baby yet, then she would do the next best thing to making him feel loved. And she did love him. Even though she used the masculine pronoun, she didn't care if the child was a boy or a girl, or if he was beautiful or plain, or intelligent or average. Her fear wasn't the pain of labor, or raising a child alone. It was that her drinking might have had an effect on her child. But she had stopped before conceiving him and the tests she'd had were all negative. She refused to dwell on the odds, for no matter how this baby turned out, he would be loved.

Finally, Jessica had something so precious that no one could take away. She may never have found the one true great love, but she did find happiness. "Wait until you see this next year," she said, as she continued to gaze out the window. "I'm going to take you for lots of walks. And I'll teach you everything I know."

She sat on the flowered cushion and looked down to her belly. She'd started talking to the baby when she had finally made up her mind to go through with the pregnancy. It not only helped her, but it made sense since the two of them were going to have to make it alone.

When everything was finally settled in her mind, the strangest thing happened to her. She was happy. Not in the usual sense of the word, but something more profound. It was as if all those ragged pieces to the puzzle of her life suddenly became smooth and fit together. Now that she had someone else in her life, someone more important than herself, she had finally found peace. And the surprising thing was that it wasn't a man. She had always thought, or fantasized, that she would meet someone who was the other half of her, and together they would create this perfect tiny human being.

Well, Keith certainly wasn't her soul mate, but he had helped give her this miracle that she carried inside of her. And for that reason, she had forgiven him for deceiving her. Someday, if her child wanted to know, she would tell him about Keith. But for now, and the next few years, she would try and provide everything he needed.

"I'll do the best I can," she whispered. It was like her mantra. She kept repeating it to the baby, and to herself. Hearing voices down the hallway, she added, "And this morning we're starting on your room. I can't wait until you're here." Softly patting her child, she left her bedroom.

When she was in the hallway, she saw Jack and Laurie trying to maneuver a box spring.

"We're putting Jack's bed against the wall in my room," Laurie said. "We already moved the dresser to the opposite wall."

"Is it okay?" Jack asked, and then looked at Laurie. "Move up a little so I can clear the door molding."

"I have moved it up. As far as it will go," Laurie said with frustration. "Maybe you'd like to try being up front?"

"I can help," Jess offered.

"No!" came the resounding chorus, as the doorbell rang.

"You are not to lift anything," Laurie ordered. "Jack and I will figure how to get this sucker unstuck."

Jess grinned. "I'll get the door."

"Let's hope it's professional movers," Jack said, leaning on the side of the mattress. "Okay, Laurie, let's just be patient and try again . . ."

She left them arguing about the best way to free the box spring. They really were funny together lately. Talk about sexual tension! They were both fighting their attraction to each other and she was afraid if they didn't find a way of releasing it, there was going to be one heavenly explosion.

Could guardian angels love? Could they *make love*?

It was a strange thought.

After opening the door, she had a moment of surprise when she saw who was on the other side.

"Dave! Hi! This is . . . unexpected." He was standing in front of her dressed in cut-off jeans and a sleeveless sweatshirt. In one hand was a hammer. In the other, a paintbrush.

"Ready to go to work," he said and smiled.

When she didn't say anything, his smile faltered. "Am I too early?"

"I thought you were kidding the other day," she said, embarrassed now for keeping him standing on the porch. "Please, come in."

He picked up his tool box and walked into the living room. Looking around, he said, "This is really nice, Jess."

She glanced at the furnishings, the high ceilings with six-inch carved moldings and nodded. "Thanks. It was my mother's. She loved Victorians. I guess I do, too. I can't think of living anywhere else." Looking back at him, she laughed. "I can't believe you actually came."

He seemed a little embarrassed when he shrugged. "I don't know—I got up this morning and thought, why not? I was just going to hang around the house and watch the Phillies game."

"Don't push!"

"Don't shout!"

Jess looked toward the stairs and laughed. "They're having a problem with a mattress. It's stuck in the hallway between two bedrooms."

Dave grinned and lifted his tool box. "Maybe I can help."

"It would certainly be appreciated," Jess said and led the way upstairs.

"Dave!" Jack looked relieved to see another male.

"Not a professional mover. But he does have a tool box," Jess said, trying hard not to laugh at the expressions of frustration on Jack's and Laurie's faces.

Dave greeted them and then looked at their predicament. "I think it would help if we removed the molding around this door. You guys have it wedged in pretty tight here."

"Laurie wouldn't move it when I told her to," Jack said, as a way of explaining that he wasn't at fault.

"I *couldn't* move it," Laurie ground out between her teeth as she glared at him. "God forbid that a male admit he screwed up something manual. It's a *man* thing. Like power tools. He must feel it threatens the size of his genitalia!"

Jess fell back against the wall in laughter. Jack's face was deep red and he looked like he was about to explode from holding back a sharp answer.

"I think you'd better help, Dave," Jess managed to get out.

"Right." Dave put his tool box on the floor and walked up to Laurie. "Why don't I take over? Just until we get this settled."

"Gladly." Laurie exchanged places with Dave and brushed her hair back from her forehead. "Thanks."

"Can I get you coffee, or anything?" Jess asked to ease the tension.

"Coffee would be great," Dave said. "Thanks. How about you, Jack?"

Jack shook his head. "I'll have ice water."

"Okay. Want to help me, Laurie?"

"Yeah, sure." Laurie followed Jess down the stairs, all the while muttering something about machismo.

When they were in the kitchen, Jess was still smiling.

"It wasn't that funny," Laurie said, bringing out the mugs and settling them on the counter.

"That's not why I'm smiling."

"What then? The baby? I swear, Jess, I've never seen such a change in a woman before. You're positively luminous with contentment."

"Thank you, but that's not it either."

"Then what?"

"You. You and Jack."

"Right. We're a great team. We can't even move a stupid bed together."

"You are a great team, and you know it. Look what you two did with my life." Pouring the coffee, she added, "And if you weren't so good together, you wouldn't be falling in love."

"What?"

"You heard me. You're both falling in love. Or you've already done it."

"That looked like love upstairs, did it? It was more like war. We're like fire and ice. We just can't be around each other without one of us losing our tempers and melting the other."

"You were pretty cozy the other morning when I found you in his arms."

Laurie poured cream into her coffee. "That. I—I was scared about something. He was reassuring me. It was nothing."

"What about the looks you two give each other when you don't think anyone's watching? I've seen them. I'm telling you it's love."

"Bull. I'll admit I thought I might be falling for him a few months ago, but that was before I realized what a troll he is."

Jessica burst into laughter. "A troll?"

"Yeah. He sits in and watches television all the time. I think he's afraid to go outside this house."

"He goes to work six days a week."

"Right. But that's safe. I gave him some information and he's scared to use it."

"Information? About what?"

Laurie took a deep breath. "About his birth mother. I think he should see her while he has this opportunity. He thinks I'm meddling in his life."

Jess smiled as she placed the mugs on a tray. "You are meddling, Laurie. It's his call. Not yours. The fact that you won't take no for an answer in anything is one of your best qualities. You're like one of those little terriers that sinks their teeth into something and can't let go."

Putting her arm around Laurie's shoulders, Jess said, "If it weren't for you being a terrier, I'd probably be an alcoholic now with no home or means of income. You saved my life. You and Jack. But this wound he's carrying around is sliced deep, and you can't sew it up. He's got to heal himself. You've got to let go, Laurie. Get your teeth out of this one."

When they returned to the bedroom, the molding

was removed and the box spring out of sight. Dave told them they shouldn't paint over the old wallpaper and Jess rented three steamers. It was tedious work for a summer afternoon and Jess felt guilty. But no one would let her do anything, except supply them with iced tea and sandwiches.

Everyone was taking a break when the wallpaper was finally removed. Laurie and Jack were sitting on the floor, with their backs on opposite walls. They barely looked at each other, let alone talk. Most of their conversation was directed at Dave. He sat on the window sill, letting the slight breeze hit him from behind.

"After we sand it and wash it down, it should be ready for the paint," Dave said. "These plaster walls really have held up."

Laurie sighed. "We have to wash it, too?" She sounded hot and tired.

"Everything doesn't have to be done today," Jess said. "We have time."

"But the crib is going to be delivered next week," Jack pointed out. "I thought we'd paint it this week and it would be ready."

"If we put our minds to it, the three of us can have it painted by tonight." Dave sounded like a cheerleader.

Jess shook her head. "I couldn't let you do that. All of you have been working since this morning. It's too much for one day."

"I don't mind," Dave answered and looked to Laurie and Jack.

Laurie nodded and Jack said, "Tell you what, Jess. Let us take care of this and you go down in the kitchen and make something terrific for dinner."

"I will, but don't you think we should ask Dave if he has plans first? We've taken up his entire day, I don't think we should presume—"

"I'd love to stay for dinner," Dave interrupted with a smile. "But maybe when we finish here, I'll run home to take a shower and change."

"Forget it," Jack said. "You can shower here, and I'll lend you something."

"Okay."

Jack looked at Jess and grinned. "So what are you going to make us for dinner?"

She shrugged. "I don't know yet. But for this job it's going to have to be special." And then she looked at Dave. Because he was sitting on the windowsill the sun created a kind of halo around his hair, bringing out hints of red in the brown. She had known him for years and had never seen that before. Nor had she noticed how expressive his eyes were behind his glasses. Or that when he smiled his whole facial expression seemed to light up with a gentle friendliness.

Jess blinked several times to stop daydreaming and saw that everyone was looking at her looking at Dave. Embarrassed, she said, "I think I'll start thumbing through some cookbooks. If you need anything, just yell."

In the kitchen, she took down her mother's cookbooks and started paging through one. But she really wasn't paying attention to the recipes.

She was thinking of Dave.

And that's what puzzled her.

Dave Sawyer had been her UPS delivery man for years. She always thought of him as nice, always with a friendly word. She never saw him as a man. To look at him in his brown uniform one would think he was average. Nothing striking, and nothing to detract. But today, seeing him show up on her doorstep in those shorts and that sleeveless sweatshirt, she'd kept looking at his arms and legs. He was like carved marble. Maybe it was all that walking and lifting. Whatever it was, it had paid off. And his smile. He'd smiled at her for years and she had never seen anything in it, except friendliness. How could she have missed it?

Shaking her head, she tried to focus her attention on the cookbook. It was ridiculous. She was almost six months pregnant and big as a house. Her thoughts shouldn't be running in this vein.

There. Her finger settled on a page. HoneyMint Spiced Chicken. Perfect for a hot summer night. She got up and checked to make sure she had all the ingredients. They would sit in the dining room. With candles and silver. Everyone had worked hard today and she would make it special. Filled with enthusiasm, she pulled an apron out of the drawer to begin.

The only problem was that the apron didn't fit around her waist. Waist? She didn't have one. The only way it fit was to tie it above her belly and under her breasts.

"Need help there?"

Turning, she saw Dave standing at the kitchen doorway.

Once more embarrassed, she laughed nervously and said, "It's like Cinderella's stepsisters trying to fit into the shoe. I'm too big."

"You're supposed to be big," he said as he came and tied the apron for her. "I think you look great."

"You're being kind," she answered. "But thanks. Can I get something for you?"

"Jack wants more water and Laurie said she'll take another Diet Coke."

When she was putting ice into the glasses, Dave said, "I wasn't being kind. I was being truthful. Being pregnant agrees with you."

"It does," she admitted.

"Is it hard, Jess?" he asked in a serious voice. "What you're going through?"

She didn't immediately answer and it was his turn to look embarrassed. "I shouldn't have asked. It's none of my business."

For some reason she wasn't offended. "That's all right," she said, and leaned against the counter. "It was in the beginning. I had major reservations about whether I could do it alone. I'm thirty-four and have an income, which puts me heads above most women faced with this situation. But still . . . it was tough."

"And there wasn't any question about whether you'd be doing it alone?"

"You're talking about the father? He doesn't exist for me. If not for this child, then I would say the entire episode was a huge mistake." She touched her belly. "But this isn't a mistake. For me, it's a blessing. I think this child saved my life."

"Really?"

She looked at him, really looked, and recognized a friend. He wasn't asking questions out of curiosity, but friendship and concern. Working here all day without asking for anything proved that. "My life was a mess, Dave, after my mother died. I was kind of lost, after all those years of taking care of her. I didn't have a social life, or any friends under sixty-five."

Pausing for a few seconds, she took a deep breath and added, "And I had a drinking problem. I used alcohol to mask the loneliness and get through the night. God only knows where I'd be if Jack and Laurie didn't come to stay with me."

"They're good people."

She smiled. "Yes, they are—and so are you."

"Me?"

Nodding, she said, "You accepted this pregnancy without any judgments. You were the first person, outside of Jack and Laurie, that I told, and you were happy for me. I can't tell you how much I appreciated that." She smiled at him. "Just like now. You're accepting what I told you about my drinking. No questions, or anything."

He looked down to the floor and then back up at her. "You know, Jess, I've been through a lot myself. Like when my marriage was falling apart. I'm not exactly proud of some of the things I did to get through that. But I guess we do what we have to do to survive emotionally. That whole period taught me a valuable lesson. Not to judge others. I sure don't want anybody judging me. I'm just trying to get through life the best way I know how, and I guess that's what most people are trying. If we fall off-balance once in a while, well, hell, we're only human.''

Jess stared at him, seeing him, not just physically anymore, but emotionally now. He was a good person, and a good friend. ''Thank you for coming today and helping,'' she said quietly.

''Don't thank me, Jess. I wanted to help.''

Something weird was happening, she thought, as he continued to stare back at her. Then, he cleared his throat and said, ''Speaking of helping, I should get back to work.''

He picked up the glasses and left.

Jess turned back to the cutting board and vowed to make this the best meal she had ever cooked. It would be an early Thanksgiving. For Laurie and Jack. And for Dave, too.

It was great to have friends again.

Chapter 18

"No, you can't go in. You have to stay out until Jack and Dave get the crib set up." Laurie held Jess' shoulders to keep her out of the nursery.

"How much longer?" Jess asked impatiently. "I can't wait to see it."

"Well, you'll have to wait. You promised."

"I know. It's just that everybody is doing everything for me and I feel like I should be a part of it."

Laurie laughed. "I think what you're carrying is a big part of it. You're the one that's going to be doing the hard work."

"Okay," Dave said with a smile as he poked his head out of the room. "You can bring her in."

Laurie released her hold on Jess and she walked very slowly into the small bedroom. Inhaling, Jess covered her mouth with her hand as she viewed the Jenny Lind crib that she had ordered two months ago. Even though she hadn't been teary-eyed for months, she cried as she viewed her child's room. The walls were painted in a soft white and accented by pale yellow cove molding at the ceiling. A white dresser with yellow knobs sat atop a matching rug, while a changing table stood waiting. But what really made her cry was a white rocker with yellow and white checked cushions that sat before the window.

Walking over to it, she lightly pushed the back and watched it rock forward. "It's perfect," she whispered and smiled at the three of them.

"Dave found the rocker," Laurie said, smiling back.

Jess looked at him. "Dave, you shouldn't have."

He looked embarrassed. "I wanted to."

"Thank you . . ." Everything was so perfect, just waiting for her child to come into this world. "Thank you all so much. I don't know what to say."

Laurie laughed. "Thank you says it all, I think. How do you like the crib?"

Jess walked over to it and ran her fingers over the spindles. "It's beautiful. Oh, and look at the teddy bear."

She picked it up and held it to her chest.

"Jack got it yesterday."

Jess turned to him. "I love him. Thank you." Burying her face into the soft fur, she murmured, "I can cuddle it until the baby comes. Look, you guys even put the sheets on the mattress for me.''

Laurie watched as Jack slipped from the room. He'd been quiet all morning as he and Dave had assembled the crib and the rocker. When he had shown her the teddy bear, he'd been embarrassed, and maybe sad. She wasn't sure. Leaving Dave and Jess, she went to look for him.

He was standing by the kitchen door, looking out at the back yard. ''Are you okay?'' she asked quietly.

He didn't turn around. ''It's really beautiful here, you know? All the trees and birds . . . She can bring the baby out here next year in a playpen, or something.''

Laurie stood next to him and nodded. ''It's a nice yard. It's a nice town. A good place to bring up a child.''

He didn't say anything and she looked up at him. His face was set in control, and the wrinkles at the corners of his eyes were deeper, as if trying to keep from crying.

''Jack, what's wrong?''

He didn't say anything for a few moments, and then swallowed hard. His voice was a hoarse whisper of anguish.

''I want to see my birth mother.''

Words weren't necessary. She quietly slipped her arms around his waist and held him.

* * *

Miriam Stanton lived in a quiet subdivision in Langhorne, Pennsylvania. The houses were small ranchers and split levels with trees that had matured in the twenty or thirty years since they had been planted. It was obvious the second wave of homeowners had begun to take over. Young children rode Big Wheels and bikes down the sidewalks or played jump rope in the driveways. It was a typical summer's day in suburbia, yet there were holdouts to the younger generation— those in their sixties who had moved in when the houses smelled of fresh paint and lumber, those who hadn't retired to warmer climates.

Miriam Stanton was one of them.

"Promise me you won't reveal who I am."

Laurie sighed. "Look, Jack, I know you're nervous, but I've already promised you twice that I wouldn't. Try and relax. We're almost there. Two sixty-four— it should be the house after this one."

"And you're sure she's expecting us?" he asked again as he slowly applied the brakes.

"Yes, Jack, she's expecting us. I told you I called and said we were conducting a survey with Philadelphia Family Court. When I asked about participating in a personal interview, she agreed. Here we are," Laurie said and looked at Jack. His hands seemed frozen to the wheel as he stared at the house.

"Are you okay?"

He let his breath out in a nervous rush. "I don't know. Maybe we shouldn't do this. Maybe she knows . . ."

Opening the car door, Laurie said, "C'mon. We're not turning back now. And she's expecting us. If we don't show, she might call Family Court to find out why. And then what would she think?"

"I guess you're right," he said and released the wheel. Shutting the car off, he opened the door and stepped out. As he walked up to Laurie, she smiled with reassurance.

"It's going to be okay," she whispered. "This is the right thing to do. You'll see."

When he didn't say anything, she grinned. "I'm so proud of you. And I'd give you a big hug right now, except she might be looking out the window. So come on, let's go meet her. Okay?"

He took a deep steadying breath and pushed himself forward. "Okay."

She answered the door quickly and stood looking at them with a nervous expression.

"Mrs. Stanton?" Laurie asked.

"Yes?" She was short and plump, with dark hair that was heavily streaked with gray. Her face was lined, and her eyes were worried.

Laurie smiled. "My name is Laurie Reese. I spoke with you a few days ago about our survey."

"Yes. Yes, of course. Please come in."

She ushered them into her living room, and stood wringing her hands together. "Please sit down," she offered.

Jack wasn't looking at the Early American decor. He was staring at the pictures that lined the wooden mantel. Laurie's eyes widened in shock. One of the men in a wedding picture looked a lot like Jack, around the eyes and the mouth.

"I'd like to introduce my associate, Jack Lannigan," Laurie hurried to explain. There were no notations that Miriam had ever contacted the Family Court after her marriage, so she shouldn't know Jack's name.

Miriam smiled at him. "How do you do?" she said with a strained politeness.

"Ma'am?" Jack sounded like a cop as he sat next to Laurie on the couch.

"Thank you for agreeing to see us, Mrs. Stanton," Laurie said. "I know this is a difficult situation for you and I'll try to make this as brief as possible." She took out a legal sized note pad and pen, to look official. "Your maiden name was Koslowski, until you married?"

She held her hands together in her lap as she nodded. "That's correct. I was married in nineteen fifty-one. Joe, my husband, died two years ago."

"I'm sorry," Laurie said. "And you have children . . . since your marriage?"

"Yes. Two sons and a daughter. And five grandchildren. Can I get you anything?" she asked nervously. "Iced tea, perhaps?"

"No, thanks. We're fine," Laurie said. "Now if we could speak about the adoption? Any questions you aren't comfortable answering, then don't do so. All right?"

"Yes. All right."

Laurie didn't look at Jack. She didn't want to see his reaction, or she might not be able to continue. "You delivered a son and placed him up for adoption. The father wasn't named—"

"I didn't think I should," Miriam interrupted. "He was a boy I had met just after high school, when I was at the shore with my friends. I wish I could say I loved him, but I didn't know him that long." She looked at Jack and cast her gaze to the rug. "Even now, this is embarrassing. I know you young people have a much broader outlook toward these things, but back then . . . it wasn't so. My mother convinced me adoption was the only choice."

Laurie smiled kindly. "We're not here to discuss your decision, Mrs. Stanton. I'm sure you did what you felt was right, and please be assured that no one is questioning that. What I was wondering was how you would feel about being contacted by your son."

"My son?" The older woman appeared startled.

"Yes. Sometimes, the person who was adopted tries to initiate contact with the birth parent."

"He already did. Years ago." Miriam stopped speaking and took a deep breath, as if the very air might give her strength. "I was so shocked to hear from him, and . . . I'm afraid I was also frightened. You see, my husband and children didn't know of him and I didn't know what to say to anyone. Not to him, or to them. I think I must have hurt him. No . . . I know I did. But too much time has passed now. I mean, I want to know about him, but I shut him out

291

of my life. How can I expect him to allow me now into his? It wouldn't be right, and I don't know if I could do it."

Laurie didn't dare look at Jack. "That's very honest of you, Mrs. Stanton. Please, we aren't here to upset you."

Miriam kept glancing at Jack. "I think about him—now, more than ever. I want to believe that he's doing well. I picture him as married, with children. And I hope that he's happy and content." She suddenly appeared embarrassed. "I suppose that's so I can believe that I did the right thing all those years ago."

"So you're saying that you wouldn't want to contact him now?" Laurie asked in a gentle voice.

Miriam looked like she might cry. "I'm saying I don't know how."

Everything in her was straining against the effort to control herself from standing up and shouting, *Well, here he is—and he's as scared as you are*. But she didn't. She had promised Jack. And she had to remember that she was here as his friend, not the terrier that tended to sink her teeth in and never let go.

She could tell that Jack wasn't going to say anything. Frustrated, Laurie stood up. "Well, then. Do you have anything more to add, Mr. Lannigan?"

Picking up his cue, Jack rose to his feet. "No. I think we have everything we need. Thank you, Mrs. Stanton."

Miriam stood up. "I hope I was able to help in your survey."

Laurie smiled as she led the way to the door. "Oh,

yes. Your input was very important, and we thank you.''

"Yes, thank you again," Jack added, following Laurie out the door.

"Excuse me . . . Mr. Lannigan?"

Jack turned around on her porch. "Yes?"

"Have we met before? You look familiar." Miriam searched his face.

Jack merely smiled as he took her hand and gently shook it. "We may have," he said. "If we did, then it was a pleasure seeing you again. Take care."

He could feel her eyes on his back as he walked away.

Laurie had started the car and turned on the air conditioner by the time he got in. "I like her," she said, as she threw the car into drive.

Jack leaned back against the headrest and sighed. "I do, too. Whew! What an experience!"

Laurie drove out of the subdivision before she asked the question. "Why didn't you tell her, Jack? I think she would want to know."

He closed his eyes and said, "Tell her what? She wants to believe that I'm happily married, with a bunch of kids and a white picket fence. How could I tell her that I'm dead?"

"I guess you're right, but it seems a shame."

Neither of them said anything for a long time. They were almost at the Burlington-Bristol Bridge before Laurie asked the most important question.

"Tell me something, Jack . . . are you glad you did it?"

"Oh, yeah. Yeah, I am. Thanks, Laurie. I'm glad you didn't give up on me."

When she glanced at him, tears were rolling down his cheeks and he didn't even bother to wipe them away. She reached across the seat, took his hand, and squeezed it.

Sometimes being a terrier really paid off.

"Now breathe deeply. Inhaling through the nose . . . and exhale. Again. Deep breaths. Inhaling through the nose . . ."

"Oh, come on," Jack whispered. "We all know how to breathe by now."

"*Shh,*" Laurie scolded, as the instructor looked at them like misbehaving children. "Just breathe like she said."

"*I'm* not the one that's going to be in labor."

"Jack, you're breaking my concentration," Jess whispered, as she applied effleurage during her breathing.

Laurie glared at him. "You're breaking her concentration." She inhaled with the rest of the class and dismissed him. He was like the class clown, always making comments under his breath. Sometimes they were funny. Mostly, they were annoying.

"All right, everyone. We've worked our way through the beginning and middle stages of labor. Now we're dilated seven centimeters and are into transition labor. Hard labor." The instructor walked up to the big screen television and inserted a cassette.

"Before we begin the pant-pant-blow method for transition, I'd like to show you an actual birth."

"Oh, no . . ." Jack held his pillow to his chest and buried his head. "I don't want to see this," he mumbled.

Jess laughed as Laurie pulled the pillow down from his face.

"Well, you're going to see it. And pay attention. You're supposed to be one of her coaches. What if she had an emergency at home?"

"Then we'd call the emergency squad."

"Oh, just be quiet and pay attention."

The film started and everyone was glued to the screen as it showed a woman in the delivery room panting and blowing and being encouraged by her husband. And then the camera panned down . . .

"What's that?" Jack asked.

"What do you think?" Laurie muttered back.

He shrugged as he strained his neck forward to figure it out. "Looks like a closeup of a bloodshot eye."

The couples surrounding them burst into nervous laughter.

"That's the baby's head crowning," the instructor said in a loud disapproving voice to once more get control of her class.

Jack's face reddened with embarrassment and Laurie glared at him.

"You know something, Lannigan? You're becoming a real nuisance." But she had to bite the inside of her cheek, not to laugh along with the others. Since meeting with Miriam, there had been a startling change in him. He was carefree and funny. It was as if a terrible burden had been lifted from his shoulders.

"Oh, God, look at that!" Jack's voice was filled with awe.

Laurie focused her attention back on the screen.

A child was being born.

Jess put her hands up to her shoulders, and Laurie and Jack each grabbed one. The three of them held on to each other in a circle of support and fear and wonderment.

He parked his Ford Bronco in front of the store and looked at the window, decorated like a Victorian Christmas in shades of white and mauve and gold. Leaning back, he rested his head against the thick velour and wondered if he had the courage to walk in to her.

Dave Sawyer was not a man given to flamboyant acts. In fact, most people would call him shy. But he had seen that look on Jess' face earlier in the day, and it had haunted him ever since.

He'd been delivering two boxes and his first thought on entering *A Woman's Passion* was always to seek out Jessica. She was standing behind the marble counter and seemed deep in thought. Following her gaze, he'd seen her staring at a man pushing a stroller and walking behind his wife as she browsed through the racks. When he looked closer, he'd been able to see that it wasn't so much intensity in her expression, but sadness.

Who was the father of her child? She never spoke

of him. What had he done to make her so afraid of men? Because she was. He could sense it every time he tried to chip away at the wall surrounding her. He could go just so far. Friendship. That's all she wanted. It was in her face and her body language.

Keep your distance. I'm protecting myself and my child. It was as if he could read her mind. Funny thing was, now he was protective of her. Like what was she doing still working at eight o'clock at night? Sure it was two weeks before Christmas and all the stores were packed. Hell, he was working overtime himself just to finish his route. But she was nine months pregnant, weeks away from delivering, and she should be home. In the last four months he'd come over to the house at least twice a week, usually on Saturday nights or Sunday. They would all sit around and talk or make dinner, or play cards. He and Jack both supported the struggling Eagles and watched the Sunday football games together.

Jess thought he was a friend—Jack's friend, Laurie's friend, her—But he'd fallen in love with her when he'd heard her giggle at Laurie's and Jack's fight over the mattress. God, it had been so long since he'd heard a woman's laughter that when she'd done it, it had stirred something long dormant. Desire.

What a pathetic situation. He was in love with a pregnant woman who only saw him as a friend. Jack knew it. Laurie knew it. The only one who refused to see it was Jess.

Opening the car door, Dave glanced at the cardboard containers on the back seat and took a deep breath.

297

It was time to make a move.

He felt like Norm on *Cheers* every time he walked into the shop.

"Dave . . ." Laurie, Jack, Mari, Anita, and even Jess greeted him the same way. And always with a smile.

But tonight Jess wasn't smiling. She was leaning against the marble counter with a scowl on her face.

The shop was crowded with women, and even men buying gifts for their wives or girlfriends. He waved to everyone and walked up to Jess.

"I can't believe you're still here. You should be home."

"It's Christmas," she answered in a clipped voice. "Can't you see how busy we are?"

"I see that you've got four others working for you and how tired you are. Or you wouldn't be leaning on the counter like that."

"My feet hurt," she said, straightening as Laurie and Jack walked up to them. "And who are you, anyway, my doctor?"

"You're also grumpy," he said with a grin. "You obviously don't want to be here, so let me take you home."

"Please," Jack cut in, "get her out of here."

Laurie nodded. "I agree. She's miserable. She should go home, but she won't listen to us."

Jess scowled at the three of them. "And what is there for me to do at home? Sit around and wait. I'm sick of it."

"She's had this nesting urge for weeks now," Laurie said. "Everything's ready for the baby. The house is spotless, so I guess she's just restless."

"Why do all of you talk about me like I'm not here? I just want to keep busy."

Going back to her customer, Laurie said over her shoulder, "My, aren't we testy? Go home and put your feet up, Jess."

Jack softly patted her shoulder. "Why don't you let Dave bring you home? We'll take care of everything. We close in an hour, but by the time we clean up, it'll be past ten."

"I have Chinese, Jess, waiting in the car. Shrimp Lo Mein," Dave said, trying to tempt her.

She looked at him, then at Jack. "Well, never let it be said that I couldn't take a hint. I know where I'm not wanted."

A half hour later, she sat at the kitchen table and picked at her food. "I really shouldn't have this," she said. "My doctor says that shrimp is high in cholesterol."

Sitting next to her, Dave glanced in her direction. She really was in a bad mood. "A little bit won't hurt you. And I know you like it."

She shrugged. "What's weird is that before I was pregnant, I could take it or leave it. Cravings . . . they're hard to explain."

Grinning, he nodded. "It is hard to figure out how you could eat shrimp and then raspberry sherbet at the same meal."

"Are you making fun of me?"

"Yes, Jess. I am. What's wrong? Do you want to talk about it?"

She didn't say anything for a few moments, as if she was considering his question. Finally, she said, "I'm fat, irritable, moody, unattractive. The customers are ignorant. They have no patience or Christmas spirit. Jack's too busy to get a tree until Sunday, and I wanted it decorated by then. Laurie is the Eternal Maternal, acting like she's my mother and fussing around me all the time." She put her fork down, sighed deeply, then added, "And my feet are killing me. There. Is that enough?"

Dave sat back in his chair and smiled at her. "I suppose it is," he answered. "First of all," he said, as he reached down and picked up her foot, "you are not fat and unattractive. You're pregnant, and you're beautiful." He took off her tasseled loafer and began massaging her foot through her sock. When he felt her resistance, he held on and continued talking. "You're irritable and moody because you're impatient. You're ready to have this baby, and it isn't time yet. Now the customers have Christmas spirit, or they wouldn't be out shopping, though we both know that isn't spirit, but it's like this every year. It just bothers you more because, this time, you're more emotional.

"What else?" he asked himself, as he kneaded his thumbs into the sole of her foot. "Oh, yeah. Jack." He held back a grin as she sighed with pleasure. "He's busy at the store, so I'll pick you up tomorrow morning and we can get the tree. We can have it all set up and

300

ready for decorating by the time he and Laurie get home tomorrow night.''

"I can have dinner ready and hot cider," Jess offered, liking the idea. "And we can have Christmas carols playing, and make it an old-fashioned Christmas.'' She sighed again as he massaged her ankle. ''When was the last time you had an old-fashioned Christmas?''

"Probably when I was a kid," he answered. "I guess since then I was caught up in the rush. I used to dread this season, working twelve hours a day and hustling just to finish my route before eight o'clock.''

Keeping her foot on his lap, he reached for her other one. "Real trees, hot cider . . . I don't think I've had the Christmas spirit since I left home.''

"Not when you were married?" She asked the question easily, comfortable enough with him so that it wasn't prying.

He shook his head. "Promise me you won't laugh?''
She nodded.

"Ellen, my ex, was into modern art. Our Christmas tree was made out of wood, with holes cut into it to hang ornaments. She thought of it as a sculpture. I thought it was weird. Kind of hard to muster up the same feelings with a piece of wood cut out like a tree and painted green.''

"Gee . . . I don't know what to say," Jess murmured. "I'm trying to picture it." She started to giggle and covered her mouth.

"You promised not to laugh," Dave said, trying to be serious.

"You're tickling my foot," she answered.

"No, I'm not. You're laughing because I had a wooden Christmas tree. But at least you're laughing."

She smiled at him, relaxed in his presence. "Yeah, I am laughing. Thanks. It's better than my constant complaining. Everyone must be sick of it. I know I am."

He shook his head. "Everybody understands. But tonight I don't think it was the customers, or Jack or Laurie, that set you off."

"You don't?"

"Nope. I think it was something else. And I think it started this afternoon when you saw that man pushing his baby in a stroller."

Her body tensed; he could feel it in the muscles of her foot.

"I don't know what you're talking about," she said in a defensive voice.

"Yes, you do. Look, Jess, the reason I brought it up was because you don't have to be sad, or scared. You're not going to be alone in this. You have Jack and Laurie." He paused for a second. "And you have me."

They stared at each other. He stopped rubbing her foot, and she nearly stopped breathing. It hit her then, the sudden realization. It was as if a fog had been lifted from her brain. Dave Sawyer was interested in her as more than a friend. Scenes flashed through her mind: Dave at the store, always talking to her. Dave showing up on her doorstep to help with the nursery. Dave

302

always helping her, wanting her opinion, making her laugh. He had become a part of her life, and all this time she had thought he was here for Jack. It wasn't Jack. It was her.

"Scared?" he asked softly, as if reading her mind.

She swallowed. "Stunned is more like it," she whispered, acutely aware of his fingers on her foot. What she had thought of as a friendly touch now became a caress. His fingers were strong and warm as he ran them over the soft pad of her foot, sending a shiver up her leg. "I'm pregnant," she stated. "With another man's child."

"I know that. I think you're beautiful."

She was embarrassed. "Beautiful? I feel like one of those dancing hippos in *Fantasia*."

He didn't laugh. "This may sound corny, but when I look at you . . . you're ripe with life, Jess, and it's beautiful. I don't care who the father is. All these months . . . I thought you'd see how I felt, but you didn't and time is running out. I want you to know now, while you're pregnant, how important you've become to me. I admire you more than any other woman I've ever known. I don't know if I could have done what you did with your mother, and then you turned your life around. Now you're ready to give birth, and—"

"But you've never even kissed me," she interrupted, totally shaken by his declaration.

He gently placed her foot on the floor and knelt in front of her. "That's easily remedied," he said, and held her face in his hands. Looking deep into her eyes, he whispered, "I love you, Jess. And if you want me, you'll never be alone again."

His lips were warm and gentle, almost reverent, before deepening into hunger. Her hands came up and touched his back, feeling the muscles under his sweater, as she pulled him closer. A sweet awakening occurred, making her blood thick and heavy with desire, and her child chose that moment to deliver a sound kick.

They both broke the embrace and laughed.

"I don't know if that was approval, or not."

She ran her hand over the lines of his face in astonishment. He loved her! He'd seen her at her worst, from morning sickness to whining about her feet. He'd watched her body swell up and her moods swing, and he still loved her. Dear God, was it possible? Was she to be given another chance?

"I think it was approval," she whispered, as tears ran down her cheeks.

Ten minutes until closing, and Jack was counting them. It had been a tough day with the Christmas rush, customers who had gone over their credit limit on their charge cards and a leaking water heater in the storeroom. He'd spent over an hour shifting boxes to save the inventory from water damage until he could find a plumber. And then he was charged double because it was an emergency. Did anyone call a plumber if it wasn't an emergency? He didn't know if it was the time of year, but he was getting real tired of playing storekeeper. He was a cop, not a bean counter, and after nearly ten months of this existence, he'd had just about enough. It wouldn't be so bad, he thought as he started closing out the register, if he was allowed any contact with his old life. But he wasn't . . . and he missed it. Reading the Philly papers every day, devouring the crime reports, didn't satisfy him. He wanted to be a part of it again.

Just then he looked up and saw Laurie holding up a sexy, silk teddy for a customer's inspection. When she placed it against her, as if modeling it, their eyes met for a few moments and Jack felt as though someone had reached in and twisted his stomach.

He couldn't leave her. He didn't want to leave her. It wasn't just the strong sexual pull that they were both fighting. It was more powerful than that. She had turned him around, entered his mind and cleaned it out of old garbage. Again, Laurie had been right about him. Seeing his birth mother, listening to her tell about her own struggle with her decision, had been a turning point for him. He saw Miriam Koslowski as a young girl, alone and terrified, with no where to turn for help. He saw what Jess was going through as a woman with support, and finally understood Miriam's decision. She honestly wanted him to be happy, carrying a mental picture of him with wife and kids and the picket fence. Well, maybe he never got the wife and kids. Or the fence. But he did get something equally important.

All the loneliness and ache that he had carried around with him since he was a soldier and a cop was gone. How ironic that, in death, he was able to find what he was looking for in life. Peace within himself. That he was worthy, and lovable.

Looking up again, he was startled to find Laurie still watching him. God, how could this happen now?

He was falling in love.

Falling? Hell, he was knee deep in it . . . and there was no way out.

Chapter 19

Glancing at the alarm clock on her night table, Jess sighed. Five o'clock in the morning. Christmas morning. Not a creature was stirring, as the poem goes—just a very pregnant woman trying to summon the strength to heave her body out of bed and waddle to the bathroom. Again. She couldn't find a comfortable position in bed, no matter how many pillows she used, and the pressure on her bladder was annoying.

Grabbing the edge of the mattress, she rolled up to a sitting position and tried to take a deep breath. "C'mon, baby. Your birthday is tomorrow. Don't disappoint me," she whispered as she stood upright. Though after examining her yesterday afternoon, Dr.

Greenspan had said he would probably see her in the office next week. She wasn't ready. Yeah. Right. She was as ready as she'd ever be. Although she was scared, she was ready for labor and delivery, whatever it took to get this baby out and in her arms. She was tired of being as big as a tank, tired of getting up three times in the middle of the night to use the bathroom. Tired of the hiccups, the leg cramps, never being able to take a deep breath . . . and tired of complaining to anyone who'd listen. She never used to be like that. Now, it seemed she was focused only on herself and her body. She didn't care about the store, or anything else.

Well, that wasn't quite true. She cared about Dave. "Aww . . . geez," she muttered, as she shuffled to the bathroom. The soles of her feet were screaming at her to get off them. Settled on the commode, she rested her arms on her huge belly and sighed. How could she be in love when she was thirty-eight pounds overweight? When her face looked like a ripe cantaloupe? How could Dave love her? Maybe he was weird. What kind of man falls in love with a pregnant woman?

She smiled. A wonderful man. A sweet, funny, sensitive man. And sexy, too. Behind those tortoise shell glasses were eyes that seemed to speak to her of future promises. It had all happened so quietly, going from casual friends, to real friends, to lovers. Not really lovers. That would definitely have to wait. But two people who discovered each other with love. There were no fireworks going off, like with Keith. This was peaceful and calm and dependable. There wasn't anything frightening about it.

It felt right, that's all.

When she left the bathroom, she started to go back to bed, but changed her mind. She couldn't sleep. Instead, she put her robe on, slid her feet into slippers and headed back to the bathroom to brush her teeth and her hair. There was something she had to do, something she had thought about for weeks. And she wanted to do it before the baby came.

She was very quiet as she came down the stairs. Jack was asleep on the couch and Dave was tucked inside a sleeping bag, like a big present under the tree. Jess stood for a moment, looking at the men, smelling the pine sap from the Douglas fir. How different this was from last Christmas when her mother was dying. She hadn't even put up a tree down here. The only sign of the holiday had been the three foot artificial tree from KMart that she'd put in her mother's room.

It was very strange how someone's life could change in a year. Last Christmas she had been praying that God would take her mother, to end her suffering, and terrified that when he did she would be alone in this world. Now here she was, pregnant. Her home was filled with friends and a man that said he loved her. Truly, this Christmas she was blessed.

Turning, she smiled as she walked into the kitchen. She flipped the light switch and squinted until her eyes adjusted. Then she walked over to the cabinet by the refrigerator and opened it. The bottle of Old Grand-Dad stood on the shelf, untouched in the last ten months. Keith's presence in her life had done two positive things: the baby, and she'd stopped drinking. But it was for her child that she now took the bottle down and held it in her hands. She remembered a time when she couldn't get through a day without it. What a lonely and unhappy person she had been. All she had wanted was someone to love, and now she was about to have a child. And she loved this child with every fiber of her being, for it had saved her life.

She never thought of herself as an alcoholic, certainly not the stereotypical drunk falling down in the street. She could function, but alcohol altered her life. She could withdraw from reality, and now . . . now she welcomed it.

Unscrewing the top, she held the bottle over the sink and poured the remaining bourbon down the drain. Her arm encircled her stomach as she whispered, "This is for us, sweetie. I want to be the best parent I can be, and I don't need any reminders anymore. I'll have you."

"And me."

She spun around to see Dave standing in the doorway. He looked like a kid. Sleepy and tousled. He was blinking from the glare of the light and wiping his glasses on his undershirt as he smiled at her. "Up kind of early, huh? Can't wait to see what Santa brought you?"

She smiled back at him as he put his glasses on and walked up to her. He took the empty bottle from her hand and threw it in the trash, then slipped his arms around her.

"I don't know," she speculated as she glanced down to her stomach. "How do you think Santa will call this one? Was I bad, or good this past year?"

"Good, Jess," he said as he kissed her forehead. "Very, very good. And to prove it he left something under the tree for you last night."

Jess laughed. "And I suppose you saw him, sleeping as you were under the tree."

"Absolutely right. He was big and fat and jolly—"

"Not unlike myself," Jess interrupted, trying to keep a straight face. "Are you sure you didn't see me walk by a few minutes ago and think it was Santa? There is a resemblance. My robe is red."

"As I was saying, this person was jolly . . . and frankly, my dear, that hasn't been your strong point lately."

She playfully slapped his shoulder.

"Hey, we all understand. Hormones. The pull of the lunar tides on your body. All that mysterious pregnancy stuff. Anyway, it wasn't you. It was Santa. The genuine article, and he left something specifically for you."

"He did, huh?"

"Yup. Told me I was to give it to you the first thing on Christmas morning." He looked out the kitchen window to the beginnings of dawn. "I just didn't think it was going to be *this* early."

"Well, I'm up. And you're up. So where is it?" It felt wonderful to be in his arms, all warm and secure. And if she needed another sign to tell her this was right, how about laughing at five o'clock in the morning? Any man that could laugh, and make her laugh, at such an ungodly hour was her Mr. Right. "So how about it? Where's this gift?"

"I'll be right back. Don't move—unless you want to sit down, or something."

She did sit, but only because her back was bothering her. Massaging her lower muscles, she smiled with happiness as she waited for him to return. It didn't take long. He held out a small box wrapped in gold foil and tied with a thin green velvet ribbon. It was jewelry, she could tell, or she really was bad this year and getting a lump of coal. Really, what else would someone get for a pregnant woman? It was probably a pin, or a locket, and she just hoped his taste in jewelry didn't run toward the ornate.

She carefully untied the ribbon and then the paper. Holding the small black box in her hand, she was afraid to open it. Her heart started beating faster in her chest, and the baby seemed to bang its head on her pelvic bone.

"Go ahead," he said, as if reading her mind.

She looked up at him, and his expression was anxious. Maybe even worried.

Taking a deep breath, she opened the box.

A solitaire diamond was nestled inside, the prisms reflecting off the kitchen light with a startling brilliance.

"Oh, Dave . . ." she murmured, glad she was sitting down. "It—it's just beautiful!"

He quickly knelt in front of her. "If you'll have me, Jess, I'd be honored if you'd be my wife."

312

Stunned, she couldn't answer him. She immediately stood up and stared at the ring.

"I'm not an executive, or someone like that, but I promise to take care of you, and love you. And the baby—she'll be mine. We could be engaged for as long as you want, until you're comfortable with the idea of marriage. I know it's scary for someone that's never done it before, but—"

"Dave," she interrupted as she looked down. "You're either going to have to move back about two feet so I can see your face over this belly, or I'm going to have to kneel down. And I don't know if I could get up again."

In spite of his nerves, he grinned, stood up and held her hands, cupping the ring inside. "Say something, Jess. I'm rambling here."

"Oh, Dave," she whispered, as tears ran down her cheeks. "I can't believe you want me . . . like this."

"I want you," he answered in a firm voice. "And the baby. I spend so much time here everybody in town probably thinks she's mine. And that's the way I want it."

Jess sniffled. "I don't know why you insist that it's a girl."

"Because I know it. But if I'm wrong, then I'll take him for rides in the truck and teach him how to play baseball. What do you say? I want you . . . both of you."

She tried to take a deep breath. "Then . . . we want you."

He kissed her with a mixture of relief and joy.

"We'll make it work, Jess," he whispered into her mouth. "We'll do it . . . all three of us . . . together."

Taking the ring out of the box, he slipped it on her finger. It was tight, but he got it on. Smiling, he looked into her eyes. "I love you, Jessica. Will you marry me?"

"I love you, too," she murmured, feeling it fill her heart and her mind and her soul. "Yes, I'll marry you. As soon as you want." She wrapped her arms around his back and put her head on his chest. Closing her eyes, she felt his heart beat and offered up a mental prayer. *Thank you for my child and for bringing this man into my life. I know they're precious gifts, and I'll be careful . . . I promise.*

"What's going on?"

They turned and saw Jack scratching his head and yawning. The fly on his jeans was zipped half way up and his toes were curling against the cold linoleum.

Keeping his arm around Jess' shoulders, Dave grinned broadly. "This woman has just agreed to be my wife."

Jack blinked several times and Jess giggled at his shocked expression. "For real?" Jack demanded, finally awake.

"For real," Jess said, holding out her hand to show him the ring.

Jack came closer and took her hand. After admiring the ring, he looked up at them and grinned broadly. "I *knew* it! You two were meant for each other. Wait until I tell Laurie."

"Well, you might as well wake her up," Jess said

with a laugh. "You know she's going to be really upset that she wasn't the first to know."

Jack's eyes widened mischievously. "Yeah . . . I'll be right back."

Huddled under the covers and softly snoring, she appeared young and innocent. He grinned as he gazed down at her in the tranquil light of dawn. He would have thought in their state that they would be perfect, untroubled by human frailties such as snoring and indigestion. But it was just like being alive, except they existed in someone else's world. Their own was shut off to them.

He sat on the edge of the bed and pushed a tendril of hair off her cheek. She sighed and unconsciously turned her face toward his touch.

"Laurie?" He whispered her name, needing to break the sexual pull. "Wake up."

"Huh?" She opened her eyes, dazed. "What? The baby?"

He smiled. "No. It's not the baby."

She rolled over and immediately went back to sleep.

"C'mon, Laurie," he said, running his hand over her shoulder. "Wake up. Jess is getting married."

It took a few moments for her to comprehend. "Married?" Her voice was low and sleepy, and she turned, lifting her arms above her head in a slow, feline stretch. As she lowered her arms, she ran her fingers down his. "Oh, Jack . . . we can't be married," she muttered. Her eyes were still closed and a lazy smile appeared at her lips. "We're . . . you know . . . angels, or something."

315

He chuckled. She still wasn't awake. Bending, he planted a big kiss on her. "Hey, sleepyhead, I was talking about Jess. Dave just gave her a big diamond ring."

Laurie sat up and pushed the hair away from her face. "Really?"

"Really. Some Christmas, huh? I was right about them. How about that? *I'm* the matchmaker!"

She stared at him for a few seconds. "Jess is getting married?" she asked in disbelief.

"Yes, Laurie. I guess we did a good job, after all."

She tossed the covers off her, hitting him in the face. He pulled them down in time to see her legs cross over him as she bounced out of bed.

"When? And *I'm* the last to know?" she demanded, throwing on her robe and slippers.

His grin of satisfaction was as wide as the proverbial Cheshire cat's. "Usually, that's my position. But I beat you out on this one. As to when, I guess that's what they're talking about right now in the kitchen."

She ran a brush through her hair, threw it on the dresser and then hurried to the door. "A wedding! We can have poinsettias and mistletoe and holly. We'll have to contact the florist, the bakery, maybe a caterer . . ."

He never heard the rest as she ran downstairs.

The newly-engaged couple was fixing a huge Christmas breakfast while Laurie and Jack cleaned up the living room, folding the sheets and blankets and rolling

Dave's sleeping bag. As Jack tied it together, he glanced under the tree to the presents. Most of them were for Jess and the baby, but there was one . . . a small one . . .

"Hey, Laurie," he called out, picking it up and walking over to her. "This one's got your name on it."

Adding a folded sheet to the pile of bed linens, she turned to him and grinned. "Oh, yeah? I think we're supposed to wait until after breakfast to open presents. That's the way Jess planned it."

He shook his head. "I want you to open this one now. Jess won't mind."

She accepted the small present and then hurried to the tree. "Okay, then you have to open yours."

She held out a flat box, and felt silly for being so shy about it. "Go ahead. Open it."

He tore off the paper and lifted the lid.

"I know you don't wear jewelry, but when I saw it I thought of you."

He picked up the gold link chain with a Claddagh disk hanging from it.

"It's an Irish symbol—two hands holding a single heart," she said nervously.

"It's beautiful, Laurie," he answered, his voice rough with emotion. Looking at her, his eyes seemed to be telling her he understood. "Thank you."

He put it on and she stared at the gold hands nestled against his chest hair. It took a tremendous amount of will power not to reach up and touch it. Touch him. She didn't know how much longer she would be able to fight the urge. She knew what was at risk. Something awaited them, and they both knew it had to come soon, for Jessica's happiness was now established. How could she stand to give up Jack, and this life they had fallen into?

"Go ahead, open yours," he said, interrupting her thoughts.

She wouldn't cry, even though the thought of an existence, even a heavenly one, without Jack was unbearable. "Oh, Jack . . ."

An aquamarine was surrounded by tiny diamonds.

"When I saw the ring it reminded me of your eyes."

The tears came, as he took the ring out of the box and put it on her finger. Third finger. Left hand.

"Merry Christmas, Laurie."

She looked up from the ring and stared at him through the tears. "I love you, Jack. I don't care what happens anymore. I love you . . ."

His eyes filled with emotion and he forced a smile, as he gathered her into his arms. "I know . . . I can't fight it anymore. I love you, Laurie Reese. Whatever the repercussions are from this, we'll face them together."

They held each other tightly, as if waiting for a bolt of lightning to strike them.

It never came.

Chapter 20

Jess glanced at the sheet of paper Dave was filling out. "Vernon? Your middle name is Vernon?"

He grimaced. "Okay . . . so I was named after my grandfather."

"I think it's a very distinguished name," she said, rubbing her lower back as she looked down to the form in front of her. They were in the Municipal Building applying for their marriage license and, Margaret, their witness, had just left. "You don't hear of it very often."

"I know," Dave mumbled, and then looked up at her. "Hey, are you okay? Your back is still bothering you?"

Shrugging, Jess said, "I've had this annoying ache since Christmas Eve. If I had known it was going to be like this, I would have gotten myself in shape before getting pregnant. My muscles weren't prepared for carrying this kind of a load."

"You're doing fine. Better than fine. And it won't be long now." He went back to work on the questionnaire.

"You sound like Doctor Greenspan," she muttered, finished with the form. She didn't have to fill out as much as Dave, since her parents were deceased and she had never been married before. The wedding was in three days and Laurie was in charge of planning it. With her usual gusto, Laurie had organized the entire affair in one afternoon. It would be very small, with just the girls from the shop, Margaret, and Dave's parents as guests.

"What time are your parents coming in?"

"Their flight is due in at seven-fifty tomorrow night, and they're staying at my apartment. You know all this," he added, while looking through his divorce papers for some information. "Just calm down. They'll love you."

"Yeah. Sure." Jess started pacing in back of him, impatient for him to finish. Dave had called his parents and told them he was getting married. He also told them the baby was his. They would get a daughter-in-law and a grandchild all at once. It wasn't going to be easy. In fact, it was going to be damned difficult to pull this off. She didn't want to start her marriage with a lie, but Dave insisted that he already felt like the baby's father and it would be much simpler to let everyone else believe it. Why did she ever go along with him? She wasn't a good actress, and she knew his parents were going to see through her. They would think she was using him, and they'd hate her. How could she explain that she'd fallen in love with him after she became pregnant by another man? It didn't even make sense to her!

She tapped him on the back, and pointed to the opposite wall. "I have to use the bathroom."

He grinned, reading her expression. "Nervous?"

"No. Pregnant."

"Okay. I'm almost done here."

She waddled over to the door and just as she was about to push it open a sudden gush of water ran down her legs and puddled at her feet. She let out a tiny yelp, but was so startled that she could only stare down at the floor.

"Jess? What's . . . ?" Dave saw the dark stain on her maternity jumper and leaped to her side. "It's okay," he said soothingly. "It's only an accident. I bet this happens to all pregnant women. We'll take care of it."

She looked up at him and blinked for several seconds, before grabbing his arm for support. "It's not an accident," she said as her eyes filled with tears and embarrassment. "I think my water just broke."

Dave's eyes widened with shock. "Here? You're going into labor *here*?"

His question was so ridiculous that she started laughing. "It's not like I picked this place." She held onto his arm and nodded toward the bathroom door. "We'll go in here and get some paper towels to clean this up and—"

"Are you crazy?" he demanded. "We've got to get to the hospital!"

"Is there a problem?" a clerk politely asked over the counter.

"Yes, my wife's in labor! Call an ambulance or a doctor—"

Jess squeezed on his arm to stop him. "I'm not your wife yet," she said calmly, and then smiled at the startled woman who was taking their marriage application. "I'm fine. My water just broke and, as soon as I clean this up, we'll get in the car and drive to the hospital." She looked at Dave. "That is, if you're capable of driving."

"I can drive," he stated in a controlled voice.

"Good. Now go in the bathroom and bring out some paper towels. A lot of them."

He looked up at the sign. It was the ladies' room. Shaking his head, he pushed on the door.

"You don't have to bother," the clerk said with a nervous smile. "I'll call maintenance. Can I do anything? Do you want to sit down?"

In spite of everything, Jess smiled back and shook her head. She was going to have her baby. Finally! After all these months of waiting, the time had finally come. She was so happy that she wanted to dance— but that would have to wait.

Dave burst out of the bathroom with his arms full

of paper towels. He threw them on the floor by her feet and said, "Okay, now let's go."

The clerk gathered up their papers and said, "Mr. Sawyer, you didn't sign this, and you don't want to leave your divorce papers here."

Dave hurried back to her, scribbled his name, and scooped up the divorce papers. "Could you put a rush on this?" he asked in a worried voice.

The woman smiled. "Sure. And good luck!"

He put his arm around Jess and said, "Maybe I should carry you to the car."

Jess leaned on him and giggled. "I don't think it's a good idea. One sore back in this family is enough. Now let's do this calm and peaceful. That's the way I want our child to come into this world. Calm and peaceful. We go to the car. We go to the hospital. We have this baby."

"Right," Dave sort of agreed. "Calm and peaceful. I can do that . . ."

Laurie slammed the phone down and shouted to Jack, "Jess just went into labor! That was Dave. Her water broke when they were getting their marriage license."

Standing in front of the cash register, Jack stared at her. He felt the color drain out of his face as he watched her race into the store room. She had their coats and her purse as she rushed up to him.

"C'mon," she urged, throwing him his coat. "Let's get there."

"Laurie, maybe we should let them be alone. Dave's going to be the father and—"

"What are you saying?" she demanded with an incredulous expression. *"We're* her coaches. We made it through this entire pregnancy and you're not going to chicken out now—So you can just forget it! She's depending on us, Jack. Now get a move on. I'm driving."

Following her out the front door of the shop, he told himself that he'd been in worst situations when he was a cop. This should be a piece of cake. Jess was the one that was going to have to do all the work. So why then was he breaking out in a sweat when it was the dead of winter?

Calm and peaceful!

"I want drugs!" Jess gasped, as another hard contraction hit her.

"Just breathe, dear," the elderly nurse advised, then looked at Dave. "Are you her coach? You should be helping her."

"I'm not her coach," he said helplessly. "They're on their way."

"I don't care about breathing and coaches! I tried it and it doesn't work! This . . . isn't like what they said . . ." Jess groaned as the contraction subsided. "Please," she begged. "Give me something. Morphine. Anything!"

"I can't give you any medication until your doctor arrives. From what you've told me, you've probably been in labor for some time now. You're already dilated six centimeters, so you should be happy it's going so fast.''

Jess grabbed Dave's sleeve and brought him closer to her. ''Don't listen to her,'' she ordered in a voice straight out of *The Exorcist.* ''Get my doctor, and *get me drugs*!''

''We're going to put this monitor on you so we can tell when you're having contractions,'' the nurse said, ignoring Jess' outburst.

Dave moved out of the way as Jess cried, ''*I* can tell when I'm having a contraction—when I feel like I'm being torn in two! Oh, God, not again!''

''Breathe, like you practiced,'' the nurse said in a strict teacher's voice. ''You're not trying, Jessica.''

''I am!'' Jess moaned in agony while rolling to her side. But nothing would stop the pain . . .

''We're here!'' Laurie announced as she and Jack burst into the room dressed in hospital scrubs. ''How're you doing?''

Dave looked at them with a helpless expression. ''Not well.''

The nurse said, ''Are you her coach?''

Laurie nodded. ''Both of us are.''

''Then who's this?'' she asked, indicating Dave.

''He's the father,'' Jack answered. ''He wasn't here for the classes, so Jess' doctor said all of us could assist her.''

There. It was settled. The nurse waited until the contraction was over, put on the fetal monitor, and checked the machine next to Jess' bed. She looked at

Laurie and said, "She's losing control, and she's well into the second stage of labor. Get to work before transition begins."

Laurie nodded and took Jess' hand when the nurse left them alone. "Okay, Jess," she said soothingly. "We can do this. We practiced—"

"It doesn't work!" Jess cried. "I tried, and it doesn't work!"

"Sure it does. Now we have to concentrate. Oh God, where's her bag? We forgot the bag!" Laurie looked at Jack with panic in her eyes. "She's supposed to concentrate on the music box!"

"I'll go back and get it," Dave offered.

Jess grasped his wrist and shook her head. "It would take too long. I want you here."

When the next contraction came, Laurie tried to make her breathe in the correct pattern, but Jess was losing it. She would start off right, but when the contraction reached its peak, she would break her concentration and writhe in pain.

"What do we do?" Laurie looked at Jack with a frightened expression. "It isn't working like in class."

Jack, standing at the foot of the bed, knew he had to push down his own panic. They were all too close, too involved, and the labor hadn't progressed as they were taught. All of them were losing it. Forcing himself to remember what he'd been taught, Jack knew he had to stay detached. All those years on the force came back with a vengeance.

"All right, Jess," he said in an impersonal voice. "Now I want you to listen to me." He grabbed her foot beneath the sheet and held it tight as another contraction began. "I want you to look at my face, and nowhere else. We're going to begin with a deep breath and start blowing out in short breaths. We're doing it together. You, and me. *Now!*"

He talked her through the contraction and when she looked like she was going to lose it, he became more firm and applied more pressure to her foot so she would concentrate on something else beside the pain.

Dave and Laurie backed off, letting him take control. Even when Jess went into transition labor, Jack wouldn't let her slip into panic. She was doing beautifully, working with Jack to ride out each contraction, and Laurie and Dave became her cheerleaders. It was a team, all four of them, that joined the doctor in the delivery room.

"Now, push, Jess—and hold it!" Doctor Greenspan worked between her legs. "I have the head . . . just have to turn the shoulder a bit."

Dave was behind her, supporting her shoulders. Laurie was on one side of her, clutching Jess' hand, letting her tears soak into her face mask. Jack was on her other side, next to her legs so she could see his face.

"All right, now blow!" Jack commanded. "Don't push anymore. Not yet. Hold on, we're almost there." He was breathing with her and the front of his mask was going in and out of his mouth.

"A few more seconds here," the doctor said, and then, "now push, Jess. Come on, let's see if we have a boy or a girl here."

Everyone seemed to strain with her, bearing down and pushing this child into the world.

"It's a girl," Dr. Greenspan announced, holding the slippery infant in his arms.

"A little girl . . ." Jess' expression was filled with wonder as she stared at her child.

"A girl," Dave said, pulling his face mask down and kissing Jess. "I knew it!"

Laurie was crying, holding her hands over her mouth as the baby joined her with a healthy, lusty hail of life. "Oh, Jess . . ." she exclaimed, ". . . you did it!"

Jack pulled his face mask off and closed the distance between them. He looked down at Jessica, soaked with sweat and white as a sheet, and bent to gently kiss her cheek. "I have never been so proud of anyone," he said, his voice filled with emotion. "Congratulations, you have a daughter."

Jess grabbed his hand and brought it to her lips. "Thank you, Jack. I could never have done it without you."

"Who's going to cut the cord?" the doctor asked.

Laurie and Jack looked at each other. Jess had asked that they do it together, but it was as if they understood their task was at its end. They really weren't needed anymore.

"The father will do it," Jack stated, looking at Dave.

Dave smiled his thanks and took the instrument from the doctor. When the mother and child were separated, a nurse cleaned the baby and handed her to Jess.

Laurie and Jack stood to one side, looking at the new family. Jack's hand reached for Laurie's and he pulled her into his arms.

"Thank you, guys," Jess called out to them, her face beaming with pride. "Thank you—for everything. Now, come meet Laura Jacqueline Sawyer . . . your godchild."

It was the first time they were ever alone in the house for the night. Something was strange. Laurie could feel it ever since they left the hospital. The ride home was oddly silent. Questions about the baby were answered with single words. When they'd come into the house, Laurie had announced that she was taking a shower. Jack merely nodded as he fell into a chair in the living room, waiting his turn. While she towel dried her hair in her bedroom she could hear the shower running, and her thoughts were scrambled inside her mind as she sat on the bed. She kept picturing Jack as he had worked with Jess. If she wasn't already in love with him, that certainly would have done it. God, she admired him. He was so strong and yet gentle. And he was scared, too. He'd been scared since the first Lamaze class, yet he put another before him because that person was in need. He must have been one hell of a cop.

She looked down to the ring on her finger and wanted to cry. For herself. For Jack. For what would never be . . .

It was as if something was crawling up her back,

making her break out in goosebumps. She felt his presence behind her and turned around. Standing in her doorway in a white terry cloth robe, he looked as tortured as she felt.

She stood up and stared at him, her heart beating in her ears.

"I don't care anymore," he said roughly as he walked up to her. "It's over now, and we both know it." Pulling her into his embrace, he whispered against her ear, "I can't lose you, Laurie. Not now. Not now . . ."

"We don't know what we're risking," she whispered back, almost choking on her tears. "It could mean eternity."

"If it's with you, then I'll welcome it."

His kiss was possessive and filled with love, and Laurie moaned as she clutched him to her. It was feverish and uncontrollable. Hands stroking and fondling. Lips hungry and voracious. He untied her robe and slid it down her arms.

"Oh, God, Laurie . . . I've waited so long. You're beautiful." He admired her body while she took his robe off.

Touching the gold pendant of two hands clasping one heart, she whispered, "Come close. I have to feel you against me."

It was a searing heat of two bodies consumed with passion, a passion that had been denied for almost a year. Both of them cried out with pleasure and a bittersweet pain, twin emotions that mirrored their souls.

"I love you, Jack Lannigan. I always will. Whatever happens, I'll love you!"

He started to tell her that he would risk damnation, anything, for her, when the dizziness began. It was swift and vicious, making him weak. His knees buckled and Laurie tried to hold him up, but she was fading before him, disappearing into the white tunnel.

"Laurie!" He tried to call out to her, but his throat was raw as if he'd been screaming.

It sucked him in with a frightening speed. All around him he heard voices telling him not to look at the light. To turn away from it. Part of him wanted to follow Laurie, to find her, and yet he felt helpless against the shadowy voices that told him to turn away.

He was floating somewhere, drifting with a current that was peaceful and warm. He felt protected and safe, as if he were a child again. There was a riverbank in front of him and he saw his grandfather smiling at him from the side.

"You must go back, Jackie," he said in a gentle voice. "It isn't your time. Your task isn't finished yet."

He tried to speak, but couldn't.

"Be a good boy now, and go home," his grandpop said. "Your mom is calling you."

Jack listened and he could hear her voice.

"Do you hear me? Jack! Do you hear me? Open your eyes . . ."

He fought the heaviness in his lids and it took a few seconds before he could do as his mother commanded.

When he did, he saw her face in front of him. She was crying and shouting for a nurse.

"Oh, thank God. You've come back to us! I never gave up hope . . . never!"

Her tears fell over him as she kissed his face.

Chapter 21

"I know you can hear me. Open your eyes this time. Please . . ."

She heard the male voice commanding her, but it seemed like her eyelids were weighted down. Fighting the heaviness, she tried again. The light hurt her eyes, and she shut them quickly.

"You're doing it," the voice said with excitement. "Come on, Laurie. Show me."

And then she knew who was speaking to her.

It was her father.

Confused, she opened her eyes and attempted to focus.

He was leaning over her, looking so old, and . . .

and crying. She tried to open her mouth to tell him he needed a shave, but it hurt too much and a garbled sound came out. Machines were all around her, and she could hear beeping noises coming from them.

"Oh, baby . . . you're going to be okay. Don't try to talk. Let me call for the nurse." He did something out of her line of vision, and then came back to smile at her. Wiping the tears from his cheeks, he said, "Wait until your mother hears this. We've been taking turns and she went home this morning. But, you know her, she's probably at church."

A young nurse came into the room, carrying a chart and approached the bed. "Well, hello," she said with surprise as she picked up Laurie's wrist and took her pulse. "We've been waiting a long time to meet you."

Laurie could merely stare, as the woman listened to her heart.

"Good and strong. I'll page your doctor. I'm sure you have a lot of questions, even though you can't talk right now."

"I don't think she knows what happened," her father said, and the nurse nodded as she picked up the chart and read it.

"I'll try to explain it, but when your doctor comes he'll give you a more detailed description. Let's see. During surgery you aspirated, because there was food in your stomach that shouldn't have been there. Tonsillectomies are tough on adults and you had a bad reaction to the anesthesia. You went into cardiac arrest, and they coded you for forty minutes."

She looked up and explained. "The OR team worked on you with closed chest massage and different medications, but they weren't getting anything. It seems they were ready to walk away when everything kicked in and you came back. But your brain was denied oxygen and you've been unconscious for well over a week now."

Confused, Laurie tried to talk but there was a terrible pressure in her throat and she started to fight against it.

The nurse grabbed her hand before she could do anything and said, "We'll pull that tube out for you. You're on a respirator; I know you don't like it, and it's uncomfortable and unnatural. But we can give you something to help you until we get a hold of your doctor and get it out. In fact, I'm going to call him now."

She patted Laurie's arm. "I'll be right back. Hold on."

Her father came into view and started talking about how worried he and her mother were. She tried to make sense out of it, but couldn't. It was as if her memory had failed her, and she was too tired to think . . .

"Technically, you suffered a fractured skull complicated by severe cerebral edema. It wasn't localized, and there was nothing we could drain, so we had to wait it out and see if you came around on your own.

We can never predict what's going to happen until the patient wakes up. And you took quite a while waking up."

Jack's mom squeezed his hand. "Now you're going to be just fine. Isn't that right, Doctor?"

The man closed his chart and smiled. "Let's put it this way, Mrs. Lannigan. Your son isn't about to walk out of here just yet, but I would think he should make a complete recovery."

Jack's dad seemed to be trying to keep his composure. "How long, Doctor, before he can come home?"

"We're not going to rush anything. Remember, we almost lost him in the beginning; we had to work on him for twenty minutes to bring him back. And we've just taken him off the respirator. I know the two of you have been through a lot, but be a little more patient. All right?"

Jack forced the words out of his mouth. They finally took the tube out of his throat, and disconnected all the machines, except the heart monitor, but his throat was scratchy and raw. And he had one hell of a headache. "I . . . I thought I broke . . . my neck."

Everyone looked at him. The doctor shook his head. "Why did you think that?"

Jack didn't know why. He vaguely remembered someone telling him, a man, but he couldn't remember who he was. Everything was confusing.

"Don't worry if you can't remember things. Everything should come back to you in a couple of days. I'll check on you in the morning," the doctor told

Jack, and then shook hands with his father before leaving.

His mother continued to hold his hand. "Oh, Jack, you should have seen all the flowers and baskets of fruit. We took the fruit home with us, and the flowers died, but I saved all the cards for you. Even the boys on the street came in to see you. Poor Joey Marchetti. He's been so upset. His mother said he feels responsible, and he's even gone back to serving Mass during the week. Oh, and he left this for you . . ."

She opened the drawer in the table next to the bed and took out an old football. "He said to tell you when you woke up, that you made the touchdown."

Jack tried to smile. That's right. That's how it all started. He was playing touch football with the kids on his parent's block. He'd hit a tree and somebody told him he'd broken his neck. Who was *that*?

His mother started to close the drawer when she said, "And, Jack, the strangest thing . . ." She pulled something else out. "One morning your dad and I came in here and you were wearing this."

She held up a gold chain. Attached to it was a charm of some sort. He looked closer.

It was an Irish symbol.

Two hands holding a heart.

"We couldn't figure it out," his dad said, as he came to stand by the bed. "Somebody must have come in here and put it on you. We asked the nurses, but no one seemed to know anything about it."

Jack kept staring at it, feeling almost sick to his stomach.

"She had blue eyes," he whispered.

"Who?" his mom asked.

"A woman you know?" his dad suggested.

Tears sprang into his eyes and he looked at his parents with a helpless expression. "I can't remember."

He was nervous. He walked around her room, fussing with flowers or straightening her blanket. When her lunch arrived, he sat by her bed, making sure she ate. He wouldn't leave her alone, and her mother had to force him to go home at night.

"What is it, Dad?" she asked, pushing away the movable tray. She really wasn't hungry. Her mother told her he had practically camped in her room since they were called about the complications with her surgery. She found that piece of news hard to believe, since he rarely had time for her when she was growing up, and even less since she had left home. But then everything was confusing now. Especially the dreams at night. Those scared the hell out of her, because they seemed so real.

Charlie Reese tried to smile, but it wasn't successful. His lower lip trembled with emotion. "I want to talk to you, Laurie, and I don't know how to begin."

"Just begin," Laurie said, wondering what he could have to say to her.

"I . . . I wasn't a good father. And I'm sorry."

Laurie's stomach tightened. She didn't want to have

this conversation. Too many years had passed. "Dad, don't—"

"No. I need to." His eyes filled and he looked at her with a pleading expression. "I . . . I was so busy trying to make a living, and I didn't . . . have time for you and your mother. Not like I should have. I gave your mother a lot of grief, and I'm not proud of myself. But it wasn't until this happened to you that I realized how much I had missed. I worked and worked, but I never really accomplished anything. You, Laurie— you're the only thing in my life that turned out right. Despite me, you turned into a terrific woman." He was pouring his heart out to her and pleading for forgiveness. "And . . . and when I thought you might die—when they told me your heart stopped on the operating table and that you were clinically dead for almost an hour—I realized that I had never told you that I loved you . . . and how proud I am of you."

He was crying freely, clutching the sheet in his fist, and begging her to understand.

Laurie wiped the tears from her cheek and said in a shaky voice, "Something happened to me, Dad, when . . . when I was out. I don't understand it. Maybe it's part of the dreams I'm having at night . . . I don't know anymore. But I can remember almost floating above the operating table and looking down at the doctors and nurses working on me. I wasn't upset; I didn't have any feeling for that person on the table. I was . . . detached, I guess. Then there was a darkness in front of me, something circular and moving, with a white light at the end. It's impossible to describe.

Except as I moved through it at an incredible rate of speed, I was filled with such peace . . . almost joy. And then I was in a valley, a beautiful place, and a woman was talking to me. I can't remember what she said. When I try, I get dizzy and frightened, but I know something important happened. Something that changed my life.''

She placed her hand over his and held it tightly. ''I was so angry with you growing up. I never felt you cared about Mom or me. And I didn't respect you, for a lot of reasons.'' Her voice was shaky, but she forced herself to continue as she repeated, ''Something happened to me, Dad. I've changed. I wish I could remember, because I've realized what's important in life. It isn't money or security. It's people. Mom. My friends. And . . . and you. Maybe we can get to know each other now.''

He stood up and wrapped his arms around her as he cried against her hair. ''I do love you, Laurie. I'm so sorry for all the wasted years.''

She smiled and sniffled back her own tears. It was the first time she could remember her father hugging her.

''I love you, too, Dad.''

''That's right. Just put one foot in front of the other. Man . . . you are shufflin' now!''

Jack couldn't even smile as he concentrated with the effort it took to walk down the hallway of the hospital.

Simon, his physical therapist, was watching the slow progress.

"Is it true? You're a cop?"

Jack nodded, shaky and frustrated with his weakness.

"Damn, I wish you were the one that saw me smokin' weed last month. I *know* I could've outrun you."

In spite of everything, Jack laughed. "You got busted, huh?"

"Can't figure it out, either. Me and my woman was sittin' in the car, ready to go into a club. It wasn't like we was driving, or anythin'. And this young cop comes up to us and busts us. For what? Everybody knows reefer is better for you than booze. Maybe not better, you understand . . . makes you mellow, not arrogant. You ain't gonna pick a fight on reefer."

"It's the law," Jack answered, looking up to the nurses' station. That was his goal. He couldn't wait to reach it, and turn around to go back to his room.

"Then the law should change," Simon pronounced. "People got to have somethin' to make life bearable." He put his hand under Jack's arm to support him while they moved aside for someone being discharged.

A woman carrying flowers bumped into him, and a mylar balloon hit him in the face.

"I'm so sorry," she said in an excited voice, and then looked down to the patient in the wheelchair. "I guess I was so happy to be bringing my daughter home that I wasn't looking."

"It's okay," Jack muttered, envious of the blond haired woman that was being wheeled to the elevator. He couldn't wait to get out of here.

"Think you can do anythin' for me, Jack? My hearing's in two weeks."

Jack looked at Simon as they approached the nurses' station. "He caught you red-handed."

"But I wasn't doin' nothin'! One of the charges is a thirty-seven, thirty-somethin', about driving with drugs. And I wasn't drivin'!"

"I'll see what I can do, Simon," Jack said, to stop his outburst. "Write everything down. But I can't promise anything." Suddenly there was an odd drawing sensation taking place inside of him.

At that moment he looked up in time to see the woman being wheeled into the elevator. The attendant turned the chair around, so she was facing out and pushed the button for the doors to close.

His heart skipped a beat and then started hammering in his chest. Sweat broke out on his forehead and in his armpits, and began to run down his back.

"Wait!" He wanted to shout, yet only a hoarse whisper came out. But the doors closed, and she was gone.

"What's wrong?" Simon asked, supporting his arm. "You look like you just seen a ghost."

"Who was that woman?"

"Huh? What woman?"

"The one that just got on the elevator. Who was she?"

Simon looked at the elevator and shrugged. "How

342

would I know, man? Somebody being discharged. There's eleven of them goin' home this mornin' from this floor alone. Why?''

The craziest thing was that he didn't know why he needed to find out. There was something about her . . . he couldn't put his finger on it. Maybe he knew her, or saw her in the hall before. It was more than that. He felt connected to her in some way. It was stupid, as crazy as the dreams he was having.

"Come on," Simon urged. "Let's get you back to your room. We've done enough today. I don't need you flippin' out on me with your first look at a pretty face."

He felt foolish for his reaction, and nodded. More tired than ever he shuffled back to his room. After Simon left him alone, he opened the drawer in the table next to his bed and took out the gold chain. He held it in his hand for a few moments as the pendant warmed next to his skin. Claddagh. That's what the Irish nurse told him it was. A symbol of love. In his entire life he had never worn jewelry, except for his high school ring in his senior year. He thought men that did looked silly, adorning themselves with gold chains and rings with diamonds to show off their station in life. That was a woman's thing. Not a man's.

So it was totally illogical for him to slip the chain over his head and press the pendant against his skin. But then, nothing was making sense any more.

* * *

"There's a cocktail party next week to benefit Children's Hospital, and the week after that a dinner for

Women in Business. I haven't got a thing to wear. Melissa is bringing out her St. Laurent *again*. Good God, she wears it to everything—Are you listening, Laurie?"

Standing at the window overlooking Rittenhouse Square, Laurie glanced at her friend. "Yes, Rita, I'm listening. A cocktail party and dinner. And Melissa's St. Laurent."

Rita was flipping through her filoFax. "Good. Oh, and a 10K race through Fairmont Park on the twenty-eighth for the Diabetes Foundation, but no one would expect you to go to that one. Can I borrow your Donna Karan for the Children's Hospital thing?"

Laurie smiled and nodded as Rita continued to tick off the many social functions that her crowd supported. Looking out the window of her apartment, Laurie tuned out Rita's voice. It was good to be back in her own place. She had stayed with her parents for a few days after leaving the hospital, but she knew she couldn't continue to hide out there. She had to get her life back in order. The funny thing was, her life seemed so meaningless. At one time she would have been thrilled to know her social calendar was filled, and would have felt she was doing something important for others. But all the dinners and cocktail parties and races for charities were really just a way for people to meet—For men and women to meet, would be more honest. It was her generation's alternative to a dating service, or being fixed up with the single accountant your mother met. Through charities it was possible to see, and be seen, by people with the same outlook on life. Ambitious Professionals. That's what they really were. Maybe she should start a new organization. She could see the brochure . . . *Materialistic? Self-centered? Want to reminisce about your investments in the '80's, and the great money you made in junk bonds? Come meet the Post-Yuppie of your dreams.*

"Laurie, will you come and sit down? I'm talking to your back and you're not even listening."

Leaving her view at the window, Laurie sat opposite Rita in one of the love seats she had bought from Bloomingdale's French Country Collection. She had spent more on the furniture in this apartment than some heads of households make in a year. What a waste . . . "I'm sorry," she apologized. "I guess I was daydreaming."

Rita nodded and sipped her espresso. "Well, I was telling you about this new girl in the office. Charlene. Calls herself Charlie, can you imagine? Right out of Penn, and Alex was letting her use your office while you were out."

"Does she have long, blond hair?" Laurie didn't know why she asked.

"Exactly . . . you know the type. Young, bubbly, energetic. Anyway, she wants to join Women in Business and she's looking for a sponsor. She's in your department, so when you go back to work maybe you could check her out. When are you coming back?"

Laurie shrugged. "I don't know. I'm just not ready yet. Soon, I guess."

Rita nodded. "Well, be prepared to hear all about

Alex's holiday on the Cote d'Azur. If he shoves those pictures in my face one more time, I swear I'll tell him I don't give a *merde* about the color of the Mediterranean, or meeting Joan Collins in Port Grimaud. Oh, and then there's Sam—he thinks he's finally met his princess. All the right qualifications. Age. Family. Religion. Social standing. Already planning the Reception Atop The Bellevue. I'll give him three years and his first child, and he'll be back hanging out at the River Cafe in Manyunk looking for fresh meat.''

Rita sat back against the down-filled cushion and sighed. "You know, I really admire you, Laurie. You never needed a man in your life to feel complete. I mean, if one was there, it was great. But if you were alone, you seemed just fine. I wish I could be more secure.''

Not wanting to comment, Laurie looked down to the ring she wore on her finger. Her parents told her the nurses had removed it and had given it to them with her other personal belongings when she'd been in the coma. She didn't remember when she got it, but it seemed important to her and, for some strange reason, she felt less frightened when she wore it. The woman Rita was talking about seemed like a stranger to her. Independent and secure? Now there was an emptiness in her heart. She felt a loss, as if she were grieving. As if she had something, or someone, very important to her . . . but now it was gone.

"You seem changed, Laurie. More quiet, or something.''

Laurie looked up from her hand and smiled. "I am,

Rita. My father found a support group for people who have gone through similar situations and he thinks I should go. Maybe I will.''

"It's got to help to talk about it. My God, what a nightmare you've gone through.''

Laurie looked surprised. "But it wasn't a nightmare, Rita,'' she said with certainty. "I can't explain why, but for some reason, I know it was something wonderful.''

Chapter 22

"Hey, how're you doing?" Phil Polis asked with a smile and held out his palm. "Heard you were back."

Jack slapped his hand and grinned. "Couldn't keep me away."

"Yeah, right . . ." Phil laughed and continued out of the department.

Looking at the man walking away, Jack felt an eerie sense of déjà vu, as if this had all happened before. He mentally shook himself. Of course, it did. He must have seen Phil four times a week for the past seven years. But there was something odd about seeing him again. That dull ache began in his head and he made his way over to his desk.

The doctors had cleared him to go back to work on limited duty, but he hated working inside, typing reports and shuffling papers around like a short timer ready for retirement. He was a street cop. He should be out there doing his job, not filing arrest reports for the rest of the department. He felt like a damn Kelly girl.

Frustrated, he started to put the reports in numerical order when a cup of coffee and a glazed doughnut appeared at his side.

"Sure you're ready for a sugar high?" Mike asked and fell into his chair opposite Jack. "Might be a jolt for someone with your delicate constitution."

Jack grabbed the sticky doughnut. "Screw you," he said, before biting into it.

Rafferty grinned. "I wish someone would. Theresa says I smell like a dumpster and won't even sleep in the same bed with me."

Laughing, Jack picked up the coffee. "Smart woman. She was always too good for you. And you do smell. When was the last time you bathed?"

"It's these clothes," Mike said defensively. "No matter how many showers I take, the stench continues."

Mike was working undercover with the ninth district as a homeless person and he was dressed for the part. Unshaven, wearing layers of tattered clothing, he looked like he lived on the streets. "Then leave the clothes in your locker, or something," Jack said and leaned back in his chair to get away from the distinct aroma.

"I'm not gonna stink up my locker. I'd never get rid of it." Mike shook his head. "Scampeca's a mail man, do you believe that? And he's bitching about his feet. *I'm* sitting on the sidewalk, like Pepe Le Peu, checking out the entrance to this Chinese Restaurant, and a woman comes up to me and tries to steal my hat!" He ran his fingers over the brim of his old White Sox baseball cap, just to make sure it was still there. "*A woman!* What the hell is the world coming to?"

Jack laughed and it felt good.

"Glad to hear that chuckle, pal. You had me worried there."

"Yeah? Why?"

Mike shrugged. "I don't know . . . a lot of people are talking about how different you are. Quiet, I guess."

Nodding, Jack said in a low voice, "I feel different, Mike. I don't know—this is going to sound crazy, but when they were working on me I knew I was dead. I was just pissed off because after Nam and all the years on the force, I bit it from some stupid accident playing football with kids."

Mike leaned closer and Jack didn't seem to mind the smell. "You mean you actually *knew* you were dead? Like one of those near-death experiences?"

Jack looked at Mike's expression to see if he could detect any ridicule. Not finding it, he decided to continue. Hell, he needed to talk to somebody. Who better than his best friend?

"Mike, the damndest thing happened. I was told I was dead. By some man, and I can't remember him.

350

Hell, I can't remember a lot of what happened, but I *know* something did. Something important. I keep having these dreams about clothes, boxes and boxes of clothes. And a baby. It's Christmas, and there's a woman . . . a woman with blue eyes. There's something about her. Like I've lost her, or something, and I don't know how to find her."

"A woman," Mike asked, with definite interest.

"She's important to me. I can only remember her eyes. When I try to fit a face to the picture, my head starts pounding like a son of a bitch."

"Maybe you're not supposed to remember."

He shook his head. "Then why does it bother me so much? Why can I remember things like floating in a stream and seeing my grandfather standing at the side and telling me to go back, that my mother was calling me? And then I actually hear my mother and that's when I wake up in the hospital. No, Mike. This woman is important. It's like a case I can't solve."

"I don't know, Jack. I think maybe you're reading too much into it."

"All right. How about this?" He unbuttoned his shirt and pulled out the Claddagh. "My parents said this was on me in the hospital, but I didn't have it when I was brought in. I'd never seen it before. *Somebody* put this on me. When I look at it, I think of the woman. Or, at least see her eyes. I'm telling you, Mike, it's driving me nuts. I can't sleep because when I do, I have these dreams. If I try to remember I get a headache. I have to do something."

"Okay. What can we do?"

That was the reason Mike was his closest friend, why they had remained partners for six years. No matter what happened between them there was always total acceptance.

Jack sighed with relief. Mike didn't think he was crazy, but then again Mike had walked the edge of reality a few times himself. And he believed in all that New Age crap and actually meditated, so this one should be right up his alley.

"There was this woman in the hospital. She was being released and, for some reason, I thought she might be the one. I know it's a long shot, but I want to check it out."

"So what's the problem?"

"This guy, he's in physical therapy, was picked up for sitting in the car with his girlfriend and smoking a joint. Some rookie in the fourth district collared him." Jack pushed the report across his desk for Mike to read. "It's a zero, and he's got no priors. Can you call your friend in the D.A.'s office and see what she can do?"

Mike flipped through the papers. "I don't get it. He'll probably only get a suspended, no prob, or anything."

"Yeah, I know, but the guy is paranoid about it. And if I take care of this, he can go through records and get me the names of all the women who were discharged on that day. If I try to do it officially, it'll cause problems—and I don't want to explain this one to Rosselli."

Mike glanced up at their lieutenant's office and nodded. "Yeah . . . I don't think he'd be too pleased." He threw the file on his desk. "Okay, I'll call downtown and see what I can do. Now what do you say we go to Kelly's? It's time you bought me a beer."

Jack picked up the phone and dialed Simon Carter's home phone number. As he waited for someone to answer, he put his hand over the speaker and muttered, "I'm not going anywhere with you like that. Jesus, you stink!"

There were five of them, all of them quiet and anxious. They sat in metal chairs, clasping their hands together, or shifting in their seats and glancing at each other with nervous smiles. Three women, two of them in their sixties, looked at the men sitting next to one another as if for male support.

The room was really a large office in the hospital, Laurie realized, for on the desk were pictures of children, a small asparagus fern and personal belongings that make working a little more tolerable.

A woman entered the room and shut the door behind her. She looked at the group and smiled. "Good. I'm glad you're all here." She sat on the edge of her desk and introduced herself. "My name is Carol Bailey, and I'm a psychological counselor here at the hospital. The reason I formed this group is because six years ago I was in a car accident on the Roosevelt Boulevard, and the most amazing thing happened to me. I seemed

353

to walk away from the wreck, as other people were rushing to it to help. I could see them, but they didn't seem to notice me. They would just keep running up to the car, with their eyes straight ahead. I remember thinking how strange it was that no one was concerned about me. And that's when I realized they couldn't see me.''

She had everyone's attention and continued. ''The next sensation was one of floating above the scene. I saw them trying to get me out, but I wasn't concerned about it. Everything appeared to be getting further and further away and, when it all receded, I entered, head first, into a very dark passageway. I couldn't see the edges of it, but I perceived them to be rounded, as if in a tunnel. It was very peaceful. A wonderful, worry-free, experience. At the end of this tunnel was a yellow-white light and I thought I must have died, but I felt no pain at all. As I entered this exquisite light, I was filled with love, great, great, love. Complete safety. Perfection. I felt euphoric.

''There were beings around me. I say beings because I couldn't see their faces distinctly, but they could communicate with me, and it was total love. Then I saw my aunt, who had died twenty years before. She spoke to me, telling me I should go back, that it wasn't my time yet. In what seemed like an instant, I awoke in the hospital, in pain and totally confused.''

Carol took a deep breath and walked around her desk to sit down. No one in the room spoke as they waited for her next words.

"I kept trying to make sense out of what I had experienced. At that time, when I attempted to talk about it with others, they tended to look at me as if I'd gone temporarily nuts." Everyone nodded, or smiled in agreement.

"Then I did a little research and found recorded histories of life after life experiences, as far back as a sixth century monk. And the fascinating thing is that so many of these experiences are the same. So . . ." And she looked at the five people seated in front of her. ". . . I started to counsel others who had gone through the tunnel. You aren't losing your minds. Or suffering from contagious hysteria. And it isn't wish fulfillment. Each of you are profoundly changed by what you have experienced, and this is a safe, accepting place for you to share your thoughts if you chose to do so."

No one wanted to go first, so Carol said, "Okay. Maybe the best way is to introduce ourselves and what we do for a living."

One of the older women was a retired bookkeeper for a major oil company. The other was a homemaker. The heavyset man was a long distance truck driver and the taller, well dressed one was an architect. Laurie closed the circle, thinking how different each of them were.

They began speaking slowly, revealing how each had "died." The homemaker had a heart attack. The bookkeeper was shot at a convenience store robbery. The truck driver was in a seven-car pileup on the turnpike, and the architect had been drowning after a boating accident. They started talking about distancing themselves from their bodies, about the tunnel and the brilliant light. They spoke of communicating with others, judgments . . . being accountable for actions and even thoughts. But no one related anything like what was troubling Laurie, so she remained more quiet than the others. After about an hour and a half, Carol ended the meeting by inviting them all to come back in two weeks.

Laurie didn't think she would.

When she was leaving, Carol asked if she would remain.

"Something more is troubling you," Carol said in a gentle voice. "Would you like to talk about it?"

Laurie shrugged. "I don't know how to talk about it. I can't even remember what it is. I only know I went through the tunnel and the light, and I came to a beautiful valley where someone talked to me. I think it was a woman, but I know she wasn't a relative, or anything. Something happened to me there that was different from anything the others were relating. I . . . I have this feeling that I existed somewhere else for a long time."

"Are you talking about a past life experience?"

Shaking her head, Laurie said, "No. Not like that. I was . . . in some place, and I lived just as I am. As Laurie Reese. I think I had a task. Some job, I was supposed to accomplish. But when I try to piece any more together, I become dizzy and feel frightened. I dream about it. About a man and a woman and a baby. And I can't see their faces. But it's the man that affects me the most. I feel empty inside when I think about him. As if I've lost him."

Her eyes filled with tears. "I know none of it makes sense. My experience isn't . . . typical."

Carol touched her arm in comfort. "What I didn't tell the others is that before my accident, I was an agnostic—that, for me, no one could prove, or disapprove, the existence of God. Or know with a certainty the nature of ultimate truth. But I know it now. And so do you. We know now what's important in life, and it isn't making money or leaving our mark. Every day is precious to us, because we know there's an end to this existence. And we've been given this gift. We aren't afraid of death, right?"

Laurie thought for a moment. "I'm not afraid of dying anymore. But I am afraid that I'll die without finding this person that was so important to me. It was as if we were connected in some way. I wish I could explain it better."

"There are thousands of recorded cases, and in some of them people talk about connecting with beings that aren't old friends or members of their family. They describe the person in terms of being an angel, or a God-like presence. Sometimes they say this person is wearing a long white robe or a flowing gown—"

"Yes!" Laurie said with excitement. "It was a woman in a beautiful gown that I talked to and she gave me an assignment. A mission of some sort.

Maybe that's where I met the man." A wave of dizziness washed over her, making her weak and she grabbed the edge of the desk for support.

"Sit down a minute," Carol gently ordered. "And don't be afraid because you're remembering. Nearly all who witness what you did associate this with the presence of a Supreme Being. And as far as being away for a long time—that's the one thing every single account agrees with . . . there is no perception of time. A year could be a minute. Or vise versa. You'll remember what you're meant to remember. No more and no less. That's the one thing I've learned. To stop questioning everything. Life's too precious, Laurie."

She looked up into Carol's eyes and recognized the wisdom in them.

Life was too short.

But which life?

Simon Carter paced in front of the window of the coffee shop. His hands were curled into fists of anxiety and shoved into the pockets of his Sixers jacket, as he looked at each car slowing down for a red light. He'd watched the traffic light change six times and was starting to fear that he'd been stood up. Or, maybe he'd just screwed up the instructions. What the hell did he know about police shit, anyway? He'd managed to stay clear of 'em his entire life, not an easy accomplishment for an inner city kid. That's why being busted for pot struck fear into him. But what he really feared was his mother. Hell, he didn't even know his father. Only met him but once. It was his mother that raised him, worked two jobs, and put the fear of God into him about the street. He was supposed to be an example for his younger brothers and sisters, and if she found out about this she would put him up against the wall and beat the crap out of him. Funny thing was, he was a man now and could laugh at her slappin' away at him. What he couldn't take would be the disappointment in her eyes.

When a hand grabbed his upper arm, he let out a yelp and nearly jumped out of his skin.

"Sorry, I'm late. I had to park four blocks away."

Simon released his breath and squared his shoulders while his heart pounded away inside his chest.

"No problem," he said nervously. "I got what you wanted."

"Good. How about a cup of coffee?" Jack asked and nodded to the restaurant behind them.

"Can't. Got to get to work."

"I'll drop you off at the hospital on my way downtown. Let's go in and talk."

Jack looked around him, as if checking out the street and Simon quickly agreed. Damn, it wouldn't look too good to be standing around acting really chummy with a cop. A vice cop, at that. He knew too many people running numbers, and running women, for that matter. It was a way of life in his neighborhood. "Yeah, okay," he muttered and hurried to the door.

They were seated at a table with a chipped formica overlay, and Simon ran his finger over a loose section. "Never saw a man go to so much trouble just to find out a woman's name. Sure this ain't got nothin' to do with some case you're workin' on? I don't want to be hauled off to court to testify I was snoopin' through hospital records.''

Jack grinned. "I told you this was personal. What you ought to be worried about is being hauled off to court if you're ever picked up again for doing dope. I pulled some strings for you this time, but if it happens again you're on your own. I can't bury files, and you've got one now with your picture inside of it. Along with your fingerprints and an arrest report.''

Simon shook his head, as if not believing it himself. "I know. I'm scared to get a parkin' ticket in this town.''

"Just use your head. You've got too much going for you to be stupid. And I'm not going to lecture you. I did some pot in Nam, so I know what I'm talking about. It ain't reality. The real world's tough to get through, but you're not a loser, Simon. You've got a chance at a decent life if you don't flush it away.''

Simon nodded and looked over to the counter in time to see a man, in his late fifties, carrying a plastic container of dishes into the kitchen. It scared the hell out of him, for he'd seen too many men with that same lifeless expression. He always wondered what they had been like when they were young. If they had been filled with dreams, and thought they could whip the ass off the world and bend it to their wishes. What the hell happened, what wrong path did they take to wind up one of the walking dead? Maybe they just gave up.

"Okay, so it was a lecture," Jack added with a

smile, as he picked up his cup of coffee. "Just don't make me look like a fool for doing it."

Simon glanced back to the man across from him and grinned. "What makes you look like a fool, man, is bein' obsessed with findin' a woman you didn't even get a good look at." He took the piece of paper out of his jacket pocket and slid it over the table to him. "I hope she's worth it."

Looking down at the list of names, addresses and phone numbers, Jack murmured, "If she's who I think she is, then she's worth it."

One name stood out from the rest.

Lauren Reese.

Chapter 23

It was in one of the best neighborhoods in the city, close to the theater district and the classiest restaurants. A uniformed doorman stood behind a fancy desk in the spacious lobby, waiting to hold open a door or greet the tenants. It wasn't just a place to live, Jack thought as he stood on the sidewalk across the street and looked at the building. It was a symbol of money and class—two things Jack didn't have.

He couldn't go in.

He knew all he had to do was walk up to the doorman and ask for her name. The guy would buzz her and then he would see her face to face and have his answer. That had been his intention when he'd come here, but now he just couldn't do it. What if she wasn't the one, then what? And what if she was? Even though every instinct that he had depended on for twenty years on the force was pointing to it, he still had this irrational fear. What was he supposed to say to her? I think I died and met you . . . some place? Want to have a drink and find out? She'd slam the door in his face, and he wouldn't blame her.

He was losing it, that's all there was to it.

Disgusted with himself, he spun around and walked down the street toward the parking lot. He cursed himself for letting his imagination run wild. This wasn't like him. He was practical and—

Suddenly he stopped and turned, looking back at a phone booth. He could call her. At least that way he'd hear her voice.

Pulling out the paper Simon had given him, he slipped a quarter into the machine and dialed the number.

It rang four times, and he was about to give up when she answered.

"Hello."

Her voice sent a shock through his system and he leaned against the glass panel for support. "Is—is this Lauren Reese?"

"Yes?"

He had no idea what to say to her. Why didn't he prepare something?

"Hi, this is Jack Lannigan. You . . . ah, you don't know me. At least I don't think so. But you might." Christ, he sounded like an idiot! "Listen," he hurried to add before she hung up, "I know this might sound crazy to you, but could we meet? I have something important to discuss with you."

"Who is this?" Her voice sounded frightened, and he couldn't blame her.

"My name is Jack Lannigan and, just so you don't think I'm a lunatic, I work for the police force." He paused, waiting for a reaction. There wasn't any, so he then added, "Of course, with the press we've been getting lately that might not be a good recommendation."

She didn't laugh and he hurried to fill the awkward silence. "My badge number is eight six eight eight, and my lieutenant's name is Steve Rosselli—"

"Am I in trouble?" she interrupted in a voice so low that he had to strain to hear it over the noise on the street.

"No. No, not at all. I'm sorry if I gave you that impression. I only need to see you for a few minutes."

"I was just about to walk out the door."

He heard that evasive tone in her voice and knew he had to do something or she was going to break the connection. "I can meet you anywhere you want, anywhere you're comfortable. I need to talk to you about the hospital."

"The . . . hospital?" Her voice sounded frightened again.

"Yes. I'll explain it when I see you. I'm at a pay phone and it's really hard to hear over the traffic."

There was a pause, and then she said quickly, "I

have to pick up some books at Borders on Walnut. I should be there in fifteen minutes.''

''Great. I'll see you there.''

She hung up and Jack placed the receiver back on the hook. He stared at the phone for a few seconds and then looked up and down the street.

Borders? Where was it? Walnut, and what? And why the hell didn't the phone company put phone books in booths anymore? More scared than he was on his first date, he picked up the phone again and called information.

It was less than two blocks from her apartment and she made it in seven minutes. Out of breath, she gave the clerk her name and paid for the books she had ordered on near-death experiences. Taking her package with her, she hurried to the section of the store that was an espresso shop and sat down to wait. This was the most bizarre thing she had ever done . . . meeting a stranger who called her on the phone. She should have told someone, even Miguel, the doorman. But there was something about his voice. It frightened her . . . and excited her.

Jack Lannigan. Just thinking the name caused her pulse to quicken. Who was he? Did she meet him at the hospital and forget him? Her memory wasn't proving to be reliable, so it could be possible. But why did he make it sound so urgent? Jack . . . Jack . . . That name. That voice. They were so familiar. She must have met him before. Trouble was, how would she ever recognize him?

Ordering a cup of decaf, she brought out her books and pretended to read while scanning the store.

It wouldn't hurt to check him out before they met. But he never said what he looked like. Turning a page in the book, she realized it was upside down. She quickly righted it and glanced once more to the front door. Sighing, she looked over the racks. There were several men in the store, but none of them seemed to be meeting anyone. This really was stupid. She'd give him fifteen more minutes. If he didn't show then she would just go home. Home, where it was safe, and . . .

She felt him before she ever saw him. It was the strangest sensation, as if the nerve endings in her skin were picking up his presence. She turned her head slowly, afraid of what she would see.

And he was there.

In front of her.

Her mouth opened, yet no sound emerged as he closed the distance between them. Her stomach tightened painfully and her pulse was hammering at her temple, making her dizzy.

"*It's you!*" he whispered in shock, as he stared at her. "The eyes—your eyes . . ."

"Jack. . . ?" Her eyes started to burn with tears and, for some reason, she wanted to throw herself against him and hold him tight to her body. Crazy. Irrational. Overwhelming.

As their gaze deepened, lightning flashes of memory

366

occurred in each of them. It was like wiping away a mist from the windows of their minds, as quick pictures were revealed. "You were with me, weren't you?" she muttered.

"Oh, my God . . ." Jack sank into the chair opposite her. His hands were shaking as he placed them on the table. "I don't understand this."

"I don't either," she answered in a muffled voice. "But I know things about you. Like you were adopted and you never married because of it. And you were playing football with some kids when you . . ." She didn't know how to finish.

"When I died," he said what she couldn't. "And you were getting your tonsils out and you ate toast. And you don't go by Lauren. It's Laurie. That's it! That's the name that has been haunting me. Laurie."

"This can't be happening!"

He looked down to the books in front of her and said, "This *is* happening. You went through it, too, or you wouldn't be reading those."

She started crying then. Really crying. Emotional sobs were choking her. He looked about him, got to his feet and came around the table to her.

"C'mon, let's get out of here." He took her books and held out his hand to her. "We need to talk."

Wiping her eyes, she looked around at the people surrounding them. More than a few were staring. "We—we can go to my place. It's not far."

"I know. Rittenhouse Square."

She didn't question his knowledge, or the fact that she was inviting a stranger into her home. Placing her palm inside of his, she instinctively knew he wasn't a stranger.

No. This man was not a stranger.

They didn't speak as they walked the two blocks to her apartment or passed Miguel in the lobby or closed the door behind them. He dropped her books on the narrow table in the foyer and followed her into the living room.

"Would you like something to drink?" she asked in a hesitant voice, for she was suddenly shy in his presence.

"Yeah, sure."

"I'll get you a beer." She turned to go into the kitchen but stopped to look back at him. "That is what you drink, isn't it?"

He was staring at her. "It is. And you're addicted to Diet Coke."

Shaken by his knowledge, she covered her mouth with her hands and muttered, "This is so weird. It's ridiculous . . ."

He hurried to close the five feet that separated them and took her left hand away from her mouth. Staring at the ring on her finger, he whispered in an awed voice, "I gave you this for Christmas because it reminded me of your eyes."

And then she saw the scene in her mind. She could smell the sap of the pine tree, see the Christmas presents that sat under it. She could feel the love in her heart for this man.

He let go of her hand and slowly undid the top three

buttons of his shirt. Pulling out the Claddagh, he held it out as if waiting for her reaction.

Her mouth dropped open as she stared at the gold charm. "Oh, Jack . . ." she murmured, filled with emotion. Her hand shook as she reached up to touch it. "It reminded me of us—two hands reaching out for love, and . . . and finally finding it." She tilted her chin and looked up at him, sure now that he was the other half of the puzzle, the one that fit together with her so perfectly.

"I love you, Laurie Reese," he said, his voice muffled with feelings he could no longer control. "I know it sounds crazy, and I've never said that to anyone else in my life. But I know I said it to you before, in another life, or another time. I love you," he said simply, beautifully, and took her into his arms.

She melted against him, wanting to feel his heart beating with hers. Holding on tight, she whispered through her tears, "All these weeks I didn't know why I was grieving. It was for you." Her lips trailed down the side of his cheek in near desperation. "For you . . . for you . . ."

His mouth met hers in a sudden irrational hunger, and they clung to each other in an embrace that was both fierce and possessive. While she gasped for breath when they parted, a strangled, joyous sound emerged from the back of Jack's throat.

"This is a long time in coming, isn't it?" he asked, while breathing hard against her mouth.

"It is," she managed to whisper in return, while

running her hands up and down his back. She couldn't stop touching him, wanting to feel that he was really with her. It was as if she'd lost something priceless and now it was found. Afraid to let go of him, she held him close, pressing against him, wanting to fuse with his body and become a part of him. "This has all happened before. Holding you. Wanting you. Loving you. I can feel it."

He pulled back and gazed at her. "I'm not going to let you go again. You know that, don't you?"

She stared at his eyes, his nose, his mouth. "I know it," she breathed against his lips. "We've been given a second chance."

The intensity of the kiss left her shaking. His hips pressed into hers, his desire obvious and igniting her own with each second that passed. They didn't ask permission as they quickly started to remove the other's clothing. The passion building between them became an overpowering energy, so strong, so potent, that it couldn't be resisted. When a shoulder was revealed it was brushed by eager lips, tasted by a hungry mouth. Jack's hands left her waist to slide up her rib cage and capture her breasts. Laurie felt a wild yearning inside of her when his lips touched her, tracing an elaborate pattern over her skin. She threw back her head and reveled in the glory of it as he moved lower, pulling away any barriers in his path. His mouth was hot and moist and fervent. And when his tongue touched her intimately, her knees buckled beneath her.

Catching her in his arms, he lowered her to the rug. There was a desperate intensity to their lovemaking.

It was as if they silently agreed that tenderness would come later, for there was an urgent, burning need to be united in an act so old and primordial that it confirmed life itself. And that's what filled Laurie's mind as Jack moved above her, staring into her eyes, reading her thoughts . . .

"We're alive!" she gasped in a strangled voice, as she clung to him, claiming him as her own, and moving with him in the age-old ritual that celebrated the human spirit. *"We're alive. . . !"*

He ran his fingers up and down her back in light, feathery strokes, and Laurie moaned with pleasure into the pillow. A seductive smile played at her lips as she remembered the lovemaking. After the first time, Jack picked her up from the rug and carried her into her bedroom. It was the first time she was carried anywhere, the first time that she could remember. She had a moment of uneasiness. The feminist part of her brain had kicked in and had protested such a possessive male action. But she didn't feel helpless in his arms. She felt feminine and secure. And then they had leisurely rediscovered each other with tenderness and a quickly renewed passion.

Only one word could describe what she was feeling. Peaceful.

An insistent ringing noise sounded from the living room and Jack jumped up from the bed.

Leaning on her elbow, Laurie watched him run out of the room. "What is it?"

"My beeper. Wait a minute."

He came back into the bedroom and she smiled at him. Only a man could be that totally unaware of nudity, and Jack was quite spectacular in his.

"Can I use the phone?" he asked, nodding to the one on her night table.

"Of course."

He sat down on the edge of the bed and she immediately curled up next to him, wanting to feel the texture of his skin against hers. Her hand instinctively started caressing the curve of his spine as he dialed a number, and he sighed when her fingers descended to the small of his back.

"Mike? It's me. What's up?"

He waited a few seconds and then said, "No. Nothing's wrong. In fact, everything's finally right. I'll tell you about it later."

"Yes . . . I'm with her now." He chuckled, and added, "That's none of your business. Tell Rosselli I'll be in tomorrow to finish the paper work. After that he's going to have to hire a temp. I'm ready to go back on the street." There was a pause, and then he said, "Thanks, Mike. I promise—you'll meet her."

Hanging up, Jack smiled as he slid back beneath the sheet. He brought her body against the length of his and the grin widened with happiness. "Mike wants to meet you."

"I'd like to meet him," she answered, astonished that she could begin to feel aroused again.

"I don't know if I'm ready to share you yet."

She knew what he meant. "I want to be a part of your life, Jack. I'd like to meet your friends. And your parents. I feel like I know them already." Sighing, she added, "That sounds crazy, doesn't it?"

"Not to me. Look, we can't explain what happened to us, but we both know it did. We connected . . . somewhere. And fell in love. I've never been in love, Laurie. Not once in my entire life. And I'm afraid of outsiders questioning it."

"All we have to say is that we met at Borders and it was love at first sight."

He kissed the tip of her nose and grinned. "No, love at second sight," he corrected.

She held him tightly to her. "Jack? What do you remember about . . . about that time?"

He slowly shook his head. "It's funny. Some things are so clear, so vivid. Like your eyes. And the rest is vague, like a dream. I remember boxes and boxes of clothes. And a woman—"

"She was sad," Laurie interrupted, and Jack nodded.

"I think we tried to help her," Jack continued. "When I saw the ring, I remembered Christmas. It was in a house. A nice house. I think I liked it there."

"Me, too," Laurie murmured. "Sometimes when I'm dreaming I hear a baby crying. Was there a baby?"

Jack thought for a moment and shrugged. "I don't know."

Laurie froze as a thought came to her. "Oh, God, Jack! We didn't . . . have a baby together and—"

"No," he said emphatically. "To do that we would have had to make love. And, woman, I would have remembered that!"

She giggled and relaxed in his arms. "You're right. Then it must have been her baby. I wish I could remember. When I try too hard, I get dizzy and frightened . . . as if I'm falling off the edge of a cliff."

Pushing a stray tendril of hair behind her ear, he said softly, "Maybe we're not supposed to remember. Whatever we did, it's over. We both came back, and we found each other. Maybe we should just let it go, and go on with our lives."

"We're not the only ones, Jack," she whispered. "Last week I went to a . . . a sort of meeting with others who had near-death experiences."

"Really? Tell me about it."

She snuggled against his shoulder. "Well, nobody told of falling in love and losing anybody, but there was a common thread. They all described the dark tunnel with a brilliant light at the end and seeing relatives or emissaries of God . . . kind of angels who spoke with them. I can remember entering a beautiful valley where a woman in a white gown spoke to me—"

She could feel him shaking his head. "No, no, that wasn't it," he interrupted. "There was a man in a dark business suit. He was in an office and I sat on a metal chair opposite his desk."

"Jack, nobody described anything like that. It was more spiritual, and—"

"Hey, I'm telling you what I remember. And it wasn't spiritual. It was cut and dried, like a business interview. For some reason I remember reviewing my life. It was real quick, like a fast flip of slides, you know—like flashing scenes of my life before me. I think I realized then that for every action I had taken in my life there really was a reaction. That whatever I gave out to others came back to me at some time, in one form or another."

Laurie sighed. "It changed my perception about God. I was never a church-goer, and I couldn't become one now, but I'm positive of His existence, and that He, or She, is more merciful and loving than I had imagined. That all the crap that surrounds us *we* create. We were given a list of instructions on how to live on this planet and we're ignoring them. I don't know—I can't change the world, but I can change myself."

He kissed her forehead. "I don't want you to change. I think you're perfect the way you are."

Closing her eyes, she laughed. "Why do I have this very strong feeling that you didn't always think so?"

He held his breath for a few seconds. "You're right. I don't think we liked each other very much when we . . . first connected. In fact, now I'm getting a strong feeling of intense *dis*like. I have this image in my mind of a rich, snotty woman who tried to run everyone's lives like she was—"

"Hey," Laurie interrupted and playfully slapped his hip. "Watch it. I am not rich. Nor am I snooty. I'm . . ."

375

"What?"

She thought for a moment. "I'm easy," she said finally, and could feel a chuckle building up inside his chest. "You find that amusing?"

Shaking his head, he laughed out loud. "I was just thinking how that could be interpreted. I mean, we meet in a bookstore and twenty minutes later we're tearing our clothes off and making hot torrid love on your rug."

Pretending to be offended, she pushed him away and slid off the bed. She took her robe from the hook in her closet and wrapped it around her like protection. "I will have you know," she said in a proper voice, ". . . that I am not *easy*. I'm a lady. This was a . . . a unique situation. That's all."

He sat up against the pillows and grinned at her. "It was a lot more than that, and you know it. Now where are you going? Come back to bed."

"I'm hungry," she stated with amusement.

"Me, too. So come back to bed." He patted the sheet next to him.

"For food," she said, ignoring his last statement as she started to walk out of the bedroom. "How about grilled cheese? You want ketchup on yours? Now, that's disgusting!"

In the hallway, she stopped and turned around. He was staring at her with that same intensity as in the bookstore. She knew then that they were a part of something special, that they were meant for each other. That they had journeyed an incredible distance to find each other—twice. Suddenly she was running back to him, hopping on the bed with a carefree, girlish enthusiasm.

Laughing, he caught her in his arms and held her tight.

Laurie pulled back and said, "Hey, Lannigan. Want to marry me?"

He became serious, tracing his finger down the curve of her face. "Geez, Reese, I thought you'd never ask."

"So? What's the answer?"

His eyes filled with tears as he tried to control his emotions. "The answer is yes. *Yes!* We've been given this gift, Laurie, like you said—a second chance, and I'll do everything in my power not to screw it up."

"I'll make sure you don't."

"And how about you? I'm a cop. I work crazy hours—"

"And you eat grilled cheese sandwiches with ketchup."

"I couldn't afford to live like this." He nodded to her bedroom.

"I don't want to live like this anymore."

"Sometimes I'm opinionated and make rash judgments."

"No kidding? Me, too."

"I hate plays, museums and the opera."

"You'll learn."

"I like to watch sports. Football, basketball, baseball."

"I'll learn."

He closed his eyes briefly and sighed. "So, do you still think you could spend the rest of your life with me? It won't be easy."

Her answering smile was filled with love.

"Geez, Lannigan, I thought you'd never ask."

Epilogue

She smoothed the sweater across her belly and looked into the mirror. The cranberry color was festive and made her appear healthy. Maybe that was just wishful thinking.

"Jack? Are you ready?"

Turning sideways, Laurie examined her reflection in the glass. She looked more like a house. She was too short to carry this much weight gracefully. Fluffing up her hair for added height, she said in a louder voice, "Come on, Jack. We're going to be late."

Not getting a response, she picked up her purse from the bed and walked through the house toward the living room. She loved the old brownstone, each room silently holding memories from the occupants of the last hundred years. It was a comfortable home and she was pleased that everyone who entered felt that way. Next week they were having a huge Christmas party and she smiled as she thought of the strange mixture of friends that would attend. Cops and yuppies would mingle and argue and come to understand each other a little bit better in the spirit of the holiday. It would be interesting, to say the least.

She stopped short and her eyes narrowed with annoyance as she saw her husband crouched in front of the TV. "I can't believe it! You promised!"

Jack glanced up, looking like a little kid with his hand in the cookie jar. "I'm sorry. I just thought I'd catch some of the game while I waited for you."

Laurie found herself placing a fist on her hip, unconsciously duplicating the age-old stance of feminine irritation. "Look, Lannigan, you dragged me, seven months pregnant I might add, to that damned hockey game last week and you promised this Sunday we'd go to Wanamakers. No football."

"But they're playing Chicago," he tried to explain.

"Hey—I promised to love, honor and cherish. Not love, honor and become a sports fanatic. You're about to be a father and we're going to start an annual tradition in this family, today, right now. Not after the Eagles lose to Chicago."

"Oh, ye of little faith," he muttered, as he stood up and shut off the set. "They could still make a comeback. I can't wait until Junior arrives so I can get a little understanding about the finer points of football. I guess it's just a male thing.''

Laurie cringed. "I have asked you *not* to call this child Junior. It makes me think of beer bellies hanging over belt buckles and gun racks on pickup trucks.''

Laughing, Jack came up behind her and wrapped his arms around her stomach. Softly caressing his child, he whispered into Laurie's ear, "And you're barefoot and pregnant. Sort of fits, doesn't it?''

She giggled, her annoyance gone. "I am not barefoot. I have socks on." She leaned back against him, loving the feel of his arms around her. She felt secure and happy, and sighed with contentment. "Seriously, Jack. Call him by his name. Conor. Conor Lannigan. It's a strong name. Someone with a name like that will do something special with his life.''

"I don't want to call him by any name until he's born. They could have made a mistake with those tests. They aren't foolproof. What if it's really a girl? We haven't even agreed on a girl's name yet.''

Laurie shrugged. "Then we'll call her Conor, too.''

Pulling back, Jack looked at her with a shocked expression. "You wouldn't do that to a kid. Would you?''

She grinned. "I'm pregnant, not cruel. Don't worry, we'll come up with one. We have time.''

"Yeah, I guess you're right.''

Turning around, she poked his chest. "What we do

not have time for is this delaying tactic of yours. I know what you're doing, Lannigan, and it isn't going to work. You promised we'd go to Wanamakers for the Christmas show, and we're going."

He looked down to the rug. "Hey, I'm not the one without shoes."

She made a face and left him to pull on her Italian leather boots. Stuffing the bottoms of her jeans into them, she thought that her feet were the only part of her body that hadn't changed in size. But it was worth it. She loved being pregnant, and Jack had proved to be an amazing father-in-waiting. He was a great labor coach. Even their Lamaze teacher said he was a natural. When she stood up, Jack was holding out her jacket for her.

"You know," he said with a soft smile. "Even after two years, you're still the most beautiful woman I've ever seen."

Pleased, she turned and put her arms into the sleeves. "And here I was thinking I'm fat and moody and wondering how any normal human being could live with me. Thanks . . ."

"Yes, but we're not exactly normal, are we?" He spun her around and tried to zip the parka over her rounded belly. It was an impossible task.

Laurie tried, but gave up. "See? I told you. I have two more months to go, and if I keep gaining weight like this you'll have to roll me to the hospital." The smile that was at her lips only moments ago was replaced by a dejected pout.

Jack tilted her chin so she was forced to look into

his eyes. "Listen to me. You're the mother of my child, and you're beautiful. Every morning when I wake up and look at you sleeping next to me I can't believe how lucky I am that you came into my life. Don't you realize you're the best thing that ever happened to me?" He kissed her lips and the pout disappeared. "And if this coat doesn't fit, then we'll buy you a new one after the light show. We're going to be in a department store."

"That's just another added expense. We've already spent so much on the nursery, and I'll never wear it after the baby comes."

"I don't care. I'm not going to allow you and my child to go unprotected in the winter. Don't argue with me on this one."

She put her head on his chest and breathed in the scent of him. "I love you, Lannigan."

"I love you, too, Reese. Now let's go, or we'll never be able to start this annual tradition of packing ourselves in with hundreds of whining, fidgeting kids and crying babies. Sounds wonderful. I know I can't wait."

She lifted her head and kissed his chin. "You'd better get used to that," she whispered. "There's no turning back now."

"Want to know the truth? I *can't* wait. Sometimes I feel almost giddy, like a kid waiting for Christmas morning."

"Speaking of Christmas morning, my mother let it slip that she and my father are teaming up with your parents for a special present for the baby. I'm afraid of what they're going to try to shove through the front door.''

"So they'll be doting grandparents."

"They already are, and the baby's not even here yet.''

"Everything's so perfect, Laurie—we're very lucky.''

Her smile was serene. "No, Jack,'' she corrected in a soft voice. "We're blessed.''

The center court of John Wanamakers was exactly as Jack had anticipated. By the huge bronze eagle that was a hallmark in the city, hundreds of families sat on the marble floor, waiting for the show to begin. Children did fidget; babies did cry. Yet there was an air of expectation as everyone looked up to the second floor where a grand Christmas tree was decorated, its lights blinking in holiday colors of the season.

Laurie smiled as she raised her head with the others around her. Even the baby sensed the excitement, and Laurie massaged an elbow or a knee away from her abdominal wall.

"I'm going to get something to eat,'' Jack whispered.

Turning, Laurie frowned. "Don't you dare try and get lost on me. The show's about to begin any minute.''

"I know. The candy counter is right over there. I'll be right back. I promise.'' He squeezed her arm and shouldered his way through the crowd.

She watched as her husband approached the elaborate display of candy and then shook her head. Despite his objections, Jack was catching the enthusiasm for the event. She wasn't sure how many years Wanamakers had been doing it, but she remembered hearing about it from her friends in grade school. Strange that she had lived so close to the city all her life and had never attended. But then, she had never been to a hockey game, either, before meeting Jack—and he'd never been to a museum. They were both trying to build a lasting relationship, having seen so many marriages fall apart. It was good that they were older, for in matters of the heart wisdom had come with age.

Laurie felt suddenly hot. She took off her parka and held it by her side. Maybe she shouldn't have worn the heavy sweater. It really was crowded and—

"I told you she wasn't fat. See? She's gonna have a baby."

Laurie looked down to a boy about seven years old who shoved his companion in an I-told-you-so gesture. They both glanced at her with embarrassment when they realized that she had heard them.

Laurie smiled at them and said, "That's okay. Hard to tell, I guess, with a coat on. But I can't even zipper it over this belly anymore."

The bolder of the two answered, "My mom was like that. But then *she* came." He indicated his baby sister in a stroller.

"She's cute," Laurie said, still smiling. As an only child she had never experienced sibling rivalry.

"She cries a lot, and gets everything she wants."

"Babies are like that." Laurie answered, realizing she sounded like an authority on the subject. She had read over twenty books on childbirth and childrearing and knew that book knowledge could not compare with experience. And she couldn't wait to become a mother.

Looking over heads of the adults, she searched for Jack. He was paying for his purchase, and a wave of tenderness washed through her. He was going to be a great father. Her only worries were related to his job. Loving someone who was an officer of the law wasn't easy, especially when that person worked undercover in vice. How many times had she wanted to say to him, "Let someone else do it. I'm scared . . ." But she'd held her tongue, knowing that was part of his makeup. He'd be miserable if he wasn't a cop.

Her gaze turned to the Lancôme counter in back of him. After the show, maybe she could buy some makeup. She had two closets filled with clothes she couldn't wear, but she could do something with her face. She almost giggled when she admitted how typically female she was. A new hairstyle, freshly painted nails, or brand new makeup was a veritable safety net against falling into depression over a body gone out of control.

Jack held a bag out in front of her. "Want a chocolate-covered pretzel?"

Looking up to the sixty-foot Christmas tree, she shook her head. "Now, that's just what I need," she muttered. "Why don't I apply them directly to my hips? That's where they'll wind up eventually."

"You're too sensitive about your weight," he answered before popping a pretzel into his mouth. "When's this thing going to start?"

He asked the same question as most of the impatient children surrounding them, and Laurie found herself using the universal parental tactic of distraction. "Look at the architecture of this building," she pointed out. "Isn't it beautiful? The curved archways . . . the white and gold columns . . . the huge ornate organ. Doesn't it remind you of an old, elegant opera house?"

"Since I've never been in an opera house, I wouldn't know, thank God. Museums and plays. Even art shows. Okay. But opera? Forget it. If it's before Buddy Holly, then I don't need to hear it. Especially if it isn't even in English."

They'd had this discussion before and she knew it was useless to argue with him. She'd have to go to the opera alone.

The lights on the tree stopped blinking and a voice announced that the show was about to begin. Laurie slipped her arm through Jack's and held her breath.

The tree lit up with lights in different series of colors, and on either side, colored sprays of water shot up in the air about six feet, swaying back and forth like dancers in time to the Nutcracker Suite. The soothing voice told the story as Toy Soldiers were lit up and then the Sugar Plum Fairy. Murmurs of appreciation were heard from both children and adults. Christmas carols followed with Rudolph's nose blinking on and off and Frosty waving to the children. When Santa materialized, kids and their parents clapped their hands. It was a beautifully executed production of lighting, music and sentiment.

Standing in awe, Laurie felt like a child at the grand finale when everything lit up at once. For the first time, every one of the hundred thousand lights on the tree sparkled with a breathtaking brilliance. It was as if a huge Christmas card had come to life in front of her eyes.

"Oh, Jack . . ."

"I know . . ." he breathed, putting an arm around her shoulders. "Thanks, Laurie."

It only lasted about fifteen minutes. One by one, everything disappeared until only the tree was left. When the organ stopped, children rose to their feet. Parents stuffed little arms into snowsuits while promising to see it again.

Observing the scene, Laurie felt part of something far bigger than the confines of her world. It was the continuation of life, of establishing and passing traditions. It was becoming a family. Still holding Jack's arm, she leaned her head against his shoulder. "I'm glad we came," she murmured with happiness.

"Me, too. What time's the next show? We could find a coat for you and then come back to catch it."

"First I want to get some makeup," she said, turning toward the counter in the distance. She nearly stumbled to an abrupt halt.

"Laurie—What's wrong?"

Her body froze in shock. Her voice seemed trapped in her throat. Lifting her arm, she pointed to a couple by the Lancôme display. The man with glasses was holding a little girl with a mop of curly blond hair, while the woman buttoned the child's coat. It was the woman that held Laurie's attention. There was nothing unusual about her. She had brown hair. A pleasant face. And she was pregnant.

"Laurie? What is it?"

"Jack," she managed to finally say. "Look at that woman! The one over there by the makeup counter."

"There are four of them. Which one?"

"That one." She pointed with an urgency. "Where it says Lancôme. Hurry, before they turn away."

Jack looked above the heads of the crowd to where Laurie was pointing. "My God," he exclaimed. "It's her! She's the one!"

"Go stop her!" Laurie ordered, shoving Jack into the crowd. "And hurry! Don't let her get away!"

Once all the adults stood up, it was impossible for her to see them any longer. Desperate, Laurie tried jumping up, but it wasn't any good. Finally, she entered the crowd herself, determined not to lose the woman. Over the last two years she and Jack had tried to piece together the missing segments of their memories. They knew they had been sent on a mission to help a woman, but they couldn't remember anything about her. Not her name, nor where she lived. And now here she was at a Christmas show! They had to catch her, to speak with her. They had to know that everything had turned out right.

"Excuse me," Laurie muttered, as she pushed her way to the counter. "Excuse me. I'm sorry . . . I'm sorry . . ." she murmured over and over as she moved through the crowd.

She saw Jack turning around in a circle, searching the crowd, and Laurie leaned up against the glass counter in defeat.

They had lost the woman.

When Jack saw her, he rushed to her side. "They're gone. They just disappeared. It was like they were swallowed up in this mob. Hey, are you all right?"

Laurie was sweating and breathing heavily. "I can't believe she's gone. It *was* her, wasn't it, Jack? I mean, she was the one, right?"

Jack again scanned the dispersing mass of Christmas shoppers. "I think she was. No. You're right. It was her. We both felt it. And the guy with her . . . something about deliveries. I don't know." He sighed deeply and ran his hand over her back in a comforting gesture. "I'm sorry I lost them."

Laurie slowly shook her head. "Maybe we weren't meant to connect with her. Maybe it should be enough that we saw her and she was happy. She was pregnant. Did you see that?"

"Yeah. I saw. I found out that when your wife is pregnant, everywhere you go you seem drawn to every other woman in that condition. But that must mean she's doing okay, right? The baby must be the one we remember. And now she's going to have another."

Nodding, Laurie stood quietly and looked down to the boxes of makeup. If they just knew something more about her . . .

"C'mon," Jack urged. "There's nothing we can do. Why don't we look on this as a special Christmas present? We know she existed and we know we helped her. Not many people get a gift like that."

"You're right, I know. It's just that I wish we could check up on her. I have this feeling. This unexplainable bond. We were important to her, Jack—and she was important to us. Somehow our meeting changed all of our lives."

"Then we'll come back here every Christmas. If we're meant to meet with her, we will. If there's one thing we should have learned, Laurie, it's that we're not really directing our own lives. Somebody else up there is pulling the strings."

He took her hand and led her to the escalator. "Now, do they have coats for pregnant women? Or do you just buy a larger size?"

"Let's just try a larger size. They're making some really great things now for women who aren't a size three." Her brow furrowed with thought. "I don't know why I just said that."

Jack wasn't paying attention. "Listen, I just thought of a great name if Junior, there, is a girl."

"Come on, Jack. No jokes now."

"This isn't a joke. I'm serious."

Stepping off the escalator, she stopped and turned to him. "Okay, let's hear it." She knew she wouldn't like it. Every name he'd come up with had sounded like an old woman's. Bridget. Agnes. Martha.

"Jessica."

Laurie's mouth opened in shock. *"That's her name!"*

"It is?" he asked with surprise. "Well, thanks. If it's a girl, we'll name her Jessica. I didn't think you'd like it. Every other name I've said you—"

"No," she interrupted. "The woman downstairs. Don't you remember? Jessica? Jess? You *have* to remember!"

"Okay . . . if you say so."

Frustrated, Laurie started to walk in front of him into the women's department when she suddenly stopped and turned around. "You remembered half of her name. You're a cop. You have connections. Missing persons and stuff. You could find her, Jack."

"I don't want to."

She was shocked. "What do you mean? You don't *want* to?"

"I meant what I said downstairs. If we were supposed to connect with her we would have. She's our past." He looked down to her belly and then back into her eyes. "We have to go on with our future, *our* family. Let it go, Laurie. It's time."

He held out his hand to her and smiled with affection. "Wanna buy a coat, and then go home so I can jump your bones?"

She burst out laughing at his ridiculous proposal.

She hated to admit that he was right; it was time to move on. She had a life now, a good life . . . a good future.

And she hadn't said the words in almost two years.

Placing her hand inside of his, she answered with all the love in her heart. "Geez, Lannigan, I thought you'd never ask."

Afterword

"Memories . . . that's all we can really leave behind."
Virginia Maureen O'Day McLellan
1944–1992

Acknowledgments

I would like to thank the following for their assistance, their patience, and their encouragement during the writing of this book:

Carin Cohen Ritter, Walter Zacharius, and the production staff of Zebra Books. Adele Leone. Kristen and Ryan Flannery. Colleen Quinn. Linda Cajio. Dale Fountain. Vernon Edwards. Vicki Shandel. Pat Trowbridge. Carol Jenick. Mary Martin. Donna Julian. John Sandell. Brian Bailey. Kevin Jordan. Scott Hamlett. Eileen Dryer. Anne Berman. Anthony Massaro. Sandy George. Dave Noto. Joe Paggi. Lou Small. If I have forgotten anyone who made the last year a little easier, it's unintentional. Each and every one has my gratitude.

CATCH A RISING STAR!

ROBIN ST. THOMAS

FEEL THE FIRE IN CAROL FINCH'S ROMANCES!

BELOVED BETRAYAL   (2346, $3.95)

Sabrina Spencer donned a gray wig and veiled hat before blackmailing rugged Ridge Tanner into guiding her to Fort Canby. But the costume soon became her prison—the beauty had fallen head over heels in love!

LOVE'S HIDDEN TREASURE   (2980, $4.50)

Shandra d'Evereux felt her heart throb beneath the stolen map she'd hidden in her bodice when Nolan Elliot swept her out onto the veranda. It was hard to concentrate on her mission with that wily rogue around!

MONTANA MOONFIRE   (3263, $4.95)

Just as debutante Victoria Flemming-Cassidy was about to marry an oh-so-suitable mate, the towering preacher, Dru Sullivan flung her over his shoulder and headed West! Suddenly, Tori realized she had been given the best present for a bride: a night of passion with a real man!

THUNDER'S TENDER TOUCH   (2809, $4.50)

Refined Piper Malone needed bounty-hunter, Vince Logan to recover her swindled inheritance. She thought she could coolly dismiss him after he did the job, but she never counted on the hot flood of desire she felt whenever he was near!

DISCOVER DEANA JAMES!